"What will men say of him?" was the question asked following the great battle fought on Bosworth Field.

They would say what they had said of Richard III while he lived—and worse. That he was a tyrant, usurper of his nephew's throne, murderer, hunchback; that he was adored by the Princess Elizabeth of York in ways suitable neither for a princess nor a niece; that his queen and wife, Anne, loved him with a passion rare in royal marriages; that he was hated by his enemies with a passion equally rare in any reign; that he was a heroic warrior, dynamic leader, regicide, and blood-thirsty despot. History and his own age have not been kind to the man who was one of England's great enigmatic kings and whose image even today is surrounded by mystery.

THE
BROKEN SWORD

Rhoda Edwards

MANOR
BOOKS
INC.

A MANOR BOOK

Manor Books, Inc.
432 Park Avenue South
New York, New York 10016

Library of Congress Catalog Card Number 75-44522

ISBN CODE 0-532-22132-X

CONTENTS

Acknowledgments

I should like to thank everyone who helped me to write this book, and all those whose research has enabled us to know as much as we do of the period. The Richard III exhibition held at the National Portrait Gallery in 1972 brought together much of this knowledge, and its compiler, Dr. Pamela Tudor-Carig, has kindly offered her advice and given me permission to use the translation of the prayer from King Richard's *Book of Hours*.

My friends Carolyn and Peter Hammond and Francis Celoria assisted in the project from start to finish, tracking down many books and little-known facts. Ruth Schmidt and Dorothy Thorn were helpful critics. Miss Rosemary Sutcliff's kindness and encouragement helped enormously—especially by making such a distinguished writer as herself "godmother" to the book. Ruth Parker, who typed the finished book, deserves especial thanks for all her hard work and patience.

THE BROKEN SWORD

I

The Reiver

Told by Anne, Duchess of Gloucester

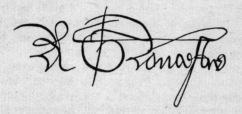

The Duke of Glocetter, that nobill prynce
Yonge of age, and victorious in batayle
To the honoure of Ectour that he mygte comens,
Grace hym folowith, fortune, and good spede.
I suppose he is the same that clerkis of rede,
Fortune hathe hym chosen and forth with hym will goo
Her husbande to bee, the will of God is soo.

Written after Edward IV's victory at Barnet in 1471

On the wall under the nursery window, where the arras
left the gray stone bare, some boy had chipped out the
initial letter of his name—R. I wondered who had done it
and if he had been caught. My husband? No, it looked too
worn and grimed with the dirt of generations. Over a
hundred years, many boys with that initial had lived in
this castle of Middleham, among them three Richards—
my husband, my father, and my grandfather—and my
great-grandfather Ralph Neville, the legendary old Earl
who begot twenty-three children to ensure that our
family ruled the North ever after. So they have done,

though many who stood upon the top of Fortune's wheel have been cast down, like my father the great Earl of Warwick, maker of kings. Now the wheel turns full circle, and my husband is lord of the north country.

Voices at the door brought news we were all eager to hear. "Duke's nearly home—past Masham an hour ago!"

"In this?" Outside, a blizzard was blowing; the draft from the window drove an icy knife against my cheek.

I smiled. It would take the Helm Wind that shrieks down Fiend's Fell out of Cumberland like forty thousand demons, or ten feet of snow instead of two, to keep my husband from riding home, once he'd made up his mind to do it. Richard, Duke of Gloucester, the King's Lieutenant General in the North, does not live his life ruled by the whims of northern weather.

My son, Edward, stood on a stool, trying to see out of the window and beyond the walls to the road. I could feel his excitement, though he did not wriggle or squeal as some children do. "My lord father," he announced, "has been to the Kings's Parliament." He said this in a serious, breathless way, as if Richard were a knight gone to seek the Holy Grail.

"Your father has been honored by Parliament for his success against the Scots."

"He captured Edinburgh, didn't he, mother, and burned Dumfries? How long does it take to ride from London?"

"Five days—a week this time, the roads are bad." I knew that the moment his brother King Edward dissolved Parliament, Richard would have left the court, which he greatly dislikes, to set out for home. Two hundred and forty miles is at best a long, tiring journey, and the last stretch from York now lay in the grip of winter's spiteful ending. Though the first week in March had passed, the sky was as leaden as it had been in January.

"Mother, will he stay at home now? How long will he stay?" He didn't turn to look at me. Richard had been away two months, which to a six-year old is an eternity.

"Until after Easter." I wished I might have said, "All summer." Easter fell at the end of March. Then, thinking this sounded too bleak, for myself as well as for Edward, I told him, "Until the Scots make trouble again." With luck, that would not be before May. "We might go to Carlisle with him this summer, now things are easier."

I expected a further spate of questions, but he was too intent on the scene outside the window. I looked out over his head. Snow had congealed in the corners of the leads and piled up thick as a pillow on the sill. It looked like the poulterer's sheds after plucking goose down; so soft, on wanted to touch, even knowing it was not fluffy and dry, but icy wet. Driven flakes splattered on the glass, clinging as goose down does, so that I had to peer in order to see anything at all. Out there, the cold must be cruel. In such weather it is dangerous to stray from the white road into the white land. Just as well that we who live here know the road as we know our own faces. I wondered how near they were, maybe riding over Cover Bridge—the river not frozen, but swollen with snow water—barely a mile left, uphill against the wind. The child's breath and my own filmed the window with steam; his hair brushed it, leaving a pattern like crushed grass blades. I wiped it with my hand, but it steamed up again. I turned away to gather everyone together, so that we might be ready to welcome home our lord Duke.

Anne Idley, Mistress of the Nursery, who is in charge of the younger children, set Edward's hat straight and inspected his face, to make sure it was not sticky. She made a sharp sound of annoyance, because he was trying to squeeze his curled-up fists into his gloves without using the fingers. He looked from her to me, decided on obedience, and put the gloves on properly by himself. She said, "Madam, when his Grace has greeted the children, I will bring them back here, out of the way. The travelers will want to dry and warm themselves."

I led the procession along the covered bridgeway, high above the yard, which crossed to the hall in the keep. Wooden pattens clattered in my wake; the children were warmly wrapped for outdoors, as it is hard to prevent them from running into the snow. They usually make enough clamor for a pack of scenting hounds, but today they were not the only cause of a din; everywhere in the castle we heard pounding feet and shouted orders. At the

open doors of the keep I paused, bracing myself against
the cold and holding the hood of my foxskin cloak
around my ears and face. Behind me the children
crowded expectantly, held back by Mistress Idley and
their tutors, like a flock of cheeping sparrows under
sheltering eaves.

After the frenzied preparation for my lord's
homecoming within doors, outside seemed frozen into
stillness. The wind had dropped and snow drifted idly
down. Beyond the walls lay a great silence, apparently
empty of birds, animals, and human beings. Usually the
comings and goings at the castle are events in which the
whole town joins nosily, but no crowd would turn out in
this weather, and snow deadened the clatter of
approaching hoofs. When the riders reached the
drawbridge, trumpets blew a fanfare, and a loud
whinnying arose from the stables, for horses like to greet
their returning companions.

There were fewer of them than I had expected—less
than a hundred; the rest of the household and the baggage
carts must have been left at York, to follow on when the
roads cleared. I walked down the steps to meet them.
Everyone looked like the snowmen that the boys build in
the meadow. I recognized Richard by his horse, which
was gray-white, treading noiselessly, like a huge ghost.
There wasn't much of him visible because, like everyone
else, he'd muffled his face until only a narrow gap for his
eyes remained. He was white all over; snow had filled
every fold and crease in his cloak and boots; even his
breath hung white upon the air. The horse blew out smoke
like a dragon. As I came near, it regarded me with dark,
mild eyes, not at all dragonlike, its whiskers dewed with
melting snow and its mane dangling slushy icicles. It
snorted as if pleased to be home and stretched out its neck
to snuff at my furs with fluttering, inquisitive nostrils.

Grooms came running, their feet kicking up flurries of
snow. They held the horse while Richard dismounted. I
thought: He'll be frozen rigid. But apart from a slight
stiffness of movement, he had his usual air of taking his
surroundings just as they were. He pulled away the layers
of wool cloth from his face and mouth, and I smiled, for

he looked so strange; white hair, brows, and eyelashes
seem absurd on a man of thirty. He smiled too and shook
himself so that snow flew off his clothes in a thick shower.
I'd have happily put my arms around him and risked a
soaking, but this wouldn't have been dignified, as I'm
twenty-six and ten years married. So I paused, while he
dragged off his wet gloves, took hold of my hands, and
kissed me. Though his face was icy and rough-skinned,
the inside of his mouth was warm. I ceased to feel cold.
Standing on pattens, I was taller than he, though
barefoot we are the same height, just four fingers more
than five feet. Among other men, he looks small. He let
go my hands, so that the others might greet me.

At this point, someone let out the dogs. A dozen of
them dashed into the yard, barking. They tore around in
circles, sniffing snow, gulping it and shaking their heads
at its chill, even tumbling head over heels in it. After that,
they made for us and hurled themselves on Richard, the
big ones leaping up, trying to lick his face. I could scarcely
see him in this smother of snow and wagging tails. He
laughed at them making fools of themselves, cuffed them
gently, and ducked out of the way of their more
exuberant greetings, while the servants bawled at them. It
seemed to me that not only the dogs, but all the people in
the castle had gone crazy, now my lord was home.
Everyone was kissing, chattering, laughing, or shouting
orders; the children were jigging up and down excitedly.
The chapel bell was ringing, shattering the snow silence
for miles around. The great iron gates clanged shut. In
this ferment, only the cause of it appeared calm. Though
he was smiling and obviously happy to be home, Richard
let the others do most of the talking, as if news of
Middleham were more important than any he'd brought
from London.

Our son, in the firm grip of his tutor, was on the verge
of losing his temper at this restraint, so, not wishing to
deny him his pleasure, we went up the steps to greet him.
He kissed Richard's hand solemnly, because he's been
taught that in a duke's son, manners come first. Then
Richard bent down, sat back on his heels, and kissed the
child on his cheeks and mouth. He looked at his father,

and his face lit up with a smile of such complete
happiness, it spread to all who watched. Seeing them
together again, the child and the man, two faces so alike
in feature, though different in coloring, I was infinitely
content.

Late in the afternoon, as I had promised, we visited the
nursery. Of Richard's three children, only Edward is
mine. The other two are bastards, born before he married
me. Katharine is thirteen and soon may be married
herself; John, who is eleven, serves his father as a page,
having left the care of Mistress Idley when he was eight, for
the tougher rule of the Master of Henchmen. Besides
these three, there are about a dozen girls and boys, whom
my husband either has in ward or who have been sent for
their knightly training in our household. There has
always been a full nursery at Middleham, though I wish
that more of the children were my own.

Whenever Richard has been away, he brings back
presents. As his visits to London had been the first for
two years, we expected something special. Edward was
awed to receive a book, *The History of Alexander,* in
English. It was not new, but of good quality and meant to
show that his father trusted him to look after it. He
opened it and turned the pages, looking for pictures.

"Father," he said in incredulous joy, "elephants!" From
babyhood, pictures of these monsters had fascinated him;
he used to think they had two tails, one in front and one
behind.

"Numberless elephants," Richard said. "Read this—
about the army King Darius of the Persians sent against
Alexander."

The children stood around, looking over his shoulder.
Edward, priviledged as the youngest, was tucked between
his father's knees. Richard put his arms around him, so
they might hold the book together. He read slowly but
clearly, his delight overflowing with every word.

> "Forty-thousand, all astore,
> Elephants let go to-fore,
> Upon every elephant a castle,
> Therein twelve knights armed well...

"Look, there are castles on the elephants' backs—and one, two, three ... Saracens, with crossbows and spears. Your Grace, father, forty thousand is *so many* elephants. Are they really high as houses?"

Richard raised one eyebrow slightly in my direction. "As a house with three stories and a gable."

"Could we keep an elephant here, at Middleham?"

"No!" he hadn't expected that one. I hid a smile.

"Is there an elephant in England?"

"No. One came from Calais just before you were born, but was taken back."

"Father, wouldn't you have liked some elephants at the siege of Berwick? Forty thousand! Their big feet would have squashed the Scots flat!" He grinned broadly at the thought.

Richard treated the question as if it were a serious military possibility. "At the siege of Berwick, forty thousand elephants might well have frightened the Scots to death, but four would have been enough to turn my hair white! You see, Edward, because elephants are so big, they eat a great deal. When you have as large an army as ours was at Berwick—twenty thousand men and thousands of horses—it's hard to feed them all. I had to see that my army got enough to eat, so elephants wouldn't have been welcome. Besides, since they live in dry and sunny lands, they wouldn't have like the rain and mud of Scotland."

"What do they eat?"

"Hay and horse bread, I suppose. They wouldn't have liked our moldy hay, either. It was full of mice. Elephants are afraid of mice."

"Are they?" Edward seemed disappointed that his favorite beast had such an absurd weakness. Then he grinned and said loudly, "Mistress Idley is scared of mice. She..."

Richard silenced him by tightening an arm around him and putting a finger over his mouth. "To speak of ladies in their presence is ill-mannered," he said sharply. The poor woman was very embarrassed. She is used to children's appalling remarks, but felt her discipline at fault if they were made in front of the Duke. I thought

Edward had been about to say that she had jumped on a stool, thus adding to her discomfort. I hoped my son knew that to make such a remark would mean banishment from his father's company and a certain spanking from Mistress Idley. I did not want him to spoil his day. The idea of that large, capable woman in a panic at the sight of a tiny mouse secretly amused me, for they do not alarm me at all.

After a slightly crestfallen pause, Edward smiled angelically up at Richard and said, "Did *you* have enough to eat?" continuing his previous train of thought.

"Yes, but too much boiled mutton and brose."

"What's brose?"

Richard was flagging a little. He looked at me, and the corners of his eyes crinkled into a smile. "Oatmeal," he said. "Edward, take your book to the table and sit up to read it properly. Let me talk to the others."

When no one could possibly feel left out and all were occupied with their gifts, I was able to claim all Richard's attention. He'd brought me a rosary, made of what I took to be large, plain beads of dark brown agate stone, with narrow gold bands around them. As it swung from my hand, Richard said, "Look," and slipped his thumbnail under the gold binding of a bead. It opened on a hinge; inside was a tiny relief picture of the Annunciation, colored in bright enamels. The archangel Gabriel had wings of gold and blue. It was a jewel maker's triumph, of great value.

"I brought it from a Venetian merchant," he said. "Work so fine does not often reach England; it's the privilege of princes."

"Even the Queen cannot own a rosary like this one."

"No doubt she would covet it." Richard spoke shortly. I looked at him. His lips were shut in a perfectly straight line. I thought: How he detests the Queen and her great tribe of a family, and he is not a man who hates easily or without reason. Now that my husband was home, I did not want our time together spoiled by sour thoughts, so I took hold of his hand and kissed the fingers one by one. I got what I wanted, a softening of the set lips and then a smile. He held my wrist, playing with the other gift he'd found for me in London.

This was an eaglestone—one of those hollow pebbles which contain another, rattling pebble—cased in gold and hung from a bracelet of coral beads. I'd asked him specially to get me one; it's said that women who wear these stones are sure to start a baby. After six years I'd begun to think some falut existed in my body, which made what was so easy for other women impossible for me. Even when I was first married to Richard, and seventeen, I had to wait three years for my son, and miscarriages made me anxious that I would lose him too. The physicians said it was as well no more babies came; I am made so small and narrow in that part that each time I would risk my life. At first Richard had felt guilty and tried not to make love to me, but this had driven us both to distraction. When we found that whatever we did made no difference, he seemed content to see our childlessness as God's will. It made Edward special, though, because he is heir not only to the greatest lord in the kingdom, but also to royal blood. I wish so much to give Richard another male child—if anything should happen to this one, which God forbid, then there would be another to take his place.

I looked at my son, sitting at the table reading his book. He's not a sturdy child; his knees are bony and poke baggy holes in his hose, and his arms are like sticks, but many little boys of six are as thin and not in the least frail. Richard, when he came to Middleham to be educated in my father's household, had been both small and skinny; and I could see no reason why his son should not grow up as strong and hardy. Edward is quick at his lessons, but spoils his work by spells of dreaming and carelessness. Richard says he used to feel the flat of his tutor's hand even more often for the same faults, and now no one could be more conscientious. Though our son is the only one, and precious, we are both determined that he should not be coddled or have preferment over the other children in any way other than rank. Life is still easy for him; he had one more year of women's rule and the small indulgences allowed those not yet seven.

When I looked at Richard again he was staring into the fire, though he still fondled my wrist absently. Under his obvious pleasure at being home I thought something nagged at his mind.

"How was London?" I wanted a truthful not a stock answer.

"As it usually is." This meant: as unpleasant as ever.

"And your brother the King?"

For a moment I got no response. He was frowning. "I thought my brother had become a stranger to me, since ..." He broke off. I knew what he meant and why it was left unsaid. Since their other brother George of Clarence had been accused of treason and excuted in the Tower, Richard had kept away from court, meeting the King only five times in as many years.

"He wouldn't let me out of his sight. He kept me up every day into the small hours of the morning, saw me out of pocket in gambling, and made me drink too much. But no women in our company—he preferred me." He gave me a little, sideways half smile that died instantly. "The King is not well, Anne. I saw his physicians, but they could tell me nothing definite. He's become so fat—there's no other word for it. He always did make me feel the size of a small boy, but this time I was dwarfed. It's not only his bodily health. He seems overburdened with melancholy."

"Melancholy?" This sounded so unlike the King.

"He's still smarting from the treachery and duplicity of the King of France—old Louis electing to betroth his half-witted Dauphin to Maximilian of Austria's child, instead of to Edward's daughter Elizabeth."

"And the Prince of Wales?" The talk of the King's worries and ill health had disturbed me.

"Well enough." His voice took on a hard, offhand note I didn't often hear in it. "No, not well enough. The child's not strong. Pale as a weed grown in the dark. He's too bookish. If Rivers had his way, the Prince would be Archbishop of Canterbury, not King of England!" Lord Rivers, the Queen's younger brother, is in charge of the Prince's education. He is a man of many talents, some think too many, especially for book learning and political, as well as tourney, jousting.

"Did he sit in Parliament?" The Prince is twelve.

"Yes, though it's a wonder his mother allowed him to mix with us provincials, in case he caught some ailment."

"The Queen's family were as much in evidence as ever?" One could scarcely avoid Elizabeth Woodville's four brothers, three sisters, and two sons!

"Those hounds always did hunt in a pack. Anne, when I sat among the lords in Parliament, I was thanked, flattered, and rewarded, only to hear, in the next bill, Nevilles disinherited once again by the Queen's relatives."

"You mean the marriage intended for Dorset's son?" The Marquess of Dorset, the elder of the Queen's sons by her first marriage, is the same age as Richard, though he would pass for younger. With his mother's silver-gilt hair and perfect features, he has the beauty of an angel but the habits of a tomcat and a turnip between the ears.

"That carpet captain! His son is well provided for— he's getting my sister Anne's daughter and the Holland estates." He can never contain his anger and contempt at a mention of Dorset, whose knightly valor is confined to the bedchamber. During the Berwick campaign he had been obliged to serve a while under Richard, who had said disgustedly that he'd been unwilling to get his pretty feet wet.

I thought it best to stop talking about the Queen's family. Between supper and bed we would hear Vespers in the castle chapel, and one shouldn't meet God thinking un-Christian thoughts.

"Will the King give you a new title—Lord of Liddesdale or Duke of the Debatable Land?"

"No! Anne, you're poking fun at me. Duke of the Debatable Land indeed! My brother has granted me the most Godforsaken, desolate stretch of peat hag on the western March, and I'm not sure what use it is, apart from a defense against the Scots. Over thirty miles of it and not a tree in sight—oh, and as much more as I can seize from the borders of Scotland. If that means more raids into Liddesdale and Tarras Moss, then I'm not sure I want it."

James III of Scotland talks publicly of "the reiver Edward, calling himself King of England," but it is Richard who had to do the reiving. I had hoped three wouldn't be any more raids for a while; they sounded so rough and terrifiying, ridden at dead of night with no moon. I didn't want to be a Border widow.

Richard might make light of it, but King Edward had given him more than just this Border haven of cattle thieves and murderers. "King of Cumberland, Westmorland, and half Yorkshire" would be a more appropriate title for him now. I did not say so, for it implied that he had become an overmighty subject in his brother's realm, and he would not like to hear this said. The Earl of Warwick my father kept the state of a king in the North until, like Lucifer, he fell in all his pride and splendor. When I was a little girl I thought my father as wondeful as King Arthur. He was not, but men followed him as a lodestar, and when they called him the maker of kings, it was with awe, not censure. Now my husband has more power than my father did, and I do not know whether to be glad or a little afraid for the future. Richard himself is glad of this new grant of a principality on the Borders of Scotland, to be ruled by him and his heirs forever as hereditary Wardens of the West March, because he cannot see himself as anything but a loyal subject—the most loyal subject of all. I do nót wish to spoil things by thinking too far ahead of how loyalties between our son and the King's son may not be so strong. Little Edward has no glorious elder brother to make a hero and serve faithfully for a lifetime, and the Prince of Wales, who will be King one day, is so very much the Queen's son. Though Richard has avoided any open quarrel with her, the Queen is his enemy. But, thank God, the future is not with us now, in this year of 1483; we are strong and England is at peace.

"Lord of Liddesdale sounds very fine," I said, keeping my doubts to myself.

"I hung a sheep stealer once who called himself that— Earless Sim Armstrong was his name. He lived in a pele tower and shared his hearth with fowls and a milch cow. We burned his steading."

I laughed, and all the children joined in. "Come," I said to Edward, "my Lord of Salisbury should be in bed."

For me there was too much of the evening left. It could not be cut short, for important guests had come to the

castle with Richard and had to be entertained at supper.
Fish, because it was Lent; some fine carp, tench, and
bream, made sluggish with cold, had been taken from the
stew pond, so the travelers might make up for their
dinnertime spent on the snowy road.

We put on fur gowns to go to Vespers, because the
chapel, even with braziers of glowing coals set around,
was icy as a cellar. When we walked into it from the great
hall, which was made warm by huge fires, and stuffy by a
crowd of people and food, I shivered. We knelt on
cushions of green velvet sewn with Richard's silver boar
badge, and in spite of the arras hung all around the walls
and doorways, the draft found my feet, and I kept
wriggling my toes in my fur-lined shoes. I huddled my
chin down into my fox furs, watching my breath rise like
incense smoke. On the altar stood a silver-gilt reliquary,
studded with rubies, emeralds, sapphires, and diamonds,
that held a piece of St. Cuthbert's robe, and a Cross of
even greater richness that came from my mother's family,
the Beauchamps, and used to be at Warwick.

Fingering the smooth, cool beads of my Italian rosary,
I tried to restrain my mind from wandering and to rebuke
it for thinking thoughts during Mass that it should not.
Out of the corner of my eye, when it should have been
closed in prayer, I watched Richard. He was so close I
could have touched him by leaning a little in his direction.
I wanted very much to do this. I could let my arm rest
against his or shift sideways on my cushion so that our
knees touched. I promised guiltily to say ten extra *Aves*
tomorrow for contemplating such a thing in church, then
decided if I really thought it sinful, I'd have to say them
tonight, before I went to bed. Tomorrow would have to
do! I didn't move, for shame; the people of our household
were meekly kneeling behind us. What would they think
if the Duchess couldn't keep her hands off her own
husband during prayers!

I shut my eyes, but opened them again well before the
chaplain had got halfway. Even if I stopped myself from
touching Richard, I couldn't take my eyes off him. It
seemed to me that each time he came home, he had to go
away again before I'd had time to look at him as much as I

wanted. I thought: How weather-beaten he's become.
The side of his face toward me was relaxed and his eyes
were shut, but lines ran out from their corners as if cut by
a knife, more scored his forehead and between the brows,
other fainter ones marked the corners of his mouth. None
of them had been put there by ill temper, but by the harsh
northern weather and the harsher demands of the life he
has led. His rough soldiers, the reivers who ride the
Border hills, gazing into the bright distances or more
often into lashing rain, have lines like those on their faces.
It gave me a twinge of heartache to see him so worn;
fourteen years of the anxieties of power and war and an
ever-increasing responsibility for the lives of other men
had left their mark. But I consoled myself with the
thought that if one looks at him whole, instead of only at
that weathered face, one sees a man who looks younger,
not older, than his thirty years. He's so full of life, a quiet
energy that drives him hard always, often leaving other
men exhausted. It's a thing I know every minute he's in
my sight, even when he's sleeping I can feel it, in the
warmth his body gives, the strong heartbeat.

I wondered if within his head, he'd be alert and
thinking, of God, of me? I didn't know; strange how far
away we are from those we love. His right eye opened,
blinked, and shut again, so that the black lashes lay still.
He didn't look at me, though I'd have liked him to. His
eyes, deep set under straight dark brows, are gray-blue,
like slate; eyes the shifty do not care to meet. I've never
met anyone so quick at detecting lies, which is an art
learned through years of ruling all sorts and conditions of
men. Maybe he is too honest with himself; some people
usually those more accommodating to their own
weaknesses, think him a hard man. I suppose, if hardness
is taken to mean strength, this is true, but if harshness is
meant, then they are quite wrong. He has too much
humanity for that.

Even when calm and at prayer, his face is not soft. I
cannot honestly call him handsome, though I would not
change him for one of the archangels. His face is too
bony, too thin—the features strongly marked, too much
jaw, too much nose—with hollows under the cheekbones

that are as aging as the lines in his skin. Also, and this is something not at once apparent, his shoulders are lopsided; he carries the right higher than the left. A bad fall from a horse when he was a child—I can remember it happening—had smashed a bone that did not set straight. It has never troubled him much, and the tailor contrives to hide it almost entirely, though when he's wearing armor it's easy to see, because the right shoulder-piece is made bigger. His left arm is scarred almost from wrist to elbow; a narrow-bladed dagger, run under the armpiece, had done it at Barnet field. Not much of a wound, he had said. I shuddered to think what a serious wound would be like. Altogether, life has left him a little battered.

When we sat back in our chairs to listen to the boys of the chapel choir sing a motet by Dr. Banaster, the King's Master of Song, I was able to watch Richard less guiltily One or two gray threads showed in his hair at the temples, but no more than when I last looked. When I offered to pull them out, he winced and said six were sure to spring up for one gone, and they'd come soon enough without encouragement. For a man who has broken bones, been bruised black from head to foot, and wounded in battle, he hates a little tweak—he can't bear to watch me pluck a hair out of my eyebrow. His hair is a nice brown color, thick and curly, good to touch—when he was a child it was a fluffy mop that always stood on end when he tried to be tidy. I think it must be his only vanity—a secret one, as he denies any good looks—for he wears it as long as the coxcomb Dorset's.

I sometimes wonder if other women find my husband attractive. Once or twice I've heard odd questions asked about whether he was born with some deformity that caused the imbalance of shoulder; people have excessive interest in the persons of princes and are ready to shrink from any bodily peculiarity. Their fear usually disappears when they meet him. But these stories do not seem to have brought him bad luck with women; in the years before he married me, he provided himself adequately with bed-fellows. That has never mattered much to me, but I'm still a little jealous of those years I did not have with him. He was sixteen when he had his first lover,

Katharine's mother. It's hard to imagine what he must
have been like for her, the young boy's body, the rather
serious face, his shyness. Had he been clumsy at first,
eager to learn? I looked at the chapel floor, ashamed at
my roving thoughts again. There was his son John, too, a
couple of years after Katharine, and, some said, there
might have been others. That winter exile in Burgundy
had been so cold and miserable—the day before his
eighteenth birthday, he'd almost been drowned in the
North Sea—and the women of Bruges are most expert in
the pleasure of love. Each day, when he was young, he
never knew if he would see another. O God, I
thought, don't let him live like that ever again, but it was
foolish to ask so much. Before long, he'd have to go raiding
on the Border—the Scots won't disappear because I want
them to.

"Per Christum Dominum, amen," the chaplain was
saying. As Richard opened his eyes, mine were still fixed
on his face. He looked startled. I hadn't realized my
thoughts were revealed so clearly in my eyes—the
message stared out of them—my lord husband, darling,
love me. Though he did not smile, his mouth looked
softer than anyone else ever sees it, and his eyes said—
soon.

After Easter, in the first week of April, when Richard
had been home one blissful, fleeting month, the sun shone.
Master Chaucer the poet talked most delightfully of the
sweet showers of April that pierce the drought of March,
but he had been a Londoner and had not known these
dales, where heavy snow and a thaw in March had made
us willing to do without the showers. Because the day was
the first of the year which could be called springlike,
Richard decided that we would go out for pleasure,
hawking, taking with us only a small party of friends. We
rode up the southern side of the dale, high into bare
mooreland, where in spite of the sunshine, snow still lay
in grubby patches on last year's flattened grass and
heather. All the land up there was still a lifeless brown, the
whins and bilberry bushes like so many heaps of dead
brushwood. Only the middle of the broad valley below

us, by the river Ure, showed green. Though the wind blew from the south, it was not warm and so strong at times we could have leaned sideways on it without falling out of the saddle. Wind and sun made a clear day, and the distant fells, so often hidden in mist or drizzle, seemed unusually sharp and near. The ring of soft purple-brown hills around us stretched away forever and ever, like ripples on a sun-lit pool; one could not tell where they ended and the sky began.

We looked very fine that day, Richard and I. No one for miles around could mistake the Lord and Lady of Middleham when they went out riding. Following a whim, we had gowns made from the same cloth—green velvet, embroidered with gold in a pattern of roses, little scrolls bearing our motto, *Loyaulte me lie*—loyalty binds me—Richard's pledge to the King and ours to each other, and love knots linking our initials, R and A. I had a little flat hat of black velvet with ear flaps, so that the wind should not tug out my hair, though Richard says it's a pity women always hide their hair. His own hair blew about all over his face, which slightly spoiled his elegance—long boots of crimson Spanish leather, a velvet hat with an emerald pin, and green gloves with gold tassels. Our horses were perfectly matched grays, brother and sister. Grays are popular hereabouts; Richard could mount three hundred horsemen for the King's service, all on gray or white horses. We rode knee to knee, touching often. I used to ride pillion sometimes behind my husband, which was nice, because I could hug him, but I enjoy handling my own horse and carrying my own hawk.

On the road we met a shepherd, alone except for his dog, which crouched at his heel and took no notice of our hounds. The man carried a lamb around his neck and used his crook as a walking staff. He took off his greasy cap as we passed and bowed awkwardly, as if unconscious of the lamb's little hoofs dangling over his shoulder and straws stuck in his hair. He gave us good day and said something about it being middlin' fair, and the lamb bleated in unison, much to our delight.

I put my merlin up after a lark, then regretted it, for she was blown away, disappearing into the sky to the south. A merlin is too small to fight a high wind, especially if she is young and inexperienced; she will give up and go with it. I felt annoyed at having let this happen. Richard saw me frown and smiled. "I haven't flown away from you," he said, coaxing. As I didn't want to seem put out on a day when we were so happy to be in each other's company, I smiled too.

The silver horse stood waiting for the signal to move, his ears pricked, watching the dogs run about the hillside. Richard was staring out over the great expanse of sunlit dale, as if he would see from here to Scotland, over all his lands. He's like a king, I thought, watching his kingdom. then the spell broke and he turned his gaze back to me. "I can never tire of looking at it," he said. "If I were a prisoner in a faraway land, this is the picture I should carry in my mind, the dream I should dream. Two things I can never tire of looking at, this and your face." Even now, after ten years of marriage, he can make my heart jump by saying things like that.

"Love," I said, "my own dearest lord, this is our home, our kingdom. We'll stay here all our lives, together—until we are called to God's kingdom."

He looked at me and smiled very gently, his eyes creasing up in the sunlight. "Yes," he said quietly, "if He is willing."

2

An Earthly Prince
Told by Dr William Hobbes, the King's physician

O noble Edward, wher art thowe be-come,
Which full worthy I have seen goyng in estate?
Edward the iiijth I mene, with the sonne,
The rose, the sonne-beme, which was full fortunate.
Noon erthly prince durst make with hym debate.
  Art thowe agoo, and was here yestirday?
  All men of Englond ar bound for the to pray.

The Death of Edward IV (c. 1483)

The skin upon the inner side of King Edward's arms was, I observed, as fair and tender as an infant's, the veins under it thick and blue, swollen with the juice of life. "At the joint of the elbow, Master Halliday," I said to my assistant surgeon, "where the vein shows at the surface."

The King was lying with his arms outside the sheets, his hands slack, the candlelight turning to gold the chestnut hairs on his thick wrists and wide, white chest. The counterpane and tester were crimson silk, gleaming with golden suns and roses. "Would Your Highness be so kind

as to brace your arm ..." He sighed and scarcely opened
his eyes, though he did as I asked obediently enough. He
clenched his fist, and the big muscles in his upper arm
swelled and stood out surprisingly hard. I say
surprisingly, because he had put on much flesh in the last
ten years, and those once lean, muscular shoulders were
cushioned with fat. That fist might well be relied upon to
knock many a lesser man into Purgatory still, and the
large hand with its long, flexible fingers would no doubt
grip a weapon to as good advantage as before— and I
looked at his left arm not the right, the sword arm.
Halliday took about a pint from the vein—it only needed
a little nick—and the blood flowed into the silver bowl as
dark and syrupy as hippocras. After it was done, he
bound the cut with a strip of linen. The King never
flinched. He lay there inert, like a felled tree, a heavy,
majestic oak, a very big man indeed. The mound his body
made reached almost to the foot of the huge royal bed; six
feet four inches in his skin, heavy-boned, and carrying a
belly on him fit for a gross old alderman. When he had
collapsed at Mass this morning it had taken half a dozen
strong men to get him to bed. There never had been such a
youth as Edward for growing, I remember, two yards tall
at fourteen, with enormous hands and feet. By eighteen,
though, he'd have looked well as St. Michael the
Archangel in a pageant, and later, as Mars the mighty
warrior.

When I had first completed my surgeon's apprenticeship, I had been fortunate enough to obtain, through the
good offices of a grateful patient of my father—he was a
well-known surgeon in the city of London—employment
in the household of the Duke of York. The Duke was
newly home from Normandy, the French war over, and
his eldest son Edward five years old. I served the Duke of
York for twelve years, traveling with him to Dublin,
returning to England, and seeing the outbreak of war
when at last he made claim to the throne. He was a good
master and an uprightman; I honored him greatly. I
served him as surgeon in peace and in war, and he
rewarded me by supporting me at Oxford and
Cambridge, when I studied to become a Doctor of

Medicine, which is no easy thing for a professed surgeon, because the universities are reluctant to admit them. During that time York was killed at the battle of Wakefield, and young Edward became King.

Not young Edward now, he was nearly forty-one years old and looked older in sickness. His eyelids flickered open, and he gazed at me without moving his head or trying to heave himself higher upon the pillows. His eyes were dull, with bloodshot whites.

"Your Grace must rest," I said severely, as if he were a boy again. "A light diet, milk, much water in the wine. I'll bleed Your Highness again tomorrow." I expected to hear a groan at this or some blasphemous expletives, but he made no comment and shut his eyes, as if he cared about nothing.

He'd been taken ill just after the feast of Easter. Because the weather had turned suddenly fine and unseasonably warm a fishing party had been suggested, upon the pleasant stretch of the Thames between Chelsea and Brentford. The King was fond of fishing now that he had become so heavy and afflicted by spells of poor health and unable to take part in more strenuous sports. So there had been much laughter, competition for a place in the King's boat, and gallons of wine drunk—they'd rowed along with big jars of it slung over the side in nets, to cool in the water—and a few fish caught. Late in the afternoon the fickle weather had turned petulant, and rain had poured down. The royal party had returned with the servants bailing out the boats and the King, like everyone else, cold and very wet, both inside and out. It was hard to tell how much he'd drunk, because through much practice, a great deal shows in him very little. He was certainly flushed and merry, as much from the conviviality of the outing as the wine. At supper he ate overheartily of a green salad and several oranges, washed down by yet more wine. This combination of heat and cooling food is not good, and disastrous for a man who suffers many stomach disorders.

For the fifth year King Edward had been excused by the Pope's indulgence from eating fish in Lent and on Holy Days. This had been obtained on my advice, for fish upset him so severely, forty days of eating it might well be the death of him. I always kept a strict eye on his diet, though there were times when, like a rebellious boy, he decided to eat what he liked and suffered for it. Because the King frequently dines in public, people noticed if he made a sudden dash for the basin waiting in an anteroom, his stomach in upheaval. As with such occurrences, gossip foolishly said that the King would induce vomiting, like the old Roman gluttons, so that he might gorge again after it. Knowing what I did of his low state of health and spirits, I was greatly alarmed at his sudden collapse. The fainting fit had been inexplicable. It might have appeared to onlookers a stroke of apoplexy, but I noticed that he had none of the bluish color about his lips that usually comes with a seizure, and no pain. Now his face had a yellowish tinge.

In the night the King succumbed to a fever. The squires who were watching over him came rushing to fetch me and any of the other royal physicians who were within the palace. I gave drafts of herbs in an attempt to reduce the fever, and the others crowded around with their own sovereign remedies, but nothing provided ease. William Lord Hastings, the King's Chamberlain and close friend, kept asking me anxiously for reassurances, which I could not give. He kept watch night and day at the King's bedside. They had been friends, these two, since before King Edward was crowned. Hastings was a dozen years the elder, though he did not look it, handsome, debonair, and amiable, managing to be both a man's man and a woman's man at one time. He and the King loved women; a favorite form of wager at court was on their latest conquests in bed. This might seem indecorous, but it caused them both to laugh and make a great many improper remarks themselves. That their friendship went beyond mere convivial companionship, however, was testified by Hasting's present distress.

In his delirium the King grabbed his friend's arm and began calling someone by name. We thought that he said, "Edward," at first and that he wanted his son the Prince.

"Safe at Ludlow," Hastings said, to soothe him.

"Ludlow's a shambles—in ruins—not safe ... Don't

go—Edmund! Edmund!"

"Merciful Christ!" Hastings said. "He's babbling about his brother Edmund of Rutland, dead twenty-two years ago! I can't even remember the boy's face. He was seventeen when Clifford cut his throat at Wakefield Bridge."

"They were close," I said. "A year between their ages."

By the time the King had been ill three days, all Westminster was certain that he was dying. His collapse had sent rumors of poison flying around, and everyone lived in great apprehension of the future. I was afraid myself that if he did not rally in a day or two at the most, he would indeed die; he was coming to the end of his strength. He was coughing painfully and bringing up brown phlegm. Every so often I got him to pass water into a glass urinal, so that we physicians might observe the signs of the progress of disease. "The mirror of mankind, Hobbes," he croaked, "in which you read all things about all men. I want no mirrors of steel or glass any longer, to tell me the havoc time has wrought on me. Self-indulgence too—I don't need to make my confession to you, Hobbes, you've known me too long. Why, I can remember a time when you put me across your knee, and your surgeon's hand was harder than my tutor's!" He grinned feebly, a shadow of his old humor in his eyes. He'd always been a great one for laughter in the past. Men had called him the handsomest Prince in Christendom. Now, he'd lost much flesh through the fever, and his face, with its prominent cheekbones, big jaw, and long straight nose, could have been the face of his youth, if it had not been so ghastly with sickness.

That day the King summoned his executors. In a spell of weak and sweaty calm, he made what provision he could for the future of his realm and for his heir the Prince. He'd made a will years ago, before he went on his French expedition, and the substance of it remained unchanged. He dictated portions that he required to be altered, then asked the lawyers to draw up a codicil.

"I wish," King Edward said, his breath wheezing like an old bellows, "I wish to make provision for the

government of this realm after my death—no, Will, we've
faced Death too many times not to know his face by now
... It is necessary that the realm is left in the hands of a
strong man ..." A ripple went through the assembly, a
new tension was felt. "A man of my blood," the King went
on, "who is qualified by rank and experience to rule for
my son until he is of age, to guide and teach him. My
dearest brother, Richard, Duke of Gloucester, shall be
appointed Protector and have the tutelage and oversight
of the Prince and all my other children. Let it be known
that I put my entire trust in his ability and known
probity—he is the best of brothers."

Amid the murmurs of astonishment and approval
from one side, Lionel Woodville, Bishop of Salisbury, the
Queen's brother, said, "But Your Grace has already
appointed my brother Rivers as tutor and governor of the
Lord Prince in letters patent issued only a month ago—
shall he lose his office?"

King Edward's congested lungs let out a gusty,
impatient breath. "My Lord, Anthony is well suited to
oversee my son's education. I have always admired his
talents. This should continue, as it would if I lived, but he
must accept Richard in my place, until my son is his own
master."

There was no concealing the dismay of the Bishop nor
the grim triumph of Lord Hastings. If all our remedies
failed and the King died, the realm would be riven in
two—a house divided. There they were, ranged on either
side of the bed, two factions, as hostile to each other as
the Turk is to the nations of Christendom. I am not fond
of deathbed spectators; they gathered around the King
like kites, some holding musk balls to their noses. I
thought: You'll be less dainty when your time comes,
when you suffer the humiliations of sickness, too weak to
get up to the stool and ministered to with bedpans. Kings
are not spared the weaknesses of humanity. No one knew
the enmity of the two factions better than King Edward,
for it was himself that kept them from each other's
throats. He also knew that as soon as he was dead, they
would leap at each other like unleashed mastiffs, to fight
for that bone of power, the person of the Prince, who

would be King—God help the child—at twelve years old. The only man with any chance of keeping them apart was Gloucester, and even he might not be strong enough. I wondered if the King knew the perilous situation he was leaving to his brother, then was left in no doubt that he did.

When the King had settled himself, half upright on bolsters and pillows, and recovered his breath somewhat, he said to Hastings, "Will, before I consign my soul to Almighty God, there is something I'd have you swear." Hastings nodded, unable to speak. The King looked at his stepson, the Marquess of Dorset, who stood there, his beautiful face resentful of Hastings, his shallow mind registering only fear for his own skin. "And you, Tom, if you respect nothing in this life, will you respect the wishes of a dying man? Will you swear to quarrel no more with Lord Hastings? And you, William, by the faith you've always kept with me, will you make peace with my lord Marquess?" The two men stood as if turned to pillars of salt, like Lot's wife, glaring at each other across the bed. "My son," the King gasped, "shall not be bequeathed a realm split by factions. If you bear me and the Prince any loyalty, patch up these differences. For God's sake, help Richard my brother. Will, you stood by me always, in the bad times. Stand by Richard now. All that we have won together will be sacrificed if this quarrel continues— swear to end it, swear on the Blood of Christ! Do not let me die thinking I have built my house on sand."

"I swear," Hastings said instantly; he would have denied the King his friend nothing and, being a generous and tolerably honest man, would sincerely try to keep his word. Dorset looked askance at first, then smiled disarmingly and grasped Hastings's proffered hand. "So be it," he said, with every appearance of sincerity. So a weather vane moves and stands firm, when the wind blows hard. Then the others joined hands, feeling some gesture of good will was needed, if only to please the dying King. On one side the Woodvilles; Lionel the Bishop of Salisbury, Sir Edward, and Sir Richard, the Queen's brothers; her younger son Lord Richard Grey; and various of their followers. On the other, those lords

of the realm who were present in Westminster; the Earl of
Lincoln the King's nephew, an energetic and decisive
young man of twenty, already known to be a close
associate of Gloucester; William Herbert, Earl of
Huntingdon, a quiet man in his mid-twenties, who had
survived a dozen years of marriage to the Queen's sister,
been deprived of his father's earldom of Pembroke, and
watched the ascendancy of the Prince's council,
dominated by the Queen's family, in his old Welsh
inheritance. Then there was Lord Stanley, one of the
older lords, whose allegiance would go to the strongest,
as it always had. Now, he seemed to favor Lord Hastings.
Seeing him take the hand of the Bishop of Salisbury,
Kind Edward said, "Watch your wife, my lord Stanley,
her son Tudor in Brittany may think my death offers him
some advantage." Stanley, quick to protest, said that the
Lady Margaret's only hope was that her son would come
home to England of his own free will, thus implying that
Tudor's claim to the throne was all but forgotten, a
protest that deluded no one. Then, as if unable to believe
in this show of comradeship taking place at his request,
King Edward heaved a huge sigh and rolled over onto his
side, turning his face into the pillow, dismissing them all
from his sight.

By the seventh and eighth days, the King's fever
worsened. The bouts of delirium grew more frequent, and
he raved like some of my mad patients at the hospital of
St Mary of Bethlehem. People, many of them dead,
passed across his mind like shadows. I've seen so many
men make such a variety of ends, good, bad, and
indifferent. Some fear Purgatory's fire and the
punishment for their misdeeds in the life after death,
others are loath to leave the splendors of this world. A
king, God knows, in the nature of things, must suffer a
lifelong sore conscience, and King Edward though I bear
him much affection, had committed some grievous sins.
The worst of these, in my opinion, was fratricide. His
brother of Clarence's wine-sodden shade haunted the
King's fevered mind like some mischievous, taunting
Bacchus, much as he had haunted the court of
Westminster in the last years of his life, the ruin of a

beautiful and talented but destructive young man. King Edward often cried out his name, and when it was not Clarence, it was the name of his own son the Prince Edward, as if he feared less his going from the world, than the troubles he'd leave behind for others.

All the time Lord Hastings stayed with him. By his side often was the King's mistress known as Shore's wife, though her marriage to William Shore the mercer had been anulled seven years before. King Edward had possessed many, many women, but this one, I think, he had truly loved, after his fashion. "The kindest and merriest of my Elizabeths," he had called her, to distinguish her from numerous others of that name, including his wife the Queen. Now she showed much dignity, not weeping, holding the King's hand when he lay quiet. Once, in a lucid spell, he knew her and stroked her thigh and smiled, as if he found her presence comforting. Even at such a time I knew that Hastings wanted her; he could not disguise the desire in his looks. I thought him old enough to know better, for everyone knew that Mistress Shore had cast her fancy upon the Marquess of Dorset, a man more than twenty years younger. In the days to come she would need protection and had already made her choice. King Edward had gone beyond the complexities of the loves of men and women. Soon he asked for his confessor, and we left him to make himself ready to meet his Maker. In an outer room the Host and Holy Oils were ready; the Archbishop of York lay nearby, waiting to be called to administer the rites.

On the ninth day of April, our sovereign lord King Edward IV died.

Before the day was out a horseman galloped from Westminster Palace, taking the road west. I had no doubt that he carried a frantic letter to Ludlow. I wondered if Lord Rivers had returned there yet from his Norfolk estates. No one reported a similar man riding north, though the Duke of Gloucester was known to be at one of his Yorkshire castles. I noticed many confused comings and goings in the next few days. Westminster was suddenly swarming with men in Dorset's livery of murrey and white and an equal number bearing Lord Hastings's badge of a black bull's head. Men were going about wearing brigandines—even when covered with fine cloth, a metal-sewn jacket is bulkier than ordinary—or carrying swords.

Exhausted though I was by my constant attendance upon the King, there remained a number of tasks for me to do, none of them pleasant. King or not, the anointed flesh of a royal corpse is still a human carcass and is dealt with as other men. After death King Edward was laid out upon a board in a room in the palace, naked except for a cloth covering him from the navel to the knees. All the lords spiritual and temporal filed past him as he lay; the Major of London, the aldermen and citizens came. Many wept to see him dead, especially the women; they waited hours to get a glimpse of him. He was buried ten days later in his chapel of St. George at Windsor.

A day or two before the beast of St. George, a council of Lords met. Not being present at such events, I could only draw my conclusions from the gossip that came out afterwards. A clerk of my acquaintance, who had been on duty in the Star Chamber, told me that the Marquess had asked for a fleet to put to sea under the command of his uncle, Sir Edward Woodville, against the French pirates. Lord Hastings had been furious, for he was Captain of Calais, and he feared that this Woodville fleet would attack him if he put to sea himself and cut him off from his garrison. The lord Marquess wanted a date agreed upon for the young King's coronation—May the fourth, he suggested. This threw the meeting into uproar. Lord Howard asked grimly why this should be decided before the Lord Protector arrived in London—surely it was a desicion that should not be made in his absence? To this the Marquess replied coolly that Protector or not, Gloucester was only one voice among many; the many were present and the one not. Then Lord Hastings had dropped his hot brick into the proceedings by announcing that he had been in communication with the Protector ever since the King's death and that plans were already made for the Duke to ride south to take up his office and that he hoped to meet my Lord Rivers on the way. At this, the Marquess got very red in the face and said that Lord Rivers, as his letters patent allowed, was already raising men in the Marches of Wales; he would be sure to come to London with a strong force. If Rivers came with an army, Lord Hastings then shouted, he would leave at once for Calais, washing his hands of English affairs, and only a siege would dig him out. This threat had such a sobering effect, dismaying the lords who looked to him for leadership, that Dorset had to agree to River's escort being limited to two thousand.

Lord Hastings, whose nerve I had to admire, then played his trump card. He had Hastings pursuivant declaim at Paul's Cross a letter that had been sent to the council of lords by the Duke of Gloucester. The tenor of this was heartening. He had been loyal to his brother King Edward, Gloucester said, at home and abroad, in peace and in war. He would be equally loyal to his brother's heir and all his issue. He wished that the new government of the kingdom should be established according to law and justice. By his brother's testament, he had been made Protector. If the council were debating the disposition of authority, he asked them to consider the position rightfully due to him according to the law of the land and his brother's ordinance. Nothing that was contrary to law and King Edward's will could be decreed without harm. The people were impressed. The Duke, though known mostly by reputation only in the South, was popular, his name a byword for justice and straight dealing. Men began to speak openly against the Queen and to suspect that she meant to keep the Protector from his rightful place. The atmosphere at Westminster had become as dangerous as a strike-a-light near a powder barrel. A few frivolous-minded souls made bets on whether Gloucester or Lord Rivers would reach London first.

I'm not one to waste good money on making wagers, but Gloucester would be the man for me in a tight situation, not Rivers. King Edward used to say that his brother throve upon danger and difficulty. His task of defending England against the Scots certainly provided both. I had served under him on his last campaign at Berwick and Edinburgh, sent with a team of nine

surgeons, to minister to the English army. There had been
no pitched battle. We had made the usual sort of war
upon the Scots, clearing towns and villages of
inhabitants, then letting in the soldiers, burning the
places flat to the ground, and rounding up the livestock to
feed our own army. It's quick work and brutal; the
homeless often die of hunger or of exposure to the foul
Scottish weather. Gloucester gave the towns fair warning
for the people to get clear away. He refused to allow
looting, murder, or rape. He gave his men the orders in a
characteristic way, by riding out in front of them and
telling them straight that anyone caught disobeying him
would be punished. He had an army of twenty
thousand, which is a big army by any standards, and
discipline of this sort is hard to enforce among so many.
But after the first offender had been strung up in full view
of all the rest and left there to rot, with his spoils hung
around his neck or one who'd molested a Scotswoman
equally publicly flogged, these orders were obeyed. Yet
no one was afraid to bring their injustices and injuries to
the Duke. He went so openly among his men that they
only needed to walk up to him to gain a hearing. He
would talk with them in their own northern speech, of
which I could understand very little, but I saw that, in his
way, he had as much of the common touch as his brother
King Edward. The Queen's family would have been wiser
not to make an enemy of the Duke of Gloucester.

On the evening of May Day I was returning to my
lodgings at Westminster when I came upon the Lord
Hastings and Howard standing by an upper window that
looked out over the Sanctuary, apparently fascinated by
what they saw, and letting out great guffaws of laughter.
As the past weeks hadn't afforded much mirth, I was
curious, and pleased when they turned around and
greeted me in a friendly fashion.

"Take a look out of here, Dr. Hobbes," Hastings said,
grinning and making room for me at the window. I
looked out. It was almost dark, and the yard below was
ablaze with cressets and torches; I had a feeling Hell
would look like that when you looked down into it. In the
spring dusk, above it all, a blackbird was singing from a

roof pinnacle, when he could make himself heard over the din of human voices. I looked again into that Hades lake of light and saw that it was in fact men moving furniture, rolled up arras, big coffers, and bulky bundles through a hole in the Sanctuary wall. Judging by the tumble of bricks and mortar they kept stumbling over, they'd had to take pickaxes to the wall in order to get the goods through. A huge painted cupboard was stuck halfway, like a ship aground.

"What goes on?" I said, stupefied.

"Her Grace the Queen," Lord Howard said, "is moving her household, her younger son and five daughters, into the Sanctuary. No one may touch her there; the Church protects her from the law."

I gaped at him. "Holy Jesu, why does she need protection?"

Hastings, triumphant, burst in with the news. "Gloucester has the King. Rivers is arrested. The Queen is in flight!"

3

Lord Protector

Told by Francis, Viscount Lovell, the Duke of Gloucester's friend

The power and auctoritie of my lord Protector is so behoffulle and of reason to be assented and established by the auctoritie of thys hyghe courte, that amonges alle the causes of the assmeblynge of the parliamente yn thys tyme of the yere, thys is the grettest and the most necessarye furst to be affermed. God graunte that thys mater and syche othir as of necessite owithe to be furst moved for the wele of the Kynge and the defense of thys londe, maye have such goode and breff expedition yn thys hyghe courte of parliamente as the ease of the peuple and the condicion of the tyme requireth.

Speech drafted by the Bishop of Lincoln for the intended Parliament of Edward V on 25 June 1483, proposing a continuation of the Protectorate

"Protector's an ill-omened title," Richard had said. "It brought my father to ruin and Duke Humphrey of Gloucester before him."

I could appreciate his gloom. As we rode into Northampton an air of unease infected our party. The day before, scouts sent out to spy upon the road between Warwick and Daventry had reported that Lord Rivers brought the young King from Ludlow with an escort of two thousand and that they carried arms; cartloads of armor, sheaves of arrows, bundles of crossbows and spears had been noticed. They should reach Northampton on the last day of April. I looked around at my companions. We numbered a little above five hundred. Richard had brought no more than a usual riding household of knights, squires, servants, and priests, which, together with the attendants of the other northern lords who rode with us, made up the number. If Rivers planned an attack, we were more than likely to end up dead, captive, or running for our lives. I had been in favor of our setting out better prepared, but Richard had shut his lips tight in that stubborn way he has, and said, "No. It usually takes two bellicose parties to make a fight. Rivers has more sense than his sister the Queen. I do not wish to be accused of storming down from the North with an army to seize the King, even though I am lawful Protector. Better to let Rivers show his hand first. The Woodvilles are not popular. I've a feeling they'll be their own undoing."

Upn the journey south he had been uncommunicative. I had often traveled in his company, and he is a man easy to talk to, especially among his friends. I had known him as a boy, when I had gone at the age of eight, just before my father's death, to be educated in the Earl of Warwick's household at Middleham. Richard, who is a little more than three years older than I, had been sent away soon after to Westminster, because of his brother's quarrel with Warwick. Our friendship was formed later, after he had returned to the North and I at seventeen had escaped the tutelage of the Duke of Suffolk, whose ward I was, and looked for the favor of a lord of high rank who was to my liking. Richard, at twenty-one, appealed to me, because he stood in such favor with the King and because of his youth, fame in war, and reputation for honesty. I wanted his good lordship but soon found we fell easily into friendship.

Now he was wrapped around in his own thoughts. He

had the stark, striken look of the recently bereaved. The news of King Edward's death had arrived at Middleham just after I had departed from a visit that began with the meeting of Richard's ducal council at Lady Day and lasted over the feast of Easter. I heard when staying at my brother-in-law Lord Fitzhugh's castle of Ravensworth, so did not see Richard in the first shock of it. King Edward had been the lodestar of his life. He hadn't had much time for an outward display of mourning, but I thought the loss would afflict him for a long time to come. Richard has never been one to take life lightly, and he has had more than his just share of trouble and sorrow. Now we were in for troubled times again.

So, riding down the main street of Northampton, we looked over our shoulders and fingered our daggers, as if the Queen's men lurked behind every alebush. We had only just dismounted at the inn where we were to lodge for the night, when Lord Rivers himself rode up. He was not accompanied by the young King.

Anthony Woodville, Lord Rivers, had arrayed himself in ostentatious mourning. His long gown of cut Genoa velvet was patterned with water flowers, his sister the Queen's device, and sumptuously lines with foxskins dyed black. Around his shoulders gleamed a gold collar of linked suns and roses, with a pendant white lion of March—the collar all King Edward's followers had worn, but studded with enough diamonds and pearls for the necklace of a Westminster whore. I wondered if, as rumor had it, he wore a hair shirt under the rich garments, as though by his perpetual mortification of the flesh he might do penance for his outward display. He dismounted, servants holding aside his magnificent fur gown in case it caught up in his very large gilt spurs—he even had diamonds in his spurs. He strode across the yard—nothing womanish here—he combines muscular activity with his extreme elegance. His fair-skinned face was illumined by a smile of great charm and friendliness; he courteously doffed his hat and stretched out his hand in greeting. Richard made no move toward him. River's sudden arrival had produced an entire lack of expression in his face, as if one had turned the page of a book and been confronted with a blank sheet. Rivers bent his knee, lower than he need have, to Richard and kissed his hand. "Your Grace of Gloucester keeps prompt time on the road. May I offer my condolences to Your Grace upon the sudden death of our late sovereign lord King Edward, your brother. Believe me, I most sincerely share your sorrow. Remember, all three of us endured many vicissitudes—why, we have even shared a crust of bread, as fellow exiles!"

"Yes," Richard said, almost inaudibly. Then, "My Lord Rivers, I had hoped to offer my own condolences to the King my nephew and to promise him the faithful service I always gave his father. It seems that I must wait to do so."

"My nephew the King will receive Your Grace soon, of course. The reason for his absence is, I am afraid, a mundane one. Your Grace's person and these northern gentlemen will no doubt occupy all the inns in Northampton. In order that the King shall not cause them inconvenience he decided it better if his own household were lodged at Stony Stratford. If Your Grace will do me the favor of accompanying me there in the morning, we may greet our nephew together." He was most convincingly conciliatory; one could almost believe that he meant to accord Richard his rightful place as Lord Protector. We could not know what he intended—a brawl now, the unfortunate death of Gloucester? Or soft words, to lull suspicion until some other trap was set? The fact that Stony Stratford is fourteen miles nearer to London was not lost upon us. Whoever held the King's person held the realm. The sooner Richard made sure it was himself, the better.

Beside the elegant figure of Lord Rivers, who is a middling to tall man, Richard was at a disadvantage. He was bareheaded, out of courtesy when speaking to Rivers, and the wind ruffled up his hair. A servant stood holding his mourning robe, and he wore the plainest black worsted, decorated only with a row of black silk buttons. This midnight garb made him look sickly pale and very tired; he could have been about the same age as Rivers, who is fully a dozen years older. There's no denying, the Queen's family are beautiful people—a pity their minds do not match their bodies. Though Anthony Woodville does not have the startling silver fairness of his sister the Queen, he is smoothly blond, with an extraordinarily unlined skin, fitting firmly over his regular features. I suspect that he puts creams and pastes on it, like a woman. Not that he is a self-indulgent man; he avoids excess. At past forty he still prides himself on the fitness of his body and on his prowess in the tourney, at tennis, wrestling, and all the manly sports; one cannot deny that he is expert in all of them. Strange that with his repute in handling weapons in the mock but dangerous battles of the lists, he has never won any distinction in real battles.

The next thing I knew was that Rivers had invited himself to supper—at least, I think he had; Richard didn't seem to be saying anything, either yea or nay. It was a good supper. These big inns that serve travelers on the north road are used to receiving guests of the highest rank. We ate in a room the size of a hall in a castle, warmed by giant fires in two hearths. The tables were spread with white damask, the candles set in silver holders, and the best serving dishes were silver gilt. We washed our hands in basins filled with hot water in which camomile flowers had been steeped and dried them on the finest linen towels.

After Grace was said, we scarcely had time to sample the first dish, of brawn with mustard, when a tremendous clatter of hoofs was heard in the yard and a voice at the door announced: "His Grace the Duke of Buckingham!" Buckingham walked straight in, still his boots and cloak, ignored Rivers, marched up to Richard, and knelt to him as if he were the King himself. Richard got up, took his cousin's hands, raised him up and kissed his cheek. "Harry," he said, smiling for the first time that evening, "you're more than welcome. You'll dine with Lord Rivers and myself?"

"Very willingly—I'm late; the roads from the Severn eastward have not yet recovered from the winter. I hope you'll excuse the intrusion, cousin, in the middle of supper."

It was an intrusion we all welcomed. Buckingham and his two hundred Welsh Marcher followers had been expected. He had sent word to the Lord Protector soon after he'd heard of King Edward's death, offering his entire support and suggesting that it would be wise to join forces here.

When the flutter caused by his arrival had died down and he was seated on Richard's right hand and Rivers on the left, I wached the three men talk. Harry Buckingham was about my own age, of middle height, with bright chestnut hair and odd-shaped black eyebrows that didn't seem to match it. His nose was largish and longish, his mouth wide, with a quirky smile. It was a face remarkable chiefly for its mobility; those eyebrows moved up and down often, the mouth smiled or grimaced emphasizing his words. Soon the warmth, wine, and food put a high color in his cheeks. I noticed that as Buckingham talked to him, gesticulating and shrugging now and then, Richard smiled often; once even he laughed. I was surprised, then pleased, that his cousin had such a cheering effect on him. I'd not had much success in cheering him the last weeks. I caught parts of their conversation. Of Rivers, Richard inquired after the enterprises of Master Caxton the printer, whose workshop at the sign of the Red Pale near Westminster Abbey we had visited once again while attending the last Parliament. It is his generous patronage of such arts and his scholar's love of learning and literature that set Rivers apart from the rest of this family. Later I think he began telling a tale of his pilgrimage to the shrine of St. James of Compostela in Spain. I remembered how he had announced his intention to go on this pilgrimage not long after the battle of Tewkesbury, and King Edward had been annoyed, saying that Rivers had a habit of absenting himself when there was work to do—in fact, calling him work-shy and a coward.

Toward the end of the meal, when we were served the last course of wafers and hippocras, dates, almonds, hard-sugared caraway comfits, and quince preserve, some of the musicians of Richard's household played to us upon lute and viol. Buckingham had brought a Welsh

harper in his train, who made a strange, wild music and
was well rewarded, though we did not understand the
language. One of the north country lords had brought a
ballad singer—a woman. It's a custom of the Border
lords to keep pipers and ballad singers, to tell of the deeds
of their families in fighting the Scots. This is an
entertainment that Westminster might well scoff at. I
wondered if this woman were one of those who follow
their men in war, a knife hidden in their skirts and no
hesitation in using it. She stood with her arms and hands
stiff and straight at her sides, a curiously wooden, dumpy
figure, who left one unprepared for the huge voice that
came from her. It was not sweet or even womanly—she
wailed like a bagpipe, setting the teeth on edge and, with
me, the hair prickling and blood tingling. I could just
understand her words, though she might have been as
much Scot as English.

> "There came a man by middle day,
> He spied his sport and went away;
> And brought the king that very night,
> Who brake my bower, and slew my knight.
> He slew my knight, to me sae dear.
> He slew my knight and poind his gear;
> My servants a' for life did flee,
> And left me in extremitie."

In every song made by a minstrel, he has locks of golden
hair and builds his love a bonny bower, but it always ends
the same way—the worms get him. I'd never yet seen a
Border pele tower clad about with lily flowers either.
Most of them have a huge midden by the wall and are so
dark and smoky within, men come out pickled like a side
of bacon. I wondered what Rivers made of it. He listened,
but could not follow the words. His face expressed polite
interest, like a traveler who finds himself in the land of the
paynims and is invited to observe their customs. After the
singer had done and collected her coins, he said, "A harsh
music, from a harsh land. I once heard the like in the Earl
of Warwick's household."

Richard was sitting back in his chair and playing with
his set of table knives, slipping them back and forth in
their case. His face betrayed no reaction to River's

remark, but I knew better than to imagine it went unnoticed. Soon, I thought, Warwick will be avenged and the Queen's rapacious family brought low, with few to mourn their fall.

It was late when Rivers left us, to ride down the street to his own inn. His farewells were as calm and friendly as his greetings had been. He should have been warned, by the obvious deference Buckingham accorded Richard.

"There goes our pilgrim," Buckingham remarked, looking from the window. "I suppose he chose that scallop shell to mark his men because it is the pilgrim's sign."

"It has been known for pilgrims to be ambushed on the road," Richard said. "Harry, I want to settle our score with Rivers quietly—no show of force. It must be done before he returns to the King, before he deals with us as he has no doubt planned. I cannot allow him to reach London before us. Sir Richard Ratcliffe, will you take sufficient men to surround his inn, request the keys from the landlord, and have the yard gates bolted. He'll find himself unable to leave in the morning—in short, under arrest, for plotting to deprive me of my power as Protector. We'll ride for Stony Stratford very early. It should not take much more than an hour. None of River's men must be allowed to warn Grey and the other of our coming."

"Or," Buckingham said with a smile, "our little royal bird will have flown."

We retired to bed. My squire shook me awake at three, shaved my bleary-eyed contenance, thrust me into the black clothes he had brushed down the night before, and pulled on my riding boots. I breakfasted in the big room downstairs where we had dined. Richard was there already; Buckingham joined us in a few moments. We ate standing up, a few mouthfuls of still hot, white bread, a slice or two of cold sirloin, washed down with hot, spiced ale to keep the chill out of us. There were a number of other things on the table we didn't have time for. Richard was still in his shirt, though he had his boots and spurs on. His squires were more or less dressing him as he ate. I noticed they dressed him in a coat of brigandines covered

with black velvet. Buckingham was wearing one too. I
sent my squire to fetch me a similar protection, to be on
the safe side. We didn't want to look warlike and arrive in
armor, but preferred to guard against the knife in the
back. I wondered if Rivers had awakened yet and found
himself a prisoner, just when he thought himself in
command of the situation.

As we walked out into the yard I shivered. The day was
gray, cold, and inhospitable, drizzling halfheartedly. We
rode as fast as we could, slowed only by miry patches of
road. Richard kept the lead almost all the way, his great
black horse had a long, easy stride that ate up the miles.
We were only just in time. As we pounded down the long
street of Stony Stratford, the inn where the royal party had
stayed was in a turmoil, horsemen spilling out of the yard
across the road. Richard's horse slithered to a halt. One
of his men grabbed the reins as he dismounted. He stood
there, looking at the milling assembly of the King's men.
After a moment, when the shouting ceased, they stared at
him, then a single yell went up—"Gloucester!"

The throng parted and a boy rode out of the inn yard,
followed closely by a man a little younger than myself.
The King wasn't dressed in mourning, but in a purple
cloak and a hat with a blue ostrich feather. When he saw
the man standing at the end of the path his men had
made, he drew rein. Richard walked toward him, alone,
between the ranks of the King's men. It made my hair
stand on end to see him—Jesu! they could have ridden
him down in an instant. But they let him through in
silence. The King's horse backed a little, shaking its head,
feeling the uncertainty of its rider. The boy's voice was
gruff with adolescence at first, then high as a child's in
query, "Your Grace of Gloucester! We did not
expect...Where is my Lord Rivers?"

I didn't hear Richard's reply, for he was speaking
quietly. He knelt to the boy, in a token of homage, though
the road was muddy. When he got up, the King
dismounted, I think because Richard told him to. They
stood facing each other, one confused and angry, the
other quiet and immovable as rock. The King, quite a tall
boy for twelve, was as big as his uncle. Buckingham went

next to Richard's side; he knelt to the King and kissed his hand. Ratcliffe and I followed him. The King's face was white as his shirt, and though he held himself upright, he was trembling from head to foot. His hand, when I kissed it, was chill and clammy. It was plain to any onlooker that he was extremely frightened. "My lord of Gloucester," he said, his voice flying up and down with fright and anger, "my uncle Rivers has been my guardian for ten years, all my life, I will not have him made a prisoner!" He was making a valiant attempt at royal authority.

"His Grace your father, King Edward," Richard said patiently, "has left me Protector of his kingdom and his children. It is a lawful precedent and cannot be disregarded. Lord Rivers has tried to disregard it. Your Grace, I give you my word, as your father's brother, that I will serve you faithfully as I served him. He has left you a great kingdom; I wish to help you rule it wisely."

The boy's face showed only unfeigned astonishment. "If my father made you Protector..." he began. Clearly he had not been told that this was his father's will.

The King's Chamberlain, Sir Thomas Vaughan, an elderly Welsh Border lord, looked nervous but spoke up bravely, "Your Grace of Gloucester has not right..."

Lord Richard Grey, the King's half brother, did the rashest thing possible—he drew his sword. A gasp went up—it is a treasonable act in the King's presence. Two of Buckingham's men grabbed him, knocking the hat from his hair into the mud; two others took Vaughan. Richard, still alone and unarmed among his enemies' followers, did not speak until Vaughan and Grey were both disarmed. Then he merely said, in a voice cold as iron, "Those who wish to question my right may do so before the council at Westminster."

We rode slowly back to Northampton and, while the town enjoyed its May Day games, spent an uncomfortable time trying to overcome the King's hostility. The boy was too old to comfort as one might a smaller child and too young to realize that men cannot be clearly divided into those who are good and those who are wicked. He obviously adored his uncle Rivers. Strange, that a man we find so unlovely should receive such unstinted affection. Young Edward had been at Ludlow since he was three, in his uncle's care; I suppose Rivers had taken the place of a father.

At supper the first night the sight of the King's bloodless, pinched little face took the edge off my appetite. He began by refusing to eat, which was a pity, for the waterfowl and fish were particularly good—Northampton is conveniently close to the river Ouse and the fenny parts of Huntingdonshire. Richard, despite every effort to make a dent in the uncompromising armor of hatred that met him, could get nothing out of the boy. The one thing that he thought would succeed—their shared love for the late King—did not. He talked of Ludlow, trying to convince the boy that he was human and could remember being a boy as well.

"Your Grace has been lucky, living his life at Ludlow. It's a good place for a boy. When I was seven your father took me fishing there. He taught me how to catch trout in the river Teme. He was nearly eighteen and Earl of March, yet he hadn't forgotten how to lie flat on a riverbank with his sleeves sopping wet, tickling the trout's bellies. When we got back, I never minded that I got beaten for getting my clothes muddy and he didn't. Did you go fishing, Edward?"

"No," muttered the King, hating to be drawn into conversation, then, grudgingly, because a gleam of interest did lie under his prickle-backed manner, "I had a proper rod. My brother Dick Grey put the bait on and taught me to make a cast. I caught a fish once—oh, that big ..." He made the customary gesture of a proud fisherman with his hands, indicating an impossible, pikesized catch. "The village boys caught the fish with their hands, as you did, Uncle." The Prince of Wales clearly hadn't been allowed the freedom of the Duke of York's sons. I didn't much like the way he said the village boys went tickling trout as Richard had.

Richard said, without rancor, "Will Your Grace take some of this? You must eat. A king can't do his work on an empty stomach. Look, we'll send this dish over to your uncle Lord Rivers, as a token of goodwill. Things are not so black—he's alive and well and dining with us here."

The King became suddenly eager. "My uncle Rivers and my brother Grey may be released?" But then fell instantly sullen again, having read in Richard's face the answer.

Richard sighed. "Perhaps," was the only reply he could make. It was, of course, impossible. Richard had already decided that Rivers, Grey, and Vaughan should be escorted north and be detained under guard at Sheriff Hutton, Pontefract, and Middleham. They would be allowed plenty of servants and comfortable lodgings, but would have no chance to plot against the Lord Protector—his men would see to that—and there would be no danger of insurrection in their favor, as there might be if we took them south to London.

Afterward he said to me sadly, "The boy knows so little of his father and cares less. He's more Woodville than Plantagenet." This was true. The boy had been taught by his mother's family to fear and mistrust Richard.

We rode into London on Sunday, the fourth day of May. The Mayor, Sir Edmund Shaa, the alderman, and citizens turned out in full splendor of scarlet and violet gowns to meet us at Hornsey. The crowd gave the young King a hearty welcome, because he is his father's son and the Londoners had loved King Edward. At this open acclaim, the boy looked happy for the first time since leaving Stony Stratford, and he received the Mayor's compliments with smiles. The crowd lining Cheap and Ludgate Hill gave Richard a warm welcome too, pleased that he had dealt so successfully with the Queen's kin, whom nobody loved. The church bells rang joyfully and they cheered, as they had two months ago, when he was thanked for his success against the Scots. To show that the Queen and Rivers had resorted to arms in order to forestall the Protector, men went in front of the procession bellowing out the fact and showing all the carts of armor and weapons taken with their badges on them. Because the day was the King's first in his capital city, Richard and Buckingham purposely made themselves inconspicuous in plainest black, riding one on either side of him, while he wore blue velvet and ermine. When the procession was past St. Paul's, the lords and citizens dispersed. I went to my own place, Lovell's Inn, by Paternoster Lane—Westminster was out of the question, for his mother lurked in the Sanctuary there and refused to come out, Richard went to his town house in Bishopsgate, Crosby's Place.

Among the first to greet us in London was Lord Hastings. He clasped Richard's hand, kissed him, said that he'd never been so relieved to see a man and that he heartily supported all Richard's actions, especially the arrest of Rivers and Grey. This one bold stroke had prevented untold violence, he said; the Queen's upstart family had been put down with no more shedding of blood than might issue from a cut finger. Now the realm was safe, in the hands of two powerful men, Richard and himself, as King Edward had wished. To express his friendship and support, he presented Richard with a great wine cup of silver gilt, a six-inch chunk of unicorn's horn set in the lid, which, significantly, is supposed to render all poisons harmless.

Before we had been in London a week, I realized that Hastings, whatever his ideas to the contrary, was not the man of the moment. Perhaps he discovered this too and found it irksome. As he had said, two predominated— but they were Richard and Buckingham. It would have been easy for me to predict the former. Richard is not the man to be Protector in name only or to be content with the position of merely the highest ranking member of the King's council of lords. Those who think he may be wrought to any temper that suits them are gravely mistaken; it'll be he who wields the hammer. In the North I have heard men remark, he has done a job that would have broken the back of many a tough Border lord twice his age, and, the same men say, they've never known anyone do it better.

Harry Buckingham is cast in a different mold. At twenty-eight, he has never been of much use or importance in the realm, apart from duties of bearing swords at ceremonies and Dorset's helm at joustings— that last must rankle! Now, I've never had any great ambition for political power above that due to my rank and necessary for safety, I'm too lazy, but I've led a more active life than he. At least I served as a soldier with Richard against the Scots on three years hard campaigning, and King Edward rewarded me with the title of Viscount for it. All I knew of Harry Buckingham was that his father had been killed at St. Albans in the cause of Lancaster when he was a baby and that he had been made a ward of the Queen. Before he was ten the Queen had married him to Katherine, one of her brood of younger sisters. For this I was disposed to be sympathetic to him. He has lived beyond his means, trying to outshine his Woodville relatives, is over ears in debt, with five children to provide for. I suspect that his eagerness to support Richard is prompted by desperation as well as resentment. Good service goes well rewarded, and Richard is the only man able to give him rewards that might restore him to solvency. In this hope, then, set free by events, he is soaring as high as a young eagle.

He didn't take much notice of me. It has been a custom with us, Richard and I, when finding ourselves in London or away from home, to sup with each other, play at chess, listen to music, and talk in the evenings. Richard is not one who seeks pleasure out of his wife's company. Now, when there was time, I went to Crosby's Place, only to find Harry Buckingham there already. Being an easy sort of fellow who does not jealously covet the exclusive company of his friends, I greeted him in an amiable way, tinged with just the right amount of deference a newly created viscount might allow a duke of royal blood. He was prepared to be lordly with me, but when he saw my familiarity with Richard, he made himself affable and charming.

At the end of the first week Richard sent a letter to Anne, asking her to join him London. "It should be safe now, so far as I can predict," he said. "I need her with me. Poor Anne, there'll be so many wives to entertain while I deal with the husbands. She'll have to be prepared for a long stay."

Harry gave him a look, as if he envied him. "I've only had the pleasure of meeting your wife a few times, Dickon. It was a pleasure, too, a rare one. Westminster has so many overblown flowers, too many cankered blooms!"

He had been eating dates and slung a handful of stones onto the fire, where they jumped and popped viciously. He had a queer expression on his face, unpleasant and vindictive. Richard gave me a startled look. We refrained from passing any remark on Harry's own wife. She had been left behind at Brecon, no longer able to rule him through her sister the Queen.

Then Harry, with a swift change of mood which I was to notice many times in him, said, "I met my lord Archbishop of York today, taking his barge at Palace Stairs for York House in Battersea. He greeted me like a long-lost cousin ..." Here Harry got up and gave an imitation of Rotherham's peculiar manner of combined cringing and superciliousness. I laughed outright. Harry seemed able to age thirty years at will; he shuffled about, heavy and stooping of frame, nodding his head like a popinjay on its perch and washing his hands with invisible soap. "I inquired after the Great Seal," he said with a grin, "if it were safely tied up in its bag again! He looked ready to choke!" I nearly choked myself at the thought of Rotherham's face. He'd been relieved of his office of Chancellor and Keeper of the Great Seal, because at King Edward's death he had gone running to the Queen, offering her the Seal so she might rule the kingdom as she chose.

In the week before Whitsuntide, two huge grants were made under that Great Seal in the name of King Edward V, by direction of his uncle the protector, to Harry Buckingham. He was given the offices of Chamberlain and Chief Justice of both North and South Wales, constable of all the royal castles, and steward of all royal manors therein. Being a made man, Buckingham began to spend his expected income. The numbers of his servants in London multiplied daily; they strutted about, flashing with gold Catherine wheels and Stafford knots on scarlet and black, like imps of Hell. They even appeared wearing the swan badge of Bohun, as if to draw attention to Buckingham's claim on a sizable portion of crown lands. These had belonged to the wife of Henry IV, the Bohun co-heiress, and with the demise of the House of Lancaster, Harry had considered them his right but King

Edward had not. This caused a few raised eyebrows in council. I heard Hastings say to Lord Howard, "Well, Jack, we have a new 'Prince' of Wales and our King not of an age to get his own!" He sounded sour. So, already in mid-May, jealousies and rivalries began to be seen within our own camp.

Fortunately, our enemies were in disarray. The Queen and her son Dorset were holed up in the Sanctuary like foxes. Soon after we'd arrived in London, Richard had discovered that a large portion of the royal treasure—jewels, gold, and minted coin—had disappeared from the strong vaults at the Tower. Dorset, who was Deputy Constable of the Tower, had ordered its removal without the knowledge of Lord Howard the Constable. Some of it had gone to sea with Sir Edward Woodville; the rest, we were certain, lay in coffers behind the Sanctuary wall. When he learned of this, Richard was more angry than I'd seen him in all these weeks. "He's no better than a robber," he said, of Dorset, "like his companions in the Sanctuary. It's the last time the Woodvilles line their purses at the realm's expense. If I catch him, I'll bleed him white." But Dorset lay low and did not run. We failed to catch Sir Edward Woodville when his fleet deserted him for our offer of pardons, and he fled to Brittany. Misfortune makes strange bedfellows, for there he joined the little group of Lancastrian exiles, who for ten years had lived in threadbare hope at the court of Duke Francis.

Another cause of annoyance and embarrassment was the Queen's determined retention of the little Duke of York in the Sanctuary. This gesture of defiance made it plain that she regarded the Protector as the King's jailer and held her younger son as a weapon to use in the event of harm befalling the elder. What harm she expected, with the King proclaimed and served not only by his uncle but by all the lords spiritual and temporal, I could not imagine.

The young King was moved from the Bishop of London's house to the tower, both to prevent contact with his mother's agents and to await his coronation in the accustomed place. He was to be crowned on the

twenty-second of June, a Sunday. It would followed by a
week of feasting and holidays, over the Nativity of St.
John the Baptist. Parliament was summoned to meet
upon the twenty-fifth, and all the lords and commons
were to be in London by the eighteenth, for the making of
the Knights of the Bath and other ceremonies. Because of
the dangers of the young King's minority rule once he was
crowned, with no one having authority to govern, most of
the lords were determined that Richard should be given
that authority by Act of Parliament and the Protectorate
extended until the King's coming of age.

On Thursday, June the fifth, Lady Anne arrived in
London. Richard had by now moved from Crosby's
Place to the greater convenience of his mother's riverside
house of Baynard's Castle. The next day Anne sent word
asking me to come there to see her. She wanted my honest
opinion on affairs in London. She had the situation
summed up for herself.

"Francis, my husband is in great danger."

"Yes." She had to look up a little into my face. She
wore black and white still, in mourning for King Edward.
This magpie coloring did nothing for her looks. Richard,
whatever else he saw in her, did not marry a beauty, no
Helen, whom wars were fought over. At the best of times,
she hasn't much color, but that day she was
unbecomingly pale and smudgy about the eyes. Bluish
veins showed through the delicate skin at her temples and
over her ears. In the soft hollow at the base of her throat
there was a mark the color of mulberry juice. I think she'd
tried to hide it with some paste, but the heat had made the
color show through. I didn't want her to think I'd noticed
this small evidence of private lovemaking. As my shadow
moved across her face, the pupils of her eyes swelled, then
shrank again as the sun fell into them. In those clear gray
eyes so many motes of color swam: dark blue, sea blue,
green, amber, brown, and even black. The lashes were the
color of a thrush's feather and cast a shadow. Her nose, a
little too long and high-boned for perfection, was slightly
shiny. I felt protective toward her without finding her
particularly desireable, for I was more familiar and at

ease with her than with my own sisters, being her own age
and brought up with her. I'd have preferred to see her
smile. When she was a little girl, she had looked as meek
as a mouse, until one noticed the cheek dimpling when
she smiled and that firm, neat, uptilted chin. Her elder
sister Isabel had attracted more attention, being prettier,
but it was Anne who occasionally reflected her father's
proud image. Like all the Nevilles, she was fiercely loyal
to her kin and most of all to Richard. When he was with
her, she bloomed into something approaching beauty.
When he touched her or held her in the dance, she would
turn in his arms languidly, with a graceful movement, as
if all her bones had softened, a movement any courtesan
would give her jewels and finery to be able to imitate. The
bawl of a passing waterman came suddenly through the
window and she turned her head, quick as a wary bird.
There was apprehension in every line of the tautened
neck, the hands that had clenched at her sides. I didn't
like to see her frightened, she was usually so unruffled.
"Francis, have I come to London to be made a widow?"

I took hold of her hand gently. "Hush," I said. "You
mustn't say such things. Richard has lived with danger all
his life."

"This is different. It might not be now, or even soon.
What will happen in five years, when the King is eighteen
and wants his revenge for all this?"

I could not answer her; the truth was too ugly. I led her
to a chair, sat her down, and made her drink some wine.
The wide eyes regarded me over the edge of the cup. "I
haven't said any of these things to Richard," she said. "I
don't want him to know how afraid I am—it would worry
him so much, and God knows, he's overburdened with
worry already." I stood looking down at her bent head.
Through the gauzy linen of her hennin veil the bones in the
back of the white neck showed. The fingers holding the
cup were extremely slender, with very small nails cut
close as a child's. Why, I thought, are some women so
very vulnerable? In four days, she would be twenty-seven;
she looked younger.

"Five years is a long time," I said. "So much can
happen in five days, weeks, months. The situation is

unpredictable. Don't lose hope, Anne. Will you
remember this—whatever service I do for Richard, I will
do for you also."

Within three days Anne's fears were justified. The
Queen was discovered to be plotting to murder Richard
and Buckingham, to seize the King, to release Rivers and
Grey, and to set up herself as regent. Richard's personal
danger was, of course, lessened as soon as the plot was
discovered, but he sent urgent letters to the Earl of
Northumberland, who was still in the North, asking him
to bring armed men quickly to London. Sir Richard
Ratcliffe took letters to other northern lords and to the
City of York asking for support. It had become clear by
now that the Queen intended to stir up a situation that
would probably result in rebellion and bloodshed; she
had too many enemies among the lords of the realm who
would not accept her rule. There was only one way to stop
her—by immediate, forceful action.

We'd made the discovery of the Queen's plot a little
before her allies were found out. She had suborned her
old enemy Lord Hastings into her conspiracy. We were
first warned of it by William Catesby, a lawyer who had
frequently worked for Hastings and who had taken alarm
at his master's dangerous plans. Lord Hastings, Catesby
said without relish, had a new bedfellow—Shore's wife.
I'd heard it said that he had hankered after her ever since
she became King Edward's mistress—there'd even been
tales that they had shared her, three in a bed! If he'd
hoped to have her after the King's death, he'd been
disappointed at first, for she went straight to the
Marquess of Dorset. It was well known she'd declared
herself the ally of her lover and his mother the Queen.
Dorset did not scruple to use her as a means of turning his
old enemy Hastings from friendship with Richard, nor, it
seemed, to send her into another man's bed. Will
Hastings had landed like a greedy wasp in the honey trap.

In a couple of days we had all the evidence we needed.
Mistress Shore was well watched. Her days were spent
plotting in the Santuary with the Queen and Dorset, her
night in Hasting's bed. Their aim—to set up a new
Protector—Lord Hastings himself. He was doomed;

Richard could not let him live.

On Friday, the thirteenth of June, an unlucky day, a council meeting was convened in the Tower for nine in the morning. It was a day of brilliant sunshine, hot already by nine. As I came in from the glare and climbed the shadowed stone stairs of the White Tower, the contrast of the heat outside with the cool interior was enough to make one shiver. In the council chamber there was the quivering tension one feels before a storm; it made my skin twitch. Everyone suspected that Richard had discovered something, but none dared to be absent from the meeting. There were others known to be in the plot, those who felt they did not fare as well under the Lord Protector as they had under King Edward.

When seated, I looked around the table, noting the chief among them. Rotherham, Archbishop of York, who'd lost his position as Lord Chancellor, was looking nervous. His face, which has a great deal of flabby, surplus flesh, resembled a cream cheese standing in a strainer, the whey oozing out of it. He kept wiping it and his dewlapped neck with a handkerchief the size of an altar cloth. Morton, Bishop of Ely, who was chagrined because he'd wanted the office of Chancellor himself and it had gone to the Bishop of Lincoln, is a very different sort of man. He's quite as old as York—over sixty I suppose—but looks younger, thinner, and harder. His face is sharp and beaky, like a bird of prey, and he has a quick pouncing manner to match it. A lack of front teeth made his rather prim little mouth look lipless, cut at either end by deep, vertical lines. Old vinegar chops, I thought, twice as clever as Rotherham and twice as dangerous; he moves men as he might move pawns on a chessboard. Dr. Oliver King, the most innocuous of the ecclesiastical bunch, had been King Edward's secretary and now had his nose put out of joint by John Kendal, Richard's own secretary, who was very clearly taking his place. Lord Stanley, one of the older lords, an important man in the northwest, was known to consort with this trio, though he also cultivated Lord Howard, who is most firmly Richard's man. Stanley keeps a foot in both camps. He greeted me pleasantly, but his forehead was glistening

like a skinned grape. I thought he would rather be seated
with the Protector's men than with Lord Hastings's allies.
All the company were strained and lacking in
conversation, murmuring desultorily to their immediate
neighbors. The windows of the chamber were closed, and
trapped bluebottles smacked and buzzed hopelessly
against the panes.

When Hastings came in I was shocked. He had aged ten
years overnight, which meant that he looked nearly as
bad as Rotherham. Christ! I had thought him a
handsome man. The bloodshot eyes had discolored bags
under them; the firm, cleft chin had developed flaccid
jowls, like some ancient hound. He appeared to have
been shaved hastily. Straight from Mistress Shore's bed, I
had no doubt, after a taxing night. He was also afraid. He
looked like a man who had played all his cards, who is left
empty-handed at the end of his game.

Harry Buckingham entered, in a swirl of black and
violet velvet, bringing into the room a strong scent of
ambergris. His eyes traveled, as mine had, from face to
face. He had the air of a man expecting something to
happen, as we all did, but he seemed the only one to be
pleased about it. He spoke to Bishop Morton first, in a
mildly obsequious way—youth deferring to ecclesiastical
old age—which only those who knew Harry well might
construe as mocking.

"I rode past Your Lordship's garden in Holborn this
morning," he said. "You have a fine crop of strawberries this
year. This sun is ripening them to perfection."

"I will make Your Grace a present of some of them,"
Morton said, smoothly, as if we were all sitting down to a
convival dinner.

"That's very kind of you, Dr. Morton. I must confess,
your strawberries tempt me to the sin of gluttony. The
Lord Protector would no doubt appreciate some of them
too; he is very fond of strawberries."

"I am delighted to do him a service." The Bishop
looked as if he were about to add a Benedicite, and I
thought; he'd make as good a player as Harry. I hope
Hell-fire roasts his corrupt and stinking marrow!

When Richard came in, he left armed men outside; we could hear the clash of metal on the stairs. His face was as bleak and inflexible as stone. He still wore black, which did nothing to soften his aspect. He looked as if he'd had as bad a night as Hastings, but lacked the defeated air of the older man. His face said: Beware, push me no further ... Every muscle in it was stretched tight. At the sight of him, Hastings's face crumpled still further into dissolution. Having given us a formal, toneless good morning, he took his seat at the head of the table. There was a short, uncomfortable silence, while Kendal placed some papers in front of his master. Richard had picked up a pen and was pulling the filaments away from the quill, one by one. Suddenly we were interrupted by the captain of guard, who came in hastily, leaned over Richard's shoulder and whispered urgently to him. He rose and quickly left the council chamber. Buckingham followed him. We could hear the low, tense voices, the running feet on the stairs, a few barked orders from below, outside. The flies were still buzzing in the window.

Buckingham came back after what seemed like an hour, but was in fact about twenty minutes. Richard followed, and his face, when he sat down again, was frightening. He began to speak at once, in abrupt sentences with short pauses between them. "Five days ago, my lords, we had dared to hope that the threat of war was removed from this realm, that England might continue in the peace my brother fought to preserve. No more bloodshed, as my Lord Hastings would say, than you'd get from a cut finger." His voice grew quiet—the moment when the cannon is primed, the powder waiting. Rotherham was busy at his face with his handkerchief. My heart was thumping and my shirt sticky against my back.

"It seems, my lords," Richard went on, "that we were deluded. The enemy has found itself new allies. They would murder the Protector, and the Duke of Buckingham his cousin. They would seize the King's person. In this last half hour armed men have been restrained from doing so—here in the Tower, under my nose! They would meet any who opposed them, with force. They would have armies out in England once more, in the name of another evil queen." He was speaking faster all the time, and louder, beating on our ears like a drummer. "Do you remember, my lords, how Margaret of Anjou's men looted and raped from Tyne to Thames? Does my brother's reign, his achievement of peace, now mean nothing?" A passion of anger was pouring out of Richard now. Faces stared at him, every shade of red from rose to empurpled crimson, then white with shock. Suddenly he stood up, as if he'd been tied to his chair and just managed to break free.

He began to speak again. Words shot from him like bolts, harsher and more furious every second. "These Woodvilles care nothing for England. They'd give us bloodshed again. War between brother and brother, father and son!" It was an anguished yell. Then he did something that startled us out of our skins. He pulled back the sleeve from his left arm, baring it to the elbow, breaking the fancy lacings, turning the upper side to face us. Though he's small, the muscles in it stood out like cords, the old scar twisted across them like a white snake. He'd begun to shake from head to foot. "This—was done to me at Barnet ..." His right hand closed over the bared arm. "Worse was done to many others—too many others. Did I shed my blood in battle for nothing? Did my friends—your friends, my lords, die that day so the Queen and her family might live in whoring luxury all their lives? They have lived like maggots off the poor carrion we left on two battlefields—on the wasted lives of my friends—in both armies, for that's how civil war rends us—your friends, your fathers'. They who intend it should cringe before God! Fourteen years ago I risked my life to bring England out of it ..." He let go of his arm, and the marks his fingers had made were red across the white scar. That terrible, rending voice went on, bursting out of him like blood from a torn artery.

"I ask you, what sin have they committed, these men who plot to drown England in blood? What is their punishment? They sit here in our midst. Look at their faces if you doubt me ... You!" The word hurtled across the table like the thwack of a clothyard shaft. Rotherham jumped as if hit at twenty paces, then huddled back in his chair, terrified.

"You, my lord Archibishop of York—you, my Lord of Ely—you, Dr. King—you were my brother's trusted servants—would you undo at a stroke twenty years of his work? You, Stanley, you whisper with these men—do you see the battlefield as a market where you sell your wares to the highest bidder?"

Oh God, I thought, Richard, stop—you injure yourself more than them. I could not recognize him in this state. The bitterness of a lifetime was erupting as if a torch had been set to a great bombard. Even Morton, who's a cold-blooded old bird, looked afraid. I knew what was coming.

"And you!" Richard's voice subsided briefly unto a snarl, then rose again. "You!" He was snarling, too, over the table at Hastings, his teeth showing, like a boar about to gore the hounds. "You, who were my brother's friend, who fought with us, who was loyal. What have you done? I'll tell you. You've driven my brother into his grave before he was old, by your friendship. What sort of a friend is it who spends his days with a man in swilling and guzzling, and procuring whores for him?" They all gasped. Richard was really savage now, shouting at the top of his voice. "You killed him! You and that goat Dorset and that woman Shore! Now you and Shore's wife plot to kill me. Well, I'm not so easy to kill. I've not lived soft, and I'm not ready to die. Shall I tell you your offense, Lord Hastings?" A tiny pause, in which Hastings sat immobile, as if he did not understand, and the fury had slid unnoticed through an empty mind. There was no fight in him. Then Richard brought his fist crashing down on the table. We all jerked in our seats. Ink slopped out of the pot in front of me, making a creeping puddle on a sheet of paper,

"Treason!" Richard yelled. The door burst open. Soldiers with halberds and drawn swords rushed through it; the word had been their signal. The churchmen were seized easily, without too much affront to their dignity. Stanley struggled, protesting loudly, but a man-at-arms promptly clouted him over the head with a halberd. He

fell to his knees, blood flowing over his left ear, and
crawled under the table, where he crouched, nursing his
head and wearing.

Hastings put up no resistance. I looked at him and felt
sick. Tears flowed unchecked down his face; his mouth
was working. It was as well King Edward could not see
this—the two men he cared for most—one destroying the
other.

Richard was leaning his hands on the table, staring
downwards, his shoulders hunched forward. "He is guilty
of treason," he said. "Let him pay the penalty. I will wait."

"N-n-now?" The captain of guard stuttered with shock.
"Your Grace, there's no scaffold ready."

"I will have no waiting. See he is shriven. At once!"

So it was done. At the door, Hastings seemed to come
out of his inertia and began to struggle. The guard dealt
very summarily with him. They hoisted him up by the
arms and legs like a frog, shoved him through the door
and down the stairs. Richard turned his face away. I
thought he sickened, as I did. But he did not relent.

We waited in the council chamber until word came
back that Hastings was dead. No one spoke. Richard
leaned against the wall, his shirt sleeve hanging down
over his left arm, the points trailing. Even from where I
sat I could see how he trembled. The anger had gone now,
leaving only a knowledge of the finality of the deed. I
could do nothing for him. Buckingham did not dare
approach. The captain of guard returned soon, white
faced. He told us that the Lord Protector's order had
been carried out. Richard barely gave him a nod. "Let
Hastings be taken to Windsor," he said dully. "Bury him
beside King Edward. It was my brother's wish."

The news of Hastings's beheading had to be explained to
the people. The Major was sent for immediately and
hastened to the Tower. He had been worried over the
danger of riot in London in support of Hastings and seemed
relieved to find the affair resolved, if in this alarming way.
The City of London is always on the side of order and
strong government and Sir Edmund Shaa willing to do
whatever necessary for the safeguard of trade. A herald was
sent to Paul's Cross to read a proclamation of Lord
Hastings's treasonable plot to murder the Protector and

seize the King, and of his execution.

In the council chamber the Duke of Buckingham urged that Rivers, Grey, and Vaughan should be tried and executed. Their implication in the plot was sufficient reason. There and then a commission was sent north to the Earl of Northumberland to try these three and condemn them. I could see the necessity of it. Richard did what was required of him, affixing his signature without a word. Rivers, Grey and Vaughan were sentenced as quickly as a terrier deals with rats. The scene had an unreal quality, as empty of emotion as a disguising, now that the agony of Hastings's accusal was over. Stanley, because nothing was proven against him, was allowed to go free, which was more than he deserved. Morton, Rotherdam, and King were consigned to the Tower. Within hours, Dorset made a bolt from the Sanctuary. Men with dogs were sent to search the fields beyond Westminster, but he got clean away.

As I left the Tower, I averted my eyes from the graveled part of Tower Green. The blood was still there, covered by sawdust, and the lump of carpenter's timber they'd used as a block. It lay stained and discarded on a heap of ropes, pulleys, and planking. I shuddered. Dickon, I thought, this is the worst day's work you've ever done. Hastings would have died, I suppose, for his folly and treason, but not like this, with scarcely time to swallow the Host when his neck was severed. There should have been some kind of formal trial. Richard would be censured for it in the eyes of the world and, worse, in his own heart. He must have acted for so many difficult, tangled reasons, some of them only half understood. The office of Lord Protector is indeed ill omened; it entails a constant, murderous battle to survive, from which no man, even of Richard's probity, can come unscarred.

4

Vivat Rex!
Told by Queen Anne

Loyaulte me Lie

Richard Gloucestre

And herupon we humbly desire, pray, and require youre seid Noble Grace, that, accordyng to this Eleccion of us the Thre Estates of this Lande, as by youre true Enherritaunce, Ye will accepte and take upon You the said Crown and Royall Dignitie, with all thyngs therunto annexed and apperteynyng, as to You of Right bilongyng, as wele by Enherritaunce as by lawfull Eleccion: and, in caas Ye so do, we promitte to serve and to assiste your Highnesse, as true and feithfull Subgietts and Liegemen, and to lyve and dye with You in this matter, and every other just quarrel.

Petition of the Three Estates to Richard, Duke of Gloucester,
later passed as Act of Parliament

Poor Bo in his spaniel's coat must have been even hotter than I was. He lay on his side near my feet, and his pink and white belly palpitated in time with his panting. Where his tongue lolled out, he had dribbled a small puddle onto the floor, and the petal fringes along his jaws blew in and out with his breath. One of his orange-tawny

ears had turned inside out and fell like a skein of silk over
his head. I turned it back the right way with the toe of my
shoe, and his feathery tail flopped feebly on the tiles,
though he did not bother to raise his head. Richard had
given him to me a few years ago, thinking him small
enough to be a lady's pet, but not a silly size like some tiny
dogs. A winter gift, I remember. Richard had come to me
one day smiling in some secret amusement, and the furry
sleeve of his gown had looked peculiar, swollen and
heaving as if something were squirming inside. Then he'd
given a yell, as needle puppy teeth had sunk in his wrist,
and a little domed white head with orange ears and round
brown eyes had popped out. We named him Hercules at
first, but as this seemed ridiculous, he became plain Bo.
He preferred to stay near me rather than to explore the
corridors of Baynard's Castle. Richard's deerhound bitch
Eilidh—this means Helen in the Scots language—looked
even more miserable, panting under the table and too big
to fit into the shade.

Like the dogs, I'd have preferred not to be in London,
stewing in June. My chair had been set in the shaded part
of the room, but the sun shone blindingly in the window;
I'd ask for the shutters to be closed soon, though this
made me feel more mewed up than ever. Outside, under a
cloudless sky, the Thames shivered with light. The river
traffic plied as usual, and London went about its business
as if this were just another sweltering summer day,
hoping plague would stay away and indifferent to the
deathly games played in high places. Because of the plot
against Richard's life, which had been discovered three
days after my arrival in London, I was not allowed to go
out even under armed guard. I had now been immured in
Baynard's Castle for a week.

I drowsed, heavy-eyed in the heat, and hoped that
Richard would come home in better shape than he had
last night. Yesterday Lord Hastings had been executed
on Tower Green over a log of wood, within half an hour
of my husband's ordering of his death. Richard had
returned from that terrible council meeting and poured
out his remorse on me. I knew that a great bitterness
against the Queen and her family had lain hidden in him

for many years, but I had not guessed how deep and
dangerous it was. He'd spent all the night telling me
things from the past that I'd never heard before. When he
was just fourteen he had been taken away from our
household at Middleham, where he was happy, because
the King had married the Queen, who was a widow and a
nobody, and as a result quarreled violently with my
father. So from the first, he'd resented her as the cause of
this unwelcome change in his life. Two years spent at
Westminster had turned resentment into hatred. He told
me so many little things, cruel things, that made me weep
over him, because I'd never known how much he'd been
hurt. It's a bad time for being hurt, fourteen—I know.
Then he'd told me about Barnet, things he'd never told
before because he didn't want to harp on the battle in
which my father had been killed. At Barnet most of
Richard's friends had fought against him and died for it:
my father, who'd taken the place of his own father; my
uncle John Neville, Marquess Montagu, for whom he'd
had a great affection; and worst of all, his boyhood friend
John Parr, who was merely my father's squire and had no
quarrel with anyone.

I looked around at the ladies who were my friends and
servants; they were the daughters and wives of Warwick's
men, almost all north-country women, with a comforting
variety of north-country voices. There's Anna, Francis
Lovell's wife, who is my cousin; Joyce Percy and Grace
Pullyn, my special friends; then Elizabeth Parr, Margaret
Huddleston, Anne Tempest, Katherine Scrope, and Alice
Skelton; all their husbands are Richard's allies. A
backgammon board was laid out on the table, and one for
merels, but we were disinclined to play because of the
heat and made little conversation. A bowl of roses, put
out fresh in the morning, had blown and begun to drop.
The petals lay limp and shriveling on the silk-carpet table
covering, their scent fading. Beside them in a jar was a
sheaf of violet-blue columbines and a little pot of purple
heartsease, the Trinity herb. Flowers for Our Lady, the
Holy Ghost, and the Trinity—I wondered if the summer
weather had been warm enough at home yet to make
them bloom in the gardens at Middleham. The only

sound in the room was the chirp of the linnet in his cage on the wall. He liked the sun and hopped to and fro on his perch, cocking his head on one side and eyeing us. Then he began to sing as if he'd never stop. The sound reminded me of my son and his bird whistle. Some misguided person had given him one of these—a little green pot in the shape of a bird, with a spout to blow through and an open beak for putting a spoonful of water inside. Blowing produces so lifelike a trilling that they are used as lures by men netting small birds. In the manner of little boys, my son knew no moderation in his blowing, and soon every child in the place had a bird whistle; we were driven mad by them. As a result, they were banned indoors at Middleham. I wished that the children might be here. If I am to stay in London as the Protector's lady, I may see my son only a few times a year. This thought brings me to the verge of tears every time it enters my head, but I cannot let Richard see. I dare not begin to think how much I will miss my life in the North or how lonely a woman's lot can be in strange places.

I had to wait a long time for Richard's barge to return from Westminster. When at last he joined me, he seemed more tired than ever, wanting to do nothing but sit by the window, in silence. The heat had laid hold of him as much as it had me; I could see he wished himself a hundred miles away from London. I sent for food, so that at least we might have supper quietly together, though we were not likely to remain alone for long. Richard showed no interest in eating. I didn't know where, or even if, he'd dined. He was still brooding over the events of the previous day.

As if he read my thoughts, he said, sighing, "I have to see someone tonight, Anne, in private. You'll forgive me if I talk to him up here? It should not take long; there's no need for you to go. I couldn't refuse a bishop."

"You've had a hard day," I said, resenting the threatened intrusion. "Which bishop?"

"Bath and Wells—Dr. Stillington." He fell silent again, an unquiet, taut silence, in which he drummed his fingers nervously on the chair arms and slid the dagger he wore ceaselessly up and down in its sheath.

I went to stand beside him. "Won't you eat now?"

"Not yet." He took my hands and held them to his face, so that they covered his eyes, as if we played a child's game of hoodmanblind. "Your hands smell sweet," he said, pushing his face against them. "They're cool. We fried at Westminster today." His face was warm and slightly sticky. He slid one arm around me and held me close against his shoulder. I wished the Bishop of Bath and Wells anywhere but on his way to Baynard's Castle. As I had thought, we did not have long alone together. Within minutes an usher came knocking at the door, and Richard let go of me.

The Bishop of Bath and Wells was a smallish, elderly man, with the face of a monk, parchment-skinned and deeply furrowed near the mouth. He walked very slowly, as if his body were exhausted with heat or some longer-standing ill health. When he was settled in a chair, Richard said, "My Lord Bishop, you asked to see me privately. Is this some matter of importance?"

"Yes, Your Grace, I would prefer us to talk alone." He sounded nervous and looked at the usher, who prepared to leave, then looked apprehensively at me. Richard noticed his glance.

"My wife will remain with us, Dr. Stillington," he said gently. Stillington colored briefly; he probably did not approve of women knowing too much of men's affairs.

"I'd be obliged," Richard said, still gentle, "if your Lordship would be brief. I am so seldom allowed privacy myself, it is difficult for me to grant interviews alone to all those who desire them."

The Bishop bent his head in apology. His hands were twisting his episcopal ring round and round on one of his thin, knobblyjointed fingers. "For a number of years, Your Grace," he murmured, "twenty to be precise—I have lived greatly troubled by my conscience. In the year 1464, you will remember, our late sovereign lord, King Edward, was married—in a strangely furtive manner—to Lady Elizabeth Grey, a widow."

"Yes," Richard said, grimly, his mouth becoming very tight.

"Since then, Your Grace, Lady Elizabeth Grey has been

Queen, and her numerous relatives have made many
enemies in England. Men have gone in fear of their lives if
they dared oppose the will of the Queen's family. I have
lived in great fear myself for many years. I have suffered
unjust inprisonment..."

"My Lord Bishop, I am as aware of all this as you are,"
Richard's voice had a very sharp edge to it now. "Come to
the point."

"I do, Your Grace, I do. I have suffered these things
because I had a secret—a secret which caused the Queen
to fear me greatly. It is this: when your renowned father
the Duke of York still lived, your brother, then Earl of
March, plighted his troth to a lady. That lady was not the
Queen."

"What?" Richard stared down at the Bisho. "Be
careful, my lord, what you say!" Shock and fright made
me move suddenly, closer to Richard's side. He took my
hand, gripping it uncomfortably tight.

"It is the truth, Your Grace," Stillington looked
frightened, but surprisingly determined. "The vow of
betrothal is a solemn one, taken before an ordained priest
of Holy Church. That priest was my chaplain, I swear it,
by Christ on the Cross!" He said this with his hand
clutching the crucifix that hung around his neck.

At the sight of this and feeling the man's sincerity, I
became very afraid. My heart began to jump, sending the
blood rushing up my neck, into my face. Richard's fingers
were hurting me, but I did not try to pull my hand away.

"You swear my brother was bound to another
woman?" He sounded unbelieving, stunned.

"Yes, to the Lady Eleanor Butler, who was daughter of
the Earl of Shrewsbury."

"Old Shrewsbury—the great John Talbot?"

"Yes. Your brother was seventeen, and she every day of
five and twenty, a widow..."

Richard cut him short. "You are telling me, my lord,"
he said grimly, "that my brother married Elizabeth the
present Queen when he was already troth-plight to
Talbot's daughter. You are telling me that this marriage
was unlawful in the sight of God. In short, he lived with
his Queen in adultery. You do know, Dr. Stillington, how

serious this is?"

"I do, Your Grace, I have spent twenty years thinking of it. I have lived in guilt and fear, which is not good for a priest. The concealment of truth is as grievous a sin as a lie—*mea culpa.*Could I watch my lord Cardinal—the Archbishop of Canterbury—anoint a king before the High Altar at Westminster, before God, Himself, knowing that king to be a bastard."

"Be silent!" The order whipped out before Richard could control his anger. His fingers dug painfully into my hand, making me gasp.

Bishop Stillington shrank, but said nothing to excuse himself or refute this monstrous revelation.

Richard said carefully, "Where is Lady Eleanor Butler?"

"Dead, your Grace, in a convent at Norwich, fifteen years ago."

I said, "My lord Bishop, if this is true, why did you wait until the woman we've known as Queen bore King Edward ten children and abused her power in the realm for nearly twenty years? Why?"

"Out of fear for my life," he said, simply and bitterly. "Others lost their lives, like my unfortunate chaplain. The Queen was aware that I knew of the matter. I was not the only one she hounded. Your Grace's own brother, the Duke of Clarence ..."

"Blood of Christ!" Richard shouted so loud that I jumped. "Did *he* know of this?"

"He found out. I was sent to the Tower immediately after he—er—died. I was let out because I swore an oath—God forgive me, I'd have denied thirty times three—that I would never speak any words against King Edward. Thus I concealed his sin from the world with my own."

"You mean my brother George died for that? I never knew why, that last time, he was not forgiven, as he had been before. I know now. The Queen—the pretended Queen—killed him, for fear it might be discovered that she was nothing but a whore. She made one of my brothers kill the other because he'd begotten the heir to the throne of England in adultery and was terrified of being found out. Oh, Jesu, I cannot bear this...have you proof?"

"Beyond my word—nothing."

"You expect me to accept your word?"

"The word of a bishop, on the Holy Book if necessary."

"Richard," I said, clutching him, "don't detain the Bishop any longer—he's spoken in good faith. You must wait until tomorrow, before anything is done."

"Very well. Dr. Stillington, leave us now. I may require you to make a sworn deposition to the council. Give me a little time."

When the Bishop had left, Richard pulled himself away from me, went back to his chair, and sat down. He covered his face with his hands and groaned. "Oh, Lord God," he said "why have you laid this burden on me?"

A great fear welled up in me. I had to ask him. "Will you be King, Richard?"

"Christ help me..."

"Will you?"

"I don't know." He sounded angry with me—desperate.

"Listen to me," I said. "Ever since you first asked me to come to London I've been thinking. Consider your position. The King hates you. If he hates you now, what will he do in five years, when he is eighteen and wants to be his own master? He'll kill you. If you remain as protector, you'll run the risk of attainder on some trumped up charge of treason at the end of that time, and your son will have nothing to inherit. I shall be sold in marriage to one of their lackeys or pushed into a nunnery until I die."

"Stop it!" he said, anguished. "I know, I know. Do you think I want to face the block at thirty-five, with half my life to live? Whatever I do, I will betray someone I love— my dead brother, who trusted me to serve his son, you, my own son. Oh God, what must I do?"

"Take the crown." I was kneeling on the floor at his side, fondling his hands, smothering them with kisses.

"I cannot!"

"Prouder men have gone to the block" How could I convice him that if he did not act now, then as sure as the hours follow one another, he'd pay, sooner or later, with his life. "Your father held back because of his conscience, and it cost him his life and the realm a bloody conflict. You need not hold back—with you it is lawful and right. You must do it, for the sake of the realm. For yourself, your son."

"No!"

"I love you. What should I do if you were taken from me—if I had to wed another man?"

"Oh God," he groaned again, "Lord God, help me!"

"Tell the council," I said. "They'll see more clearly what should be done."

"You're right. Nothing should be done without the approval of others. Whatever is done, if they wish it, then it is my duty. I cannot stand alone in this—it's too great a decision for one man to take. It would be easy for men to brand me as a usurper.

"All my life I've witnessed the evil abuse of earthly power. God has raised me up to great power and wealth; already I've sinned by abusing His gifts. I have snapped my fingers and sent my brother's friend Hastings to his death. I have been Protector nine weeks—what might I be willing to do after twenty years? After seventeen as a king, Edward killed his own brother. A king's soul is in perpetual peril. Why, even you might live to fear and condemn me."

I touched his cheek. "No," I said. He turned his head stiffly away, as if unable to face me while thinking such a thought.

After a pause, he said, "He was betwitched."

"Edward?"

"That old harridan Bedford and her daughter the Queen plucked my brother like a fruit off a tree—an everlasting, bountiful, golden apple. Old Lady Bedford made wax images and cast fortunes—everyone knows that."

I shivered. "Don't. He was young."

"Old enough to know the smell of brimstone and never, ever, a fool. I poured out all my callow youth's love on my brother, and most of it did not touch him, because of *her*."

We sat in silence after that, for a long time, until the room was dark. Servants came to light the candles and to find out if we wished to be made ready for bed; Richard sent them away. I watched the nighttime world through the open window, my thoughts racing and turning over and over. In spite of the lateness of the hour, boats and barges were moving like glowworms on the river, lit by torches or lanterns, going home before the tide turned and began to ebb. It was lapping against the castle walls now, creeping upward, making craft tied up at the jetty bump gently at their moorings. On the southern bank the shore was marked out by a beading of lights. Trade at the inns and stews of Southwark's bankside is at its height when more sober people are going home to bed. Those lights would not dim until dawn. Downstream, lights still showed on London Bridge, strung like a necklace from shore to shore. If I had been at home, looking out at a June night, I'd have seen nothing but the black humpbacks of the hills and the pale, half-dusk, half-dawn glimmer in the sky that haunts the midsummer nights in the North. I am not used to a world so crammed with people. The air smelled stale, too, of river water tainted with bilge, green-slimed timber, and nameless stinks that came and went, cramping my stomach with nausea. I can't smell London without feeling sick; it brings back too many memories. After twelve years I had not forgotten those four nightmarish months, when I hid myself from my enemies in the kitchens of a cookshop. there is a little white scar across the knuckle of my left thumb—I had not been able at first to slice onions thinly and evenly. There were other scars too.

When I was fourteen, my father had sold me in marriage to Queen Margaret's son, whom none of us ever believed poor Henry VI had fathered. My marriage had lasted four months, until the Prince was killed at Tewkesbury, and it changed me from a child to a woman. Civil strife made my father grovel to a woman he hated, abuse two daughters he loved, and brought him to his death. It killed a young man about whom I did not care; he was seventeen. He died, and it might have been Richard, not he. I can scarcely remember his face. I have always dreaded memories of that time. Because it was Richard who healed my scars, one by one, over our years together. I live for him, by him and through him, and the child he gave me. This made me speak as I had. I did not know yet if Richard would heed my words.

On Monday the Queen was at last induced to give up her younger son the Duke of York from the Sanctuary. Now that her plot with Hastings against Richard had failed, she had no choice; neither could she rail against Cardinal Bourchier the Archbishop of Canterbury and Lord Howard, King Edward's most highly respected councilor, who went into the Sanctuary to collect the child. It was impossible to reveal the story Dr. Stillington had told us until both little York and his brother were together in the Tower, from where no one could abduct them to use in the making of rebellion against the Lord Protector. If the young King was to lose his crown, there must be no chance of setting up his brother in his place.

I went to see the boys on the following day, because I felt guilty, knowing of Dr. Stillington's story, and distressed at the thought of children taken to such a grim, foreboding place. Their lodgings were pleasant enough, however, with a garden where they could shoot at the butts or play at ninepins or closh. There was even a battered old quintain there, painted with marvelous ingenuity in the likeness of the King of France, crowned by a filthy old hat stuck with a cockleshell pilgrim's badge. I shuddered at the memory of King Louis, his interminably long nose with a drip on the end, his greasy hat, and having to kiss his grimy hand; I'd have preferred to kiss his dogs.

As I kissed the hand of our sovereign lord, King Edward V, I felt guilty again. He did not kiss my cheek. I had seen him only twice since he was taken out of swaddling bands. He was a thin boy, as tall as myself, though he would not be thirteen until November, and very fair like his mother. His face was pale, like a prisoner's who has been kept in the dark, with bluish rings around his eyes. In the last weeks he'd been unwell, in bed with a fever. Dr. Argentine, one of the learned physicians who had attended King Edward's deathbed, visited him daily, but could report no signs of any special disease, only the malaise, which did not respond to physic. Besides that, he was very unhappy. I looked about at his surroundings. There was nothing to suggest that he was a prisoner, except for the unnaturalness of his being alone with his brother among servants who were strangers to them both.

"If there is anything Your Grace would like to have here ... You may tell me, and I'll see that it is brought," I said, feeling shy of him, as I had of his father, though for quite different reasons. "Anything that might pass the time, though you won't be here much longer..." I decided not to say that his coronation had been postponed until the ninth day of November. Richard had insisted on offering this alternative date, which had been announced by the Mayor, because he had not yet decided what to do.

"No," he said, looking at the floor.

I felt nearly as awkward as he, snubbed by his manner, yet sad, because he was no more than a child, miserable and frightened.

His brother York, who'd been eyeing me up and down, took his chance and said, "Madam, Aunt Anne, may I have my dog? He got left behind at Westminster, in the palace. I hope he's not lost." He looked up at me, the beginning of a hopeful grin on his freckled face.

"Tell me what he looks like and what name he answers to," I said, "and we'll find him."

"He's called Merryman. My father the King called him that, because he was for me and I was a merry man too. He's got a lot of hair over his face and a white tail and wears a red collar. The servants know who he is." He managed to grin. He was a sturdier, more handsome boy than his brother, more golden in coloring, and looked as if he would be taller. He was the one most like his father. The King looked at him in a resentful way, as if his brightness intruded on his own moodiness. The two boys had met no more than half a dozen times in their lives.

"It's better here than in Westminster Sanctuary," he volunteered. "There wasn't a garden there."

"It must have been crowded, in a little house with all your sisters," I said.

He pulled a face like a small gargoyle, to show what he thought of his five sisters. "Bess is nice," he said, "but she's old—nearly as old as you, Aunt Anne." I doubt if this would have pleased his eldest sister, Elizabeth, who is seventeen.

"I won't have to get married again, will I?" he asked, anxiously.

"Didn't you like your wife?" He'd been married when he was four to Lady Anne, the six year old daughter of poor John Mowbray, Duke of Norfolk, who had died quite young, leaving her heiress to vast estates. Thus King Edward had acquired a wealthy dukedom for his younger son. Little Anne had been a pretty child, delicately made, with soft auburn hair. At her wedding she had been considerably more solemn than her husband. She died, God rest her little soul, almost two years ago.

He said, "It was like having *another* sister. I didn't see her much. Will I see Bess again soon?"

"Of course you will, and your mother."

"Her Grace my mother cries a lot," he said. I could believe that. She'd very likely reached the difficult time of life—she had her last baby three years ago and was approaching forty-seven. I felt embarrassed, rather than triumphant, thinking of her sitting in that poky house at Westminster, weeping hysterically, swollen eyes and patchy red flushes spoiling her looks. I envied her once, because she had borne a dozen children and stayed beautiful. Now I felt nothing for her, neither pity, fear, nor hate.

In order to avoid the subject of his mother, I told the King that his stay in the Tower would soon be over. He gave me a strange look, then cast down his eyes and did not say a word. To my dismay, I felt myself blush hotly, though I'm a grown woman and should have learned to suffer discomfiture without this reaction. I am cursed with a thin, pale skin that betrays even the faintest coloring. I hoped that the King had not heard the tales spread already by mischief-makers through London, that Richard aimed to have the crown out of envy and ambition. I believed now that this would come about, that he would be King, but for many serious, unhappy reasons, which included neither envy nor ambition.

I was immensely relieved that the King had not asked after his uncle Rivers and his half brother Grey. I knew that word had been sent to the Earl of Northumberland at Pontefract, ordering their trial for treason and their immediate beheading. I was glad that Grey, who'd been kept under guard at Middleham, would not be beheaded there—I didn't like to think of my son watching headings yet.

Richard put Bishop Stillington's deposition first to his inner circle of advisers, then to the entire council. The news leaked out. By Friday, there wasn't a tavern in London where bets were not made on the Protector becoming King within the week. The words written in the Wisdom of Solomon were often quoted: "Woe to thee, O realm, that thy King is a child and thy nobles feast in the morning. Blessed art thou, O realm, when thy King is a son of champions." I believed that I might count on the fingers of my hands the lords in England who did not now agree with Solomon. Many of them heard Dr. Stillington's story of the precontract eagerly; most were willing to accept it, whether they believed it or not. There seemed no reason to disbelieve it. As for Richard, I'd never set eyes on a more reluctant son of champions. Though the outcome of events now seemed so certain, he still held back from making formal claim to the throne. He felt unable to bear the responsibility for such an act alone. But indecision was unendurable, and enormous pressure was put on him by other men, who were perhaps more certain because the burden of kingship would not fall upon themselves. Richard's usual reaction to pressure being put on him is to dig in his heels and keep his own counsel. This time he could not. At night he did not sleep, and because he was so restless, I did not either, so we suffered the strain together. I had no wish to be Queen and felt frightened and inadequate to the burden of it. All I wanted was to return to my quiet, happy life in the North. But this was impossible; those days were gone forever.

On Sunday, the twenty-second day of June, Bishop

Stillington's tale was made public. A sermon was preached from Paul's Cross by Dr. Ralph Shaa, the Mayor's brother and prebend of St. Paul's, on the text: "Bastard slips shall take no root." A large crowd turned out to hear him. They were strangely quiet for a London gathering. I felt that they did not much like talk of King Edward's sins, his precontract, and adulterous marriage. He'd been very popular in London. When Dr. Shaa had finished they went away to their homes, muttering. Richard looked uncomfortable, as if the sermon had been preached against himself, but the others were pleased to note that the crowd had not been actively hostile and that Dr. Shaa had not been bombarded with rotten eggs and cabbages.

The Londoners liked even less the sight of Shore's wife doing penance as a whore. When she had been discovered in the plot with Lord Hastings, Richard had been sufficiently angry and bitter against her to sentence her to imprisonment for abetting in treason and to hand her over to the Bishop of London's court, to answer for her carnal misdeeds. The Bishop's court had given her the usual sentence accorded common whores: to walk through the streets in her shift, wearing a striped hood and carrying a white wand. Her shame was greatly lessened because of the sympathy of the crowd, for she was, like them, a Londoner—her father, John Lambert, was one of the most important members of the Mercers' Company. They thought she'd acted only out of care for the children of her dead lover the King and to protect the handsome Marquess. Maybe she had. I saw no reason to pity her; she'd lived like a Queen for ten years as King Edward's mistress, and she had plotted against my husband's life. It was unusual for Richard to be so harsh with a woman. Because he would not put the blame of leading a dissolute life on his brother, he unloaded it squarely on the associates in that life. I thought King Edward equally to blame, but refrained from saying so, knowing that Richard would be angry, even with me.

I'd seen him in anger too often in the last days. Someone put about the old, often repeated story that King Edward himself was offspring of the Duchess of

York's adultery with a captain of archers called Blayborne. This story had been used often as an insult to King Edward, but I'd never met anyone who really believed it. I could not imagine my mother-in-law stooping to consort with archers or being a woman to cuckold her husband. I suspected Harry Buckingham of having mentioned it, in his zeal for pleading Richard's cause, for he had been heard to say meaningfully, that Richard was the only one of the Duke of York's sons to be born in England and indeed the only one to remotely resemble his father in appearance. Richard was furious that the smear had been made on his mother at a time when he was living in her own house—Barnard's Castle— with her approval and exchanging letters with her often.

Whether the Londoners favored Richard or not, it was a timely week in which to create a public stir. London celebrated its two greatest feast days, the Nativity of St. John the Baptist or Midsummer, which fell on Tuesday, and Sts. Peter and Paul, the dedication day of its cathedral, on the following Sunday. All the most important citizens were in town. On the eve of St. John the Baptist, the torch-lit procession of the City Watch marched through the streets, three thousand of them, the Mayor riding in state in their midst. The Midsummer bonfires were lit and banquets held out of doors in fine weather. People hung garlands over their doors, as they do in York at Corpus Christi, made of green birch, fennel, St. John's wort, and white lilies.

On Monday and Tuesday Harry Buckingham made two long speeches, the first to the lords at Westminster, the second to the City dignitaries at the Guildhall, who were assembled for their St. John's Day festivities. No one had realized he was so gifted at speech making. Francis Lovell told me that he had not hoped to hear Richard's case put so convincingly. Harry had held his audience as a seasoned player might—his voice carried well, his mobile face and dramatic gestures riveted the eye—he used no notes, needed no prompting. So convincing was he that on Wednesday, when most of the lords spiritual and temporal, and the commons, met in the Parliament Chamber at Westminster, a bill

petitioning Richard to become King was almost
unanimously approved. Edward our son was to be
acknowledged heir apparent, and his heirs in turn to
succeed forever. Because he had a son, Richard could
offer England a safe royal succession, and because he was
a young man, the child would have time to grow and not
be thrust upon the throne in a minority.

On Thursday, we gathered in the great central
courtyard of Baynard's Castle—bishops, lords, aldermen, all jammed elbow to elbow. Harry Buckingham
read out the petition agreed on by the three estates of the
realm the day before. On his lips the legal language ceased
to sound tedious and became moving. The good
government of King Edward IV, he said, had been
corrupted by the evil counsel of the Queen and her family,
so that "no man was sure of his life, land, or livelihood,
nor of his wife, daughter, or servant, every good maiden
and woman standing in dread of being ravished or
defouled ..." Harry gave this part a burst of righteous
relish, though I thought it somewhat unnecessary.
Everyone knew what was meant—it was said that no
woman anywhere was safe from the attentions of the
Marquess of Dorset.

Harry went on to tell how the Queen's marriage had
been unlawful in the sight of God, because the King was
already trothplight, and how he had been lured into sin by
the witchcraft of the Queen and her mother. The claim of
Clarence's son was dismissed because of his father's
attainder. Richard was therefore undoubted heir to the
throne.

I watched Richard. Knowing how he was torn apart in
his mind between what he wished to do and what was
forced upon him by circumstance. I could understand his
look, which was more that of a man hearing a death
sentence than one being offered a crown. I wished with all
my heart that he might have had it in him to look more
cheerful. They'll say later that he dissembled and put up a
show of reluctance—some folks always find evil to say of
their betters.

At the end of his speech, Harry Buckingham walked
forward to the foot of the stairs where Richard stood, and

knelt. A silence fell. I held my breath. Then Richard walked slowly down the stairs, coming to a halt in front of Harry, took the parchment petition from him, and stood there, a little uncertain. Harry, still kneeling, took his hand and kissed it—the mightiest subject's gesture to his King. "Will Your Highness accept this petition of the Three Estates of the realm?"

Richard said quietly, his voice not carrying well, "Would you place this burden on me? Am I worthy?"

"Will Your Grace accept?" Harry was urgent in his supplication; he hadn't expected this last minute reluctance.

"Is this the wish of the people?" Richard's voice had sunk almost beyond hearing.

"Of the lords spiritual and temporal and of the commons of England. Highness, will you accept the royal dignity and estate?"

Richard bent his head then, twisting the parchment in his hands. We did not hear his answer. Harry did though, for he jumped to his feet, flung his arms wide, and gave a triumphant cry: "King Richard!" A crowd of citizens, who'd been primed for it, took up the cheer: "King Richard! King Richard!"

The day of our coronation was to be Sunday, July the sixth. This is not the best time of the year for the event. I prayed that the weather would not be hot or drown the spectators with thunderstorms. As there were only nine days between Richard's assumption of the crown and the coronation, we were caught up in a tempest of preparations. Work had already begun weeks ago, but much of the clothing had to be replaced and altered, especially now that there was not only a king to be provided for, but a queen and all her household. Peter Curteys, the Master of the Wardrobe, was in demand in a score of places at once; his flat, Leicester voice soon began to gabble orders, quantities, and measurements like a litany. For such a solemn occasion the colors my ladies might wear were limited; they all had to be dressed alike and had very different ideas about what suited them. I had to arbitrate and soothe those who felt their

complexions suffered by the final choice. They all wore
blue, crimson, and white, except for the old Duchess of
Norfolk, Richard's aunt, who is well over seventy and
insisted upon a gown of purple and crimson, to mark her
status as elder sister of the King's mother.

Richard's mother herself, did not attend. This was not
because of any disapproval of her son's actions, but
because, since the execution of George of Clarence, she
has attended no court ceremonies and lives the life of a
Benedictine nun at her castle of Berkhampstead. I was
frankly relieved at her absence; she would have been sure
to take entire charge of all the women's part of the
proceedings, leaving me to feel like a little girl playing
queens. Richard, who in some ways, would have
preferred his mother to be present as a sign of her
approval, understood my feelings, saying that the
Duchess of York ordered him about unmercifully too
and, King or not, he was very conscious of being her
eleventh and youngest child.

My own poor mother would not attend, either. In the
dozen years since my father was killed she has lived cut
off from all society. I think she has never had a happy life.
She wanted to be a support and helpmate to my father,
but often managed to offend him by her timidity and
complaints. She has more affection for Richard than for
me, born of the days when he was fostered in our
household and of her pathetic wish for a son. Sometimes
I cannot abide her and feel guilty because of it and of my
relief at her absence.

I had to make a great effort to welcome Richard's sister
Elizabeth, Duchess of Suffolk. She is much too like King
Edward for a woman, very large, handsome, and well
padded. She turns her eyes on me with a calm,
contemplative stare, reminiscent of a chewing cow, and
suggests that I should eat more—following her example,
I suppose. She is thirty-nine years old and has produced
ten children, most of whom are thriving, and looks as if
she has suckled each one herself, like a farmer's wife. She
and her husband come rarely to court, living mostly at
their manor of Wingfield in deepest Suffolk. The Duke is
supposed to suffer from ill health, though it hasn't

affected his ability to father children. Her usual statement, "Suffolk is not well today," could generally be taken to mean that he was laid up with the gout and vile tempered into the bargain. He has taken a fancy to me, and at the sight of his very red face, I take refuge among my ladies, who giggle behind his back, for his mind runs dreadily on oats and barley and the feuds he has with the Paston family.

The day before the coronation was kept, according to custom, at the Tower, which I hated, because I kept thinking of the poor deposed King and his brother, prisoners now in the Garden Tower. Richard had told the boys himself, which he said afterward was the worst thing he'd ever had to do in his life. Young Edward, as might have been expected, turned on him in venom and fear, calling him usurper and raving of the punishment of God that would come. Yet the bewilderment of the younger child had been worse, when he asked if he were now no different to Arthur—this was his half-brother, King Edward's bastard by Elizabeth Lucy. There was no time, however, to be sad. In the afternoon we rode in procession from the Tower by way of Cheap and Fleet Street to Westminster. I thought Richard looked very fine; he is always at an advantage on horseback, because people do not notice that he is small and so different from King Edward. He knows how to ride to get the best out of his horse, to make it arch its neck and tuck in its chin and mouth at the bit, to use just a touch of spurs to make it dance around a little and step up high. He rode White Surrey, the largest and showiest of his horses, who is trained for war and unafraid of crowds and noise. He is beautifully milk white and looked even better in a saddle, bridle, and trappings made of red cloth of gold. Richard himself wore a long gown of purple velvet and ermine over a doublet of marvelously rich blue cloth of gold, patterned with pineapples. He had to show himself bareheaded to the people, which I thought was good, because it made him look younger. He looked more cheerful too, now that most of the waiting was over.

Behind Richard rode Harry Buckingham, looking as triumphant as a necromancer who had conjured up a

king out of the air. Both he and his horse were trapped
from head to foot in blue and gold. It reminded me of
how my father had ridden in splendor so often at King
Edward's side, and I did not find the memory pleasant.
Harry loves to act the pageant master, and every day
seems bursting with new ideas. Wherever he goes there is
laughter and animated talk. I laugh with the others, for he
is very entertaining and goes out of his way to be
charming to me—a little too far, I have begun to think.
He puzzles me, because I cannot see deeper in him than
the quick wit and laughter, the constant mimicry, but
deep down, I feel he does not laugh. His wife is still
banished to Brecon.

I rode in a litter carried by two white horses.
Everything was white, so I made my ladies paint my face a
little, in case I were too pallid. I wore my hair hanging
down my back, though I am a married woman. It is the
custom for a queen to go to her coronation with her hair
loose as if she were a virgin. My hair is long enough to sit
on, so I spread it out over the cushions, wishing it were
golden and more suitable to a queen, instead of plain
mouse brown. The sun did not come out to gild it either,
and I wondered if I would ever look the part, in spite of all
the ermine, jewels, and trappins of majesty.

In the morning at six o'clock we walked in procession
from the White Hall near St. Stephen's chapel to
Westminster Hall. Striped cloth had been laid down for
us to walk on, and we went without shoes, me in my white
stockinged feet and Richard in his hose of crimson satin.
In Westminster Hall, Richard took his seat in the King's
Bench, and we waited for the Abbot, the Cardinal
Archbishop of Canterbury, and the other lords spiritual
to come and escort us in procession to the Abbey. The
royal trumpeters and heralds in their coats of arms went
first, then the Abbey Cross was borne in front of the
priests in their gray fur capes, the abbots and bishops in
their miters carrying their croziers, and the Bishop of
Rochester bearing a Cross before Cardinal Bourchier.
The Cardinal had several priests to help carry the hem of
his vestments, so that the weight might be taken from
him. I prayed most fervently that he would get through

the service without fainting or, worse, dropping down dead. He is over eighty, not in good health, and slowed the procession to an agonized creep.

I tried to get a glimpse of Richard between all the earls and barons who walked behind him and in front of me. Harry Buckingham, as Great Chamberlain, was his trainbearer. The Barons of the Cinque Ports carried a canopy of rich red and green silk over his head. There was a canopy held over my head too, hung with gold bells that chimed as we walked. I wore robes of crimson velvet, with a very long train, which was carried by Lady Margaret Beaufort, Lord Stanley's wife, who is less than five feet tall and had to be assisted by several henchmen. She was wearing pattens on her feet, hidden by her robes, to make her appear taller, but she still looked tiny beside the Duchess of Suffolk, who walked in solitary state behind her. I was entirely at the mercy of the trainbearers; without them, I was certain, I'd be unable to move a step, the weight of my robes was so great. Nearly fifty yards of velvet had been used, loaded with miniver and ermine and gold trimmings. My hair was hanging loose again, and I wore a circlet of gold, crusted with precious stones. I was hot already, uncomfortable, and shamefully hungry. The King and Queen have to go to their coronation fasting, because of their receiving of the Blessed Sacrament at the end of it. I kept telling myself that I must not faint, even if the ceremony, from the time we assembled in Westminster Hall, did last more than eight hours. I had been told that the crown itself was very heavy, though only half the weight of the King's but I should not have to wear it long. The Bishops of Exeter and Norwich would be standing on either side of me, and I was to tell them if I felt faint, so they might hold me up.

Inside the Abbey a large wooden platform with steps leading up to it had been erected and all covered with red cloth. On it were St. Edward's chair for the King after his crowning, and two other great chairs. We were seated in these first. I sat there with my back so rigid it did not touch the chair. Every muscle in me was tense, for the awesomeness of what was to happen had laid hold of me as soon as we entered the Abbey doors. I looked around at

the people; I could scarcely believe it possible to cram so
many in. I doubted if many of them could move even their
arms, they were wedged so close. Faces peered around
pillars and down from galleries. Many would be able to
see nothing at all, some might well not hear much either.
They were all watching us, the King and Queen. I was
frankly terrified and prayed that I should remember what
to do and say.

Holy Mary, Mother of Christ, please help me to be as
strong as a man today, and help Richard to endure this
too, for it is even harder and more solemn for the King. I
added a prayer for the Cardinal, who looked as if he
needed it more than either of us. As he began his
presentation to the people, walking to the four corners of
the dais to ask if it were their will that he should crown the
King, he seemed very slow and shaky, his voice old and
not strong. He said, "Sirs, here present is Richard,
rightful and undoubted inheritor to the crown," and the
crowd all shouted, "Yea, yea, yea, so be it, King Richard,
King Richard, King Richard." When Richard got up and
in the same way showed himself four times to the
people, inclining his head in submission to their will, I
held my breath, though they had already answered. I
began to cry then, and I cried on and off all through the
service, though not in a way that anyone would notice at a
distance. My whole heart and body were so seized and
overwhelmed by emotion, I choked and my eyes kept
blurring, until the tears spilled over and ran down my face
as the wax ran down the flaring candles. Richard's face
wavered before my blurred eyes, every line so familiar,
yet the face of a stranger. He looked exhausted and
battered by kingship already, his face sheet white and
thinned with strain, in contrast with those around him,
who were flushed with heat. The choir began the anthem,
"Firmetur manus tua...." A king needs strength. I'd
wanted him to be king, but now I was afraid, the burden
was so great. It is both marvelous and terrible to be a
king.

Because the King must not come empty-handed into
the sight of the Lord God, he next made an offering of
gold at the High Altar, then I did the same, after which we

both had to lie prostrate before the Altar on golden cushions, while the Cardinal said the orisons over us and the Bishop of Lincoln delivered a short sermon to the people. Then I sat on a stool on the left side of the Altar, while Richard took the royal oath, making his answers with his hands on the book of the Holy Gospels. His voice was clear and unfaltering, but I did not think it would be heard in every part of the Abbey, except for the end, when he said: "All these things and every one of them I Richard, King of England, promise and confirm to keep and observe, so help me God, and by these Holy Evangelists by me bodily touched upon this Holy Altar." The hymn, *"Veni creator spiritus,"* was sung most beautifully, as if by a choir of angels, and I could scarcely see anything for tears.

Afterward we went to the Altar together, where I had to kneel praying while the King received his anointing. First Buckingham, the Great Chamberlain, removed the King's crimson robes. Then he knelt, while the Cardinal untied all the lace of the openings in his shirts so that he could be anointed in the eight places: on the palms of both hands, on his breast, his back, his shoulders, on the inside of both elbows, and on his head. I blinked hard, to get the tears out of my eyes, because I wanted to see as much as possible. Cardinal Bourchier poured the Holy Oil from the dove ampulla into the spoon held in his decidedly shaky hands and made a little cross with the oil in each of the places. Then the crown of Richard's head was annointed with the Chrism, which is the most solemn moment of all, the consecration of the King, which sets him apart from other men. Each time the Cardinal touched the King, he blotted the place with a cloth, which would be afterward burned so no others should touch the Holy Oil. He also tied a linen cap over Richard's head, such as judges wear, so that the Chrism should not be touched for a whole week afterward, when the Abbot of Westminster would come to wash his hair. When Richard held out his hands for the anointing, I saw that they were shaking far more than the Cardinal's and that he trembled from head to foot, as if he felt the presence of the Holy Spirit and waited in dread and awe for the moment of consecration.

After the anointing, the King was clothed in the white silk tabard, the coat with images of gold, the hose,sandals, and spurs, the sword, which he buckled on himself, the stole, and the square robe with great eagles of beaten gold. Then St. Edward's crown was blessed, and the Cardinal took it in his hands. I watched, half in awe, half in fascinated horror, for the old man seemed to have difficulty in raising his arms with the weight of the crown in his hands, but after an initial wavering, in which he nearly cracked Richard over the head, he managed it. Then the ruby ring was blessed and put on the third finger of his right hand—the marriage finger—to show that the King is wedded to the people. Lastly came the gloves of cloth of gold, and the scepter with the dove was put into his right hand and the rod with the cross into his left.

Then I received my own anointing from the Cardinal. Lady Margaret had to undo the lacing of my gown in front, so that the oil might be touched between my breasts,which with the head, are the only places where the Queen is anointed. A linen cap was put on my head, and I was crowned and invested with a ring, as the King had been. The Queen's scepter and rod were put into my hands. As the bishops led me back to the dais, I had to make a deep obeisance to the King, who was already enthroned there. I wished that I might have knelt to him, as the lords temporal did, their hands laid between his, and sworn to live and die in faith with him.

When she had been close to me, I noticed that Lady Margaret Beaufort was in quite alarming floods of tears and having to snivel into her handkerchief. Her nose was very red. I had no time to ask what was the matter—I'd have preferred to give her a sharp smack across the face to stop her. I had a feeling her tears were caused by the sight of Richard being anointed instead of her wretched son Tudor.

After the anointing Cardinal Bourchier began Mass. During the *Gloria* the priests swung their censers around us and I began to feel faint, although sitting down; the incense smoke wreathed about our faces, the light of the candles hurt my eyes. The Abbey smelled like a huge kitchen where incense, candle wax, and sweating people were being slowly cooked. As I sat there I could feel my shift stick to my body and sweat running down the back of my knees. During the *Credo* the Holy Gospels were brought for us to kiss, and after the *Agnus Dei,* when the *Pax* had been given, we went together to the High Altar. When we had knelt to say our *Confiteor,* a silk towel was held up to screen us from onlookers. The Cardinal took the Blessed Sacrament and broke it, dividing it between us, to show that the King and Queen are united in one flesh by the bond of marriage. Then we were given wine from a chalice, to purify us. For me, this was the moment of moments in the whole ceremony, when I received the Body of Our Lord with my husband, and we were as one, King and Queen.

After Mass we went in procession to St. Edward's Shrine,where the Cardinal took the crowns. Then we retired into little rooms screened of by arras. I fell into the chair set ready, no longer able to hold off faintness, exhaustion, and hunger. My ladies hastened to bathe my face and to make me drink a little wine and eat some bread, for I had touched nothing since the night before. I was stripped of the crimson robes and immediately loaded with an even greater weight of purple velvet and ermine. When all was ready we went in procession back to the dais in the middle of the Abbey and then, crowned, in our purple, to Westminster Hall. Because the coronation banquet was not yet ready, we left our crowns and robes in the Hall, and went to sit for a while in a room apart. We were too exhausted to talk much. Richard looked much as a man might who had fought a long hard battle, and I did not dare look in a mirror, for tiredness spoils any looks I might have and I had never been so tired in all my life.

The banquet began at four o'clock and went on for more than five hours. I shall never know how I sat through it all. The service of the courses was lamentably slow and the food in consequence cold, but I wanted little to eat. I told my cupbearer to water the wine, for if he did not, I'd be certain to fall asleep. When the second course was served, the King's Champion, Sir Robert Dymmock, rode into the Hall, on a white horse trapped in red and white silk, the colors of England and St. George. He called upon any man who disputed the King's right to declare himself and fight, throwing down his gauntlet on the floor. At this the whole company cried out: "King Richard, King Richard, King Richard!" The Champion was given wine in a cup which he claimed, according to custom, and rode out of the hall.

By the time the third course of wafers and hippocras was served, it was dark in the Hall, and candles and torches had to be brought in. Soon after , the feast came to an end, with everyone too exhausted to endure any more, and we went from the Hall. Outside, the summer darkness fell kindly on my tired eyes, and the warm, soft air soothed my aching head. In the torchlight we walked back to the palace. The bell boomed out the hour of ten to a city wide awake still and celebrating our coronation with bonfires and feasting. I thought of all the kings and queens who had gone before, doing as we did, going from the Great Hall to their Palace; the same river flowing strongly with the tide, silent but for a little lisping lap upon the walls. The black line of the Lambeth shore lay on its other side, pinpricked with light, and behind us the bell tower in Palace Yard, and the fountain that had been made to flow with wine instead of water. I asked God to grant Richard a long and successful reign, and that he should shine among the kings who were his noble predecessors, and that I would not fail in my duty to him and to the realm. Now that the thing was done, we should forget all doubt and regret, for we were crowned and anointed and nothing could ever undo it. So be it, *ita fiat, amen.*

5

The Common Weal
Told by King Richard

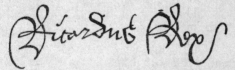

I trust to God sune, by Michelmasse, the Kyng shal be at London. He contents the people wher he goys best that ever did prince, for many a poor man that hath suffred wrong many days have be relevyed and helpyd by hym and his commands in his progresse. And in many grete citeis and townis wer grete summis of mony gif hym which he hath refusyd. On my trouth I lykyd never the condicions of ony prince so well as his; God hathe sent hym to us for the wele of us al.

Letter from Thomas Langton, Bishop of St David's (1483)

I'd never have thought to see John Kendal my Secretary in such a dither of excitement. He is not a man who demonstrates extremes of feeling. His letter to the Mayor and citizens of York, requesting them to prepare for our visit, overflowed with anxiety and pride, for John is a man of York himself. Kendal's letters are a joy to receive, each one an example of the writing master's art—his neatness and attention to detail is fanatical. He sent direct to the City on the day we left Notthingham, though I'm sure York did not need to be prompted into making us welcome. The crux of his letter—and this amused me a little—was that the men of the South would be watching and waiting to find fault with anything that was done in the North, as it York could not be expected to equal the pageantry of London. The men who served in the city levies, who came south just before the coronation, might well be smarting still from the rude scoffing of the Londoners. "For there come," Kendal said, "many southern lords and men of worship, which will mark greatly your receiving Their Graces." I have to admit, I shared his hope that they would be impressed.

This homecoming to York was the climax of a six-week progress through England, and the pageantry the citizens prepared the eleventh civic welcome, and the happiest, though this should not belittle the efforts of other towns. In Reading, Oxford, Gloucester, Tewkesbury, Worcester, Warwick, Coventry, Leicester, and Nottingham I had been surprised and delighted by the warmth of my welcome. On the journey I particularly wished to show my intent to rule with justice and mercy. In every town a special court of judges and lords was set up, over which I presided, to hear the cases of poor men who had no other means of redress and to try the oppressors and punish evil doers.

This is only the beginning. When I was crowned I swore an oath to myself that I would undertake the fifth labor of Hercules and cleanse of corrupt practices the Augean stables of public administration. This cannot be achieved entirely, I am willing to admit, but some measure of it can be done, even if it takes a lifetime. Within the government of the realm, injustice, peculation, usury, and extortion flourish; I'd die happy if I saw these things wither in my time. For this reason I had not wished to make an example of selling my good lordship and refused the gifts of money offered by the citizens during the progress.

I left my wife the Queen at Windsor after the coronation. She'd looked so tired and pale that I'd wanted her to rest a week or two before coming north with me. That way, she did not need to start traveling until after Lammastide, when she joined me at Warwick. She brought with her an ambassador from the Queen of Spain, a lord called Geoffrey of Sasiola. He had come in friendship, and I suspect his geniality was increased by his journey in the company of the Queen of England, whom he treated in his grave, Spanish manner as if she were made of glass.

During the happy interlude of the progress it would have been easy to forget how many clouds lie upon England's horizon. In France the old enemy King Louis is dying and too busy begging the Almighty to prolong his life to trouble us much, which is as well, for we are in no position to trouble him. At the beginning of August I received a note from him, short and offhand to the point of rudeness, as is his way. I sent him a reply, pointing out that while willing to observe the truce between us until it expired next April, I'd be obliged if he'd make clear whether the terms of the truce regarding English ships trading to France were still valid, because the attacks by French pirates had rendered them nonsense. If the crafty old spider thinks he may deceive me as he did my brother, he will have to think again, and if he makes rude gestures to England, he will be paid back in his own coin. To give this point, I had a letter delivered to him by a stable groom—Kendal remarked that next time it might be a dog boy from the kennels, for Louis cares more for dogs than men.

In view of King Louis's precarious hold on this world, the position of his nearest neighbor, The Duke of Brittany, becomes even more uncertain. A week after the coronation, we discovered that Elizabeth Woodville had hatched yet another plot, this time to smuggle her daughters out of Westminster Sanctuary and send them abroad, to Sir Edward Woodville in Brittany. The eldest, Bess, she had promised in marriage to Henry Tudor, the Lancaster pretender. The Woodvilles would treat with the Devil himself if it benefited them. Before, Elizabeth acknowledged Tudor for what he is, an unknown adventurer. What right has he? Son of the bastard half-brother of Henry VI, Edmund Tudor—not even Harry V's half, but the mad, sickly blood of his French Valois wife, who was served by some Welsh squire—and through his mother, Lady Margaret, descended from a Beaufort bastard of John of Gaunt. His claim to the throne of England is far inferior even to that of my cousin

Harry Buckingham. Even the title he uses, Earl of Richmond, is spurious, belonging to his mother only. If Elizabeth wishes to aid her sons, then she seems to have allied with a man who is as much their enemy as he is mine.

The conspirators who carried her letters were caught within a week. While staying at my friend's house of Minister Lovell, just after we left Oxford, I wrote to the Lord Chancellor, asking him to make the usual arrangements for their trial by a commission of lords. There is a danger in these meddlings of a foolish woman. Elizabeth may try to have her sons "rescued" from the Tower by raising a rebellion in the South. Rivers had a following in Kent, the lord Marquess in Devon and Somerset, and their minions Cheney and Stonor in Wiltshire and Berkshire. The last thing I want is an attack on London and the Tower, like Fauconberg's in 1471; those who hold the Tower and London are well on the way to holding England.

This convinced me that the best policy would be to remove my brother's sons from the Tower, to keep them from the hands of my enemies. Tudor dreams of invading England, Elizabeth Woodville dreams of revenge, and I've no urge to be a three-month wonder. I decided that the boys should be sent to a secret, country place and guarded by my most trusted servants. The North has many such places and men. Sir Robert Brackenbury, Constable of the Tower, is also Constable of Barnard Castle in Teesdale, which might prove a suitable place.

I entrusted the moving of the children to Sir James Tyrell for several reasons. He has been my faithful servant for a dozen years; his duties as Master of the Henchmen make him responsible for the boys in the household; he travels frequently unremarked as Master of the Horse and is discreet and resourceful. A servant was sent to London to arrange the business with Sir Robert Brackenbury. Later Sir James set out from Warwick to fetch the children and bring them north. He is now back in York.

It is no use pretending they do not gnaw at my conscience, those two children, who must suffer so cruelly the bitterness of the disposed. The very thought of them brings a dark mood on me, and I wonder if by my acceptance of the crown I have not condemned them to death already. Children are not too difficult to guard, but when they are young men, others may try to use them against me, as pretenders to the throne, and then there will be only one end—the block.

One pretender is enough for the present. As I have said, we are in no position to make war on anyone, though perhaps the time to strike at France is not so far off. I'm not much older now than Harry V was at Agincourt and see no reason why I should not bear the rigors of a French campaign better than he; I've been trained in a hard school.

Strange, to think that this summer I might have spent in much the same way as the last seven, in keeping the Border against the Scots. A letter had arrived from King James, asking for an eight month truce, as a preliminary to a longer peace. No one would be more pleased to see an end to Border forays than I, but it is impossible to rely on a king who is kicked about his realm like a football by his own nobles. His faithless brother, the Duke of Albany, took refuge at my court, to await a further chance of scoring off the King. Henry Percy of Northumberland, who has had ample opportunity to observe the weaknesses of the Scots, said, "Will Your Grace treat with poor Jamie? I think, Richard, that Albany means to cause trouble again."

"I'll accept his offer in good faith," I said, "but we must be prepared for his inability to enforce a truce on his unruly subjects. I've a feeling you'll be kept busy, Henry; it's a relief to know I have a warden on the Marches who knows the Scots as well as I do." Though he preened himself under this small piece of flattery, I was well aware that he wanted more. He had hoped to take my place as the King's Lieutenant in the North, but since I have found him a man lacking in decision, I intended my nephew Lincoln to head my son the Prince's council, because he seems to possess the qualities for the job, and to make Lord Dacre my deputy on the West March. Percy's nose may be out of joint, but he can no doubt be appeased by other means.

"Does Your Highness have any intentions to replace the late King's council in the Marches of Wales?" He tried to make this sound a disinterested inquiry, but I knew that finding himself restrained from a complete rule in the North, he was jealous of Harry Buckingham's position in Wales.

I gave him a straight answer. "My mind is not yet made up on what is best for Wales. The King needs a strong deputy there, of course, and I think the Duke of Buckingham will serve me well in that capacity for the time being." I turned to my Welsh bishops, Richard Redman of St. Asaph and Thomas Langton of St. David's, for their opinions. They are two of the best of the churchmen in my service, though neither is any more Welsh than Percy or I, both being north-country men from my own country of Westmorland. Redman, in particular, I have a great admiration for; he combines the office of his bishopric with that of Abbot of Shap and the burdensome duties of visitor of all the Premonstratensian houses in England and Wales. He looks like the rest of his family, big, burly Westmorland squires from the hill country, and is one of the most energetic, efficient, and moral men I know. There can be scarcely a highway in the land he has not traveled in the course of his duties, undeterred by dangers and bad weather, or a monastery that he has not visited in person.

He said, "A council of lords may well be the answer in Wales. Some answer is certainly needed there. I hope, Your Grace, that we may be able to do as I have done at my cathedral of St. Asaph and build a new edifice from the ruins of the old."

"You think as I do, my lord Bishop," I said, "I hope Dr. Langton is in agreement."

"In view of my recent appointment, Your Grace," he said, smiling, "I am willing to rely on the judgement of my brother of St. Asaph. I must confess, I tend to forget that I am a newly made Welshman!"

I thought that I could offer Harry Buckingham many trustworthy advisers to help him bring Wales into some sort of order. Though he is largely untried in government, he has shown himself willing and talented and left me indebted to him; I am hopeful of his success. Though I have much liking for him, I will have to take him on trial for a time; it is Wales itself that will make or break him.

"If I may divert Your Grace into lighter matters," Dr. Langton said, "I have discovered several young boys in my diocese with singing voices of incomparable beauty. The Welsh may present us with many problems, but they can compensate us with their singing. I'm sure that some of them could join the choir of the royal chapel, and it would be a pleasure to send them where they will be appreciated." He obviously intended to compliment me on my taste in music, which pleased me, for I would like it to be said that the King's choir was the finest in the land.

I thought then of my own son, who can sing tolerably well if required, but would not, alas, ever attain the standard of the chapel royal. When we departed from Nottingham, he traveled from Middleham to meet us at Pontefract. We did not reach the castle until after dark on St. Bartholomew's Day. The Prince, I was told, had been sent to bed at his usual time of eight o'clock and informed that we would not arrive until the following day. Anne said, "We'll see him in bed, just for a little while," and looked at me, knowing that I, any more than she, would not leave greeting our son until morning.

At the door of his room, I told our ladies and gentlemen to wait outside, for the Prince is only just seven and would be sleepy and not ready to play his part before strangers. The servants in the room were nervously waiting, wondering whether to wake him. His eyes must have been open, for as he turned, the light from the door, which stood ajar, fell on his face and he sat up and saw us. He threw back the covers and jumped out of bed in a single, flurried movement and rushed across the floor. Before he could land headlong against our legs, he remembered his manners and who he was. He stopped and knelt down in front of us, quited naked, concealing his private parts with his hands, for his mother's benefit, and said in a voice with a halt and a question in it, "My lord father is the King's Grace now and my lady mother, the Queen ..." He couldn't manage any more but stared,

tongue-tied, at me, as if he'd expected me to be wearing a
triple crown at least, like His Holiness the Pope, and his
mother to be garlanded with roses like the Blessed Virgin
Herself. His eyes were the size of plates, his mouth very
slightly open, revealing that since we saw him last he had
lost two milk teeth in front.

Anne said, shaky with laughter, "Come here ..." He
jumped up, unself-conscious again, and ran to her. When
he left his mother and came to me, I sat back on my heels
and put both arms around him pressing the warm, eel-
smooth naked child close to my chest, while he kissed me
with noisy, damp enthusiasm, as he always used to do. He
smelled of soap and linen sheets, and his small bare feet
were standing on my own, on top of my dusty boots, I was
absurdly relieved that he was not as much in awe of me as
I first thought.

"Oh, Father!" he said, between pressing his nose into
my cheek and his fingers into the back of my neck. "It was
a hundred and twenty-three days—I counted!—since you
went away."

Anne, who was holding on to me, her hand on my knee,
said, "No more days to count now. You must try to make
these last long, not wish them to fly away."

"No," he said. Then, curiously, "Father, you do look
ordinary!"

"I'm no different," I told him.

He looked into my face, very serious. "But you are the
King's Grace," he said. I could tell that he understood,
that it did make a difference, even for him, and that he
had accepted that I could be the same, yet different, at
one time. "May I see your hand?" he asked, solemn still. I
let him take my right hand between his. He held it palm
upward, unfolding all my fingers, turning it slightly from
side to side, so the light winked on the gold backs of the
three rings. He peered at it as if about to read my fortune.
My skin looked very hard and lined beside his. "Even
though it's washed away now, it does stay on you forever,
doesn't it Father?" I realized what he meant by this
scrutiny of my hand; he'd half expected to find signs of
my anointing still there, like stigmata on me.

"Yes," I said, "forever."

Anne had got up now, and was looking down at us. Her face was as serious as the child's. "Sometimes, Edward," she said, "things you cannot see, mean most."

"Yes." He understood.

"You must go back to bed," I said in his ear, holding him close again. "Your mother the Queen is tired now, she would like to go to bed too."

"Oh!" A half protest, then, "I could put on some clothes!"

"No," I said and picked him up, to carry him back to bed. He was excited already, and I didn't want him to become too tired; he had a few hard weeks ahead of him. He clung to me like a marmoset, with arms and legs, even his toes tried to wriggle down the tops of my boots; his sharp knees dug into my ribs. He's too old for picking up and all this hugging and kissing. I thought myself too indulgent to him, but it could do little harm, I see him so seldom. I put him back in bed, tucked the covers around him. We stood looking down at him. He must have been in the bathtub earlier, the ends of his mouse-fair hair were spiky with damp after a toweling. He lay, grinning up at us with possessive delight, his prodigal parents returned.

That very evening I got Kendal to draft a charter creating my son Prince of Wales and Earl of Chester. For his age, he understands what is expected of him and shows seriousness and intelligence—with God's grace, he'll make an honest man. I have great hopes for his future.

Five days later, on the feast of the beheading of St. John the Baptist, we set out for York. My son had been tutored on how he was to address the citizens, the lords, and the bishops; I had caught him reciting all his instructions, so I knew that he was trying hard to remember everything. He rode on his white pony beside his mother, a few paces behind me. Anne looked less tired now, as if she had come back to life again in the North; there was color in her cheeks, and she smiled often. We stopped twice by the road, for refreshment, and people came crowding up to us, offering all kinds of gifts. They brought white roses and gillyflowers, baskets of ripe plums, apples, a green finch in a cage for the Prince, and a basket of cheese cakes—the ones the wives of York made so well. My son, when offered these, promptly took one and ate it there and then, as any boy of his age might, given the chance, which gave the crowd huge delight. They blew kisses to the Queen and Prince and pressed around, trying to touch my clothes, kneeling in the road in front of me. All this on the road from Pontefract—I knew that when we reached York we'd be welcomed more warmly than even John Kendal had hoped.

We were met at Breckles Mills, near Tadcaster, by the Mayor, John Newton, the Aldermen and Council of twenty-four, all in scarlet and red gowns, mounted on fine Yorkshire horses. They escorted us into the city, one of the Sheriffs riding in front of me. At the chapel of St. James without-the-Walls, several hundred citizens in blue, violet, and musterdelvers were waiting on foot to greet us. It was here that the crowds began. Along the city walls, on either side of Micklegate Bar, people sat, leaned, or hung on every inch of the crenelations, their heads stuck out of the slit windows of the guard rooms, they packed the ground. I had been welcomed many times to the ciy, with both my wife and son, but had never seen so vast a crowd or one that more noisily demonstrated its welcome. The King, the Queen, the Prince ... I never knew, on those other occasions, that this thing would come about. Now, to see the people glad that I had come back to them in the royal state did much to ease the burden it had set on me.

The citizens came forward, carrying the most handsome present we'd ever been offered—a hundred marks piled in two basins of silver gilt for myself, a hundred pounds in gold in a great cup for the Queen, which so astonished and moved her, I could scarcely hear her murmured words of thanks. In York we would not refuse gifts. They would be repaid in kind; the city had given me twelve years of friendship, which I can never forget. Outside Micklegate Bar a pageant had been set up, showing Eborac, the legendary king of the city, enthroned. When I rode up to the open gate, he came down from the stage and walked up to me, offering on a velvet cushion a great gilded bunch of keys—the keys of

his city. Then he took the crown off his head and offered
that to me also, making a rhyming speech beginning:

> "Most reverend rightiouse regent of this rigalitie,
> Who's primative patrone I peyre to your
> presence,
> Ebrauk of Britane ..."

—which was doggerel, but sounded fine in spite of that.
This done, and the city given into my hands, the crowd
roared its approval, and we rode on through the gate,
come home to our city of York at last. Every foot of the
house fronts in the street, from Micklegate to the
Minster, was hung with arras and painted cloths and
garlands of flowers, the streets cleaned as I had never seen
then before.

At Ousebridge there was another pageant, showing
three kings: St. Edward the Confessor, my brother King
Edward, and myself. St. George with a shining gold halo
presented me with his sword. Then a child came on, and
St. George crowned him with a little coronet. The crowd
went mad, cheering my son the Prince. He stared at the
show, enthralled, recognizing himself, and smiled and
waved as if he too were a player and had done all this
before. An idea that had been at the back of my mind for
some time suddenly came to the surface, and I decided
that the people of York should be given a show for
themselves. I would formally invest my son as Prince of
Wales here, in a great ceremony in St. Peter's Minster,
with a procession through the streets. To be honest, I felt
pleased as a schoolboy to have thought of it.

On the last day of August I sent to London for the gear
needed in the ceremony of investing my son with his new
title. This left only seven days to try the speed of the
messengers to London and back, for I had decided the
day most suitable for the ceremony would be the eight of
September, the Feast of the Nativity of the Blessed Virgin
Mary. The Prince had a special gift, a saddle for his white
pony, covered with crimson and blue cloth of gold,
fringes of Venice gold, and long silk tassels of blue and

crimson. We had banners for the procession, of the royal arms, St. George, Our Lady, the Trinity, St. Edward, and St. Cuthbert of Durham, the greatest of all the northern saints. The dean and chapter had their own banners of St. Peter and of St. Wildred of York. Thirteen thousand badges of the white boar were needed for the household, all the citizens, and the men who would keep order in the streets, if only by restraining the people's enthusiasm.

In York there were many pleasant matters to be attended to. In the absence of Dr. Rotherham, whom I had not yet seen fit to restore to favor, we were lodged in the Archbishop's palace, near the Minster, a whole wing of which was given over to the children. My brother George's son, the Earl of Warwick, had joined the Prince's household. Before, he'd been brought up quietly on one of his father's old manors, until it became necessary to keep a closer eye on him, in case conspirators should try to use him against me. He is a year older than my son, and though they share the same blood, being the children of two brothers and two sisters, and bear the same name, they could not be less alike. Warwick's a handsome child, in looks rather like his father at eight, but thankfully lacking George's irrepressible bad behavior. He seems timid and solitary, and my son outshines him at lessons as if their ages were reversed. His ten-year old sister Margaret is so different, charming and intelligent. She was to stay in the Queen's household, with the other girls, who included the two youngest daughters of John Neville, Marquess Montagu, whom we've cared for since Barnet, and my bastard daughter Katharine. I'd like to see Katharine betrothed by Christmas, now she is turned fourteen. I have in mind for her William Herbert, Earl of Huntingdon, whose Woodville wife died a year or two ago. His lands lie mostly in Wales, where I need all the allegiance I can get, and he is an earl, which is a good match for a king's bastard child, though—and I give away no secrets—her mother was of noble blood. My son John had pleased me so well that I intended to make him a knight, at the same time as the Prince's investiture. His mother had no high lineage and he is a bastard, but I wish him to remember that he is my son, and though he cannot inherit, he has my affection. They are good children, for my sins. It worries me that God has not seen fit to bless my marriage with more than one son. Being King has suddenly made this more important than I care to admit, but I cannot say it to my wife, for she would be hurt. I wanted to see her happy during this brief homecoming to York.

On Sunday, September the seventh, the Creed Play was performed for us. This was a very great honor, as it is played usually only every tenth year, at Lammastide, and the rule had been broken. The scenes illustrate the words of the *Credo,* beginning with God the Father, in white robes, a long beard, and a halo on his head, saying,

> I am gracious and great, God without any beginning.
> I am maker unmade, all might is in me;
> I am life and way unto wealth winning.
> I am foremost and first, all I bid, shall it be."

The Prince was intrigued by the beard, for he had not often seen men with hairy faces, and seemed to think it almost blasphemous that God should have his beard stuck on with glue.

The next day was almost entirely given over to my son's honor. I shall never forget his face when he saw me for the first time crowned, in Parliament robes of crimson velvet furred with ermine, with a train six knights had to carry. His eyes went straight to the crown and stayed there. He was struck dumb by it. When I smiled at him, he smiled back, but looked solemn again immediately. He looked from me to his mother, and back, then to her again. She wore her hair loose and her crown on her head, which fascinated the child; he had never seen her like that before.

We walked in procession to and from the Minster, for High Mass, through the streets of the city. At the end of the service the great west door was opened, and the Bishop of Durham went out. I stood at the top of the

steps, looking out over my city of York and its people.
The afternoon sun shone straight in the door, blinding
me. The people began to roar, loud enough for a pitched
battle or a riot, but a happy noise, for all its fearful
volume. I was moved, in a way I had only been once
before—when I knelt before the High Altar at
Westminster for my anointing and received the Holy
Spirit. Tears ran down my face, and I had to blink several
times before I could walk down the steps between those
surging ranks of thousands of yelling people. They gave
me something, those men and women of York, that I had
most desperately needed ever since I took my seat at
King's Bench and became King; they enabled me at last to
believe in my right.

In the streets the soldiers looked more like drovers
faced with a stampeding herd; they had to fight to keep
the crowd back. When the people saw the Queen walking
behind me, hand in hand with the Prince, they went mad.
A young woman and a child together are guaranteed to
move multitudes, and York showed itself crazed with
delight. I was able to turn around once to look at them.
Anne was smiling, first at the crowd, who obviously
adored her, than at the Prince, who smiled back. He
seemed a little apprehensive of the noise and thrusting
nearness of the crowd, but when his mother bent and
whispered to him, he walked on between them more
confidently. As she bent her head, her pretty hair fell
forward, spreading around her shoulders. I could have
walked all day through all the streets of the city and never
tired; I was so drunk with the elation of it. In the middle
of Stonegate, as we came back toward the Minster and
Archibishop's palace, I stopped, to allow the Queen and
the Prince to draw level with me, and in sight of all the
people, kissed them. His lips were incredibly soft, as a
child's are. Anne's lips were no less soft, moist and gently
parting, as if she would prolong the moment, defying the
eyes of the city. That kiss, between the King and Queen
brought a fresh roar from the crowd—cheers, shouts,
whoops, and whistles that made the Queen blush as
bright as a poppy.

When we had come back to the Archbishop's palace, in

the great hall there, before all the lords spiritual and temporal, I invested my son with the symbols of his dignity as Prince of Wales. He had begun to look tired and big-eyed and nervous of doing anything wrong. I felt that he wanted very much to hold my hand, but was not allowed; princes have to learn the hard way. When I buckled on his small sword and put the gold ring on his finger, he was trembling like a puppy dog with a fit of the shivers. I set the gold garland on his head, thankful that it was light for him. When I put the rod in his right hand, for him to hold like a scepter, I held his clenched fist in my own hand for a moment and squeezed it until he became steadier and was able to manage a smile. Then he watched while I knighted his cousin Warwick, my bastard son John, and Sasiola, the Spanish ambassador.

After that, a banquet was held, which lasted four hours and reduced all the children present to yawning silence. Their cousin Lincoln had been briefed to see they did not eat too much and make themselves sick or drink anything but very watery wine. At the end of it, Lincoln carried Warwick out, for he was almost asleep. Francis Lovell would have done the same for the Prince, but received a polite refusal. My son preferred to walk, still carefully grasping the rod of office and very much on his dignity, though he was stupid tired and faced being put immediately to bed.

Watching them go, the two Edwards, I suddenly thought of the other one, whom we thought would be King, and his brother, who bears my own name, and all the happiness of the scene in front of my eyes was blighted. Darkness, sickness, and guilt came on me as if a demon had me by the throat and stifled me with his foul wings. There were many children there that day, but not those two. I shook off the mood quickly, but not before Anne had seen my face. I felt her touch my arm. "You look as if you'd seen a ghost."

"Not ghosts," I said. She looked around, at the departing children, and the remains of the feast, the broken sugar subtleties, the crumbling ostrich plumes.

"If there's blame," she said quietly, "I share it." She knew my thoughts; I did not have to make any reply. The unspoken words—my brother's sons, Ludlow, the other Prince—were understood and would never be used between us, one against the other.

It was too much to ask, that I might be allowed to linger in the company of my family. Those clouds that lay on the horizon were gathering nearer England's shore. I had word from several sources that unrest in the South was growing, in just those counties where the Woodvilles had always laid their bribes thickest. I took the precaution of issuing commissions for the defense of London and wrote to John Howard, Duke of Norfolk, urging him to leave his own county and go to his Sussex and Surrey estates, so that the people might take warning from his presence.

Before we left York, an envoy from Duke Francis of Brittany brought me an unwelcome request that amounted to a threat. King Louis had made his cousin of Brittany an offer; gold in return for the surrender of Tudor's person, but if this were not forthcoming—war. In order to withstand France, Duke Francis required no less than four hundred archers from me, to be maintained at my expense—and he wanted an immediate answer! Since I have never complied with any demand while under threat, though I'd be alarmed to see Tudor traded to France, I'm afraid the Duke will have to whistle for his archers. But even as Monsieur Mainbier, his envoy, spoke with me, news came that old Louis was almost certainly dying. This was a small relief, for there was trouble enough at home.

By the Feast of St. Matthew, we went to Pontefract again. I'd intended to be in London by Michaelmas, but wanted a little more time to set up the Prince in his new larger household. It was the end of the first week in October before I parted from my wife and son and rode south. Because I did not know yet when the storm brewing there would break, I wanted Anne to stay in the North for a while. She did not wish to leave me, but could not deny that she would be pleased to go home to Middleham with the Prince. Edward had begun to plead to go to London. For his own good, I cannot allow it, until he is a little older, and affairs more settled. Then he may come for Parliament, or Christmas.

This parting disturbed me a little. Too often, recently, I've crawled into my wife's bed at midnight, too bone weary to do anything but lie against her welcoming warmth and go to sleep. That night I'd promised not to be such uninspiring company and to come to her earlier. Each time we part and danger threatens, I can feel that she is afraid, though she does not say much or cling foolishly and almost never cries. I thought that she'd been tired ever since coming to London in June, into the heat, danger, and trouble. Because she cares for me, she had suffered great strain all through that time, until after the crowning. It seems to me sometimes that she is not strong; I could swear that in the last few difficult months she has lost flesh, and she has always been slight. I could circle her wrists between my forefinger and thumb and feel the separate bones in them. In spite of their delicacy, she does ordinary things with her hands and wrists and handles a horse better than most women. Her ankles are small too and finish off the best legs one could wish to see on a woman, very slim and smooth and shapely. When she turned her back to me, I slipped my hand between the long, loose ribbons of hair and ran my finger down the curve of her spine. It made out each bone, from the nape of her neck where the hair grew downily, all the way down to the little tail end, where she became soft and round again. I wished I might give her some of my strength; my own body is so tough and stringy and has never suffered a day's illness in years. I look at her sometimes and think of a bird poised for flight—a lark or a swallow. Surely it is one of God's miracles that she wishes to stay with me, summer and winter, never wishing to fly away. When I touched her, she turned over toward me. It was too dark to see her face. To find out if her eyes were open, I felt for them with my lips, found them wide open. She did not blink or flinch from the touch; the lashes stayed still. I traced the outline of her lips with the tip of my tongue; I'd know her blindfold—those lips have their own special shape, long and narrow, with shallow curves and a sharp little dip in the middle of the upper one. In her left cheek, a single dimple comes when she smiles. She was smiling now, I could feel her lips stretch, the dimple crinkled as I touched it, growing deeper as she smiled more. When she began to kiss my mouth, trouble and fear went away from us for a while.

The farewells next morning were hard to make.

"May I ride just a little way south with Your Grace, please?" The Prince was as near wheedling as he could get, though he's been taught not to whine after his own way.

"No. You must stay here to look after your mother the Queen." I couldn't be harsh with him, but he must learn that now he is Prince of Wales and seven, he is no longer a nursery child. I couldn't bear to watch his disappointment. "You can get up with me and ride as far as the outer gate," I said. One of the grooms, grinning, cupped his hands for the Prince's foot and put him up, to sit squeezed between me and the saddle bow. We rode the couple of hundred yards to the gate like this, with everyone laughing and cheering the Prince. He felt important and waved from his vantage point on the tall horse.

"When I come back," I told him, "I expect to hear you construe some Livy or Vergil and to see you make a high score at the butts." He turned his face to look at me, subdued at first at the thought of the Latin, then gave me a gap-toothed smile.

When we reached the gate I said, "No further," and lifted him up to let him slide over my knee and down the horse's shoulder into the arms of the groom. He went to his mother then and held her hand. She gave me a little wistful smile, but said nothing. In his descent from my horse, my son had managed to cover the seat of his black hose with short white hairs. That was the last thing I noticed about him as I rode south, that my Lord Prince's behind was absurdly and unfortunately piebald!

6

Most Untrue Creature
Told by Robert Bolman,
a clerk in the Privy Seal Office

Here loved be God ys alle welle and trewly determyned and for to resyste the malysse of hyme that hadde best cawse to be trewe the Duc of Bokyngame the most untrewe creature lyvyng whome with godes grace we shall not be long tylle that we wylle be in that partyes and subdewe his malys. We assure you there was never falsse traytor better purvayde for as this berrerre Gloucestre shalle shewe you.

Letter from King Richard to the Lord Chancellor, written at Lincoln, 12 October 1483

"Northerners," Bele said, "are a pain in the arse; first cousins to the Scots and the Devil!"

Strong language so early in the morning jarred on my ears. Last night's Lincoln ale seemed to have risen from my stomach and settled in my head. Bele, who has the clerk's job over mine, had drunk more ale than I had and was worse tempered than usual.

"Anyone in particular?" I said carefully. My tongue felt, and tasted, nasty.

"The whole contrary lot! Not been here five minutes

and think they know the Privy Seal Office business inside
out. Master Secretary Kendal too—where does he hail
from, Kendal in Westmorland? — They make good cloth
there, but it never stops raining. He's a hard nut to
crack—as the saying goes, 'like master, like man.' " Bele
hadn't just got up from the wrong side of the bed this
morning, he'd fallen out on his head and put his foot
in the jordan.

"Walls," I said, "have ears."

Kendal, the King's Secretary, walked through the
door, "Master Bele, Master Bolman, good morning." His
lean face was expressionless. I didn't know if he'd heard
what Bele had said. He's a man of about my own age—
just the right side of forty-five—with strong north-
country speech and a laconic turn of phrase. Bele is right;
we're surrounded by too many northern voices, using
words no Londoner can be expected to understand, and
by the blunt, rude manners that go with them.

Kendal looked out of the window at the clock over the
gatehouse. "Not to the Scots, Master Bele," he said mildly,
with his back to us. "Say that to a man of York, and you'll
find yourself slit up the middle like a blood pudding."

Jesu! He had heard. We froze. He didn't elaborate on
this cheery warning; it wasn't necessary. The clock's hand
pointed to seven. Outside the window, birds were loudly
continuing their dawn performance. The hazy, early sun
of October showed the table-top gritty with spilled
pounce.

"Right," Kendal said, "you've five minutes to clean up
in here, before His Grace the King comes." He went out
of the door again. No one can say that he wastes words.

Bele made a rude gesture at the empty doorway. I
hastened to dust off the table and to see that the inkstands
were ready, the pots full, and plenty of fresh quills lying in
the trays—right-hand quills for everyone except me and
extra ones for the King, who writes fast and often breaks
his pens. I laid out pans of wax over their chafing dishes,
the seal matrices, the silk cords and rush plaits, tinder to
light the charcoal for melting. The Privy Seal itself stays
in the custody of Dr. Gunthorpe, the Keeper. A learned
man, Dr. Gunthorpe, the Dean of Wells, who studied at

Ferrara in Italy and is even familiar with Greek scholarship; he served King Edward long and well.

When all was ready for the morning's business, I took a look out of the window. The room was on the ground floor of the Bishop's palace in Lincoln, which is comfortable quarters, even for us clerks. We enjoy the hospitality of Bishop Russell, the Lord Chancellor, though he is not in residence himself. He suffers greatly from the stone, and this has prevented him from moving out of London since the King's coronation. Yellowing fronds of a weeping willow dangled down in front of the window, moving to and from in a slight breeze, making waving patterns of sunlight across my face. Orange-yellow lichen grew on the stone window frame; it gave the place a mellow look, which made me think of autumn. The smell of a bonfire made by the Bishop's garderners drifted indoors. We were at the eleventh of October already, with only a week to St. Luke's Day, indeed, we seemed to be having his "little summer" now.

We wouldn't stay long in Lincoln. We were on our way south. Rumors had been abroad ever since we left York that the Kentish men in the Weald were preparing rebellion. It doesn't take much to stir up the Kentish men. Lord Rivers had acquired a following there, especially around Maidstone and his manor of the Mote; they may wish to avenge his death. It's too much to ask, I suppose, that the new King should be allowed to a peacful reign, taking the crown as he did, but they might have given him more than three months.

As Bele was demonstrating, we Londoners resent the arrival of the northern men in every public office, and their determination to act as new brooms. Well, many of us feel that way about the King himself. We may mock and scoff, but the north-country men are a formidable lot, no doubt of it, and among them, none more formidable than the King. Once or twice I've been close enough to him to make out his features clearly—I am near-sighted and doomed to see life in a blur. What a straight-lipped, uncompromising mouth, and eyes that look harder into your own than many a judge's on King's Bench. I wouldn't want to face his disapproval. When he turns up, I keep very quiet or scuttle out of his way. His manner is mild enough, though, and his voice most pleasant. The roughness of his Border reivers doesn't seem to have rubbed off on him. He never addresses his servants as if they were animals, a habit all too common among the lords of this land.

We worked that morning until dinner, without a break. Hard work is the order of the day now. I don't mind that too much, remembering the days when King Edward led his government at a lively pace. Bele doesn't like it though. He prefers a day that begins at nine and a four-hour break for a tavern dinner washed down by five or six pints of ale.

None of us in the Privy Seal Office are fond of Bele, because he bought his post of chief clerk simply by paying a cash sum for it, no doubt provided by some noble patron. Since he did this over the heads of several of us under-clerks, of whom I am the senior, there has been much discontent.

That evening, for want of anything better to do, I went down to the tavern with a few fellow clerks. My wife is in London; she never travels about or offers to share my lodgings. My son is a scholar at King Henry's college at Eton and does not write as often as he should. I had to wait until I was nearly thirty to get married—an under-clerk's salary is not enough on which to keep a family—and have spent most of the next dozen years regretting it. If the new King continues to travel about his realm as he has in thse first three months, I'd see even less of my family. In their eyes, I think, my failure to get promotion, even when it was my due, has branded me an unsuccessful husband and father.

The tavern was crowded, even for a Saturday evening. We elbowed our way in, and in the crush I jolted a man's arm so that his ale slopped over from his pot and wetted my gown. He turned and mouthed something at me, but the babble was too loud for me to hear his words. Every man was talking about the same thing.

"Kentish men are up in the Weald!"

"St. Luke's day they said it was to be—the rebels have shouted too soon!"

"Exeter's buzzing like a hive with treason!"

"Are they coming out for King Edward's Queen and the lord Marquess?"

"For King Edward V and the little Duke of York? God help the poor innocents!"

"Wait for it lads—who d'you say they have at their head?"

I had to hear it yelled half a dozen times across the tavern noise before I could take it in. The voice of one of those who are always in the know rasped in my ear, "the Duke of Buckingham!"

"What lunacy!" I shouted, to make him hear, and grabbed his sleeve. "You've heard wrong, my friend, surely. The Duke of Buckingham is too great a noble to become a rebel overnight! Besides, he is in Wales. Why, he's second only to the King in the realm, by birth as well as all his high offices."

"Maybe he'd like to be first!" Someone laughed.

"They say he tried to free little King Edward and his brother from the Tower and found they'd been murdered—and he cannot keep faith with Herod! Well, first bastardize those boys, then put them to silence—doesn't that follow on as surely as night follows day?"

"Hush!" a man said uneasily, looking at us, and around for the white boar badges of any King's men. "We talk treason, and I'd rather not have it in my tavern!" It was the landlord himself, alarmed and flustered.

The arrogant, know-all voice went on, "News came in from London, landlord, the story's all over the city there. The King's done in his nephews—like I said, when I heard it was King Richard instead of King Edward, it had to come—only a matter of time before those poor little bastards were finished off—stands to reason!"

Bele and I made our escape as quickly and quietly as we could. "Well, Robert," he said, grumbling, "we'll be needed back at the Bishop's palace. No sooner do we put down a pen than we have to pick it up again. King Herod or not, old Dick will drive us until we drop!

"With a rebellion on our hands," I said, "I wouldn't be surprised if we do. Is this story true, about the Duke of Buckingham and King Edward's sons? Tales fly about with the wind."

"We'll soon find out," Bele said grimly.

We did. Buckingham had raised an army in the Marches of Wales; the Woodville partisans had a force out in Kent and another in the west country. And how they had caught us napping! The King had no soldiers with him, nor even the Great Seal, without which he was unable to issue his commands correctly. One of the most urgent tasks, then, was to send for the Great Seal, which was still in the keeping of the Lord Chancellor in London. Kendal drafted a letter to Bishop Russell, then wrote out a fair copy and gave it to the King for his signature. I watched the King write a postscript to the letter. He wrote very fast, angrily. I sneaked a look at his face and was relieved that I could not see his expression unblurred. His handwriting is large and clear, but this time it would be made scrawly by haste and anger. When he turned the letter around and wrote along the side, the pen nearly went through the paper on the down strokes of the long-tailed letters; even my dim eyesight told me that. It scared me, to see his anger flow out in ink. Frankly, I'd been afraid of him before, as one is of someone unknown who is the King and to clerks next only to God Almighty, but I sometimes caught myself watching him now as if he would grow horns and a tail in front of my eyes.

In the following two days, while I was writing out copies of a proclamation against the traitor Duke of Buckingham, straining my eyes by candlelight, I wondered: In the name of all the saints, why? Why had Buckingham so suddenly and startlingly turned his coat? Until that day no one, least of all the King, had the slightest inkling of his intent. Was the man mad? He was Constable and Great Chamberlain of England. The King had been more generous to him than many thought wise, giving him lands, princely offices, and honors. Even the old Bohun inheritance, about fifty manors, worth more than £ 700 per annum, had been given him. He'd been glutted with favors, all within the space of three months; I knew, for I'd written out many of the grants. Now he was willing to risk all. It didn't make any sort of sense. I thought that the popinjay young Duke had fancied himself as the maker and unmaker of kings. I was not the only one to overhear him say that he'd soon have as many men wearing Stafford knots as the Earl of Warwick used to have ragged staves.

Buckingham had taken with him to Brecon, ostensibly as a prisoner, the Bishop of Ely. No doubt it was thought the Bishop would be safely out of the way in Wales. Having worked in this office for many years, I had heard and seen much of the Bishop of Ely. John Morton is a clever man, to whom intrigue is the breath of life. I was always frightened of him, for he is one of those who enjoy bullying men younger and humbler than himself. I've seen some of his clerks in tears after an interview, lashed by his sarcasms. I'm told he likes young men who stand up to him and return a witty answer, but despises those who are afraid of him. If I knew anything about it, the ambitious Duke of Buckingham would be as clay in Bishop Mortons hands, and King Richard's enemy was more the Bishop than the Duke.

As for the story about King Eward's sons having been murdered, it was common gossip in every tavern in Lincoln, but no one within the circle for the court or the Privy Seal and Signet Offices seemed to know anything or were giving nothing away.

Before the two rebel armies could move out of the west, meet the Kentish men, and attack London, Fortune came in on the King's side. It's always been said that the elements fight on the side of the House of York, and the fouler the weather, the luckier they are. This October proved no exception. In the middle of the night of the fifteenth I woke up suddenly, which is an unusual thing for me; I can sleep like a log anywhere. The noise that had woken me was a steady slamming. Then came a great crash. I started up, swearing, heaved myself out of bed, fumbled around for the iron and tinder, meaning to strike a light, then decided it wasn't worth the trouble. The room and the night outside the window were black as the Devil's backside. I got up, stumbled over my own shoes, and opened the window. I had to jump back as the wind knocked it out of my hands. That shutter had been blown clean off its hinges and spun away, God knew where.

Rain came bucketing in, wetting me. I backed away,
naked and dripping, while in seconds a pool formed on
the floor where I'd been. The wind screamed, hauling and
tugging at everything outside like a straining draft team. I
could just make out a cluster of narrow chimneys of
Flemish brick above the buildings on the other side of the
yard. In front of my eyes one of them snapped off and
disappeared; at the same moment a bush, roots and all,
sailed with a scratchy slap into the other half of the
casement. I had seen enough. I forced the window shut.
Jesus, what a night! Out there one could all but hear the
leathery flap, flap, flap, of the wings of all the demons in
Hell as they rode the storm, shrieking their delight at our
poor earth's discomfiture.

I climbed damply back into bed, buried my head, and
managed another hour's sleep. I woke feeling stale and
irritable. Daylight of a sort had come. There was only one
word for the sky—evil; it closed down on us like a curfew.
Rain was streaming out of it, not abated one jot from the
night before. A drip plopped onto the floor in one corner
from a weak spot in the roof; the room felt chilly. The
mellow stonework of the palace seemed to have turned
greenish with damp already. Downstairs the Bishop's
servants were trying to sweep water from the passageway
with brooms. But the water merely sloshed dirtily out
into an already flooded yard and then slopped slowly
back over the doorstep. "St Luke," one of the men said,
"has had his little summer—good and proper!"

I paddled across the courtyard, overshoes all the way,
hugging my most waterproof woolen cloak around me
and jumping along like some monkish frog. My fellow
clerks arrived in similar fashion. The Bishop of St. Asaph
strode in as if he would have walked successfully upon the
water; Dr. Gunthorpe stalked after him like an indignant
cat, and the King came with them as if he'd not even
noticed it was raining. As they walked past, I flattened
myself against the wall but was close enough to see the
King's face. It had a pinched, pallid look, as if he were
cold, and there were marks under his eyes the color of
charcoal. Yesterday I wrote out with my own hand the
proclamations against Lord Harry of Buckingham,

calling him false traitor. Only weeks ago he had been the
King's friend. I remembered witnessing something quite
trivial between them that seemed to show them as other
young men are. The Lord Harry, in a break in a council
meeting, had slipped the King a piece of paper with a
drawing on it. I couldn't see what it was—probably a
comic head of someone at the meeting—a lord who
looked like his own breed of hounds or some such thing.
We clerks often amuse ourselves with making carica-
tures. Lord Harry was clever at this and at mimicry—as
good as a player. Well, the King had taken one look at it
and laughed, laughed out loud like a schoolboy, though
he did screw up the paper in his hand so that no one might
share their joke or be offended. I remember that incident
because the King had laughed, and as he looked that
morning, I couldn't imagine him laughing in this life
again.

Not, in the next few weeks, that any of us had anything
to laugh about. On St. Luke's Day we rode to Grantham
in the rain, torrential, pouring rain that made us sodden
to the skin before we'd even left the gates of Lincoln town.
It's a long day's journey—thirty miles— and the roads
had turned overnight into treacherous lakes of watery
mud. The wind blew from the west, hard enough to send
all Lincolnshire into the North Sea. In Grantham the
King was lodged at the big posting inn called the Angel,
where he'd often stayed before when traveling the north
road. I had to put up with a billet at the Peacock and
came away flea-bitten. After a few days we moved on to
Leicester, which the King had set as a mustering place for
his army. Buckingham was expected to cross the Severn
from Wales and head south down the Watling Street to
join the Kentish rebels and the west-country men in an
attack on London. We would have to prevent him from
doing so.

It was a dismal journey. The wind and the rain did not
cease, so it was a wonder that by the time we reached the
Leicestershire clay lands around Melton Mowbray we did
not come to a halt altogether, stuck in the mud. While the
rain obscured my already poor eyesight, I listened to
angry shouts, the creaking and groaning of wheels, the

squelch of hoofs, and the splashing of marching men. Our
passing left the countryside in a fearful mess, churned up
as if by a giant plow. Sometimes I noticed the King,
riding up and down the line, talking to the men he knew.
Come to think of it, I was always seeing his gray horse, all
blurry in the rain like a ghost. His horses are beautiful
creatures, usually satin-coated and in the peak of
condition, but this one was a nasty, yellowish gray,
straggle-maned and filthy as mud sprayed up onto its
neck.

We clerks, who had charge of all the supplies of paper,
parchment, and documents, fought a losing battle with
the rain. The trussing canvas of the quires of paper and
bundles of parchments and the leather coffers, unless
packed with extreme care, were found to leak after
exposure to steady rain for eight hours at a time. Bele was
supposed to supervise these details, and being Bele, he did
not even trouble to see if a servant boy had greased all the
leather baggage every day. On the night when the worst
happened and Kendal himself could not make his pen
write because the parchment was limp-damp, Bele
unjustly put the blame on me. Kendal remarked, with his
gallows look, that it was as well he and not the King had
been sitting there unable to make his pen do anything but
strew fuzzy blots instead of letters. But I noticed
afterward that I was not reprimanded and Kendal was
curt with Bele, so accounted him a shrewd man. I
wondered if he knew that Bele never took his turn at
writing up the Signet Office register of daily business, a
task we had to do every night. It's a mark of Kendal's
efficiency that he insists on keeping this book; it is
endlessly useful for reference, however tired we may be as
we scrawl in the entries by dimming candlelight.

When we set out from Leicester we had doubled our
numbers. The wind had dropped and the rain slackened,
wetting us only on and off, instead of all the time.
Sometime while we were heaving our feet out of the
clinging bonds of Leicestershire into the not less miry
depths of Warwickshire, on the way to Coventry, a
messenger from the Marches of Wales met us. He and his
horse looked freakish, plastered with many colors of

mud. But he brought good news. The Duke of Buckingham's rebellion was bogged down on the Welsh side of the Severn. They could get nowhere near the crossings. The Severn had flooded; nothing like it had been seen in the memory of man.

A storm had hit Bristol on October the fifteenth, the day before we caught it in Lincoln. Ships in the Severn estuary were driven ashore and smashed like walnut shells. A whole hamlet called Saltmarsh had been washed away; hundreds of people and animals were drowned. The messenger had been with the King's men this side of Severn, he said, and the destruction was hard to believe. The river as far north as Worcester was as wide as the sea; the only things to be seen were trees sticking up, the roofs of houses, and the legs of floating dead animals pointing to Heaven. To make doubly sure that Buckingham remained stuck in Wales, Sir Humphrey Stafford and a hardy band of the King's men had seen that all bridges still standing were pulled down and the fords destroyed. If they hadn't been able to ride a horse or slither on foot, they'd gone in little boats, he said. Now all the hill roads into England were waterlogged gutters, guarded by the King's men. I thought of them out there, in the barren, wet territories, and gave thanks to God that there would not be a battle. As for Buckingham himself, he'd somehow got across the Wye and had been last heard of at Weobley before he left his floundering rebels and disappeared. The Bishop of Ely had, of course, abandoned him and fled, none knew where.

More good news came, that the Duke of Norfolk had dealt with the Kentish men and with bands of rebels in Sussex and Surrey. London was safe. All that was left for us to do was mop up when the rebels and the blood water had drawn back. Buckingham was doomed; no dove would wing its way to him over the waters bearing an olive branch.

We headed south fast, to Salisbury. I had a taste of campaigning, enough to last me the rest of my life. We did the hundred miles in under four days, on appalling roads, which was hard for everyone and it nearly crippled me. The ground was hilly, too—big, bare chalk hills over

which the wind could bowl a cartwheel unaided. And it
rained—how it rained!

On the road to Salisbury a small party made a
diversion of a mile or two to see the famous Giant's
Dance. I'd heard of this place, which is called the second
wonder of England. In the middle of a barren plain are
huge standing stones, built up in a circle of arches—like a
giant's game of closh. I was curious, and as Kendal
mentioned it, I asked if I might go with them. He was very
amiable about it, said I was welcome. When we got there I
was more impressed than I had expected to be, the stones
were so huge, so stark against the sky and plain, dark and
dripping in the rain. The wind whistled and crooned
around them like a dirge for the ancient peoples who had
lived there.

After I'd walked around for a bit, the rain began to pelt
down, and we huddled around and under the stones,
though they gave no shelter. Half a dozen men clustered
around the arch nearest to me, and I squeezed in beside
them. I couldn't see the men properly at first and then
realized that one was Kendal, humped up in his cloak, his
chin sunk in his collar, like a disgruntled bird. The other
had his back to me, but seemed dimly familiar. The
trouble with me is, I don't recognize people until I'm
within a foot of their faces—the near-sighted are often
accused of not greeting their acquaintances, when really
they have failed to see them clearly. Kendal opened his
mouth, and I thought he was going to speak to me, but
before he could, the other one turned around and saw me.
He rubbed the back of his hand over his eyes to get rid of
the rain and it left a smear of mud acros the bridge of his
nose. His right hand had rings on it with gems the size of
gob stoppers, and I knew why he was familiar; in fact I
saw his face quite clearly. Jesus! it was the King. I had
blundered in among all the great lords of the realm, where
Kendal was privileged by his office to go but I was
definitely not. In spite of being as cold as a wet flatfish, I
broke out in a sweat. I was about to back away,
anywhere, preferably down a coney hole, when the King
spoke to me. "Master Bolman, did you ever see the
Giant's Dance before in your travels? You've been in the

Privy Seal Office a good many years, I know." I couldn't get over the way he said it, as if I were someone he knew well, but hadn't seen for some time—he even knew my name—me, an insignificant pen pusher, middle-aged and passed over twice for promotion!

"N-n-no, Your Grace," was all I could manage at first. I knew I was stammering and hoped he wouldn't think all his Privy Seal clerks were moonstruck idiots.

"Kendal says he thinks Merlin had nothing to do with building this circle of stones, rather that it was raised by a race of people living before King Arthur, before the Romans came. I told him Geoffrey of Monmouth's story, but he's a hard man to convince. You're a clerk, Master Bolman, and have no doubt read as many books as either of us. What's your opinion?"

My head was so entirely emptied of opinions by the amazing discovery that he'd asked me for one that I stammered even more. Kendal had one corner of his mouth drawn back in what I realized was actually a smile. He didn't seem to think it strange that the King should stand in the middle of the Giant's Dance on Salisbury Plain in the streaming rain, talking to one of the underclerks in his Privy Seal Office. "Well, Your Highness," I managed, "I have read the *Chronicles of England* as printed by Master Caxton, and he thinks the manner of raising the stones and the reason for it a mystery." We began to walk back to the horses, me still at the King's side, astonished. As he walked, he kicked aside the thick, tussocky grass rather moodily, and the water sprayed off it in showers. But he spoke to me in a very friendly way.

"Geoffrey of Monmouth says it was built as a memorial to the Britons who were massacred by Hengist the Saxon and that Merlin brought the stones from Ireland by means of amazing engines. I'm inclined to believe him. The stones were raised by man's means, not by magic, whatever Merlin had to do with it. None of our masons today know their secrets. Uther Pendragon, King Arthur's father, and Aurelius Ambrosius are supposed to lie buried here, among the stones. They were famous men, who defended their land against the foreign invaders. England is still at the mercy of foreigners, and traitors." I didn't know quite what to say to that. The rain was streaming relentlessly down, blown slantwise over the plain; every time I opened my mouth, it ran in. The King scarcely seemed to notice it, though I did see him hitch up his collar a little higher around his neck, in a vain attempt to prevent the rain running straight down the middle of his back, as it was down mine. My hat, bound firmly on by a tippet under my chin, felt like a bath sponge filled to capacity. The King wore a cloak of thick wool, of some color—blue or murrey perhaps—that looked black, carrying its own weight of water. My teeth chattered occasionally, both with cold and nervousness. He looked cold, but did not show it. He seemed determined to take an interest in me. "How long have you been a clerk in the Privy Seal, Master Bolman?" he asked.

"Nearly twenty-five years, Your Grace. I entered the service just at the time King Edward of blessed memory became King."

He seemed pleased by that. "Men of your experience are an asset to us. You must be one of the chief clerks by now."

Kendal shot me a sharp look, then his master another and gave his twitch of a smile again. "Er—no, Your Grace," I mumbled, "not yet. I'm only an under-clerk."

The King looked at me very straight for a moment, an uncomfortable but not unkind stare that he had to break to blink the rain out of his eyes. "Why?" he said.

The simplicity of this question unnerved me, and without thinking, I blabbed out the truth. "Your Grace, I have no funds other than my salary. Men more fortunate than I have been able to purchase the vacancies among the chief clerks, even without the benefit of long service. I am not the only one to be passed over."

"I see," the King said, and frowned. Thinking him annoyed at what I had said, I prepared for a sharp rebuke from Kendal later. Then he said, "Does Dr. Gunthorpe know of this?"

"No, Your Grace, he has been Keeper of the Privy Seal for only a short time. My Lord Chancellor may well know of it." Bishop Russell had been the former Keeper. thought the King would soften, but he did not; he

'Who among the clerks has bought his office?"

"Richard Bele," I said, without compunction.

"I see," the King said again.

Kendal, who looked as if he wanted to be on the move again, preferring to endure the rain on horseback than on foot, said only, "Hmm." I didn't have much time for thinking about what we had said. Though I did not speak with the King again, I thought that next time I might not be quite so scared of him. He seemed so ordinary in conversation that I began to wonder if he really were the man that gossip told of, a King who had slaughtered the innocents. Kendal must know, I thought, and I found myself watching his thin, wedge-shaped face. It told me nothing.

Buckingham was taken before the Feast of St. Simon and St. Jude, when we arrived at Salisbury. The King had put a price of £ 1,000 on his head, and he was sold by one of his own tenants. If it hadn't been one, it would have been another, for such a fat reward, and Buckingham was not loved among his own men. He'd gone into hiding near Wem, north Shrewsbury. His tenant Ralph Bannaster had turned him over to the Sheriff of Shropshire, who was sending him south under guard, his feet tied to the stirrups. A long ride for one who knew that a scaffold lay at the end of it. Maybe he hoped for mercy. I heard Lord Lovell say to the King, soberly, "Will you see him?"

"No," The word was spoken softly, but had a terrifyingly bleak, empty sound to it—empty of hope for Buckingham. I couldn't see the King's expression from where I sat, but reckoned it must be as hard as granite.

I was right. There was no delay in the matter. Buckingham was tried by his peers, headed by Sir Ralph Assheton, a hard-bitten north-country man, if there was one. The sentence was inevitable, in spite of Buckingham's grovelings. He was beheaded on All Souls' day, the second of November, which was a Sunday. People said that the King was a hard man who would not stay the ax on a holy day. Later I heard how Buckingham had begged to see the King once more, in the name of the old friendship between them, which he had betrayed. Some thought the King would soften, but he did not; he hardened his heart to adamantine. It was as well that he did, for it was discovered that Buckingham had a knife hidden in his sleeve, with which he intended to murder his one-time friend.

Most astonishing of all was the discovery that Buckingham had sent letters to Henry Tudor in Britanny, arranging that his rebelion should coincide with a Lancastrian invasion from the sea! Bishop Morton of Ely, as I had suspected, had won Buckingham to his purpose. Morton always did favor the cause of Lancaster.

Tudor's plans for an invasion suffered as much from the weather as Buckingham's revolt had on land. The storms beat his ships back, and it was not until the end of October that he managed to cross the Channel. We heard this news at Salisbury and that his ships lay not far off Poole. The day after Buckingham's heading we went south into Dorset, a hurried, anxious journey. But by the time we slogged wearily into Poole that evening, the news of our approach had reached Tudor and he sailed away.

After that began a journey into the west country, which for me was a succession of damp, uncomfortable lodgings in strange towns, where I even found myself sharing a bed with Bele—a horrible experience! I was too saddle weary to notice much about the country through which we rode, except that each night I scraped mud of different colors off my boots and clothes. In the evenings there was no time for the tavern, much to Bele's disgust. Then, and at first daylight, we were busy at our clerk's duties, at the call of Kendal or of the King himself. As I sat trying to make hands stiff from clutching wet reins hold a pen and longing for a cushion under my rear end, I thought that the King and his lords had only a few advantages over us—a hot bath—if they were lucky—a cleaner bed and the pick of the food.

One of the northern soldiers, a very dirty, bearded yokel in a rusty sallet with raindrops hanging all around its rim like a string of beads, summed up my feelings. They put a lot into a few words, if one can understand them. He didn't like his grub—last week's bread and a nameless soup. After he'd swallowed it—he was too hungry to throw food in the midden—he spat accurately out of the window six feet away and gave his verdict: "Nowt," he said, "but piss and cabbages!" And he was right. Later I saw the same man mounted up on a horse much too good for him to have any legal right to it. Curious, I chatted to him a while, understanding about half of what he said. His name was John Key, and he was one of the soldiers of the City of York, a cordwainer by trade, who'd served an apprenticeship and was a respectable craftsman, though he didn't look it. He was mud-caked to the ears, hadn't seen a razor since he set out from York, and I wouldn't mind betting he was lousy. He'd been hauled up before the captain of his contingent, because they were strict in the King's army about thieving and looting, but when Key said the horse had belonged to the servant of a traitor and was thus forfeited goods, they laughed and let him keep it. It turned out that he'd picked it up from the lands of Sir John Cheney, one of the rebels who'd now fled.

Incidents like that broke the tedium of the journey. We went from Poole to Dorchester, to Bridport, and to Exeter, where we stayed put for five days and there were half a dozen more beheadings. Then on to Bridgwater, on the northern coast, a long, hard slog through deepest Devon and Somerset. This was a depressed and depressing little town, which had once had a flourishing cloth trade, but now seemed full of out-of-work weavers, tumbledown houses, and a silting-up harbor. The bridge over the muddy river seemed to be tottering on its arches for lack of repair. From there we crossed the Somerset fenlands by causeway, near to Glastonbury, heading for Salisbury again. That ride was frightening, like crossing the sea by a plank bridge. The land was still flooded after the great storms of a month ago and, the locals said, would stay that way until the end of winter. It's a watery, desolate place at best, but when I saw it, one could hardly imagine human beings had existed there. Bridgwater to Salisbury took only two days. The grooms were having great trouble now with saddle sores and lameness, and the horses looked rough and thin; some of the busiest men among us were the farriers. By the time we moved from Salisbury to Winchester and Farnham and home to London, men and beasts were all jaded and ill-tempered.

The Mayor and five hundred citizens met us at Kennington and escorted us toward London. As I rode up the filthy highway of the Borough of Southwark, I felt almost an affection for its familiar squalor. Crowds lined the street in front of the big inns, but it was a subdued welcome for the King, returning from a bloodless victory over his rebels. At the south end of London Bridge those rebel's heads had been set up on poles, the kites soaring over them.

At the house called the King's Wardrobe, near St. Paul's, the Queen met her husband. She had come south a week ago, as London was safe again. When our party rode in through the gates, she darted across the courtyard like a swallow, leaving her ladies behind. When the King had dismounted, she went straight into his arms. At first they did not kiss, only held each other very tightly. Now we were back in London, our journey done, the King's face was the color of candle wax, and if I knew anything about it, he was tired enough to drop where he stood. I wasn't sure if I could stand myself without my knees wobbling. At a rough estimate, we had ridden close on five hundred miles in five weeks. I watched the Queen's face, pressed briefly against his shoulder, a little, fine-boned face, the eyes big and bright as mirrors. After their first embrace, they kissed and parted, as if a little shy of all the spectators, and walked into the house. I thought: He's a luckier man than I supposed. I wouldn't get a welcome like that.

Back at Westminster I began to catch up with five months' news. The first piece of gossip concerned the Solicitor General. This lawyer, Thomas Lynom, as King Richard's man, having worked for him in the North when he was Duke. Lynom, the fool, had fallen arse over head in love with Shore's wife, who was imprisoned in Ludgate for her part in the treason against the King in June. He had even gone so far as to apply for a marriage license! The King, when he heard of this, had not been pleased, for a woman who was so blatantly his enemy and a notorious whore was hardly a suitable wife for a dignified officer of the law. He had written to the Lord Chancellor, asking him to try to persuade Lynom out of this folly. But, and this caused us some amazement, he had not expressly forbidden it. When it appeared that Lynom was determined to marry Elizabeth Shore, the King allowed it, letting the woman come out of prison into the care of her father. Now we were all back in London, Lynom took the wife he desired, apparently without any loss of favor with the King.

Soon after this, while I was still bewildered by the King's leniency to his Solicitor General, he did me a kindness. He sent a direction to Dr. Gunthorpe, requesting him to dismiss Bele! He had rememberd what I had told him that day we had gone to see the Giant's Dance and had removed those who had obtained posts in the Privy Seal Office by bribery. I was to have Bele's place! Pleased as I was to get my promotion at last, I was surprised that the King felt it necessary to cleanse the crown offices of corruption. If he continued in this way, he'd make enemies for sure; most men prefer those who turn a blind eye.

The King did not intend to give us clerks much respite that winter. We managed to stay put at Westminster for the whole of December. After the Christmas season, we would be busy, for Parliament was to meet on the twenty-third of January until the twentieth of February. This we'd expected—the session had been postponed from November last because of Buckingham's rebellion. What we had expected was that the King would go on progress into Kent in the two weeks between Epiphany and the meeting of Parliament. As if we had not had enough journeying about. Kent in January was a dismal prospect—the miriest ways in the kingdom. Kendal announced this and asked me if I would go—it was not necessary for us all to go—and that we would be traveling fast and light, to Maidstone, Canterbury, and Sandwich. "The King wishes to take oaths of allegiance" he said, "from those who have dabbled in treason. He intends to issue a proclamation, urging all men who have grievances at law to prepare petitions, which he will hear and determine. The King's justice must be brought to Kent."

So, I thought, the King will go into Kent, the worst center of the rebellion against him, to bring the Kentish men his justice. To my way of thinking, his care for the common weal will bring him trouble from some of his lords. Their idea of the King's justice is more likely the ax and the gallows, not the recourse of poor men to the law. Is this King, the law giver, also King Herod, who, men say, has put his brother's sons to eternal silence?

7

The Innocents

Told by Lady Elizabeth, eldest daughter of King Edward IV

Why soo unkende, alas?
Why soo unkende to me?
Soo to be kende to me.

Syne the tyme I knew yow fyrst
You were my joye and my trust.

Erly and late I am ryght fayne
Youre love and favour to attayne.

Ys ther no grace ne remedy,
But ever to morne eternally?

15th–16th century

On the Feast of the Holy Innocents, the day when King Herod slew all the boy babies in Israel, my mother refused to get up. She lay in bed and wept all morning until her face was red and puffy. It was an unlucky day—falling on a Sunday—so we'd have to beware of Sundays for all next year. The year my father had been crowned was the same, but he believed too much in his own luck to worry and went to the Abbey on Sunday, defying the omens. In spite of all the weeping and wailing and mourning for my poor little brothers, I don't think my mother had given up the hope that they were still alive. I

can't bear to imagine them dead and I can't believe that
my uncle Richard would murder anybody, let alone two
children, his own kin. My mother refused to have him
called "King" in this house. She called him names I'd
blush to repeat but mostly "the Hog." In the same way,
she was always known as the Queen, though elsewhere in
the world she was known as Lady Grey, as if she were
never married to my father. What could it matter how
titles were used, in a cramped house in Westminster
Sanctuary?

The day after she took to her bed, my mother got up
and looked at her face in a mirror. She made Cecily dab it
with a lotion called *"lac virginis,"* which is made of lead
and something else ground up and put in rose water. It's
supposed to make ladies' skin white. My mother's skin is
as white as her water flower device, the wrinkles in it no
more than the veining in a petal. Her eyelashes are the
only fault—too light; she dyes then from time to time. I
had to braid her hair and pin it up. It made a thick, silvery
rope, below her waist; there are white streaks in it now,
but they don't show much in hair so pale. I coiled it up
and stuck in the long ivory pins. She had a set of these,
each with a tiny diamond rose in the head. I put on her
black velvet hood of the latest fashion, which looked, as
almost everything does, elegant on her—more flattering,
I thought, than the high butterfly headdresses.

I felt like a servant. My mother thought she should
keep us occupied with trivial tasks, to stop us fretting. It
had the opposite effect on me; I'd rather read a book for
the fiftieth time or merely stare out of the window than
fiddle endlessly with needles, face lotions, and wailing
children. A strand of my own hair had fallen against my
mother's. It looked a dark, bright color beside hers,
crudely yellow as oat straw, with a tinge of red in it where
the firelight catches. I'm not much like my mother. Cecily
is the only one of us to resemble her closely, and pretty
though my sister is, she can't compare with the crystal
clear beauty of our mother when she was younger. She's
not young now, though her figure is good still, if a little
thick in the waist, but after bearing twelve children the
miracle is that she isn't shaped like a meal sack. I'm taller

than my mother, or Cecily; in fact, I seem to be the tallest girl anywhere. Standing back to back with my half-brother Dorset, who is six feet, I was only a hand's breadth shorter. He used to say I was too big and not going to be beautiful, but later on he stopped saying that. Everyone says I'm like my father, which always pleases me.

My mother was sitting in front of the meager fire, her skirt folded back over her knees to show her petticoats and her white stockinged feet in velvet slippers, fashionable, round-toed slippers—she managed to get some new things brought in from the outside world. Only since we'd been in this ordinary house, like a shopkeeper's, had she taken to this habit of warming her legs. It reminded me of my old nurse, whose legs had been all lumpy with veins. I wondered if my mother had behaved like that—like an ordinary woman—when she was young and lived on country manors. At court no one had ever seen the Queen's ankles, not even her daughters.

"Bess," she said, running a finger along the hem of her gown, "this velvet needs turning. The pile's molting. You and Cecily can sew it together. I'll speak French for an hour with Anne, and you must hear Bridget say her alphabet." My heart sank. Another day spent busily at nothing.

"Is that man of the Hog's outside today?" She asked this question every day, without fail. As usual, I went to the window and looked out. The twenty-ninth day of December, as dreary and dark as could be. The guard was there. He was wearing the royal livery of murrey and blue, my father's livery, ours. We'd been in the Sanctuary for eight months. The summer had been worst. In winter the rooms in the house were dark, poky, and cold; in the summer they were nearly as dark, and stifling hot. There was a tiny garden, but we never used it, because the windows of other houses overlooked it. The palace of Westminster was cleaned in August, when the court had gone on a progress. We had to shut all the windows, because the stink of this operation was so appaling. Now, facing the darkest winter days, we were running short of good, clean wax candles and were having to use smelly tallow dips.

As I left my mother's room, I almost fell over my
smallest sister and stubbed my toe on one of the annoying
little steps in the wooden floor that these houses seem full
of. Bridget, who is just three, was sitting on the floor
outside the door, pulling apart a wooden doll whose arms
and legs were fixed on by leather thongs. When I ran into
her, she howled instantly. I picked her up, but she went on
crying. Her pudgy little face was scarlet; her flax-white
hair stuck out in unkempt spikes all around it. She didn't
smell very sweet and her skirts were damp. She's growing
too lazy to ask for the pot, I thought, or her nurse is too
bored to care. I heard Katherine set up a yelling
somewhere else in the house. Very nearly five, she was
resentful of having to do her lessons, for she had no one of
her own age to learn with. Anne, at eight, was in the same
predicament. In that hateful hen coop it always seemed
to be me who had to comfort the little ones. No wonder
my mother had made only brief visits to her nursery,
sweeping in and out, never letting us forget she was the
Queen. We used to kneel to her, all in a row, like a set of
mourners in assorted sizes, each of us with long, fair hair
down our backs; butter wouldn't melt in our mouths. My
mother now coped with the indignity and incovenience of
living so close to her children by shutting her ears to the
howls and leaving the harassed nurses and few elderly
servants—and me—to deal with the troubles.

We'd had a miserable Christmas. We tried to be brave
and decked the house with holly and ivy, bays and
rosemary, but it all fell flat and sour. Cecily said, what
was the use of having mistletoe when there was no man in
the house between fourteen and sixty, and nobody
wanted to kiss the chaplain or the page. On twelfth day,
we drank each other's healths in "lamb's wool," a lovely
drink made of ale, with spices and sugar and all fluffy
from the roasted, bursting apples floating in it. The
Abbey bells rang loudly that day; the King would make
the Ephiphany offering of gold, frankincense, and myrrh
at the High Altar, in memory of the three Kings of
Cologne. He'd go in procession to the Abbey, wearing his
crown, and in the evening there'd be feasting in the White

Hall. Even in our house the sounds of merrymaking around Westminster could be heard.

When it grew dark, which was by midafternoon, my mother got out her cards. She always made a great fuss about these and wouldn't let any of us use them. She kept them wrapped in silk, in a painted wooden box that smells of incense. The cards themselves were battered and grubby, because they were so old and had belonged to my grandmother Bedford. The pictures' names were written under them in French—strange pictures, fool and Pope, justice, the world, the Devil, the hanged man. It was a long time since my mother had been obliged to make her own amusements, and she seemed less remote because of it. Her chaplain was too good humored to forbid the game. Some priests think casting fortunes is as bad as conjuring up the Devil. For my mother, it was half game, half believable magic. My fortune read too favorably to imagine it ever happening; the cards predicted that I should be a queen! A year ago I might have believed it, but not now. I knew that my mother had been cheating and arranged some of the cards as she had wanted them. So like her, to half believe and then turn the belief into a lie by her own hand.

I would never be a queen now, nor my little brother Edward a king. I was just as much King Richard's prisoner as he, but I was alive. No one seemed able to tell us for certain whether my brothers were alive or dead. Early last September Bishop Morton of Ely's agents had got into the Tower, to begin a scheme to free them. To everyone's dismay, the boys could not be found there. This was a disaster, because there couldn't be a plot to free them without them being present for freeing. My mother was convinced immediately that they were dead and that my uncle Richard had murdered them. She was so frantic we were all afraid that she would go mad. I kept saying that they must have been moved from the Tower, but she would not listen.

Then a visitor came to us in the Sanctuary. He was a little black beetle of a man called Dr. Lewis Caerleon, a Welshman who had sometimes acted as my mother's physician. He was also employed by Lady Margaret

Beaufort, Countess of Richmond, Lord Stanley's wife. We knew her well, a tiny woman with bright brown eyes, a rather ferrety nose, pursed up mouth, and black eyebrows so highly arched they gave her a look of perpetual pained surprise. She is a very learned lady and has a way of always appearing independent of men. Dr. Lewis brought a message from her to my mother—an offer.

Since King Edward V and his brother the Duke of York were missing from the Tower and presumed dead—he had to wait for my mother's fit of weeping to spend itself—what better plan than that Lady Margaret's son, Henry Tudor, should come back from exile to avenge them by killing the usurper Richard and making himself King of England? The Bishop of Ely had persuaded the great Duke of Buckingham to help us. Lady Margaret's man Sir Reginald Bray had gone to Buckingham's castle of Brecon and found the plot going well. The fact of my brothers' disappearance—murder, certainly—could be put to use, to turn the people from King Richard and show Henry Tudor as their savior from the usurper and shedder of infant's blood. The condition Lady Margaret had to offer my mother came last. It appalled me. Tudor would marry me and restore my father's blood to the throne in our heirs! I gasped; I could not help it. My mother said something very sharp to me. She was willing to grab at any offer. "But we don't *know* they're dead," I blurted out. My mother almost slapped my face. Me—to marry the Lancastrian pretender, whom my father had sworn to give a traitor's death if he got the chance. In our topsy-turvy world my father wouldn't have known us for his wife and daughters. For that matter, he wouldn't have known my uncle Richard for this brother.

But the plot failed, and the October gales blew Henry Tudor back to Brittany. I'm still offered to him, if he cares to try again. On Christmas Day, he had proclaimed himself King Henry VII, at Rennes Cathedral in Brittany, and sworn that if he should win his crown, he would make me his wife. Of course, this was why my mother had foretold I should be a queen. They showed me a picture of Tudor, belatedly, after the plot. He's got a thinnish face,

the eyebrows as arched as his mother's and eyes with
drooping lids, as some birds have. His hair looked sandy
in color. He's twenty-seven. But I'm sure he'll never get
near England again, to claim me. I sometimes pray to Our
lady that he may not and that my uncle the King will rid
us of him once and forever. Dr. Lewis Caerleon will carry
no more messages from Brittany; he was caught and
imprisoned in the Tower.

Parliament met at the end of January. News of it came
trickling in to us. Lady Margaret Beaufort had been
attainted for her part in the rebellion, her title of
Countess of Richmond taken away and a lot of her lands.
Everyone was surprised that she didn't get imprisoned in
the Tower, but she was sent off to the country, where her
husband, Lord Stanley, was told to keep her in order. I
think it's she who tells Lord Stanley what to do. So does
my mother, for she sneered and said my uncle was a
bigger fool than she thought. He's not that much of a
fool, though, because he attainted a hundred and four of
the other rebels.

King Richard's title was confirmed by Parliament, and
his son's succession. My mother cursed. When she heard
that the King had abolished benevolences, a hated royal
tax, which amounts to outright demands by the King for
money from whomever he chooses, she scoffed and said,
"That won't last!" The King and his advisers had drawn
up some good Acts. Most of them concerned the working
of the law. My father used to say that his brother knew as
much about the law as a man who'd studied at the Inns of
Court and twice as much about putting it into practice.
There was an Act to stop oppression by bailiffs and
stewards, who turned the law to their own advantage; one
to prevent men getting places on juries by bribery; and
one to protect those thrown into prison on flimsy
evidence. I didn't pretend to understand the legal things,
but it seemed as if the King would be popular with his
subjects because of these reforms. "The lords won't like
it," my mother said, with malicious glee. "All those poor
men able to turn the law against their masters, when
everybody knows the only way to rule is by keeping the

commons under the thumb of the lords." There were also
some Acts to help English merchants and one to protect
foreign booksellers, writers, and printers. Master Caxton
would not be too pleased about this one, as it gave
freedom to his rivals in trade.

Though Parliament confirmed that my uncle's son
should inherit the crown, the King wished to make more
solemn these mere words in ink on parchment.
Accordingly, all the lords spiritual and temporal were
required to swear on the Holy Gospels, in the presence of
the King himself, an oath of allegiance to the Prince,
acknowledging him as King if something should happen
to his father. My mother's face looked ugly when she
heard this. "He swore the same oath to my son. He may
well fear sudden death; the sword of God's justice will
strike. That is what I pray for."

God knew whom she prayed to. Soon after she had
uttered these wicked words, something occurred that
made me shrink from my mother's company. I would not
enter her room without crossing myself or saying a
prayer. I found the Things in a little casket hidden at the
bottom of her clothes-chest while rummaging for
something she insisted was there but wasn't. I paid for my
curiosity in opening that box for long afterward, in fear
that haunted even my dreams. At first I thought little
Bridget had hidden away some dolls. But they were no
toys. There were three of them, horrible, obscene
manikins made of flesh-colored wax. They were more
revolting than anything I could imagine, and more
terrifying. That did not stop me looking closer. Two of
the things were made like a naked man and woman, the
third like a male child. The bigger ones were each
crowned with gold paper and, most horrible of all, had
hair on their heads. I knew whom they were meant to
represent. Women could be burned for making these
things and using sorcery against the King and Queen.
How had she managed to get hold of the hair?—it must be
theirs—some very devious bribing of servants, I
supposed. It wasn't the first time my mother had dabbled
in making images. My grandmother Bedford had been
accused of the practice more than once; she made one of

the Earl of Warwick and said spells over it to bring about his death. Maybe she had invoked the aid of Satan. Trembling, I shoved the box back where I'd found it and ran out of the room. I was first violently sick, then went to my room to pray for protection against evil. I did this every day after.

On the eleventh of February I was eighteen. I cried when I woke up that day, because I was growing old, had been made a bastard, and for all the hope there was of finding a husband to look after me, I might as well have been a nun. I cried because I knew nothing of my little brother's fate. I cried because I was frightened of my mother and because my beloved father was dead. I cried also because I remembered my seventeenth birthday, last year. It had been Shrove Tuesday and Lent beginning the next day, but a banquet was held in my honor. My father was trying to comfort me for having been jilted by the Dauphin, though I think he needed comfort more than I did. He found me a special partner for that evening—not one of the single men my own age, for he was not looking for another husband for me, but his own brother, Richard. As my uncle was at Westminster for the Parliament last year without his wife, my father had honored us together. I was happy enough to fly; my uncle was the hero of the time because he'd beaten the Scots. I know he's not a flatterer or a flirt and, they say in astonishment, faithful to his wife, but he said I was the loveliest princess in Christendom that night. I had a gown of green cloth of gold, which is one of my best colors, and I wore my hair down, bound back by gold ribbons. I was shy of dancing with him at first, because of being quite a lot taller than he is. He didn't seem to mind, though, and is a good dancer, which always makes things easier. I'm the only one of us girls old enough to remember my uncle before he went away to live in the North. Until I was six he lived most of the time at Westminster. Maybe it was because of my father's affection for him that I followed suit. My father was my mentor in all things. Now, a miserable year later, I cried because I'd liked my uncle Richard so much, and he'd brought such terror and grief to us; our uncle Rivers and half-brother Grey dead, our

brother's crown usurped. As for our bastardy, in my
heart I believed it true and blamed my mother, never my
father. He must have been betwitched in some way; it was
a marriage with the Devil's blessing, not God's.

Before the end of the session of Parliament, the King
sent ambassadors to treat with my mother. He chose two
men even she could not refuse to see. They were Lord
Howard, who had been given my younger brother's title of
Duke of Norfolk, and the Lord Chancellor, the Bishop of
Lincoln. They had been two of my father's most trusted
servants, not my mother's friends perhaps, but never
openly hostile to her. I saw them come into the house.
They looked astonished to find the former proud Queen
living in such humble surroundings. They were
unsmiling; the long and the short of it, I thought. The
Duke of Norfolk always had a soft spot for children and
made a special pet of me when I was small; I hoped he
would still be kind. The Chancellor was a tall, very thin
man, with a sick, yellow face and round shoulders, on
which his gowns hung like a scarecrow's clothes. With his
big nose and white hair, he looked like a stork. The Duke
did not try to kiss my mother's hand. He was not going to
treat her as queen. He gave her a perfunctory bow. The
Chancellor looked ominous in the background.

"Madam," Howard said, "my Lord Chancellor and I
would be obliged if we might speak with you in private."
My mother nodded, her mouth pursed up, though she
looked oddly tremulous and scared. She led them into the
best room. When she came out, she looked very strange—
old, almost. As the two men left, I managed to touch the
Duke of Norfolk's arm. He stopped, and his stern face
suddenly creased up into his cheerful smile. "We'll soon
have you out of here, Lady Bess," he whispered, like a
conspirator.

My relief was so huge, I almost burst into tears. "My
lord," I said, very low, in case my mother heard, "will you
tell the King—I don't want to stay here. For love of my
father, help us."

After they'd gone, my mother called me and Cecily to
her. She was crying, weakly. "They brought terms," she
said, "from the King." It was the first time she'd called

him that. "They swore to me that the King had proofs that
my sons still alive. He wished me to send you all out of the
Sanctuary into his care. If I accept his proofs, and terms,
he will leave me free to live as I wish. Your brother Dorset
may have a pardon if he comes home. I'm too weary," she
said, "to know where I am to go, how I am to live.
Daughters, what am I to do?" She'd never asked us
anything before.

"Please, Madam," Cecily said, taking courage,
"wouldn't it be best to accept?"

"I wish to leave this place," I said, as I'd never dared
before.

"So be it," she answered, sighing. "He offers me seven
hundred marks a year, and to find husbands for all you
girls, and to give you dowries—annuities of two hundred
marks each. The sums are paltry. Gloucester's a hard
man. But what can I do? Take it or leave it, Howard said.
You see how they speak to me now." Put baldly, it didn't
sound an overgenerous offer.

"He's not panting to make amends," Cecily said.

On the first day of March the King assembled his lords
spiritual and temporal who were left in London after the
Parliament, the Mayor, and aldermen and swore
publicly, upon the Holy Gospels, to protect me and my
sisters if we would come out of the Sanctuary into his
care.

The next day we walked out of the house in the
Sanctuary and were escorted to the palace, leaving my
mother alone and tearful. It was Shrove Tuesday again. I
didn't want to think of that other time a year ago. I didn't
want to meet my uncle the King either. In the end, it was
the Queen who met us. She looked grave and
uncomfortable and kissed each of us on the cheek very
quickly, as if she did not know whether we'd like it or not.
I was curious about her, having not seen her since my
brother's wedding to little Anne Mowbray. I remembered
nothing about her appearance, perhaps because it is
unmemorable. I couldn't judge how different she'd been
then, at twenty-one. She is not beautiful. Her face is
serious and pale; the color comes and goes in it easily. I
noticed how slender her neck was, like the stalk of a

flower; in fact, she was downright thin. I was shocked, having expected to find my uncle's wife a pretty woman, who delights had kept him out of other's arms. Her perfume was delicious though—it made me aware how I'd missed these things in the past year. I resented her from the start, though I felt guilty about it, because she went out of her way to be kind. After I'd thought her a sober, full little creature, she surprised me by taking my hand and smiling most charmingly, saying, "Lady Elizabeth, I'd almost forgotten, we are sisters in a way; my father was your godfather." I had forgotten; I couldn't remember her father the Earl of Warwick. My mother had hated him even more than she now hated the King.

After the first formal greeting he gave us, I scarcely saw the King. I couldn't remember what he said to us. My eyes were fixed on the floor most of the time, and when I had to kiss his cheek, I kept them shut. He had an ordinary, warm, man's face. I was trembling like a leaf. Afterward I wondered if he felt embarrassed to be landed with five nieces, all little bastards, whose lives he'd ruined.

Cecily and I were to wait upon the Queen, while the little ones were merely added on to the already large nursery of children in her care. Before, I'd have thought it humiliating to wait upon my uncle's wife, but after nearly a year of attending my mother, it didn't seem so bad. Anne is a gentler person than my mother. I hoped her ladies would not be hostile to us. In those first days I watched the Queen. She gave me the satisfaction of being both better-looking and younger than her, yet she made me feel large, and robust as a peasant. Whenever I saw her and the King together, I seemed to grow twice as large and wanted to leave the room without exactly knowing why. When they talked in private, they used all sorts of queer, north-country words and expressions, which I did not understand. I felt shut out, though I had no right to be included. The first time I saw my uncle kiss his wife, I was reduced to hopeless desolation. It wasn't the sort of explicit embrace my father had thought nothing of indulging in public—just a touch, really—but she turned her face to him, and it was as if a shutter had been opened upon a sunny day; I wondered why I had not thought her pretty. I blushed hotly. If only there were someone to show me that tenderness, to look after me. I've never been kissed properly, and I'm eighteen. Tears swam into my eyes, and I forgot them, the King and Queen, in my longing to have my father back, to be picked up like a little girl and be enfolded in his huge, warm hug, to hear his lovely laugh.

No sooner had we girls got our freedom, such as it was, we were told to pack our belongings, because at the end of the week we were going to Cambridge, beginning a progress that would last all summer. The King wished to be in the North by the end of May, to take whatever action was necessary against the Scots. The day we set out for Cambridge, March roared like a lion. It seemed too early to be going off on a progress, though it was wonderful to be on horseback again, out of doors, and setting out to see fresh places in England. I was now convinced my brothers were alive, in the North, where we were going. My mother had sent a letter to my half-brother Dorset and expected him to come home and make his peace with the King. In spite of the cold, bleak day, life seemed better.

Many of the villagers in places we passed through left their work to watch us. In their weekday clothes, the people always look so drab, like blocks of sparrows gathering around a peacock in his pride. There were plenty of sparrows gathering around a peacock in his pride. There were plenty of peacocks among us. I found myself looking covertly around at all the young men and wondering which ones were unmarried. My sister Cecily was doing the same. Whenever we see one under thirty who is good-looking, he's bound to be married already. What seems to be missing in my uncle's household are the sort of young men who'd made up my half-brother Dorset's circle. Clothes, jewels, money, eating, drinking, tennis, gambling, and endless women; they thought of nothing else. I was kept very carefully away from Tom's friends; my mother and, surprisingly, my father were both strict about this. Beside them, so many of the men at court now would have looked country yokels. I supposed my uncle would marry me to one of his followers. I wouldn't be as lucky as his bastard daughter Katharine and be given to an Earl. There are so many north-country men; it would probably be one of them, whom I'd need an interpreter to understand. They have such absurd names—well, they sound absurd to me—one of the squires is called Ellis Entwhistle; how could anyone marry a man with a name like that!

On the road there were a few pilgrims, going to Our Lady of Walsingham, thought not many, for the season was too early. A friar or two plodded along, their brown habits bellying out in the wind. The Queen said, "I would like to go to Walsingham," and sighed. She didn't tell me why; perhaps she wanted more babies. My mother had said something about her being barren for six years and how it was a wonder she kept her husband's fancy from wandering. She had, though; they slept in the same bed every night, the whole court knew. I hated to think of my mother, working some evil on her, to make sure she stayed barren, and was almost sorry she might not go to Walsingham.

Cambridge should be a gracious place, full of college buildings and learning, but whatever it was to the eye, it offended the nose. One might think all the pigsties and cattle yards in the kingdom were there. They told me this was because the townsfolk drive their beasts to the common meadows by the Cam in the day and allow them to wander loose in the night. The streets were like middens, and though the Mayor and the college provosts had seen that loads of green rushes were laid down, we were forewarned and wore pattens.

We spent three whole days being shown colleges and half-built colleges, hearing Latin speeches and learned disputations. The unfinished chapel of the college of St. Mary and St. Nicholas, known as King's College, which was endowed by Henry of Lancaster, was a most marvelous building. The King gave Provost Field gifts toward it amounting to a thousand pounds, an enormous sum of money. He spent a long time looking at the drawings of the timber roof and fan vaulting and of the intended bell tower and talking to the architects and masons; he was really interested, I could see. The chapel was as beautiful as the one my father lies in at Windsor—more so, perhaps, from the outside. The stone was very pale gray, clean and newly hewn, rising out of a flat, muddy field against the cold March light and wide-open, scudding sky.

From Cambridge we took the road across the fenny lands toward Huntingdon and Stamford. I came that way once before, with my father. He told me the fenmen go on stilts because of the wet. My little brother Richard had said, "But you wouldn't need stilts, father, you've such long legs!" My father had roared with laughter at this. When we crossed the river Nene at Wansford Bridge we were very near the castle of Fotheringhay.

The Queen said, smiling a little, amused smile, as if she saw something that we did not, "Richard—the King—was born at Fotheringhay."

"Madam, didn't you know him when you were both small?" I asked her curious.

"I can *just* remember him when I was four, and he came to live in my father's household. When he arrived, he was very grubby and bedraggled from traveling. Poor Dickon, I thought he looked like the little owl who had fallen down the chimney of my bed chamber one morning; we found it sitting dejected in a heap of soot, with its feathers all out of place. They both brightened up later." I could not visualize the King as a grimy brat of nine, but the memory seemed to touch some special tenderness in his wife.

We came to Nottingham in mid-March. After that, we were going north to York to meet the Prince. I was curious to see this child. The title that had been my brother's was now his. I wondered if he were as clever at his books as my brother Edward had been at seven, reading half a dozen Roman authors. The Queen said that his father wanted him to have a good grounding in Latin, because it would help him with law, which is one of the most important things for a Prince to learn. It would impress people if he were taught Greek, but it was better to use that time in sending him into law courts and councils, to learn how to administer the royal justice to those who would later be his subjects. He'd soon begin his serious training in the use of weapons, horsemanship, and other sports, because a king who cannot lead his men into the field will forfeit his subject's respect—as happened to poor Henry of Lancaster. The Queen showed me the gift that had been prepared for the Prince's eight birthday, which would be in early June. It was a book, the English translation of Vegetius' *De re Militari*. This is a treatise of instruction for young men beginning their training in knightly exercises. There were some colored borders in it, with flowers, the King's arms in the initial letter on the first page, and the Prince's device of a golden griffin, to show it was specially for him. "He loves books," his mother said and looked as if she would like to tell me of his accomplishements. She longed to see him. I turned away, thinking of my own poor mother, all alone. We'd had news that my half-brother Dorset had tried to come home, to make his peace with the King, but had been caught on his way to Calais by Tudor's agents and kept prisoner by them. I thought it had cost my uncle a good deal to pardon him and face the prospect of having him back at court, for they had loathed each other since boyhood. It showed in the proclamations made against Tom—my uncle singled him out as an adulterer, traitor, and extortioner. I know there's some truth in this, but Tom has never been unkind to me, as he often is with his women.

By the time we'd been at Nottingham three weeks, I began to feel happier and less strained in the presence of the King and Queen. Cecily bloomed, now that she had fresh air, exercise, occupation, and company. The pastiness, pale skin, and spots that had come from confinement in the Sanctuary had disappeared. She looked ravishing, putting all the other young women, married or maidens, in the shade. Being a bastard, she got even more stares from men than before, when they had not dared, in case my mother the Queen should have heard of it. I got nearly as many admiring looks, which was very gratifying, as I knew tall girls are not always thought beautiful. Some ancient lady told me I looked like my grandmother the Duchess of York, whom they used to call "The Rose of Raby." The Queen gave me seven yards of green velvet, the color of a holly leaf, for a gown. She said wistfully that it suited me better than her, though it was one of her favorite colors. She already had a gown made of it, which gave her a certain snowdrop prettiness. On me, though, with my golden hair, it would turn heads, and the Queen knew it. A less generous woman would have offered me scarlet or a drab murrey.

On Palm Sunday, the children of the royal chapel made a procession around the castle at Nottingham, bearing willow palms in their hands and singing. My father always used to give thanks on this day for his victory at Towton. It was a very terrible, slaughtering battle, fought in a blinding snowstorm. My father said that when he touched his armor his fingers were burned with the cold. In armor he looked really frightening, a shining giant, even when just standing still and grinning down at us. I'm sure if I'd been a Lancastrian soldier, seeing him fight, with one of those two-handed swords only very big men can use, I'd have died of fright. In a helmet and steel shoes he'd have stood six and a half feet tall. The King my uncle, though he's quite little, fought just like my father, at Barnet and Tewkesbury. Our family breeds remarkable men. A poem had been written about my father, mentioning that Palm Sunday victory; I remember it, because I was in it, though of course I wasn't born when he fought it. My father was called "the Rose of Rouen":

> The rose won the victory, the field and the chase.
> Now may the people in the south dwell in their own place.
> His wife and his fair daughter [me!] and all the good he has.
> Such means hath the rose made by virtue and by grace.
> Blessed be the time that ever spread that flower.

That Palm Sunday had been two weeks earlier in the year than this one. At Nottingham it was springtime. I like this castle. Perched up high on top of a great rock, you can look from windows and walls over all the center of England, beyond the flat Trent valley to the high hills in the North and far away over the rolling fields in the South. Here north and south meet. The Queen said she liked it too, because she always felt at Nottingham that she was halfway home. There are two courtyards—the outer, as big as a field, and the inner, where the houses for living in are. In my father's time they had been rebuilt in timber, plaster, and stone, with lots of glass windows. In the middle of them was the high tower, containing four stories of rooms above the level of the rest. From the big windows of those rooms you can see everything from a dizzying height, the countryside like a map spread out, the water meadows below the rock, where the little river Leen winds, and the cattle in them the size of ants. The King and Queen live in these rooms, while the rest of the court fitted into the houses and elsewhere in the castle. In front of the tower flower gardens have been planted with primroses and tall yellow daffodils, growing right up to the foot of cherry trees in blossom. When the breeze blew strongly, a snow of pink and white petals drifted down among the flowers.

In the interval between Mass, the palms procession, and dinner I took the Queen's spaniels outside for a run. I stood watching them rush to and fro, skidding in the fine gravel of the yard. Bo, the cheeky tan and white one, lifted his leg and watered the flowers, which wouldn't please the gardeners. People came and went as usual from the houses and the door of the tower. I didn't take much notice of them. Things are always busy wherever the King is, even on a Sunday. After a while, I became conscious of my own idleness, called the dogs and turned to go back indoors.

A man servant came blundering out of the door, almost knocking me down. He did not beg my pardon. Before I could be angry, he gibbered at me, "I'd keep out of there if I were you, lady. There's bad news come from the north—from Middleham ... Everyone's going stark mad—may the Blessed Lord Jesu preserve us all!"

"What news?" I asked, too warm and lulled by the sunshine, to be alarmed immediately.

"The King's son," he said shakily, "is dead."

I looked around at the courtyard, at the flowering cherry trees, the daffodils, and could think of nothing to say. I felt stunned and cold, but not in the least like crying.

"I must go to the Queen," I said. I didn't want to—not to face more deluges of grief over a dead child. My mother's frenzy of last autumn was too near in time. I dared not think of her, of how she'd prayed for this to happen, of the child image she'd made. It's an only child, I thought, climbing the stairs, then: Today is ill-omened—the feast of Holy Innocents fell last year on a Sunday.

They were in the room on the third of the tower. A lot of men and women were moving helplessly about, hushed with shock. They grouped around the Queen. She was kneeling on the floor, doubled forward, hugging herself as if in pain. I saw a woman huddle like that once, who was having a miscarriage. She didn't make much noise. No weeping yet, only whimpering. The King was half kneeling, half lying over her, his arms locked around her, his face hidden against her back. He made no sound at all. No one dared touch them, to drag them up off the floor. "There's nothing you can do, Elizabeth," Lady Percy said to me. I couldn't bear it. I ran.

I heard that the Prince had only been ill a few days, taken without warning by terrible pains in his belly. After a day and a night he died. The physicians, demented, were helpless. Everyone at Middleham was terrified in case the child had been poisoned, but, as Lady Percy said, the Prince could not have lived in a safer place, and it must have been a sickness. They kept the details from the Queen, because her son had died in pain, screaming, the messenger said, for his father, as if the King had power to vanquish death. My mother would be triumphant when she heard. Maybe she would be sure that she had actually brought it about, by her strong magic. The child had died, they said, on the ninth of April, the very day of my father's death, on which we'd kept his Year Mind. Some saw this as the King's just punishment.

I could feel nothing but pity, where I'd expected to be glad. I had an overmastering urge to run to the King and fling my arms around him, as I had when a child, to say

how sorry I was and that I'd never wished this terrible
thing to happen. I couldn't bear him to think I'd wished it.
The surprise at minding so much what he thought of me
was something I couldn't explain to anyone. It troubled
me as much as my fears of the cause of the poor little
Prince's death.

During Holy Week, the King bolted the door in the
faces of even his intimates and let no one in for days. We
could hear the Queen weeping piteously for hours, and I
kept away, unable to endure the sound. "They'll go clean
out of their minds," someone said, "seeing no one, not
even a chaplain." Nottingham, where one day it had been
spring and full of hope, had become a place blackened
and blighted overnight, as if struck by some evil,
unseasonable frost. Instead of throwing off the Lenten
gloom at Easter, everyone put on mourning, mostly
white, for a child and went about with hushed voices and
apprehensive looks. We haunted the castle like specters.
The sorrow of that time would haunt the King and Queen
for the rest of their lives; he began to call Nottingham,
where the dreadful news had driven them almost into
madness, his "Castle of Care."

After another two wretched weeks we crawled
miserably onward to York, arriving on May Day.
Everywhere was sadness and dismay; the citizens did not
know how to greet the King, above the usual formalities.
The King went to Sheriff Hutton to see the Prince buried;
then we rode on to Middleham, where the child had died.
The Queen's ladies dreaded this visit, for she was already
inconsolable. She looked ill and plain. I wondered if
people really died of a broken heart or if sorcery could
make them wither and pine, even to death.

I had expected the ride north from York to be through
barren brown moorlands, amid whistling winds, and to
see half-starved peasants trying to grub a living from
stony soil. Such was my idea of all Yorkshire! Instead, I
saw green, lush pastures, rivers stocked with salmon and
trout, rich abbeys and convents. By the Ouse just beyond
Lendal Bridge in York, the cattle stood knee-deep in
water chewing the cud, switching their tails as the first
gadflies of the year bit. A barge passed us, three men

harnessed to the tow ropes like beasts of burden, pulling it along beside the bank. They stared at us in awe, but did not stop plodding along. On top of the barge's cargo of monstrous sacks, about half a dozen children were perched, hurling pebbles from a sling at passing ducks. Perhaps they were sacks of grain from fertile Yorkshire farms. Even the hills, when we began to see them, were green and fresh with May grazing. They grew bigger in the distance, a little more as I had imagined, when we came near Middleham.

Middleham Castle was not at all as I had expected, either. I'd thought of it as the grim, Border fortress my mother had told me about, where my father had once been the Earl of Warwick's prisoner. Instead, it had a mixture of homeliness and grandeur. It was set beside the market place of a small, steep-streeted town, and flanked by wooded parkland with gentle hills and meadows, where deer and many horses grazed. In the yard, in curious contrast, chickens and peacocks pecked together for grain. It hadn't been grim for a long time. We only stayed four days, because the King wanted to go on to Newcastle and Durham; I doubted if he could bear to stay longer. When we arrived, the servants there looked as if the Last Judgement had come to them; half of them would fall on their knees and burst into distressing tears.

It was at this time that I began to watch the King, where before I'd disliked even to glance in his direction. I was not sure what I wanted to read in his face—a hitherto undiscovered cruelty, guilt, were what I feared most. I saw none of these things; his face is not easy to read. I hadn't really looked at him since that banquet a year ago. He seemed older, as if much more than one year had gone by. Some days he looked as if he'd been up all night, and I was distressed to see him like that, which defeated the purpose of my scrutiny. Once started, this study was hard to stop, and he occupied my mind a great deal. His mouth when he's quiet and thinking, which is often, used to shut very firmly; now it seemed tight and hard. If my father had been thin and caught in a serious mood, he'd have looked quite like his brother, except for the mouth. Odd, how seeing them together, I'd never noticed perhaps because their sizes were almost comically different and hid the likeness.

I wondered if I would dare to ask him for news of my brothers—if they were in the North and if I might see them. I thought the answer to the second question would be no. As each day went by, I waited for an opportunity to catch the King alone, which was asking the near impossible; he is always surrounded by a crowd of people. I could not ask to see him, being afraid of refusal.

I got my opportunity by chance. I was going up the stairway to the Queen's rooms at Middleham and met the King quite alone, coming down very fast, sideways, because he wore long jingling spurs. On the spiraling stairs he almost ran into me before noticing I was there; I jerked him out of some grim abstraction. An odd look crossed his face in that moment, startled, embarrassed, and angry all at once, as if he wanted to run straight upstairs again. My knees gave way, and I sank down on the narrow step in a great spread of skirts, entirely blocking his way.

"Get up, Elizabeth," he said. His voice was stony. I stared as a coney might at a stoat, unable to move.

"You have something to say to me?" This was no more encouraging.

Then I blurted it out, too frightened for artifice or caution. "I want to know if my brothers are safe," I said.

He was standing on the side end of the steps above me and leaned his back against the wall, as if suddenly resigned to being caught in a situation he'd wished to avoid. "The elder boy's health is indifferent, but the younger is well," he said levelly.

I nearly fainted with relief. "May I ...?" I was going to say: May I see them?

"No," he said, anticipating, "you may not see them— not yet. You must trust me."

I burst into tears.

"Don't weep," he said harshly. "My ears are bludgeoned with weeping." Before I could move, he bent down and lifted me to my feet, his hands gripping the upper part of my arms. As he passed me on the narrow side of the stairs, he said, much more gently, "Men and women are born to too much sorrow. It's hard to endure, it, Bess—I know." With that he disappeared, running down the rest of the stairs and into the castle courtyard.

I cried as I never had in all my life, as if he had been unkind to me, when he had not. "Comfort me," I sobbed into the empty air, "comfort me—me—me—as you comfort *her*, and I might learn to endure it all."

Mon Seul Désir
Told by Queen Anne

A! mercy, Fortune, have pitee on me,
Ande thinke that thu hast done gretely amisse
To parte asondre them whiche ought to be
Alwey in on. Why hast thu doo thus?
Have I offended thee? I? Nay! iwisse.
Then turne thy whele and be my frende again,
And send me joy where I am nowe in pain.

And thinke what sorowe is the departing
Of two trewe hertes loving feithfully.
For parting is the most soroughfull thinge,
To mine entent, that ever yet knewe I.
Therefore I pray to thee right hertely
To turne thy whele and be my frende again,
And sende me joy where I am nowe in pain.

Late 15th century

"*Ave Maria, gratia plena: Dominus tecum* ... Blessed art
thou among women, *Ora pro nobis* ..." I'd said so many
Aves I thought the words would be graven on the air in
front of me, like those scrolls that issue from the mouths
of stone weepers on tombs, words that rise as incense
smoke to Heaven. So many prayers to be said: for

Richard, who is now always in danger, for the soul of my dead son. This June he would have been eight years old. Most Blessed Lady, help me to free myself from my anchoress's cell of sorrow. The hours of a day seem so long now, to say an *Ave* for each does little to shorten them, I want to bear my husband another son.

I opened one of the hinged agate beads of my Italian rosary that Richard had given me and looked at the tiny picture inside of Our Lord's Nativity. The heads of the ox and ass were modeled very lifelike, resting their chins on the edge of the manger. The ox was white, Our Lady's robe sky blue. Lord God, I thought, have pity on me, an earthly queen; I wish I were poor, with only a manger in which to lay my child, if it would make me more worthy to bear one. I dreaded another, yet most desperately wanted it, for Richard's sake. Our child would be begotten in love, not carelessly or in anger. Yet I do not conceive, while those women who fall pregnant so easily often seem to resent it, saying sour things about how a baby can be made in less time than it takes to say a *Pater Noster*.

The plain fact is, though for me the hand of the clock may creep ever more slowly from each numeral to the next, the King's hours fly away fast as swallows, all spent in work or traveling. How we traveled; it made me very tired. In eight weeks we went from Nottingham to York, York to Middleham, Barnard Castle, and Durham, and back to York. Then we went to Pontefract, and from there to York again for Corpus Christi, back to Pontefract, and then, at the end of June another, a longer journey to Scarborough. There Richard intended to oversee the fleet, which was to sail against the Scots. One way or another, on land or sea, we should give them a sit-up this summer, and force them to sue for peace.

Scarborough, briefly indulged by the fickle summer sun, should have put new heart into anyone, but it could not cure my sorrow. Throughout every mile of our journey from York to the sea, wind tore across the high, bare wild country as if it would pick up up from one place and set us down in another, but did not drive away the clouds that sagged out of the sky to veil the land in mist and rain, from which one came upon gray, stone villages

by surprise. Wet people in dingy woolen's watched us.
The roads were awash with chalky mud; our horses' hoofs
splashed up puddles like dirty milk. Shivering, I
remarked to my ladies that we seemed in for a right
stormy northern July.

This weather lasted almost a week. I could not drag
myself away from huge fires in drafty hearths and
coughed as if the cold sea wind that rained salt on
Scarborough Castle, probing every chink in walls and
windows, was rattling my bones together. July felt more
like January. This was the first year I'd found the foulness
of northern weather hard to tolerate in a season meant to
be summer. By the end of a week, however, the clouds
went out to sea overnight and the sun came up cheerfully,
as if unperturbed by what had gone before. The sea
danced and smiled, and the North seemed itself again.
The days became warm and clear; one could see for miles
along the coast. Whins in bloom turned the heaths
brilliant yellow.

On one of those idyllic summer days, at my wit's end
over my unanswered prayers and continuing barrenness,
I blurted out the whole trouble to my closest friends,
Joyce Percy and Grace Pullyn. Both can be trusted never
to gossip. Some women are fond of exposing their
married lives, of stripping their husbands naked in
chatter with their friends. I have always hated this sort of
talk; it seems so heartless, exposing not only the men, but
the women too, as discontented and waspish. For some
time this had made me reluctant to confide in anyone, but
I no longer knew how to live with my misery. So, as we
were walking in the rose garden, the sun warm on our
backs, the wall at the cliff edge keeping off the worst of
the wind, the sea sparkling beyond, I unburdened my
heart to them.

Words broke out of my mouth all of a sudden, louder
than meant: "It is hard, to be a queen." Then I wished the
platitude unsaid. They stared at me. Joyce, who is one of
those women born to mother everybody, opened her
mouth, then shut it, nonplused. I stood holding a blown
crimson rose I'd just snipped, waving my scissors, and
feeling the color surge up my neck. Knowing my face

must match the rose petals, my heart fluttered ridiculously.

Joyce said, "Your Grace tells the truth there. Anne, my love, you mustn't be sad today. Can't we bask in the sun and think of nothing? The others are playing closh and quoits on the lawn—we could join them." She was trying to coax me out of my gloomy mood. If it had not been for her and my other friends, I think I should have gone mad, in these last months, grieving. From the other part of the garden, we could hear the clatter of tumbling pins and the laughter of my ladies amusing themselves.

"A queen," I said, "is a precious vessel. The state ordains that her body shall exist to carry princes. It should be made the Eleventh Commandment in England: the Queen shall bear her King heirs. Well, I have not. I am twenty-eight years old. Eight years barren. My son is dead.

"I tell you both, my body is as useless as an empty bean husk. It grows thin and faded, and this cough is making a wheezy old woman of me. Surely, in honesty and by logic, I am no Queen?"

"Anne!" Joyce was aghast, more red in the face than I had been. "Your Grace must not talk in this way—as if God had abandoned you. Never, *never* let the King hear you say such things! It would be like pouring salt in an ulcer. You are young; there's time for more children."

"After eight years? I should believe in miracles, but ..." Their faces were melting in a haze of tears, and I could no longer see their expressions of shock and anxiety. "I would rather die than hurt my husband the King. Yet I injure him by my very existence. If he did not care for me, he could rid himself of me by divorce, have heirs by another wife. But he is shackled by love and conscience. I hang around his neck like a millstone. He is in such danger, his throne, his life, because ..." I couldn't go on, my voice breaking.

Grace had so far said nothing, merely standing with downcast eyes and pursed lips. She is the best listener in the world, a quiet, plain woman, the eldest of us three, wife of a Yorkshire gentleman of no account at all. She took the rose out of my hand. I'd gripped the stem so

hard, thorns had pricked my finger and blood was
dropping onto my gown, making rusty spots on the black
damask and bright red blobs where the skirt was folded
back to show the white satin lining.

"The King cares for you. He would never divorce you."
She put the rose in her basket, then dabbed my hand
gently with a handerkerchief. "You must not give up
hope."

"Hope? There's precious little hope now. Besides, I
don't feel strong enough to carry a child, even if we
summoned the energy to make one between us." A snail
was crossing the paving stones of the path, leaving a silver
trail. For one so slow, it seemed very sure of reaching its
destination. I wished I might share the purpose of that
snail.

"Do you think, then," Grace said diffidently, beginning
to perceive the unadmitted cause of my distress, "that if
His Grace the King did not hear Mass every morning at
four, and then ride to work down at the harbor on the
affairs of his navy, and not come back until all his
subjects are in bed, you might feel more hopeful?"

Thankful to be given so much lead, I said in a rush,
"You must not think the King neglects me ... He has to
work so hard. This year has been full of trouble. He's not
had the heart for ..."

Joyce, the practical, offered simple advice. "Make love
to him. Don't think yourself no longer desirable. You
have an advantage over so many of us—a husband who
has eyes and heart for no other woman. Woo him—
whatever you do when moved by passion, at the height of
bodily pleasure, do at the beginning—show you desire
him. You mustn't be shy ... Maybe it is sinful to say such
things, but a woman who is loved frequently stands more
chance of a pregnancy than one who is not."

I blushed hotly again; even the tips of my ears burned.
"Surely nothing between man and wife who want a child
is sinful?"

"No. And it is between them alone—no need to tell
your confessor anything." Joyce was very firm. "As for
feeling tired; you must sleep in the afternoons, and we'll
spend the rest of the day making you beautiful!" she

managed to raise some hope in me again; a lightening of
the spirits came from sharing the problem with friends
who love me.

On coming in from the gardens to my apartments we
were confronted by a scene of chaos. The two
Elizabeths—Elizabeth Parr and Bess, King Edward's
daughter—and Anna, Lady Lovell, looked on in
consternation. Servants were heaving rolls of arras the
size and weight of siege guns, propping ladders against
the walls, sweeping up heaps of dust and rushes. My
spaniels ran delightedly among them, heedless of cuffs
and curses. We called the dogs away, and my steward
arrived to explain that a new set of wall hangings had
been delivered, arriving from London by ship, and that
afternoon brought up from the harbor. The set of six
tapestries had been purchased from the famous
workshops of Pasquier Grenier of Tournai, by special
command of the King, as a gift for me, his wife, and the
rehanging of the room was taking place on his orders—
entirely for my pleasure, the steward said. This all but
reduced me to tears of remorse, having spent an hour
bemoaning my lot.

When all the hangings had been put up and the room
tidied, we went back to look. We stood dumb-struck in
the doorway. Joyce, not given to lavish praise, her feet
usually planted firmly on her native soil—she comes from
the East Riding—said in awe, "But this is magic,
sorcery—it cannot be Scarborough Castle, it's Paradise!"
She was right. The room was transformed from a rather
old-fashioned royal apartment in a bleak, northern
castle, to an enchanted, secret garden. It made me think
that a golden key would be needed if we wished to enter it,
but all we had in fact to do was walk through an ordinary
oak door. We spent a long time going from one picture to
another, to gaze and exclaim.

In each one, on a background of vibrant rose red, the
figures of a lady, the young girl who waited upon her, a
lion, and a unicorn were standing upon an island of dark
blue, like angels upon a cloud. The lion and the unicorn
acted as standard bearers, though in two of the pictures
the unicorn was shown in gentle submission to the lady,

which is proper behavior for a unicorn.

My ladies declared that the tapestries were the finest they had ever seen; even those who had traveled in France and Burgundy had not set eyes on their equal. Not only were color and design marvelous, but the air of mystery created by the subjects embodied the world of all the romances we had read. My room would now make a setting for the *Roman de la Rose;* the love stories of Tristan and Iseult or Lancelot and Guinevere could be re-enacted there. The tapestries were large, so enclosing us in their world of delightful deception that one had to look out of a window to discover the real, English scene of sky, cliff and gray stone walls.

Joyce, Grace, Elizabeth, Bess, and Anna engaged in a heated discussion of the lady's gowns, jewels, and headdresses; some they thought ugly, but some aroused them to ecstatic envy. Even the most daring fashions of the court of Burgundy were not as rare and strange as these.

I listened to them with only half my attention, as I couldn't keep from wondering at the lady with the unicorn. Who was she? Was she real and living somewhere in France or Italy, or had the artist dreamed her up out of his own imagination? Perhaps he built his dream on some fleeting moment, a chance meeting, never forgotten. Beside such an artist's ideal of a fair woman, I am nothing—Queen of England, yet nothing.

Joyce and Grace came back to me, smiling, obviously bursting with some idea. "Oh Madam," they explained, "dear Anne, you shall be fair as the lady who has tamed the unicorn!"

"All the glamor of that lady? I'm too pale, too ..."

"Nonsense," they said in chorus. "We'll make you more beautiful!" I let them carry me along on their own enthusiasm, and, it is true, as they got to work on me, I did begin to feel a little cheered.

First came the elaborate and tedious task of washing my hair. They set a huge silver basin on a stool and I knelt in front of it on a cushion. Grace combed all the hair forward into the basin. Elizabeth Parr poured rain water (this keeps hair silky) scented with camomile and

gillyflowers over it from a silver ewer, which she dipped
into a tub the servants kept replenished and hot. After
soaping me vigourously with fine Castile soap of Bristol,
they rinsed it away by pouring streams of water steadily
from the ewer until the hair felt slippery and squeaked
between our fingers. Water trickling down my nose, I
watched the perfumed steam rise, the mass of hair
floating like dark weed; then, as it was fished out and
wrung, the water splashing back into the basin. At the
bottom, the silver was engraved with a naked figure of the
Goddess Fortune. She wavered and undulated with the
liquid, and I thought: Maybe she will smile on me again,
for a little.

It took a long time to dry the hair, while I sat with my
back to an overwarm fire, and Grace and Bess alternately
rubbed it with towels and combed out long, wet strands.
As it dried, it lost the seaweed look and returned to its
own pale mouse-brown. However strong an infusion of
camomile flowers is put in the water, it does not approach
blonde. It has always seemed an uninteresting color, but I
only once dared to try a dye and that was when I was
thirteen and too young to know better. It turned the color
of a saffron bun, and my mother shrieked, declaring that
no daughter of Neville and Beauchamp should look like a
Flemish whore from the stews of Southwark. I didn't
know what a Flemish whore looked like, or stews, and had
never been to Southwark. But I had to bundle it all under
a tight cap for weeks until the garish color faded, in case
my father saw it, all the while made to feel wicked as
Jezebel.

Ladies at court do use saffron dyes or make brown hair
red with quicklime, but they are usually of an age when
the years cease to be counted after thirty and of dubious
reputation. It used to be fashionable to imitate the rare
shade of silvery blonde that was the great beauty of
Elizabeth Woodville, Lady Grey, until she was well over
forty, and also that new-minted coin-gold of Shore's wife.
We heard of one lady who became quite bald through
bleaching. I'm afraid I shall never set fashions.

Bess said, "How Your Grace's hair crackles from the
comb! It's so fine ..." A skein of hair spun out like a

cobweb, floating weightlessly down to mingle with the
rest. When she had finished polishing it strand by strand
with a piece of silk, it hung about my shoulders and waist
like a curtain of silk itself.

Grace, who is gentle and skillful, plucked out a few
hairs from the front with tweezers, to leave my forehead
smooth and high. At the hairline, new hair grows downily
and fair enough to be barely noticeable, so I do not have
to suffer the agonies and reddened skin of those less
fortunate. Plucking is best; shaving is horrible and has to
be done very other day, as if one had a beard! The most
she could do with my eyebrows was pluck them to a line
fine as silverpoint, for they do not possess the haughty,
arched look required by fashion.

After that, my hair was wound into a rope and pinned
up on top of my head under a linen cap, so it would not
get in the way of the bathing. I sat on a large sponge on a
plank in a wide wooden tub, with curtains of scarlet and
white silk like a tent, trimmed with gold fringes and
surmounted by a gilt fleur-de-lis. When I was finally
helped out to stand upon damask towels to be dried, they
poured so much rose water over me, I had to be dried all
over again.

At this point we felt we had earned a rest. I was dressed
in a shift of filmiest linen, and we sat eating strawberries,
still warm from the castle garden. Dusk was drawing in;
the sky had the purplish bloom of a plum. In the soft
candlelight of early evening, my prolonged toilet
continued.

About a hundred years ago a French knight—de La
Tour Landry—wrote a homily for his daughters, advising
them on modest Christian behavior. Master Caxton
printed it in English this year. My own father was strict;
to disobey him did not enter one's head, but he was a man
of the world, unlike the narrow-minded Frenchman. If
women followed Landry's advice, we'd all look plain as
puddings. He said painting the face is wicked, grooming
the hair a sinful vanity, and predicted torments in Hell for
women who pluck or shave their hair and brows—Devils
will stick red-hot pins in the denuded parts. Nevertheless,
all of us do these things in varying degrees. Richard, in

common with most men, loathes any too obvious interference with nature in the body of a woman, but he has never objected to discreet paint on the face. He'd hate me to be unfashionable or downright dull among others.

Elizabeth smoothed first lemon juice, then sweet almond oil on my hands to whiten and soften the skin, rubbed the nails with vermillion to make them rosy, then did the same to my feet. My face, after being washed with soap in the bath, was bathed with milk, then with cowslip and rosemary water to make it soft and clear and, I hoped, relax the tight little lines around the eyes that are a sure sign of being over twenty-five. As my skin is so pale, I never use the sticky white or pink ceruse that some women apply as thickly as lime plaster. It must be repulsive for a man to kiss skin disguised in this way. No blue or green color on the eyelids, either, or black lines drawn around the eyes; only whores use that much paint. But Joyce tilted my head back and told me to open my eyes wide, while she put into each a drop of nightshade juice. The Italians call it *belladonna,* or "lovely lady," because it makes your eyes look large and lustrous and the pupils swell as a cat's do in the dark. The vermilion was used again, sparingly across the cheekbones, rubbed in well, then more on the lips, blotted with a cloth, and applied again, to make it brighter. Without saying anything, Joyce began to stroke a little red on my nipples, and I almost told her not to, slightly shocked, then didn't. They wrinkled pleasantly at the touch of her finger. If my husband's reactions are anything to judge from, men particularly like this part of the female body, so there doesn't seem anything wrong in enhancing its charms. The paint made the rest look startlingly white. Last of all, they lavished precious and potent perfume on me, far too much for modesty, and applied in the most inmodest places. The heavy richness of oil of roses, musk, and amber would linger for days on me, my clothes, my bed, and transfer itself to Richard's skin and hair. I hoped no one would notice if on the following day he smelled like a Venetian courtesan!

Grace combed down my hair again, leaving it loose, but winding a string of pearls as a caul about my to set

it off. She stripped off the shift, so, like Eve before her fall,
I was clothed only in the length of hair. Then she wrapped
me in a gown of black velvet sewn with roses in silver
thread, lined with gray squirrel fur, more fur around the
hem, and wide sleeves. Joyce put her head on one side
critically, then added a necklace of Florentine
goldsmith's work, fashioned like a spider's web, a broad
collar set with so many pearls they looked at first like dew
upon the web, until one saw they made a design of
interlocked roses. Joyce showed tact, I thought, in thus
hiding the thinness of my neck. The result pleased her, as
it did me. When she held up the mirror, I appeared both
younger and healthier, lips very red, eyes enormous and
black, reflecting back the light. We are clever, I thought,
Richard will like me.

Bess my niece stood idly, playing with my comb. She
looked so dejected, her beauty was spoiled. Her face is
smooth as a peach, but now seemed pinched and drab. I
found her difficult to talk to, though she responded to
kindness with a gratitude that made me feel guilty, and
sorry for so many things that had happened. She had
fallen from Fortune's wheel and found her fall hard. We
should find her a husband.

I'd found my fall hard too. Two weeks after my
fifteenth birthday, I had been brought into London, the
traitor's daughter, a captive in the tail end of King
Edward's Roman triumph after Tewkesbury field. The
honor of leading that procession had been given to
Richard. I saw him only once, when the crowd, drunk
with sentimental joy and free wine at Edward's victory,
had milled around him, garlanding him with such a
weight of laurels and white roses he looked like a garden
hedge, his horse shying as flowers were hung on its ears.
Two months later I was washing dishes in an Aldersgate
cookshop. Bess's long, elegant hands would never know
that humiliation; she would never have to feed like a
scullion on broken meats and stale bread.

"Leave me now," I said. "Tomorrow, if it is fine, we'll
go riding along the sands." I wanted to wait in peace, for
Richard to come to me. As the night was not cold and my
furs warm, I opened a window. The night was dark as my

velvet gown, though the stars over the bay were very bright; the new moon dropped into their midst like a sliver of white apple. The air smelled of the sea, and mown hay from the castle meadow.

I knelt in front of the window and prayed, under my breath: "Hail Mary, Star of the sea, come to our aid— give us a child. You who bore the Holy Child, let me bear my husband the King a son." I'd have a bad time, I knew that. I might die. But if I bore a son that lived, it would not matter. The first one died. I prayed for his little soul, for Edward, my son, until the inevitable tears came. I blinked them away, and tried to shut out memory from my heart.

I listened to the wash of the sea, the sigh of the wind. I thought: Women's bodies are akin to the tides that wax and wane with the moon. This brought back another memory, of a day when we had visited the Holy Isle of Lindisfarne, off the coast of Northumberland. We had ridden out over the causeway at low tide, all of us together, Richard, little Edward, who was only two and had to be carried, myself, and the other children. As far as the eye could see was a desert of wet, rippled sand, across which the light and shadow of clouds passed like wayfarers. The sea had receded from us, almost out of sight, leaving a debris of white shells and pebbles, brown ribbons of weed, and shimmering pools of water. So, I thought, the tide of happiness has drained out of our lives, leaving me barren as the sea-less sand.

Not only this, the demands of kingship are draining away whatever is left of my husband's youth. What should I do to rouse passion in him now? What did those famous beauties, Elizabeth Woodville and Shore's wife, do when they made love with King Edward that I do not know of? Whores know what to do to men's bodies; each man possessing them must teach them something new. I have known no other man but Richard. The lady in the tapestry has a secret look, as if a child has been conceived in her only a little while before. I envy fecund women ...

Lost in thought, I did not hear the door open and close softly. I opened my eyes to find Richard standing at my side, eyeing me in a puzzled way. He was alone; his servants sleep on the opposite side to my ladies, in an outer room which has a separate staircase. He wears black or white a great deal now, as I do, but tonight he had been arrayed regally in the gown I had given him at our coronation. It is the most splendid thing, made of yards and yards of purple cloth-of-gold tissue, lined with silk damask and embroidered all over with the blue garter emblem and white roses. It would be fine enough to receive a foreign embassy in, worn over nothing at all. I must have looked strange, kneeling on the cold tiles in front of an open window, the ends of my hair trailing on the floor around me.

"You'll catch cold," Richard said, clasping my hands in his to help me up. His grip felt very warm. He went over to close the window.

I said, "The King's Grace is a very clever man to find such magic, perfect things to give me. Richard, I've never seen anything as beautiful as these tapestries. I'd thank you on my knees for them a hundred times over."

"You will not." He took hold of my hand, instead. "Show me them." He fetched a candle sconce to hold up, so that we might look at the pictures close to in a bright light. Every foot of the tapestries contained some fresh miracle of color and grace. Once again amazed by their beauty, I said, "They must have cost—oh—three hundred pounds?"

"Three thousand would not have been too much if it gave you pleasure. I was shown the designs in London by an agent my sister Margaret sent from Burgundy. There was another set, with the hunting of the unicorn, through forest and flowers. They showed the beast drawing poison from a stream by touching it with his horn and being captured by the virgin. But the huntsmen surround him and kill him with spears. It's a sad fable of the life of Our Lord, His Holy purity, His Virgin Mother, the hunt which ends in His betrayal and death. I thought you would prefer these."

I put my hand on his wrist, under the smooth white silk of the wide sleeve, and drew him closer to the picture.

"Did Master Grenier's agent explain to you the significance of these pictures?"

"They represent the five senses. This one is sight, the others are hearing, smell, taste, and touch."

I liked best, I think, the picture representing sight. The lady is sat alone and pensive, the unicorn lying beside her, his front hoofs in her lap, peeping rather coyly into the mirror she held up. On her other side the lion held up a standard blazoned with the King's arms and my own.

The picture of taste, which covered one entire wall of my room, was almost too big to look at properly without daylight. In this, the lady took comfits from a golden dish held by the maiden waiting upon her. A green popinjay fluttered upon her gloved left hand. Behind them grew a hedge of roses in full bloom. I did not cease to be enchanted, though I'd spent an hour looking at the pictures already. Richard, seeing them for the first time, was equally fascinated, but I think he was more taken with lifelike animals and birds or the details of flowers than by the romantic mystery of the lady.

"I had a popinjay," I said. "My father gave it to me for New Year when I was seven.

"I remember. It bit me." Richard had hated it; it had screeched every time it saw him.

"There's a unicorn foal—or is it a fawn?" he said. "He has a little beard, but his horn hasn't started to grow yet." I knelt down to examine the bottom of the tapestry, and Richard sat on his heels beside me. We counted at least ten different flowers in just one small area: forget-me-nots, violets, daisies, pansies, gillyflowers, love-in-a-mist, bluebells, lilies-of-the-valley, marigolds, and daffodils, all blooming together in glorious disregard of proper season.

"The lady," I said, "wears dresses of materials that I might use, and in some ways the cut resembles our latest fashions. How elegant she is. I wonder if her hair is really golden? Artists even paint me with yellow hair; it's supposed to be a compliment."

"Stand up," Richard said. When I obeyed, he took a strand of my hair in his hand and held it to the light. He let it slide through his fingers along all its length, until the end fell out of his hand, then picked it up and repeated the gesture. "You have pretty hair, Anne; I've told you so

many times. Look, it's smooth as satin. Don't you see
how much better a living thing is than a picture? Those
fashions are not as ugly as the one used ever since I can
remember, where you women pluck out the hair on your
foreheads. Thank God you don't do it to excess. Or shave
yourself here." He touched me rather unexpectedly, so I
gasped. "The thought makes me squirm," he said, "a
woman's so very soft and tender there," and proceeded to
demonstrate the fact with intimate accuracy. I felt so hot
and weak, my knees trembled and I clutched him for
support. He kissed the strand of hair in his hand,
"Besides, I've never cared for yellow hair."

"The French lord did, perhaps. Enough to honor his
lady by the legend over the door of her pavilion: A *mon
seul desir.*" My voice sounded odd, husky and breathless.

For answer, Richard laid his cheek against my hair; I
could feel his warm breath on my neck. "You are my one
desire," he said softly. I blushed and felt confused as a
young girl. He held me at arm's length, studying me with
the concentration of a man deciphering a mystery. "Look
at you, pearls in your lovely hair, soft fur and black
velvet, white neck, hands, and feet. You don't need that
necklace—let me take it off. You smell very sweet. You're
much, much fairer than any tapestry lady. May I lie in
your lap, like the unicorn?"

"I thought," I whispered, "that only virgins could
capture unicorns."

"Well," he said, mouthing my ear, "when did you last
catch one?"

"Oh, twelve years ago or thereabouts! I'd forgotten
what they looked like, it's so long."

After that, it was easy to do what my friends had
advised—make love to my husband. The artist who had
designed those tapestry pictures composed an elegant
play upon the five senses, in which those senses, as they
are used in love, had no part.

Sight—well, we left the candles to burn down and
gutter out in a stink of wax. I took the purple gown off
Richard, surprised at the weight of it in my arms. When
he was in bed, I asked him to fetch my eagle-stone
bracelet from a chest on the other side of the room, I must

confess, only so I might see him walk back to me naked. I like to watch him when he is unaware that I am watching.

When he lay down, his head in my lap like the unicorn, I looked at his face. He smiled at me then—he hadn't smiled much lately—and I did not see the deeper lines in his skin, the gray scatter in his hair. I thought how much I like his mouth, smiling; the lips are beautifully shaped, more than anyone would think. Gentleness suits him. We lay scarcely stirring, our mouths touching, as if we had wounds that must be healed by gentleness before our strength came back. His face and hair smelled good, of a favorite blend of spices he's always used: nutmeg, cloves, cinnamon, angelica root, and musk, mixed in rose water.

"Talk to me," I said.

The words were half nonsense, half serious, telling me how he'd bought me the tapestries so that their strange magic might provide some brief escape from the unkindness of the world in which I had to live, how much he needed me now, how he thought of me often in the long absent days. I drowned in the tenderness of his voice, and the ache of sadness was soothed in me a while.

I looked downward at myself, almost lost in deep feather beds. I'm too thin, I thought vaguely. My breasts were always small, but round; now they're more pointy. The tips are quite large, though, and red as cherries. Once, when I was very small, my sister had hung cherries—the double-stalked ones—on my ears for earrings. I could remember the feel of them bobbing against my cheek, the glossy skins warm from the sun. Richard had picked them for us, climbing a high wall rather unnecessarily to get in the orchard. He'd been caught there and duly beaten.

"What are you thinking of?"

"You," I told him of my inconsequent recollection. Equally foolish, he said,

> "How should a cherry
> Be without a stone?
> And how should a dove
> Be without a bone?"

He took one of my own cherries softly between his lips

and licked it, and I forgot to say how sorry I'd been twenty years ago, when he got caught and did not have time to eat a single one. "When the cherry was a flower, then it had no stone," he murmured. "My hinny bird, you're softer than any dove. You want me?"

"Yes."

Much later, at the other end of night, I watched the gray of day steal upon the room. We had forgotten to draw the bed curtains. Chairs and chests, black lumps by night, slowly regained their natural shapes. The unshuttered window gleamed palely On the sill outside, a gull stood, preening casually. It was too early to know if the day would be fine or dull.

We were lying head to foot of the bed, the sheet wound into a rope, our feet somewhere among the pillows. Richard's heart was jerking like a running rabbit; his face was wet. I wiped it gently with the sheet. He opened his eyes and looked at me. It would be hard to imagine a look more sad, tender, and bitter all at once. "You kept saying—'Give me a child, please give me a child.' Don't say that to me, Anne." He turned his face aside, into the tangled heap of bedclothes.

"Maybe you have," was all I could say.

That morning, and on many following, my ladies found me asleep disgracefully late. Grace and Joyce said nothing, but their glances spoke for them. They gave me water distilled from yellow wallflowers to drink noon and night for a month and tisanes of sage leaves to aid conception. I waited for the signs, ignoring a nagging little ache in the small of my back and an ever increasing lassitude. My face in the mirror grew paler, shadows around the eyes darker. This spoiled the new look of softness brought by pleasure. In all my married life there had never been so much pleasure, unexpected and exquisite in its intensity. Yet what should have been a joy was only a mask for unhappiness.

It could not last.

Richard, whom I did not often see in the daytime, began to look as bad as I did. He had the kind of pallor that revealed a shadow on the lower part of his face, even when freshly shaved. It wasn't long before I overheard a remark—not servants gossiping, but a gentleman—about the candles that burns at both its ends. Thereafter I felt shamed and became conscious that eyes had begun to watch for a change in the outline of my belly.

Why does the menagerie at the Tower of London not include a king and queen—in a cage like the lions and bears? "Here, ladies and gentlemen, we have a genuine king and queen, to amaze you with their antics. The wonder of the world is, they are very like you ordinary folk!" We'd get as big an audience as a two-headed calf. I grow too bitter at fate; it is a fault that I should confess. I must be more grateful at having been born to high estate. Unlike some foolishly romantic ladies, I do not delude myself that it would have been better to be born a peasant or to remain a kitchen girl all my life.

They were right, though, about the candle that burns at both its ends. The King works longer hours than a laborer who does overtime in his dinner break to earn a few more pence. A mason like those we saw at Cambridge starts work in the summer at half past four; then: beer and breakfast from eight to nine, beer and dinner from eleven to one, beer and bread at three to four, home at seven or three on Saturdays. Thirty-seven days in the Church's year are holidays. The King is lucky to get half an hour for his mealtimes, a little longer if he dines in company; Saturdays are no different. Only on the thirteen principal feast days can he confine his work to necessities. Sometimes he works past ten at night and is always at his desk in the morning as promptly as a foreman on a building site. In winter, though, he can work as early as six, because the King, unlike a mason, may use unlimited candles.

I'd been worried for a year now at the way Richard drove himself, but throughout this summer it almost passed the limits of reason. I think he wished to prove to himself his right to rule and perhaps to forget he had no son to build a new world for. No issue is too trivial, no detail too small, no person too humble to be given his personal attention. Things even a clerk would pass over to an under-clerk, the King will do himself. He'd even write out a warrant to the Treasurer of the Household for a payment of a shilling to a servant, if no one else was on hand to do it as quickly. As he says, he has pen, ink, and a hand, and his breath is saved by not dictating it. Kendal, his Secretary, has begun to look like a harrassed cadaver. Men groan and yawn; wives grumble at seldom seeing their husbands.

Of the great issues, the most important was to strengthen England by securing friendships with foreign countries. We could achieve less than we hoped for, because Burgundy and Brittany were weakened by civil strife, Spain and Portugal friendly but distant, France and Scotland still hostile.

Toward the end of our stay at Scarborough the fleet put to sea against the Scots and won a small but decisive fight. The enemy piled on all sail and headed home for Leith. Richard went out with the Duke of Norfolk on his carrack the *Mary Howard,* a gold whistle hung around his neck like a sea captain. They captured a Scots vessel, though the commander, Sir Andrew Wood of Leith, whom Norfolk said was the most daring reiver on the North Sea, escaped.

They were at sea two days. We watched from the castle battlements, but there was little to see except a cluster of specks on the horizon and a little cloud like a smudge of charcoal hanging over it. Fearful that the Scots might sink an English ship, I spent half the night in the chapel, praying that if anything so terrible happened, it might not be the King's ship. But by the second evening, they were all safe home in harbor.

Richard came back to the castle that night, from the house in Sandside where he often worked during the day. He fell into bed and lay without speaking or moving for some time. When I put an arm around him, he moved away, though not irritably—I think he was too tired to enjoy being touched. After a while he said, "There's not a muscle in me that doesn't ache. I could sleep for days." He must have spent hours on end standing on the pitching deck of a ship.

"Hush," I said, "go to sleep."

"I killed a man today, in hand-to-hand fight. I've not

done that for years. We boarded a Scots ship and took it.
He was a seaman with no armor, wearing only canvas
breeches. He tried to swing out of the rigging on top of
me. Someone warned me in time."

I took hold of his right hand, the hand that had gripped
the sword. His fingers lay loosely in mine, no apparent
strength in them. "Hush," I said again, "sleep now."

Some things are easier forgotten when spoken of first.
"One of our men fell between the ships when we were
grappling." I shuddered. "There weren't many Scots left
by the time we boarded her. The archers and the gunners
knew their job. The rest turned tail."

Now the Scots were finished on the sea, they sued for
peace, and we returned to York, then moved on to
Pontefract. Soon after, bad news came from London. I
think sometimes nothing but bad news ever comes out of
the south. Not rebellion this time, but reports of small
incidents of sedition and rumors, each seemingly trivial
but together to be seen as more menacing. On the
eighteenth of July, worshipers going to early Sunday
Mass at St. Paul's discovered a bill pinned to the great
door inscribed in large letters with a rhyme—neat,
impudent, and treasonable:

> The Cat, the Rat, and Lovell our Dog,
> Rule all England under an Hog.

I hated it. Richard shrugged, Catesby was flattered,
Ratcliffe swore, Lovell laughed. The author of the
treasonable rhyme had been identified as William
Collingbourne, a Wiltshire gentleman who'd been
involved in Buckingham's rebellion and a wanted man
for the last nine months. He'd once been an usher in the
household of the Duchess of York, my mother-in-law.
Though he was still in hiding, a servant of his had been
seen pinning the bill to the door of St. Paul's on that
Saturday night. Collingbourne is thought to be still in
contract with Tudor. He is not the only one; I believe
there are many traitors among us.

I'd thought a good deal about Henry Tudor lately.
While he lives we can have no sure peace. Remembering
his mother Lady Margaret's tears at my anointing, I
thought: She should be in the Tower. It is her life's goal to

see her son crowned.

In June Richard had made a truce with Brittany, agreeing to provide a thousand archers against France, in return for a closer surveillance of Tudor by the Bretons. But a month later, before the archers could sail, Tudor was warned and fled froom Vannes in the clothes of a servant, over the French border into Anjou. Now he's a snug as coney in its hole, and we can't send a ferret in after him. He waits for another chance to invade England. We have the constant worry of this and the frightening expense of defense; we cannot relax our vigilance until the winter.

Richard decided that he should go to London and went away, taking only a small household with him. I said nothing, for he had enough worries, but his going left me desolate. I was manifestly not pregnant and had to admit to being relieved, as I felt exhausted and unwell. Yet I was reluctant to lose him, even for so little. The more I had of him, it seemed, the more I wanted.

I prayed for his safety every hour of the days; there seemed so many dangers, London in August would be at its foulest; plague was bad this year, as the weather had been moist and hot. Richard would stay part of the time at Westminster and part at the Wardrobe, in the City near St. Paul's. Plague knows no respect for rank—didn't the second Richard's Bohemian Queen Anne die of it at Sheen, which is a healthy place? I saw to it that they took with them the reliquary with the blood of St. Sebastian, who is known to protect us from plague. I also sent one of my chaplains on a pilgrimage to Our Lady of Walsingham, to make offering and pray for the King and myself, that we might, with God's favor, be blessed with a son, though I now had a hopeless feeling it was too late. My prayers for Richard at least must have been granted, because after three weeks, he came back to Nottingham safely.

I discovered that while in London Richard had ordered that the body of poor King Henry VI should be moved from its obscure grace at Chertsey Abbey to Windsor, to lie in St. George's chapel. Henry of Windsor he'd been called, from his birthplace, and it seemed fitting that he should return there, to rest in an honorable place next to

King Edward, who had destroyed him. It did not need a simple, Christian act like this to tell me that my husband is an honest man.

I may know this, but rumors say other things. Because King Edward's sons have been removed from London and the people can no longer see them walking in the gardens of the Tower, they say that the King has killed them. They say God had judged us by taking our son. What can I do or say? I do not lie at night with a man who had killed his brother's children.

Another thing Richard had done while in London was to make his sister Suffolk's son the Earl of Lincoln, Lieutenant of Ireland. This is an office usually held by the King's heir. Since our son died, Richard had named no heir. Edward of Warwick is barred by his father's attainder and not yet ten. Lincoln is twenty-one and a capable young man. It seemed a sensible appointment.

In September, on the Friday before Holy-Rood day, the Scots ambassadors arrived for the signing of a truce for three years in Border warfare. One could not have told they were Scots from their dress, which was very fine, though in the French fashion, but when they opened their mouths, their speech was all but incomprehensible. Those of us from the North probably understood more of it than the southerners, who were left at sea and needed interpreters.

Archibald Whitelaw, King James's Secretary, though a venerable pedagogue, had very Scots speech. He made an interminable Latin oration—it ran into pages—I could see him shuffling through them as he read. His spectacles didn't seem very effective. I can follow some Latin delivered slowly in an English voice, but this might as well have been Icelandic; his r's rolled around like escaped marbles. Richard was sitting like a carved image, his face more wooden than usual under such circumstances. This told me he could probably understand a large part of the florid Latin phrases and, while remaining courteous, was wincing under a heavy load of gratuitous flattery. He knew very well the Scots had known him for years as a Border reiver who'd put the fear of God into them.

The Bishop of St. Asaph was attending me, standing by

my chair, and as Whitelaw said something about Cicero, my curiosity overcame me and I whispered, "My lord Bishop, what does Dr. Whitelaw say?"

He whispered very quietly back, "He's recounting His Grace the King's virtues ... 'Your goodness and generosity, your clemency, liberality, truth, great justice, magnanimity passing belief, your not human but almost devine wisdom ... You show yourself gentle to all and friendly even to the meanest of your subjects ... A poet said of a Prince of Thebes: Wise Nature never joined to a slighter frame a greater soul or more strength of mind.

The Bishop's large and beefy face remained perfectly serious, but at the last revelation, he gave the suspicion of a wink.

Someone else evidently overheard the Bishop's interpretation to me, and I would rather he had not. Sir William Stanley, Lord Stanley's brother, was standing near. He did not attempt to hide an unpleasant grin. He's a strongly built man in his late forties, with wide shoulders and a habit of standing aggressively with his feet wide apart, so he gives the impression of being made square, with angles. His face is very dark, needs to be shaved twice a day but often isn't, and his hands have hairy backs, a ring on every finger. He fancies himself with women, too; every time he kneels to me, I feel that as he descends or gets up, he is trying to look down the front of my gown. This is a habit of many men, but in others it does not seen so offensive. His kiss on my hand makes me shudder.

When Whitelaw had finished his oration Bishop Russell, the Chancellor, answered it on our behalf. When he in turn had finished and everyone was shifting their feet in relief, Stanley said to his neighbor, "The man's a windbag from eating oatmeal. Last time I heard a Scot comment on our monarch, it wasn't so nice. 'Yon wee bugger,' if I remember rightly. They couldn't believe he was King Edward's brother; thought he was some little reiver come out of Carlisle sands to get up their arse."

Dear God, I prayed, don't let me blush and look foolish in front of this coarse, horrible man, because that's what he wants. He'd better guard his tongue; it verges on the treasonable. I didn't blush. I felt my chin stick out as Richard's does when he's in a stubborn mood. I used my father's technique of blank, uncomprehending disdain; Stanley is not even worth a sneer. I got up, followed by my ladies, and swept so close to him my sleeve brushed his doublet and he was forced to step back quickly to let us pass. He is my husband's enemy, I know it, though he pretends loyalty.

Francis Lovell knows that Sir William is discontented. Francis has good cause for hate; his mother became Stanley's second wife and was abused by him. She's dead now, but Francis has never forgiven it. He told me that one day he found Sir William with his great muddy boots propped on the table, yawning and grumbling to his brother that he couldn't even get leave to go home to Ridley in Chesire for a couple of days hunting—"Old Dick'll work us to death," he said.

Sir William frightens me. Ever since I heard him break the news of her son's death at Tewkesbury field to Margaret of Anjou, I've known he's a cruel man to women. He once tried to kiss and touch me, which I'd never told Richard, in case he did anything he'd regret. To be precise, and I blush to recall it, Stanley tried to grope me with his hairy paw, and in panic I bit him. I was fourteen and he about thirty five. His eyes still mock me with it. I don't know why I should feel so frightened of him now. Perhaps it is because I feel ill, and apprehensive about everything.

By the time all the folk came crowding into Nottingham for the Goose Fair in the second week of October, deception was no longer possible. The truth looked at me every day out of my own mirror. Joyce Percy put me to bed each afternoon, urged me to eat more at every meal, as one does a finicky child, but her pleadings were in vain. I knew the nature of the sickness before any others did. The cough was impossible to hide, but the difficulty in breathing, the sharp, burning pains that cramped my chest, the degree of lassitude and despair could be kept from them, for at least a little longer. Some days it was hard to gather the strength to get out of bed, to set one foot in front of the other, to

answer sensibly when spoken to; the world swung about
as if I stood in the center of a whirling sphere or on the
teetering steps of Fortune's wheel, about to be cast down.

There wouldn't be a baby now; my body had ceased to
function as a woman's should. This wasting sickness is
common enough; people I've known have died within
months or imperceptibly over years. For me the time
would be short. I dreaded the day when Richard found
out. The doctors would part us, I knew, in case the King
should take infection from me. He suspected already that
something was wrong, for I caught him watching me
sometimes, and he looked afraid.

Another week, the Feast of St. Edward the Confessor
passed, and the thing I had dreaded happened. The cough
was particularly irritating at night, worse when I lay
down among the pillows. It was making sound sleep
impossible for both of us. In the small hours of the
morning I was sitting up in bed, trying to stifle it. Though
the fire had burned down and the room cooled, the effort
brought me out in a sweat. Richard, who'd slept only
fitfully through the night, suddenly got up and, without
summoning anyone, himself lit a taper for candles at the
embers in the hearth and brought me wine to drink. He
held the cup for me, put his arm around me so I might
lean against him, and, when the coughing lessened, laid
me down again, careful as a nurse. Then he put more
wood on the fire, stoking it into life, until the dancing
flames lit the far corners of the room and I felt their
warmth. Sitting up, I pushed back damp hair from my
neck, where it had come loose from its braid.

"Is it uncomfortable?" Richard touched the long plaint
gently.

"Yes—hot."

"Let me tidy it." He undid the braid, then combed it
out, and began to replait it. He was much slower than my
ladies, but very careful not to pull and persevered until
he'd made a neat job of it.

"You're clever," I said, managing a shaky smile.

"No, but I can make a plait." It seemed to please him,
to be able to do a little thing for me. When he'd finished
and tied up the end of my hair with a ribbon, he sat on the

side of the bed, folded back the covers, and looked at me.
He began to feel me all over, rather as one might to find
out if a bitch is sound, encircling my wrists and ankles
with his hands. I lay naked in his lap, watching him. I had
to concentrate on breathing, because it hurt, and I didn't
want him to see. After he had completed his inspection,
he sat for a while in silence, stroking me.

"I can feel every bone in your body. Anne, you're ill,
aren't you? I want the physicians to see you tomorrow.
We'll ask Hobbes."

"Not yet."

"I have eyes, my love. You grow thinner daily. What is
it?"

"Only a cough. It'll go soon."

"Don't tell me silly lies. On some nights lately, now the
weather is cooler, I've woken and felt you in a fever. Look
at this damp hair." He touched it.

It was no use hiding in pretense. He was in no mood to
be deceived. I refused to look at him. "Yes, you're right. It
doesn't matter. Dickon, I can't give you a child—that
matters."

For answer, he laid his hands over my face, shutting
out the light and his own expression. We seemed to have
nothing more to say. I lay quite still, in the warm dark,
until the thing I was always fighting happened and I wept.
Not that I made a sound, but tears like scalding water ran
out under Richard's fingers. He must have felt them, for
he took his hands away and put them over his own face.
Blinking, I looked at him. He'd sit like that when he was
old and tired, and I not there to see. Presently he snuffed
out the candles and got back into bed, pulling the covers
over us. He took me in his arms, his face between my
breasts, holding me tighter and tighter, until the muscles
in his arms stood out like iron. When I thought he'd break
my ribs and could no longer draw breath, I whimpered
and he relaxed his hold and became gentler.

"You mustn't let this matter so much."

"Richard, you've just had your thirty-second birthday;
it's dangerous for you to face the future with no heir. You
are the king."

"Yes, Christ help me. And I still don't know if it is right

or if this is my punishment."

"No one, no man on earth could have done differently.
You did right. *I* trusted you."

"Didn't God punish me enough when he took my son?
Oh my lovey, my dear, when I first asked you to marry
me, you should have thrown your dishwater in my face
and sent me away. I meant to protect you all your life.
Instead, I've done the cruelest thing possible—made you
Queen. You should not be punished for my sins—not you
..."

"No, no, no... Don't, Dickon, don't." I cradled his head
in my arms, stroking his hair that wound, soft and
curling, about my hands.

"My honey," he said, in a little, muffled voice, "my
honey, don't leave me." I thought: he knows I will die. I
can do nothing to help him suffer it.

When we left Nottingham to go back to London it was
early November, rainy and cold, the wet leaves already
fallen from the trees. Two days after our arrival, Richard
went into Kent again, to Rochester and Canterbury,
because these parts were still troubled.

He came back and, as I foreknew, it happened. At
Westminster the doctors, too many of them, asked
questions that seemed pointless and did embarrassing
things about which I did not care. I expected Richard
would not come to me that night. When he did, I knew the
doctors ordered otherwise. Over the years I'd seen him in
most moods, but never so completely tongue-tied. He
started off several times, but couldn't manage to be
coherent. His lips were lead-colored and stiff. At last I put
my hand over his mouth and said, "I know. Don't talk of
it."

Nothing in this sad, short life happens as we wish it.
Poor Richard, he'd come to me wishing to comfort me
with love, but his misery engulfed him, and all he could
do was cling to me like a child with night terrors. From
the queer way he was breathing, I thought he would break
down and weep. We lay pitifully in the absurd attitude of
love, silent. I thought: This is despair, everything is
finished for us. You are beautiful to me, my most beautiful
man; before I could even form my childish thoughts, you

were lovely in my eyes. You have given me such delight, and now I've nothing to give you; I'm skinny and marked by sickness. You'll have to watch me become like some deformity and shrink from touching me.

For a long time we lay sleepless, until full daylight, and I knew it to be late but did not dare to move. He was so still, I had a passing, stupid fear he'd stopped breathing, had died. When at last he slid from me and rolled out of bed, he stroked my face softly once, with a hand that felt lost and unsure. Watching through my eyelashes, I saw him pick up his fur gown from the chest, drag it on, and walk to the door, barefoot and silent, forgetting his shoes. He stumbled a little and put a hand on his head, as if very tired or the burden on him too heavy. Out of habit I turned into the snug place where he'd lain. I wanted to call to him, to bring him back to reassure me it was all a dreadful dream, from which I should wake to a new day, hope returned. But I lay with screwed-shut eyes, choking, until the murmuring voices ceased and I knew he'd been shaved, dressed, and gone away to his work. He'd never come back—never.

Then my heart broke. People say this isn't possible, but it is. It's quite simple. I felt it snap.

I began to weep, a horrible, loud, and ugly noise that brought my women running. Joyce held me in her arms until it was all over, and held the basin, for I cried until I was sick, then cried again and was sick again. I knew myself hideous and unhinged and felt her fright under her sturdy calm.

Later, I tried to compose myself and ask God for the strength to endure what remained of my life. I knelt before my confessor and said, "Father, I have sinned in my thoughts. Since it is wicked to wish away the gift of life, I am guilty. Father, I have wished to die. I want to die. There is no other way for me." He was shocked, stunned into helplessness. How can a celibate priest, however understanding, comfort a barren woman who has lost her child and her husband?

Richard was going to send for my mother, but I said no, not until the end. I wanted only him. I shall have to die at Westminster, too, when I long so much to go home.

If it were possible to go north again, dying would not be
so terrible. My spirit longs for so many sights and sounds
of home. If it were a bird, it would fly away and perch
near a river, to hear the sound of running water. Not a
river like the wide, gray Thames, but narrow rushing, and
peat-stained, chattering over stones, clear and cold,
bright-glancing under the sun.

The North is full of memories: warm milk drunk in hill
pastures by a lonely road, the kindness and humble
dignity of its offering; the cows standing among clover
and meadowsweet, butterflies dancing around them; to
ride up some seemingly desolate hillside, in silence
broken only by baaing sheep; clouds hanging low and rain
sweeping into your face; then suddenly to hear the
Angelus bell from some abbey many miles distant and
know that in that wet waste busy human beings are
tending the soil and worshiping God, season after season.
Perhaps the very best season is haytime, when our men and
women of the dales climb up and down hill under their
pitchforked burdens like moving haycocks. The hay is
sweet-scented with herbs, too many for me ever to have
known all their names. The borage and clover in it gave us
good honey. All those summers of sunshine and laughter.

No more than eighteen short months ago, on the first
day of spring, Richard and I had been happy, and I had
thought that we might stay in our north country kingdom
until death claimed us. Now death has come for me.
Happiness ended for us on that April day in Wensleydale,
as the lark's song ended with the merlin's strike, as the sun
was blotted out by a cloud. It was the day on which King
Edward died, and we poor blind creatures in our
ignorance dared to be happy.

I think of my son often now; he seems so close to me,
for the wall that divides the places where we dwell is frail
and soon to be broken down. Sometimes, I'm not sure, in
dreams, which child is which, my son or my husband. One
came to me when he was eight, the other left me. I've
known Richard ever since I can remember, in childhood,
youth, and maturity, and I want to grow old with him.
There's so much of his life left that I may not share. I can't
bear to think that some other woman will have him. I

shan't even know what he'll be like, gray or bald, or sad in his age. Bad things are happening—more danger threatens him. Lord Jesus, who knows what is past and what to come, help us, help him. What is his destiny?

9

The Unicorn

Told by Dr William Hobbes,
the King's physician

William Hobbys

Where as longe saying and muche symple Comunycacion amonge the peple by euyll disposed parsones contryved & sowne to verrey grete displesure of the Kyng shewyng how that the quene as by concent & will of the Kyng was poysoned for & to thentent that he myght than marry and haue to wyfe Lady Elizabeth, eldest daughter of his broder ... the Kyng send fore & had tofor hym at sent Johnes as yesterdaye the Mayre & Aldermen where as he in the grete Hall there in the presens of many of his lordes & of much other peple shewde his grefe and displeasure aforesaid & said it neuer came in his thought or mynde to marry in suche maner wise nor willyng or glad of the dethe of his quene but as sorye & in hert hevye as man myght be ...

Court Minutes of the Mercers' Company, 31 March 1485

"I tell you, Hobbes, I give Her Grace the Queen no more than three months. Some go quicker, some more slowly. There are remedies I might prescribe, but..."

The learned Doctor John Argentine, of King's College, Cambridge, lowered the glass flask containing urine from our patient, which he had been examining at the dull light of the window. He adjusted his spectacles, regarding me gravely over them. Not for the first time I observed his likeness to a barnyard fowl. He had the same blinking, parchment-lidded eye and long, flexible neck protruding from the beaver collar of his voluminous gown of musterdelvers, into which he huddled as if laying an egg. Though in his early forties and twenty years my junior, he is one of those who wear their scholarship like grave clothes. He handed the flask to me. "An unhealthy color." He clucked with gloomy triumph, as if he'd achieved his egg at no small cost.

He told me no more than I knew already, but had been reluctant to state without the opinion of the most important physicians in England. We had just spent a good hour with the flask, in reaching a conclusion that the level of turbidity in the sample told us the obvious; the seat of trouble lay in the chest. I put the flask back in its basket, to retain for further study, and we returned to our chairs.

There were ten of us in all, assembled around a table in an anteroom to the Queen's apartments at Westminster. It was upon her condition that we sat in consultation. The King, half out of his mind with worry, had begged me to convene as many expert advisers as possible. These learned colleagues now passed around a sheet of paper on which the astrologer had cast the Queen's horoscope. It appeared unfavorable in the seventh, eighth and twelfth houses, predicting unhappiness in marriage, death and sorrow. Some shook their heads and resigned the case to Fate; others pooh-poohed.

Though he had stated his disapproval of astrologers in forthright terms, the King had asked in particular for Argentine, obviously impressed by his repute as a scholar. He had sent for him before, during the time of the Protectorate, to attend the eldest son of King Edward, but the boy remained sickly. I had to conceal my dislike and mistrust, knowing Argentine's opinions to be governed by theoretical treatises. Galenist doctrines are quoted as if Holy Writ; every time he sees me he feels obliged to expound on the virtues of the "laudable pus" or induced suppuration, with which I, as a result of bitter experience with battlefield wounds, am in entire disagreement. He also adopts an air of superiority toward me, as might befit a learned lecturer at a university to an aging surgeon. I have a suspicion that he blames me

entirely for allowing King Edward to die and thinks me
no better than a skillfull butcher or a horse leech. That I
had been awarded a doctorate in medicine by his own
university when he was *in statu pupillari* there appears to
increase his disapproval to choleric proportions. My
hands, lying on the table in front of me near his clasped
claws, looked crude as a laborer's, each fist the size of a
mason's hod, with thick fingers that sprouted hairs along
their upper side, though I noticed with satisfaction that
my nails were pared shorter and kept cleaner than his.

At the window a chill November rain pelted the panes.
An arras on the wall shuddered, as if secret listeners were
concealed behind it, and showed a spreading stain of
damp in a sunny land of huntsmen and flowers. If it were
left hanging, mildew would spoil it. The fire refused to
burn well; an adverse wind blew smoke out from the
chimney that tickled the lungs. We coughed discordantly
at intervals.

Geronimo Ganducio di Verona, an Italian physician of
my acquaintance, for some years resident in London,
ventured his opinion. "The lady, Her Grace, *e cosi
triste*—how you say—said, low of spirit. Also she is
barren in the womb. Eight year ago, you say, she bear the
one child, the son. Since then she do not conceive ..." He
sniffed and shrugged in the dismissive manner of a
Lombard moneylender. "It make her sad, then, to lose
this one child. She waste away in sadness. I see death sit
beside her," he said with finality, "and I think he come as
a friend." Though he had not set eyes on the Queen until
that day, he saw clearly what to my mind was the most
unhappy feature of the case.

Another Cambridge man, Walter Lemster, who is
much consulted in his part of the country and vouched
for by the Lady Elizabeth Mowbray, the widowed
Duchess of Norfolk, said, "I have seldom seen Her Grace
the Queen. Twenty-eight years old you say, Hobbes?
Many die of the wasting sickness at approximately that
age, particularly women. I cannot see any hope of
recovery. She has lost both her youth and her looks, such
as they were. How long has Her Grace been in bad
health—years? months? She has been absent so long from

court—until eighteen months ago. The wet, cold climate in the North has infected her with an excess of the phlegamtic humor."

"On the contrary, Dr. Lemster, she showed no signs of this disease before she left the North. Not that I could say she has ever looked robust, but she has survived more than twenty winters of our climate without ailing in any uncommon way. I am inclined to think that melancholy predominates." This came from Thomas Bemmesley of York, who has had a closer acquaintance with the Queen than any of us, having acted as her physician in the North. "Her childbed was very bad, one of the miracles of God that she did not die. The child tore her ... She healed, but I think perhaps there was some other damage—no more children."

The last of our number who appeared to have anything to contribute to the verdict, other than gloomy looks and shakes of the head, cleared his throat in his usual modest, apologetic way. But we all paid him the respect due to his age and wisdom by listening to him in silence. James, or to give him his born name, Jacob Friis, had been a physician in King Edward's service almost as long as I had. His fur-lined cap concealed a shining cranium fringed by a dandelion fluff of white hair. He looked at us sadly with eyes of washed-away blue, his round, pink face crumpled as a new baby's.

"Of course," he murmured gently, "the cohabitation of the King and Queen must cease immediately." Noises of assent were made around the table, but I detected a slight embarrassment. If it had been any ordinary man, this would have been absent. But he was the King, and they feared his reaction. So did I, but for different reasons—for his sake rather than my own.

"The King has eyes, my learned friend," I said, "like you or me. He has no choice but to heed our verdict."

That verdict was unanimous, but we went on talking, reluctant to admit defeat. Remedies, tried and trusted, were bandied about the table like tennis balls. Venice treacle, that panacea for all ills, will do no harm and may be beneficial. An electuary syrup will help soothe the cough at first: a compound of horehound and comfrey,

mixed with figs, liquorice, anise, and hyssop, blended
with honey and administered in spoonfuls. My colleagues
had a number of pronouncements to make on the subject
of diet. Milk is held to particularly efficacious when
drunk still warm from the udder. That of asses and goats
is most nourishing—a goatherd I know of grazes his flock
in the fields toward Chelsea. Honey, dried figs, and a
soothing drink made from barley can do good, and the
white meats such as chicken, veal, or kid, which do not lie
heavy on the stomach. Not that any amount of coaxing
her to eat would make much difference; she had no more
appetite than a captured linnet that mopes in a cage. Six
months ago a diet of this kind, rest, and happier
circumstances might have had some effect. If I'd kept her
in the North I might have saved her. But she had refused
to leave her husband. Against such determination I
remained helpless.

I was sufficiently aware, having observed many cases at
Bethlehem and other hospitals of the ugly, irremediable
progress of the disease. Every symtom weakened the
body—the night sweats, pains in limbs and chest, the
hurried breathing, the constant flux—and resulted in
emaciation. This last sometimes reached such grotesque
extremes that the patient was reduced to a living cadaver.
No tomb sculptor could produce a grimmer reminder of
mortality than a patient at the termination of phthisis.
I've seen them lie too weak to move, speak, or swallow,
mere collapsed bladders of skin containing a perfectly
visible skeleton. I crossed myself and swore that if she
became like this, I'd forbid the King to see her at all. It's
bad enough when it is brother or sister, mother, father, or
helpless child, but where there has been love between two
bodies, this dissolution has a special, lazar-house horror
for the surviving partner.

It remained for us to tell the King of our decision,
either by advancing on him in our whole number to lend
force to the argument or by a deputation. Someone said,
shirking, "Who is best acquainted with the King?" and
everyone looked at me.

I said, "If you wish me to speak with him on our behalf,
I am willing. It is perhaps best that I do."

I had borne news that killed hope in men many times, to many people, but never found it so hard to begin. The King heard me out in silence. When I came lamely to a halt, he said quietly, "So I have lost everything."

At this, Dr. Rotherham, Archibishop of York, felt obliged to offer his churchman's comforts, though he is no friend of the King. Oozing solicitude, with the intimacy permitted by his cloth, he put a commiserating hand on Richard's arm. "Your Grace takes too harsh a view of the situation. God has performed miracles before. Sarah and Abraham ..."

Richard broke in savagely, "My lord Archibishop, since the Queen will not live to three score years, nor I to a hundred, that would be no solution."

Rotherham, realizing his blunder, quailed visibly and, as is his way, had his revenge by saying, "A divorce then, Your Highness. The Pope ..." He got no further. The King snatched his arm away as if he'd been touching a viper and deliberately turned his back on the Archibishop. He didn't say a word, but a more damning gesture of royal displeasure would be hard to imagine. Rotherham had the sense to extricate himself discreetly from the room. As he passed me, his face was ugly with anger, a rich rosemadder, glaring against his archiepiscopal scarlet. He's a haughty prelate, that one, who takes a rebuke hard and never forgets it.

It was left to me to call in upon the Queen every day, to keep an eye on her progress—decline, I fear, was a more suitable term. Four weeks out of those three months predicted by Argentine passed. The women were still trying to check the cough with simple remedies; syrup of honey and thyme, pennyroyal in hot wine, or the powdered root of elecampane, that we call "horseheal," but it worsened daily.

One day in early December I came upon her sitting by a window, staring out at wheeling gulls over the Thames at ebb tide, and was shocked by the change a month had effected. She had that hunch-shouldered posture which comes with this disease, making it cruelly obvious that the base of her neck and shoulders was sinking into potholes. Her dress was of the newest style, square-

necked and smoothly fitting at the waist—one could have
circled it with two hands—held by a gold chain girdle
from which dangled a musk ball of fretted gold. I would
have thought the style flattering to most women and the
color, a deep violet, pretty against pale skins, but she
seemed to have dwindled within it, like a poor ghost at
dawn; her outline had become oddly childlike, no breasts
to speak of. As she stared into nothing, the soft lips
trembled, and her eyes were lakes of unspilled tears.
Lovely eyes still, unusually large and limpid, but sunk in
sockets stained as deeply purplish-brown as a rotten
plum. The flush on her cheeks was brighter than ever. It
brought a deceptive look of vivacity to her face, until one
noticed the rest was the color of a tallow dip, the flesh
shrinking from the bones. I put my hand on her forehead
gently and felt it burning, though she shivered and said
she was a little cold.

"Madam, have you drunk your milk today?" I said like
a father. She asked, as if nothing were amiss, whether she
might have some dates, fancying something sweet. But
her voice, always lowpitched, was husky with tears. She
blinked up at me and tried to smile. I could not long meet
those guileless, wet-lashed eyes. The shy glance made me
careful not to move suddenly or talk too loudly in her
presence, as if she were a timid doe, easily frightened
away.

This woman, out of all others, should not die in such an
unhappy way. There is a rare quality about her, as if those
innocent eyes contemplated a deeper vision of life than
her female contemporaries. It is a quiet thing, with no
outward distinction, matching her appearance. Perhaps
this had come as a result of her misfortunes as a girl. Two
years ago she had been—pretty? no, not quite; beautiful?
no, not upon immediate judgment; but never a plain or
uninteresting woman. Though hardened to sights of
disease, I felt old and disillusioned with my profession.
Death makes a fool of the old physician. If she did this to
me, God alone knew what her husband suffered every
time he looked at her.

That early December sky seemed dark with every
imaginable trouble. News came that the rebel Tudor had

been welcomed in Paris at King Charles's court like a prince, albeit a threadbare one. The French were terrified by the story fed them by Tudor agents, that King Richard was intending to descend on them like a second Harry V, to win a new Agincourt. The Welsh adventurer seemed to them a God-given weapon to use against the English. Tudor had gained an advantage.

As if to rub salt in our wound, in November, John de Vere, Earl of Oxford, escaped from the castle of Hammes, having persuaded his jailer the Lieutenant James Blount to treason, and the pair of them fled to join Tudor in France. Oxford's escape was serious, because apart from Tudor's uncle Jasper, who calls himself Earl of Pembroke, he was the only Lancastrian of rank and military experience left. He'd commanded the right wing of Warwick's army at Barnet. Having been imprisoned at Hammes for the last ten years and now a man of about forty-two, he was desperate enough to do anything to avoid returning there. Though Tudor was unlikely to make an attempt on England this winter, the King, goaded into retaliation, issued proclamations against the rebels and set all the county levies on alert for service at half a day's notice. Beyond that, there was little he could do but wait.

Also at this time, William Collingbourne, the traitor who'd become famous for the rude couplet about the Cat and the Rat, was taken. He was tried at the Guildhall by the Earl Marshal the Duke of Norfolk, the Constable Lord Stanley, Sir William Hussey the Chief Justice, and many other peers, a commission designed to put fear into Tudor agents. The charge: on 10 July last past, Collingbourne had offered a man £ 8 to carry a letter to Tudor, urging him to land in England before St. Luke's day in October. The sentence: the penalty for treason. Collingbourne was not of sufficient rank to escape with the ax. On a gloomy, nose-dampening day, London saw its best execution for years. A great crowd turned out. I did not attend. Later I heard Collingbourne had not been granted the hangman's grace of being taken dead off the gallows for the butchery. The executioner is skillful as a surgeon; Collingbourne did not die until his belly was slit

and his entrails drawn. The crowd didn't often see that
punishment carried out. Some said his last words had
been: "Jesu, yet more trouble!" Others that he merely
screamed. Though only small fry among traitors, he was
made a grisly example to others, who, when crossing
London Bridge from Southwark, might see his head and
quarters stuck on spikes there.

Christmas, when it caught up with us in the year of God
1484, was as doleful a season as I could ever remember. I
was confined to the palace of Westminster. Four days
before Christmas day, on the Feast of St. Thomas, in the
middle of the night, the Queen suffered her first
hemorrhage from the lungs. It weakened her, though
with rest it might not have occurred again until the end.
But she refused to rest. I attempted to forbid it but she
insisted on appearing in public at every stage of the
festival, from Midnight Mass on Christmas Eve until the
dancing, disguising, and boar's-head bearing on the eve of
Ephiphany. In her stubbornness she openly defied me,
astonishing me with a freezing, hard-chinned look that
quite altered her face; it was her father to the life. She said
that the king should not be left to go through this
wretched twelve days of feasting alone.

Consequently, on the twelfth night, after sitting for
hours in the heat and glare of the White Hall, weighed
down by ermine and white cloth of gold, wearing her
crown, a winter queen, she hemorrhaged again. As she
left the hall the night frost cut into her lungs, and she
collapsed in the snow by St. Stephen's chapel, leaving a
stain like some delicate white hare caught and
disembowled by a hawk. Someone fetched the King. It
was a scene that should have belonged to a disguising. A
king in a fiery crown of gold, kneeling in the snow, his
purple velvet spread in a great lake about him, holding in
his arms a white queen, blood upon her face; a strange
pieta, lit by the pitiless flare of torchlight.

I began to pray that the sickness might take her
quickly. But my prayer was not answered for more than
two months. In mid-January, because the weather was
mild, the King took the Queen to Windsor, clutching at a
last straw of hope that she might do better in the country

air. However, the change induced no improvement;
everywhere that winter was too wet. She grew weaker,
and the length of time she left her bed, daily shorter. I
noticed she would always contrive, however badly she
felt, to be up and dressed whenever the King visited her
and insisted that her rooms should be cleared of any of the
clutter of sickness. Her women burned storax and
candles perfumed with spikenard. Sometimes she would
play chess with her husband. I thought that Friis would
have a fit if he saw them sitting on a table's width apart,
but said nothing. Soon she was content to sit still, while
the King read to her. She seemed to take much pleasure
and comfort in this, especially from the old-fashioned
speech of John Wycliffe's New Testament.

While at Windsor, I was amazed to discover that St.
George's chapel had become a place of pilgrimage, of
thanksgiving for miraculous healing. All done by
invoking King Henry VI, poor, dotty Henry Lancaster,
who was appearing on this earth to his suppliants with
more frequency than does Our Lady. Pilgrims were
coming to Windsor barefoot, bent pennies in hand, to
offer in gratitude at Henry's grave. On the Feast of the
Nativity of the Blessed Virgin in September last past, no
less a person than the Abbess of Burnham, near Windsor,
had come to give thanks for the preservation of the life of
her page, who'd fallen out of a tree and smashed his skull.
Humbly following her on the same day had come Henry
Walter of Guildford, who had received a cannon-shot
wound in his belly during a sea fight against the French
last June, when serving on one of the King's ships under
Sir Thomas Everingham. Though seeming certain to die,
he'd been healed, he said, by King Henry, who had
appeared wearing a crown (restored since his deposition!)
and the familiar blue gown. Walter had shown his fearful
scar to anyone who'd look; he'd take off his shirt for the
price of a jug of ale. A dozen other pilgrims had come
since. Most of them seemed to have been parents of the
victims of childish accidents: one child hanged itself with
the cord of its rattle, another tried to swallow a pilgrim
badge, and one adult was astonished when the bean he
had poked into his ear as a baby, fell out thirty-seven

years later!

It is nothing new, of course, to venerate King Henry,
but this raised him almost to sainthood. A saint? No. I'll
admit, in his lucid spells, he'd been a pious, unwordly,
monkish sort of man, who would hesitate to tread on a
beetle, but at times he was undoubtedly Bedlam-mad. At
this rate, they'd soon be selling latten hat badges at
Windsor, like those of St. Thomas at Canterbury and
Our Lady of Walsingham. Did King Richard know what
went on? It could hardly escape his notice. As Kendal, his
Secretary, had been heard to observe, one might think the
King had eyes in the back of his head sometimes, and too
many people were anxious to act as his ears. Kendal said
he'd ventured a remark on holy Henry's cures to the King,
who had answered gently that who was he to deny what
had been testified by sworn depositions. "Let it alone," he
had said. "The healed are so often children, and the
parent's gratitude goes me no harm." This from the King,
who'd been accused of murdering Henry in the Tower in
'71!

Time did not allow me to ponder on pilgrimages to
King Henry. Soon after our return to Westminster I
began to feel myself caught up in a waking nightmare.
The first inkling I had that the City of London was
humming with nastiness, as a dunghill does with flies,
came from my sister Katherine. I had gone down from
Westminster on frosty evening during the second week of
February to take her a belated New Year gift. I obtained a
bolt of fine murrey chamlet cheap from Master Appleby,
Keeper of the Wardrobe. Better to be on the safe side with
gifts for women. One year I bought a tiny ape from a
sailor on a Genoese carrack, thinking she would be taken
with its tricks. So she was, until on the third day it did an
indecent thing in front of the parish priest.

Since she was widowed, Katherine has lived in a
comfortable house off Thames Street. It has a small court
paved with flagstones and bordered by mulberry and
medlar trees; a vine is trained to grow along the sunnier
wall. There one may forget that the street, though wide, is
foul and unpaved and that fishy odors waft across from
Billingsgate.

"Yes, except for Will, who is in your kitchen eating eel

Katherine took me firmly by the arm and led me to a chair in her solar, plumping up the cushion as if I were an old man of infirm arse. She poured good Rhenish wine from a silver flagon and offered me figs preserved in sugar and her own almond cakes, to which I am partial, then sat herself down upon the linen chest. I could see I was in for an installment of local gossip. Possibly another episode in the scandal of Mistress Rose Williamson, who in her way is as much a success as Shore's wife at court. Men fought for her, abandoned their livelihood and put their souls in jeopardy for her. She is a whore who serves priests in various London parishes—no other men, only priests. As my sister whispered, immorality had taken place before the very altar ... After saying this, Katherine knelt under her little image of St. Anne and said a whole decade of her rosary for recounting such a sinful thing.

"Now, William," she said darkly, "will you kindly explain to me what is going on at Westminster." This foxed me for a moment. She always hopes for more court gossip than I am prepared to divulge.

"Well," I said, helping myself to another cake, "the Queen, not to beat about the bush, is dying. There was the usual great banquet at Epiphany, more than usually unenjoyable. The Lord of Misrule offended my lord Stanley ..."

"William!" She cut in on me tetchily. "Either you are being deliberately muttonheaded or you live such a monkish life you have not been in a tavern or stood in a crowd outside Westmisnter Hall and heard the talk."

"Kate," I protested mildly, "I've had a hard two weeks. As I've told you, Queen Anne is very ill. I've either been with her or waiting to be called to her almost daily. I haven't dined out in a tavern since before Christmas. What talk?" I reached for another cake.

"If you'll stop stuffing yourself with my almond cakes and listen, I'll tell you." She got up, went to the door, opening it suddenly as if expecting to find someone with an ear to the keyhole, then peered out of the windows into the pitch-black yard. "You came alone from the palace."

"Yes, except for Will, who is in your kitchen eating eel

pie and onions. What is this secrecy? I'll have you know I'm sufficiently trusted not to have watchers creeping after me into the City. Who's talking?"

"All London, by the sound of it. And it's downright treasonable." This made me attend to her seriously. She continued: "About the Lady Elizabeth."

"Which Lady Elizabeth?"

"God's blood, man! Let me finish. The Lady Elizabeth, eldest daughter of King Edward, of course. I'll tell you what I heard from my neighbor, whose husband was master cook at that great cookshop in East Cheap, at the sign of the Coney.

"*She* said, 'Your brother'll no longer be needed at Westminster when the Queen dies—he'll be giving place to a midwife!' So I said, 'What in the name of the Holy Mother of God do you mean?' '*They* say,' she had the impudence to repeat in my house, 'that the King wishes to marry the Lady Elizabeth his niece and will do when he is free of the poor sick Queen. Helped on her way to the Almighty, I daresay, poor soul. It's said he dances with her in public—the Lady Elizabeth—and a different sort of dance in private! Your William, the royal physician, will keeping mum about a swelling belly before he can say, "*Dominus providebit!*" ' "

I was appalled. "What is this—filth—the leaking of a London jakes? That my sister should give credence to such stews gossip ...!"

"It's none of my business to heed dirty tales," she said tartly, "but someone should heed this one. The King's name joined in adultery with his own brother's daughter. Why, it's incest!"

Stunned, I said, "But the Queen is dying—the King suffers greatly. He sees nothing beyond his trouble and his duty. Salome herself could dance for him and he'd go on talking about the next audit of crown revenues. Besides, he has slept alone, on *my* orders, for three months or more."

"Rumor knows that—and has the answer: three months to lie at night between a lady's legs ..."

"Katherine!" I had heard enough.

"You don't think I believe it, I hope!" To give her

credit, I doubt if she did, but like all women of her age, she is not above a little salacious speculation. The seriousness of the whole foul, fungous crop of lies alarmed me. If stories were circulating so freely in the City, then they must surely be buzzing in the palace of Westminster, where a new rumor is baptized before it is even given birth. Lies so wicked are the Devil's work, put to use by the King's enemies and spewed out by them into the London gutters. At the idea of the Queen learning of the tales, I crossed myself; it would be too cruel.

Adultery and incest were now added to accusations of murder. Ever since the Lord Harry of Buckingham had rebelled, it had been common speculation that King Edward's sons were dead—murdered, by the King's order. This news was stale as last week's loaf, but still chewed over in the London taverns. Folk had been quick to pronounce the King's own son's death as a visitation of God's judgement on the father. But in my view, God does not always judge in this life, and the child was taken by a sudden sickness, no more. I was careful not to mention any of the three children to Katherine, who would burst into the copious tears she reserved for the misfortunes of other people's children. Her own family had never aroused such a deluge of sentiment.

"Mary of the Sorrows!" she wailed. "All this on top of us not knowing what's become of those two innocent boys."

"Those who stick their noses too far into what is not their concern, get them bitten of," I snapped. "The children have been put well out of reach of dangerous meddlers." This, I realized, might be interpreted in two ways. She burst into tears. "In the country," I said, as if instructing a dull child, "a nice healthy manor house, no London dirt. There's no call for you to cry." She blew her nose on my handkerchief and was soon restored to her usual good sense.

"But, William," she said, "how can you be so certain?" To this I had no answer. One can be certain of very little in this life, but Kind Edward's sons were alive and safe; I'd stake my Hippocratic oath on it.

"I won't sit here and talk treason. If you take my advice,

Kate, you'll keep your mouth and ears closed. You can be certain measures will be taken against these scandalmongers. If it goes as far as the pinning up of lewd rhymes in public places, well, remember Collingbourne's fate." I took my leave, kissed her, and went with my servant to St. Botolph's watergate, where he obtained a decent boat with two oarsmen by yelling overgenerous terms.

We were rowed back to Westminster, lanterns bobbing in bow and stern, frost gleaming white along the gunwales. Near Temple Stars we were rolled about by the wash of a six-oared barge that passed us in gilded opulence, lit up by many lanterns and the streaming torches of servants. It was painted all over with the device of a white hart's head, smothered in gold fringing, and piled with cushions. I knew both it and its occupants; Sir William Stanley owns a barge fine enough for an earl. His loud, north-country voice carried over the water—an unpleasant, ostentatious man. His brother, Lord Stanley, was with him, perhaps on the way back from his house in the City. Sir William was laughing in a jeering way that made me suspect some unfortunate was the butt of his entertainment. They left us behind, and by the time I alighted at Palace Stairs they had disappeared.

I now felt it my duty to pass on what I had been told to some discreet person high in the confidence of the King. The obvious choice was the Duke of Norfolk, a man approaching my own age, for whom I had long had a deep regard. King Edward had many good servants, but John Howard was one of the best of them. Luckily, he had not taken barge down river to his own house for the night. Though it was late, he willingly granted me an interview, as an old friend.

The first thing that struck me upon entering his rooms was the atmosphere of warmth, light, and comfort. The furniture was of painted wood and polished oak, the arras of fine quality; some solid plate was displayed on a cupboard, though all seemed remarkably unostentatious for a newly created duke. Candles and firewood were not stinted, for he is a man without a grain of meanness, though a determined enemy of waste and untidiness. He sat bareheaded near a fragrant fire on which juniper twigs burned, his feet in lambskin slippers, wearing a long gown of violet damask, reversing to miniver, over a doublet of tawny velvet sewn with pearls. He had a chain of gold worked in suns and roses, with a pendant boar, around his shoulders. In front of him on a small table was an open book—accounts by the look of it—in which he was writing. That he acted as comptroller and auditor in his own household fitted with my measure of the man.

He greeted me with his usual broad smile that creased his weather-beaten face into as many lines as some leathery old fisherman's. On board ship, in jack and sea boots, he would pass for the skipper of a sailing barge. He still had most of his front teeth and a good deal more hair left than myself, iron gray and vigorous looking. His eyes are remarkable, large and dark gray also, their gaze disarmingly direct but full of shrewd intelligence. When he stood up, he was about my height and like me sturdy and square. He could have been ten years younger than he was.

"William," he said, motioning his page to draw up a chair for me, "I'm glad to see you here. What can I do for you?"

"Sir John, Your Grace, I make no secret; I've come on a distasteful errand. After I've told you, I'll feel like washing my mouth out with one of my own potions." He nodded, not taking his eyes from me. I looked at his firm-set mouth and jaw and took confidence.

However, the presence of the page made me hesitate, which he observed and said, "Take no notice of Tutsyn; he has cloth ears and a glued mouth." The little man grinned, winked, and made the gestures of "hear no evil, speak no evil."

When I told Howard all I had heard from my sister, his face lost its geniality and acquired the jowly pugnacity of a grizzled hound. I could see why he had been such a formidable man to oppose across a council table, especially if you were a Frenchman.

"I had hoped," he said, "that we would be able to spare the King this at such a time. Hobbes, I've been aware of this tale for several weeks, but you have enlightened me on its cruder side.

"You are a discreet man. I may as well tell you that behind this smoke screen of brimstone there is a little uneasy fire. This iniquitous idea of marriage has been dreamed up by the Lady Elizabeth herself, with the connivance of Lady Grey, her mother. The first declares herself to be in love, the second wishes to see a crown on her daughter's head at any price, as a salve for her own disposession. Well, this price is too high. The Pope may have given dispensations to uncle and niece in foreign parts, but England is a civilized country; incest, even to secure the royal succession, will not be tolerated. As for the King himself, he is about as aware of the rumors implicating him as a blind, deaf and dumb man might be.

"To put it plainly, the Lady Elizabeth is knocking her head against a stone wall. A pity she has not knocked any sense into it. I'm sorry for the girl; I've always been fond of her; but if she were one of my daughters, she would have to see reason. A husband must be found for her as quickly as possible.

"The sooner all this waiting is over and the Queen, poor young lady, dies, the easier I shall be in my mind, brutal though it may sound. Her lingering is harrowing for everyone; it's become painful to see her. After a decent interval, the King will marry some suitable foreign woman, get himself an heir, and all this scandal will be forgotten." As usual, Howard spoke sound, practical sense.

"How long," I asked, "can this be concealed from the King?"

"Not much longer, I'm afraid. His name is damaged further each day. Most people never see anything in such a tale but a wronged woman, and there's nothing your busy-tongued Londoner likes better than a wronged woman!

"The King is hideously vulnerable, through his being unknown to the London crowd and also because of his own nature. He lacks the craft in dealing with women of his brother, who learned it through long and intensive experience! King Edward was a clever man—he perfected his paths of escape. King Richard is not, so they have him enmeshed—not caught yet though—I've a feeling that horse will kick when they show it the bridle. My worry is the Woodville woman—Lady Grey. She knows where he is most vulnerable, and she is as old in guile as the serpent—forty-eight now, though it's hard to believe. I don't need to tell you, Hobbes, you're a physician; her age explains much.

"Richard married Anne Neville when he was twenty, and between you and me, I'm as certain as one can be with any man that he's been faithful to her ever since. That is probably beyond Lady Grey's comprehension. It is indisputable, I fear, that her daughter is infatuated with the King and will move heaven and earth to snare him. One of my manifold duties is to see that she does not. It's a mistake, in my opinion, to leave girls unmarried to their twentieth year; they begin to cry for the moon."

"Poor child," I said. "Whom may she turn to for comfort and advice? It's not such an unnatural thing; I remember her as a fat, toddling child of two, running after her uncle as if he were some idolized elder brother. Sir John, this situation that has arisen is horrible.

"You're right, Hobbes. If she'd been married off and her future not in jeopardy, it would never have entered her head. But the worst is to come. The King must be told. The council are only waiting for an opportunity. In his defense we have the opinions of many learned churchmen, to show that the rumored marriage is uncanonical and beyond contemplation. I'll be honest with you, William; I look at his face sometimes and, experienced old spokesman of diplomacy that I am, I wonder just what and how we are going to tell him."

A few days later, in council, they told the King. It was a mournful Monday morning at Shrovetide, by some irony also St. Valentine's Day. I was, of course, not present when they broke the news, but Norfolk told me afterward that for a full five minutes they had sat speechless, while the King, who is not given to bad language, swore an incredible string of oaths, worthy of the captain of an Iceland herring boat. Once provoked, he has a temper to match his brother's, especially, I think, when he is wounded in his emotions. But the outburst had died away into an obstinate refusal to countenance the rumor at all. No action was to be taken; the story was to be ignored, with the contempt it deserved. On this he was adamant, though clearly the others were convinced he was wrong and would have to alter his mind.

On that same morning the bells were tolled. As often happens when a king, or queen is reputedly dying, news of their demise trips over itself in its hurry to be abroad. In my opinion, bearers of false news should have their wagging tongues slit. As I say, the bells were tolled, and the poor Queen, hearing them and being told the reason, was distracted with fear. She had been sitting in her chair by the fire during the short spell that she now left her bed, but started up and almost ran from the room. Alarmed, I followed her, for any exertion greater than a slow walk could reduce her to such a state of panting, palpitating exhaustion that she might be prostrate for days or, worse, hemorrhage again.

The whole episode was a nightmare I should not wish to experience again. She went along the palace corridors so fast I could barely keep pace and broke in on the council meeting, Having got so far, she could go no further, but stood swaying on the threshold, holding on to the door jamb, panting and clutching her side. Between gasps, she managed to wail: "They say I am dead ... the bells toll for me ... My lords, do you wish me dead?"

Before anyone could stop him, the King ran across the room and flung himself on her. She fell into his arms, breaking into unrestrained tears, shaken by paroxysms of coughing. Worst of all, he began kissing her, anywhere, clumsily on neck and shoulders, because she turned her mouth away, and he murmured all the while: "Hush ... hush ... oh, my love, my love, my love, hush now ..." The words were stifled and broken as he caressed her with mouth, hands, and voice, trying to tell her that nothing was changed, "No one," he said, "no one—not in all the world—would wish you harm. Hush, darling ... please ... quiet, now, quiet ..." But she could not quiet herself; after all those months of choked-back tears, her pride had been vanquished by fools hanging on bell ropes. The King held her, trying to soothe her. She pressed herself quiveringly against him, responding to his kisses as one long starved. My eyes turned from them, stinging.

In a short while the bells ceased tolling. In great trepidation, I asked Lady Joyce, Sir Robert Percy's wife, if she knew of the rumors concerning the Lady Elizabeth and whether the Queen had any inkling of them. She said that indeed she had known, since before Epiphany, not from anything overt, but from Lady Elizabeth's face—it could be read like a book. Others must have noticed it, but she had seen that no word reached the Queen. For this I was thankful; Lady Percy is a rare woman, sensible and discreet.

God is sometimes without mercy. Death did not come to the Queen for another four weeks, until the Wednesday before Passion Sunday. She did not get up from her bed again during that time. I forbade the King to see her for more than a few minutes each day. She was in great deal of pain and he saw enough without witnessing that too. At the end she in fact bled to death, being too weak to withstand another hemorrhage. On that day, the sixteenth of March, an eclipse of the sun threw a sad, ghostly shadow across London. Some swore it was the shadow of the wings of Lucifer as he passed through the sky. All the self-appointed prophets within the palace of Westminster foretold a year of pestilence and war, of ruin for the King, a punishment for his own wickedness.

A fresh crop of rumors sprang up after the Queen's burial in Westminster Abbey. This time they had become too malicious to ignore. Suspicions of poison invariably attend the deathbeds of royal persons who do not die of that rare complaint, old age. But London seized upon the titillating conclusion that the King had poisoned his wife in order that he might be free to marry the Lady Elizabeth. The tales now implied deliberate cruelty; the bells had been tolled before the Queen was dead by the King's order, so that she might be frightened into taking leave of this world. An indiscretion over a gown was magnified out of all proportion. At the Epiphany feast, the Lady Elizabeth had appeared wearing the same cloth as the Queen, cloth of gold of a quality allowable by sumptuary law for a king's daughter, but definitely not

for his discredited bastard. The simple explanation was
that the gown had been the Queen's gift, made from
leftover cloth. No one chose to remark that King
Richard's own bastard daughter was dressed to equal
rank or that the laws of dress are less strictly adhered to
these days. Inevitably, it was said that the King had
wished the beauty of the Lady Elizabeth to overshadow
the fading looks of the Queen, to her great hurt.

I do not know how many details the King had been
told, but the sight of him in the past week had been
enough to move stones to pity. He went about his work
much as usual, granted audiences as frequently as he
always had, but what he said to them or what conclusion
these people reached about him, I felt unable to imagine.
He appeared to have bound and gagged his face into
something approaching expressionless composure, but
his eyes pleaded for respite. Pressure was put upon him to
take some action, though I felt that whatever was done
would be inadequate; the filth had seeped into too many
minds. In the end he was goaded into an extraordinary
course of action—extraordinary because instead of
condemming the London rumormongers in
proclamations read out by deputies, he met them face to
face, in public, denying the slanders by words from his
own mouth. It was at once the best and the worst that
could be done. It is difficult to know how he brought
himself to do it.

Two weeks to the day after the Queen's death, a huge
concourse of London citizens was assembled in the great
hall of the Priory of the Knights of St. John of Jerusalem,
in Clerkenwell, this being the only available hall in
London big enough to cram them in. On the Wednesday
in Holy Week, the last day but one of March, we rode
down to Clerkenwell with the entire royal household,
through Bloomsbury Fields and Holborn. As we crossed
the Fleet River at Holborn Bridge, I thought of how
fourteen years ago the King had found his wife hidden in
a cookshop near Aldersgate, in the middle of a street full
of houses of ill fame—it seemed to me scarsely more than
yesterday. To him? Well, I think he moved now as if all
his life had been but a dream, that Destiny, treacherous as

a Jack O'Lantern, had led him into barren and desolate places.

Most of us in that great train rode in silence, mum as mice as if the hand of the Almighty was raised over us in anger. So it proved to be, for when we reached the Bishop of Ely's house in Holborn—"to let," you might say, in the absence in France of Dr. Morton—the sky opened and a torrent of rain fell out. It gushed down in an opaque sheet, as if someone had turned a heavenly spigot, and like good ale it frothed merrily, bringing up a scum on the puddles. There was a hail in it, jumping about like beans, pitting the wet slush of the road with worm holes. When the first spate of it slackened, I peered through icy rods of rain at horses whose bay coats were dark with water, manes slick on necks, tails bedraggled, velvet-covered harnesses dripping. The riders had the look of a gaggle of disgruntled ravens on Tower Green in a thunderstorm, all in mourning black, with ruined plumes and ratlike fur.

We entered the gate of St. John's soaked to the skin. Within the great hall, the stink of wet wool on the backs of nearly two thousand people was enough to choke a healthy man. Whether they had donned opulent fur and best Kendal cloth or common frieze, it all smelled alike, of piss, with overtones of herbs used to guard against moths. They were packed tight enough in the hall to make the wall buttresses bulge outward, each man jammed with elbows in his neighbor's paunch. Each dripped into his own pool of water, which soon trickled across the flagstone to join one with another.

I felt I should stay as near the King as possible, not liking the look of him at all. In spite of the solicitude of the brothers of St. John upon our arrival, in proffering wine and hot towels, rain still ran out of his hair. It may have been because the water made it appear darker, that his face by contrast had a pallor like the dead. You might almost see through him.

As he walked out in front of the waiting multitude, he looked small and thin, as if the wet clothes had shrunk on him. In all that huge hall the only sound was the little clink of his spurs, and to me it seemed to echo around the roof timbers. There was no need for a silence to be called;

I could hear my own hearbeat, the gurgling in the gutters outside. Water rolled off my bald pate and down my nose, and my back ached from standing woodenly in a confined space.

The King slowly mounted the steps of the dais at the hall's end. He stood there in isolation, staring blankly over the mass of uncovered heads. He played with the dagger at his belt, then stopped, as if uncertain of what to do with his hands. St. Edmund, King of the East Saxons, had been bound naked to a stake, to be shot full of as many arrows as a porcupine has quills. I surveyed the pink ocean of faces, bearing various expressions: shocked, disapproving, grave, sly, smug, anticipatory, or downright salacious. A few, I was sure, indulged in the lechery of imagining what it might be like, pleasuring the Lady Elizabeth. These looks, then, were their arrows.

When the King began to speak, his voice was muffled and stumbling. I thought: The ones beyond the front rows won't hear a word. But he gathered strength after a sentence or two. Soon no one but the deafest, most decrepit alderman with ears sunk in fat could have missed a syllable. Most of the time he sounded coldly angry, but once or twice, when he spoke of the Queen, his voice became harsh with emotion. But they listened—almost held their breath. In the silences, one might have heard falling hair. When he said that it had never, ever, entered his head that he might marry the Lady Elizabeth, his brother's daughter, that he had not wished for the death of his wife the Queen, neither was he glad of it, but as sorry and deep in distress as any man could be, I began to sweat for him. It seemed to me grotesque that any King of England should have to stand up in front of his subjects and utter such a denial. No, more, shameful, those who had accused him should hang their heads, like the elders who condemned Susanna of adultery.

Anyone, the King said, caught spreading defamation against him was to be immediately imprisoned and not released until the source of the rumor had been traced. Masters of the city companies were to be summoned before the Mayor and ordered to exert their authority over members and their apprentices, to suppress rumors.

He came down from the dais even slower than he had gone up, like a man sentenced to the block. The spell broken, men began to shuffle their feet, but no one liked to be the first to start talking. Even Sir Thomas Hill, the Mayor, resplendent in soggy scarlet and miniver, looked chastened.

Shocked by what had been said, Prior Weston and the brothers of the order of St. John hovered around when we left the hall, but the King refused the wine they offered, and as soon as his horse was brought up, he rode out of the gate at the head of his train, leaving an embarrassed silence behind him.

The King's horse played up like a fiend all the way home, an unusual thing, as most of his mounts have perfect manners and he is a capable horseman. It threw up its head, jerking and champing until the bit jingled a carillon and foam flew in thick, white blobs. It refused to walk or trot, but jogged along erratically, swishing its white tail like an angry cat. A horse in that mood perversely sets out to put its rider through hell, to rattle his teeth in his head, jerk his backbone to and fro in a constant, whiplash motion, and make his arms feel like unraveled string. I suppose the animal felt the tension that gripped its rider and became as nervous as he. All the King could do was hold it in tight, which only made matters worse. It shied at every bush and lurking gardener's boy or wheelbarrow in Holborn, its trampling hoofs slithering about in the churned mud of the road.

When we reached the great gate of Westminster, I rode in under the arch with relief. I saw the King throw the foamlathered reins of his horse over its head for the waiting groom to catch and slide stiffly out of the saddle. He went in, ignoring friend and onlooker alike, while we flocked after him like sheep. He headed for the royal apartments by a devious route, through the river gardens. There, without warning, he ran to the stone wall where the Thames lapped at high tide, leaned over it, and was very sick in the river. When I caught up with him, he was surrounded by distraught friends and servants and still heaving like a land mariner in a gale. He sagged against the stone wall, fingers grasping at small plants that grew along its top. He was shaking, his face greenish, sweat drops gathering on it. I put my arm around him and felt every muscle shudder. His clothes were cold and wet. The rain was beginning again, blown by a gusty wind over the river. I said gently, "My lord Richard, come inside now." He gave a little groan and shook his head, but after a while let me lead him indoors.

That evening heralded the three days of mourning at Passiontide, by the singing of the office of *Tenebrae* in the royal chapel within the palace. At the best of times this is always a solemn moment for all true, believing Christians. Throughout the office, fifteen candles on a great branched sconce are snuffed out one by one, until at the *Miserere* only one solitary light is left. When this is extinguished, the priests beat together wooden clappers and stamp on the floor, to signify that chaos and darkness have descended upon the world. So indeed it seemed at this time, that we were close to the valley of the shadow of death.

Because the King appeared so unwell, I was installed in a place of privilege, beside Lord Lovell, behind the arras that screened off the King's chair from the rest of the chapel, where only he and his family, his confessor, and intimate friends were permitted to be present.

At first in the darkness I could not see well and was only made aware that something was wrong by a small sound. I thought a dog had got into the chapel and was whimpering at the door to leave. Then I saw that the King was lying flat on his face on the floor. The sound was the beginning of such a storm of weeping as I hope never to hear again. One of those glazed lions might have got up from the floor ties and leaped on his back, to maul him with claws and teeth.

"Oh Lord Jesu," I said under my breath as I heaved myself upright, "is there no end to this?" I knelt again on one side of him, Father Roby his confessor on the other, Lovell at his head. We all groped rather helplessly, as one does when a man breaks down so completely. The King lay with his arms spread out like a crucified Christ and wept without any abatement. He was past knowing what he did. Having kept an iron grip on himself for too long, his breaking was all the harder for it. I'd seen a good many men weep in my time, but none quite like this. Father Roby murmured, "My son, my son, let God heal you. Peace ..." The King had a rosary wound around his right hand, with beads of delicate filigree ivory and gold. His fingers had clenched so hard on it, some of the beads were crushed and broken.

I took a deep breath and decided to deal as summarily with him as I would with any man in such a state. I put my hands on his shoulders, gripped hard enough for it to be painful, and bellowed in my best battlefield butcher's roar: "Stop this! Stop it, I say—my lord Richard, you forget yourself!"

To the amazement of all three of us, he did stop, relapsing into a series of choking heaves. He went limp too and, though still trembling, had lost that twanging tautness that so frightened me, for it can push a man into a fit. Lovell knelt at his side in a state of shock, near to tears himself. Father Roby muttered a prayer.

"For the love of God," I said in Lovell's ear, "leave him to mop his face and recover some dignity. We intrude upon too much grief."

Father Roby, who is probably a better doctor of theology than the Archbishop of Canterbury and a man beyond the common sort in understanding and humanity, put his hands on the King's head, stroking him as if calming a panic-striken horse. "There is a prayer in which I have great faith, for those who are threatened by enemies and in deep anguish of mind. Hear these words, my son, and be comforted." He knelt, and the King followed his example, kneeling with bowed head in front of his confessor. Roby began to pray: "O Lord, who restored the race of man into concord with the Father, and who bought back with thine own precious blood that forfeited inheritance of Paradise, and who made peace between men and angels, deign to establish and confirm concord between me and my enemies. Show to me and pour out on me the glory of Thy grace. Deign to assuage, turn aside, extinguish, and bring to nothing the hatred that they bear toward me, just as you extinguished the hatred and anger that Esau bore toward his brother

Jacob ..."

The friar broke off suddenly, for the King grabbed his arm and hung on as if drowning. "Their hatred is terrible," he said in agony, "they wished to humiliate me ... They forced humiliation on me." His voice rose in a great rending cry, "Before Christ on the Cross—I am innocent!"

Father Roby summoned all his strength and began to intone very rapidly, calling upon God to rescue His son from trouble. It seemed an endless litany, a testimony of all those in every book of the Holy Bible who had been saved from peril by the bounteous grace of God and of how Christ's sufferings for us should redeem us all.

"Even so," Roby went on, "Jesus Christ, Son of the living God, deign to free me, Thy servant King Richard from all the tribulation, grief, and anguish in which I am held, and from all the snares of my enemies, and send Michael the archangel to my aid against them. Deign, O Lord Jesus Christ, to bring to nothing the evil designs which they make against me, just as you brought to nothing the advice with which Achitophel counseled Absalom against David the King.

"Even so, deign to free me by Thy most Holy merits, by Thine incarnation, by Thy nativity, by Thy baptism, by Thy fasting, by the hunger and thirst, by the cold and heat, by the labor and suffering, by the spit and abuse, by the blows and by the nails, by the crown of thorns, by the lance, by the drink of vinegar and gall, by Thy most cruel and unworthy death on the Cross ..." Roby spoke the words over the King as if they were incantation to protect him.

The King was very quiet now, his face buried in his hands. Only when the friar moved and the shadows shifted aside, I saw that tears ran out between his fingers, trickling down the backs of his hands and wrists. Lovell saw too, for he made a choked sound and, with a look at me, got up and fled from the chapel. I followed him.

Outside he said, "Dr. Hobbes, what can we do for him? What can I do?" He was wiping sweat off his forehead, ruffling up his hair into a veritable rook's nest.

"Nothing," I said heavily. "Nothing—only wait. Leave

him to God."

"I cannot endure to witness it." Lovell sounded anguished himself. He is unusually thoughtful of others, for a young man of twenty-eight, more like a brother to the King than a chance friend.

"No. Go to the King tonight, my lord; stay with him. Most likely he'll take more comfort from your silence than from anything you say. If he is so bad as to need a physician, send for me."

The remaining days of Passiontide sank in my mind without trace. I was in constant attendance upon the King. The day after our going to St. John's being Maundy Thursday, he was required to perform the accustomed duty of washing the feet of his subjects, in remembrance of Our Savior's act of humility. This year thirty-three poor men were assembled at Westminster, one for each year of the King's age and one for the year to come. After the ceremony was ended and the gowns, shirts and purses of money distributed, Lovell came to me, more distraught than ever.

"Will you go to the King as soon as he is free of all these people, Hobbes? He is not well. After the *Mandatum,* when he had given back the towels to the Abbot, he fainted. It only lasted a moment, but he'd fallen if I'd not seen it and held him. He knew what had happened, and that I knew, but he's too stubborn to admit any weakness. He can't sleep. Last night was worst of all. Is there anything you can do to ease him?"

That afternoon I visited the apothecary and had him mix juice of white poppy, hemlock, wild bryony, and henbane—I use this for rendering patients unconscious in difficult amputations. In the evening I took the King a sleeping draught in hot, sweet wine, which I was surprised to find he accepted without argument.

Each year's Good Friday is now a reminder to me that my bones are growing old. Everyone, from the King, who is half my age, to his humblest subject, goes creeping on his knees in church to the Cross of Christ. My knees creak like ungreased wagon wheels halfway up the chancel. After his sixtieth year a man should attend to his will, make his peace with God, and prepare his soul for death.

There was a time, as a young man careless of God's displeasure, when I thought the only things worth enduring Lent and a diet of stockfish for were the Easter games and the paschal lamb, succulent and fragrant of rosemary in its case of pastry, and the tansy pudding. This year the lighting of the candles on the eve of Easter and the joyful pealing of bells all over the City of London upon Sunday morning left me unmoved, either by the night's vigil or the day's joy. Years ago, in the troubled time of civil war, men bade farewell to one another with a little prayer:

> Jesu, for thy mercy endless,
> Save thy people and send us
> peace.

To which I say, never more fervently than now, *amen.*

10

Tenebrae
Told by King Richard

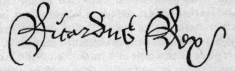

I ask you, O most gentle Christ Jesus, by all these things, to keep me thy servant King Richard and defend me from all evil and my evil enemy and from all danger, present, past, and to come, and free me from all the tribulations, griefs, and anguishes which I face...

O Lord, hear me by all thy benefits for which I give and return thee thanks and for all the benefits and gifts granted to me, because you made me from nothing and have redeemed me by thy most wonderful love and mercy from eternal damnation to everlasting life. Because of these and for other things which eye hath not seen nor ear heard, nor can heart of man comprehend, I ask you, O most gentle Christ Jesus, to save me from all perils of body and soul by thy love and deign always to deliver and succor me, and after the course of this life deign to bring me to you, the living and true God.

Part of a prayer translated from the Latin in King Richard's own
Book of Hours

Dreams are strange. Often they do not assume the distortions of fantasy, but come so startlingly lifelike as to verge upon a reincarnation of reality. One morning in winter, near the very end of a fragment of sleep, I dreamed in this way. I was carrying my son up the steps of the keep at home at the end of the day, as I often did when he was small. There appeared no vision of the place, it being so familiar, only a sense of the worn dips in the stones underfoot. I could feel the warm weight on my arm, his hair brush my face and stray into my mouth as the wind blew it up. It smelled of hay and grubby child after a long summer afternoon in gardens and meadows. When I woke, I was wiping away the imagined tickle with one hand, though it was not in fact imagined; tears were trickling down my face. When my eyes cleared, the gray dawn rattled the windows of Westminster, rain driven in dribbles between the casement hinges.

The winter had been so cold. I shivered, half smothered by furs and feather beds in the fug of Westminster, having slept warmer in the dismal Border fortress of Bewcastle in a blizzard blowing over the peat hags of Liddesdale. How I hate this place. The whole ancient warren of it stinks. I'd never have thought myself sensitive in such matters; too much of my life has been spent in garrison towns, camps, and pele towers. But this royal palace reeks of dead revels and smiling treacheries. One could turn the place over to a pack of untrained hounds and it would smell sweeter; there are too many sea coal fires, too few privies. You cannot walk down a corridor without finding men relieving themselves against the walls or dogs squatting in the rushes. Well, it's no different to what it has ever been; the distaste lies within myself. I feel like a hawk mewed up overlong, fidgeting from foot to foot, pining for light and air. Once or twice I escaped to walk in the dank winter gardens, among skeleton trees. Fog, overlying the Thames, hid the Archbishop's palace at Lambeth and the tower of St. Mary's church. Shriveled fronds dangled off the trellised vine, which looked as if it could never bear even little sour grapes. The peacock known as the Grand Turk inspected me with a disinterested eye and huddled within his feathers, trailing his folded tail behind carelessly as a sheaf of rushes. I watched him until interrupted by those who came out looking for me; Kings are denied the luxury of solitude.

That winter, how many times out of habit I had rolled over in bed, thinking to find human warmth at my back. I'd find myself on the edge, ready to fall out on the floor, before remembering Anne was not there. She never objected if I turned my back on her; often she'd curl there in her sleep. So we had become, even in affection, creatures of habit. Now, I still reach out for her on waking. Foolish, for I was often absent from her company before and seldom distressed in this way. Perhaps that valley between sleeping and waking holds more pain than the harsh daylight world.

Pain. Yes. My soul bears wounds that bleed it near death. There is no other way to describe. I could not pray. Not upon Good Friday, when Christ died a shameful death for us sinners, nor upon Easter Day, when He was risen. I almost forgot that Easter, the third day of April, was my own Saint's Day, St. Richard of Chichester. I took no comfort from the Blessed Sacrament. The child's words in the carol came sadly to me:

> Upon Easter day, mother,
> My uprising shall be;
> O the sun and the moon, mother,
> Shall both rise with me.

I could not rejoice; my utterances were sterile. The week after Easter marked the passing of a whole year since my son died, and he was a mortal child, who cannot rise from death. It was a cold week, too; we did not see the sun. Cold Easters remind me of Barnet. Father Roby, my confessor, urged me to think on the Blood of Christ, which heals and cleanses men of sin, but I cannot look on a picture of Christ, His bleeding heart, without remembering my friend John Parr, who died in my arms at Barnet, his body laid open in a way worse than any picture. We were both eighteen. He had fought as my enemy Warwick's squire. Being who I was, my brother's chief general, I was allowed no time to weep for him. Now, if I had tears left to weep, I would, and say: John, it would have been better if I had died, not you, that Easter fourteen years ago.

Father Roby begs me to give myself the solace of prayer, it being the only defense against the malice of enemies. I, who have sinned and erred in the manner of men born in high places, must, it seems, be punished.

Westminster is riddled with rumors. Immediately after

Easter I sent Elizabeth and Cecily to Sheriff Hutton near
York. My brother George's children are there; my own
bastard son, John, should be, though I haven't the heart
to send him away just yet. How far Elizabeth has been the
source of rumormongering I can only guess. That she
should conceive a passion for me, of all men, passes
belief. I would not see her, however she begged. Let her
tears flow like a river; it will have to serve as the waters of
Lethe, to make her forget her monstrous scheme. It
horrifies me. How easily a woman's schemes are turned to
incriminate a man. Why should we always be credited
with initiating lust? Am I more easily hoodwinked than
any other male within this palace? Am I, among them, an
unparalleled example of moral turpitude? I've been
harsh, examining my own feelings, but can find no spark
of lust left in me to respond to the advances of an
undeniably beautiful woman. I'm cold as a stone. For six
months now I've not touched a woman, and I couldn't
care if it were to become six years. At the end I could
scarcely bear to touch my wife, the sickness had so
ravaged her.

My trouble has had its effect upon the business of state.
Work takes longer than before; it seems impossible to
make eyes and mind move co-ordinately. The one
becomes sore and watering in candlelight, the other
empties itself disconcertingly into vacuity in mid-
conversation or in the dictation of correspondence.
Sometimes all the letters appear afflicted with St. Vitus's
dance, frenziedly lurching across the page as if to tumble
clean off it, so that I've found it difficult to follow even a
sheaf of my own notes. True, I write a vile screed for my
own use, but now it passed beyond legibility. I caught
John Kendal staring, as I was signing an exchequer
warrant, at my hands. They were shaking so, one would
think the pen had taken on life of its own. Perhaps they are
often like this; I hadn't noticed before. Kendal looks
worried half into his grave, and I cannot find it in me to
reassure or cheer him.

Hobbes, when he was free to turn his attention to me,
delivered a pithy lecture, which made me feel guilty as
when a child of five, refusing to allow him to draw a milk

tooth. If it had been anyone else, I'd not have had the patience to hear him out. In the end he gave me potions to bring sleep. Whatever the contents—the stuff has the effect he desires. I sleep leaden as a drunkard and cannot wake myself in the morning; the squires have to prod me into consciousness. They look so frightened when I am finally roused, as if caught in a treasonable act. I won't let them leave me sleeping after five o'clock, there'd be no day left to work in. They are bad days, those; Hobbe's drugs cling in the blood like a gallon of hippocras. I crawl about, as if suddenly aged, afflicted by blinding headaches. Few notice; they try to defend me when in this state from others who would belabor me with anxieties, to which my sodden and stupid head must be forced to produce answers.

Worst of all, the council are determined to badger me into taking another wife. They'd pitch a stranger into my bed and expect me to acquire an heir within nine months to the day. Please God, not yet, not yet. Anne knew very well what was expected of me; she faced it more bravely than I do. They mutter of the King of Portugal's sister, which led Sir Edward Brampton into offering to teach me his language, and a less likely tutor than that swaggering Portuguese pirate for the sweet phrases of wooing is hard to imagine. Where can I find a princess of European royal house who is not either mad, hideous, a child or a widow eager for a nunnery? I want an heir, it's true, but not of tainted blood. Most likely is a fourteen-year-old virgin, full of disappointed romance, who lies counting my gray hairs, or some sloe-eyed Iberian with a mustache who counts her beads and longs to be the bride of Christ. It's a prospect to render a man impotent for life. Well, I'm a poor bargain to set in the marriage market, possessing neither a handsome physique nor a merry face, still less the reputation of a man like Dorset, to bring the bees to the honeypot. The royal sergeant painter made what is supposed to be a likeness of me; it's no inducement to women. I'm not young anymore. Besides, no king whose throne is threatened and insecure can attract bidders. As with every other matter, nothing can be decided until after Tudor's invasion, which by summer is a certainty. In this one thing it gives me a little respite.

Though I must live in constant awareness of this threat, elsewhere the year proceeds within its usual pattern. In mid-April the Courts of Law sat for Easter term. When in London I have been accustomed to preside severally in King's Bench, Chancery, and Exchequer as often as possible during session at Westminster, or in council within the Star Chamber. My brother, for all the time spent in pleasure, did not neglect to do this; Edward worked harder at his duties than I've heard some give him credit for. This year the cases appear more tortuous and illogical than ever and the machinery of justice lumbers like an overloaded wain on a rutted road. It is sometimes possible to check interminable delays by personal investigation, though I've often had to consult the recorded proceedings of dozens of cases that have been wrangled over for years and to query the operation of the law. My presence makes the justices wary; some of them grudge me any legal knowledge or any rights on their preserve. But I cannot achieve the progress that a year past seemed so desireable. I'm so tired. No, to be truthful, I'm so exhausted as to be unable to wrestle any longer with corruption and policy or to drive others to do the same, I cannot see where all will lead—I'm too empty of purpose or hope, clackety-hollow as a coconut cup.

More worrying than any other problem is the lack of ready money. Not that the crown is become impoverished, but to pay wages and purveyors' bills, to maintain defense posts, gold and silver coin in the coffers is a necessity. Last August I squeezed more than £ 2,000 from the City of London. Though a sum this size to their combined wealth is nothing but a fleabite, London aldermen squeal as if a surgeon had attacked a vein and gone off with an illicit quart of blood in his blood in his bowl. Another month at most and I must of necessity prick them again for the same sum. I can't feel much compunction in bleeding the citizens of London, but it's a dangerous policy. The Londoners have no love for me, nor I for them; I've found them a mercenary, mucky-minded lot, too eager on seeing a stranger, to clout his head first and ask his name second. I'm a stranger, out of the north country, though my brother wore London like a jewel in his hat.

But the Londoner's loans have been spent before they were even pledged for. Ships had to be commissioned to patrol the coast from Harwich to Poole, to guard against invasion from France. By the time the softer winds of April had come, every port and seacoast hamlet was alerted, beacons stocked with firing on every shingle bank and cliff. The country levies held themselves ready to march at half a day's notice. I stood beside John Howard of Norfolk and watched the ships sail from the wharves at Stepney, where the caulking yards and rigging and sail makers had fitted them for service. Fair names they had—*Mary of Barking, the Elizabeth, the Carragon, Nicholas of London*—and made a brave sight, tacking to and fro on the ebb tide.

John Howard took me to his house at Stepney, among green fields and gardens but near enough the shipyards for a whiff of tar to drift in the windows on a southerly breeze, and fed me on his Colchester oysters, fresh gathered the day before and brought up river by a sailing barge on the next tide. He takes pride in the size of the pile of empty shells besides his plate. I do not share his passion; they taste of very little more than fishy estuary water. By way of compensation, John offered to send me melons, from beds in his own gardens, later in the summer.

From Stepney, Norfolk accompanied me to inspect the gunsmiths workshops at St. Katherine's where they wrought serventines for the Calais garrison. In the Tower storerooms there's a good stock of gunpowder, for which the account is not yet rendered. The same can be said of the bows, arrows, spears, and lead for the defense of Harwich. The Tower is not in as defensive array as could be wished and repairs in good Caen stone are expensive. After the invasion of rebels will come the invasion of creditors.

In mid-April we went to Windsor for a few days. There my wife's Month Mind was kept without pomp, in accordance with her own wishes. She saw no reason why her demise should provide more than one excuse for the court to bloat itself with a banquet. Whatever offering was made in her memory went to God, in prayer.

I succumbed to an urge for being incessantly out of doors, whatever the weather, until my conscience was pricked by the sight of Francis Lovell, waiting for me under dripping trees in the Great Park, drenched, mud-splashed from head to heel, sneezing and cursing quietly to himself. After that we went out on drier days with hawks. Francis's big gos took a heron in the river meadows by Runnymede, where our horses trod fetlock-deep in water, duckweed twining around their hoofs.

We left for London before the St. George's Day feast, though I felt guilty of shirking my duty. A deputy to conduct the Garter ceremony and the mumming was easy to find. I've no heart for feasting. It was hard enough to see the new buds unfurl upon the trees and hear unseen cuckoos calling through curtains of green willow by the river. From an orchard near Brentford apple petals blew in milky showers through the spring squalls. They lay, pinkveined white, upon the black of my sleeve or clung like a touch of grave fingers to my cheek, scarcely heeded, for my mind is in winter.

Soon after I sent Francis to Southampton, to oversee a small fleet patrolling the Channel; it's time he had an independent command. He was reluctant to leave me, and I miss his company, but strain and distress seem to have had their effect on him also.

I could not muster the decision to leave London until ten days into May. Where should I go? Nottingham, I supposed, equidistant from all possible sources of trouble. Though possessing a fair kingdom, I no longer have a home. Perhaps one day, when war is over and done with, I may have leisure to take my wife's body home to the North. I'd have her lie at York, in St. Peter's Minster, her son at her side, in alabaster tombs. My chantry at York shall be the most beautiful in the realm, the finest in Europe, perhaps, to rival my brother's chapel at Windsor. It shall see a new flowering of architecture in the North. Italian sculptors and masters of metalwork shall teach our craftsmen; John Tresilian, the Cornish smith who wrought at Windsor, shall join them. And the windows shall be the glory of St. Peter's, for our York glass painters are surely without peer. I'd like a window of the Resurrection, Christ breaking the bonds of the Tomb. Masses for our souls shall be sung into eternity by a hundred priests clad in copes of white silk embroidered with joyful angels blowing on shawms and trumpets or playing golden harps. It shall be a memorial to my years of youth, before I left the North, that shall live as long as there are men in the streets of York to see it.

By Ascension Day we were at Windsor again, and from there I rode to visit my mother at Berkhampstead, taking with me only a small escort of about twenty persons, as she now lives according to the Benedictine Rule and a great train of my household disrupting her regimen would be unwelcome.

She greeted me in the courtyard, among a flutter of women and doves, standing out from the cluster like a queen bee, partly because of her height, but also perhaps on account of her legend. We all hold her a little in awe. In her lifetime she has earned two nicknames, "The Rose of Raby" and "Proud Cis," no one denying that the rose bore some thorns; now one might call her the grand old lady of York. She carries herself very straight for seventy, her head poised on her neck with familiar, arrogant grace. The severe black robes and white linen bands of the coif binding up her chin set off the not inconsiderable remains of her beauty, an effect of which I suspect she was aware. Seeing that perfect profile in a kind light, one would take her for thirty years younger.

She made profound obeisance to me, though without humility, inclining her head and sweeping her skirts with the correctness of a fashionable lady. Then she kissed my cheek with that slightly proprietory air she bestows upon her children and grandchildren and led me in to dine. As she walked, she clanked gently, like an armed man with an unsheathed sword at his side, this being caused by the number and size of her devotional jewels hanging around her neck. She wore a reliquary as big as my fist, which held a piece of a nail from the true Cross, a gold crucifix as knobbly with gems as a cardinal's hung on a rosary of sapphire-studded gold beads, and an image in ivory and silver of Our Lady of Walsingham.

Her conversation avoided both condolences and politics, for which I was grateful. She spoke first of the chantry founded by Otto Gilberd at Marledon in Devon, where prayers were to be offered for her soul and mine, then asked after the health of old friends, of Chancellor Russell, of John Howard of Norfolk, of Lincoln her grandson, but not of her granddaughter Elizabeth nor of old friends now my enemies in self-inflicted exile in France. Forthright in her opinions though she is, she does not lack tact.

At Berkhampstead the round keep and many of the older castle buildings have fallen into disuse, my mother making herself comfortable in the smaller, timber-built living quarters. After Vespers we walked in her gardens, between low hedges of box and yew, lavender and quince. Most of the plants had been chosen for their sweet scent: a lawn of close-clipped, springy camomile that, when crushed by footsteps, releases a scent halfway between peeled pippins and balm; banks of *Rosa alba* still in green bud; wallflowers of lemon, amber, brown, and scarlet; clumps of clove gillyflowers to open in July. In her old age, gardening had become my mother's passion, having for her the additional virtue of being encouraged by her Rule. A gardener I had recommended for employment pleased her; she declared he was a positive magician with flowers and pointed out her peonies that had been brought on early by his skill—crimson and rose-colored ones fully out, the pale pink about to break their buds.

On one of the grass lawns my mother halted and looked down, a frown drawing the fine white brows together as she stubbed the toe of her shoe in the turf. "Daisies," she said pointedly, with more dislike than the offending intruder merited, "play havoc with a good lawn," I took her point. The pretty, feminine device of Lady Margaret Beaufort, Tudor's mother, is a knot of growing daisies, or marguerites.

"They're hard to get rid of," I said. "You may clip the heads, but you might ruin a lawn uprooting them all."

"Nasty weeds grow apace," she replied, "and she is a very clever woman. There may be no more of her than would fill a pint pot, but every inch of the Lady Margaret is as purposeful as any man. Make no allowances, Richard, you are too soft with women. Prim-mouthed little bitch!" This was hardly a suitable comment from a woman of religion, said with a well-remembered curl of the lip and the superiority of a woman nearer six foot than five to the diminutive. Proud Cis clearly wasn't humbling all her pride before God.

"What do you suggest I do with her, other than leaving Stanley to answer for her? He is her husband."

"Husband, indeed! You know as well as I do that she swore celibacy soon after she married him. She could manipulate him with her little finger and convince him he pursues a self-invented policy of infinite wisdom! As for that son of hers, the unknown Welshman of bastard stock, she bore him when she was fourteen—she dotes upon him as only an absent mother can. She would raise Antichrist if it would aid him. If you find her overears in treason, as I suspect she is, you should deal with her as a man is dealt with."

"You can't mean I should take her head!"

"I do." The answer was as forceful as she could make it.

"Jesu! Mother, I don't make war on women!" Frankly, this ruthless female logic left me a little aghast.

"Then you condemn yourself to be their dupe ... and don't take the Name in front of me!"

I said angrily, "Madam, do you take me for a fool?"

"No. You, my son, have more intelligence than any of my children. But in some things you're too obstinate and too upright to use it as it should be used, as Edward would have used it."

"Are you suggesting he would have headed a woman? More likely he would have bedded her and won an admirer for life. Well, I'm not made for that, either."

"You underestimate yourself, child, you always have. I've watched self-doubt hold you back too often these thirty years." I turned away from her, embarrassed.

"My lady mother," I said, my voice rather harsh and abrupt, as it is when trying to hide my feelings, "did I do right—to take the crown?"

She was silent for a space, while I stood with my back

tó her, snapping sprigs off a rosemary bush. A bumblebee, late from home, tumbled about among a border of purple fleu-de-lis. In the chapel they had decorated the altar, standing in those blue and white painted earthenware jugs from Antwerp.

"What's done," she replied, "cannot now be undone. You decided the answer to that yourself, two years ago, and you must abide by it. Have faith in yourself; without it you'll be a king stuffed with straw. You're too like your father, and doubt was his downfall, God rest him. Yet I think you are made to suffer even more. Don't scourge yourself. You do—I can see it written all over you. I neither condone nor condemn. You are my son." This was all she would say. She never was one to bolster up the doubting with empty assurances.

"You give me no comfort," I said bitterly, left unreasonably desolate by her answer, refusing to turn around to face her.

"Richard," she said gently, "you're young. You're breaking yourself to no avail. I cannot help you. No one but Christ can heal your bitter pain."

"Young! You're mistaken there. Even if spared the hazard of war ..." At that juncture the clock in the tower over the west gate began to strike seven, making me jump violently.

My mother touched my cheek with one finger. "Hmm," she said, looking at me rather fiercely, as she does when concerned, "you're nervous. Your hands shake. You've just jumped out of your skin. You're pallid as a fasting monk, and there's about as much flesh on your bones. You haven't taken to a hair shirt like that play actor Rivers?"

"No." I shrugged and tucked the offending hands into my sleeves to hide them, making no further comment. Seeing me unwilling, she did not pursue the subject.

"It is my custom," she said with dignity, "to pray a while before I retire at eight. Will Your Grace come in?"

"No. I'll walk a little. Your gardens are pleasant." I kissed her. "Good night, mother, may God give you sound sleep."

That night I slept hardly at all, though the bed was

comfortable and well-aired, with finest lawn sheets, as one might expect in my mother's house. I regretted leaving my own traveling bed, having thought that one night in a strange one would do me no harm. Well, it did me no good, and in the morning I winced at the sight of my face in the barber's mirror.

After Mass I took leave of my mother. In the graveled courtyard our horses' hoofs crunched, a groom leading Lyard Mountfort around gently in wide circles, letting him fret against the bit a little, to take the edge off him. That one goes as sweetly as a lady's p. rey after the first hour, which he spends pretending he has never been backed. It had rained in the night, and white doves strutted across the yard, dabbling in puddles and preening to their reflections in the early morning sun. In the bright daylight my mother bade me a conventional farewell: the cool kiss upon the cheek, the blessing of a woman of religion, when I bent my knee to her as a gesture of filial obedience. She is not a woman to whom the expression of affection in public comes easily—in that we are alike.

This time, however, she took my face between her hands and held me still, quite firmly, so I could not escape her eyes, looking down into my own—as she is a tall woman. She wore a strange, heavy look, as if she had come upon a derelict building remembered from childhood, expecting to find it inhabited, a look of memory disappointed, to find all who lived there dead. God knows, after last night I was the usual corpse-candle color, but she gazed at me as if she were at my funeral, about to lay me under the earth, and I already wore a shroud. She has extraordinarily bright blue eyes. I had thought her to have been dry of all tears for many years, so was surprised to find they swam with tears, had become rheumy and old.

If I were more prodigal with my emotions, I think I should have fallen at her feet and wept myself back into childhood, submerging her in the undammed flood of my own agony. But apart from a certain reserve of pride between us, I had no right to unload my burden on her. She has suffered a lifetime of sorrow and bereavements, beside which my own diminish to little grains of sand.

I detached myself from her hands and moved aside, before she should see the evidence in my own eyes of pricking tears. I had the reins in my hand and my foot all but in the stirrup, when she suddenly held my wrist to detain me. Uncertain of her intent, I stood facing her, my hand still on the saddle pommel. She embraced me with unwonted tenderness, kissing my mouth and stroking my hair. Her lips trembled. We stood cheek against cheek, inarticulate with choked emotion. I don't know if she felt me shake within her clasp.

"Mother," I managed to say, "pray for me. I need your prayers." The Jack o' the Clock over the gate swung his mace with a whirr and a clank and began to strike the bell.

"Every hour of the day, as the clock tells them, as long as you go in danger, which is all a king's life, Richard. May our sweet Lord Jesu Christ guard you and bring the evil plotting of your enemies to nothing. I have only one son." As she finished speaking, the last stroke of eight struck and Jack was still again. My mother had borne eight sons.

I squeezed her hand, but did not kiss her again or give assurance of a next time of meeting. In our family we do not make such promises, and she knew as well as I that before she saw me again, I must ride to war. While she had been so close to me, I noticed with a shock that her hair under the nun's coif had been cropped. Three feet of magnificent snow-white hair clipped close as her camomile lawn. Proud Cis had sacrificed her greatest vanity.

We rejoined the household at Aylesbury and progressed without lingering to Kenilworth. I had chosen this place in preference to Warwick, which hold too many memories, for there, in her father's castle, a month short of twenty-nine years ago, Anne my wife was born.

This part of Warwickshire is heavily wooded, secret sort of land, where the sky is glimpsed in patches and the wind filtered by leaves, in which, if left too long, I'd feel enclosed. In Kenilworth chase, the game almost falls out of the trees and cover; hawks and falcons grew indolent with the abundance of quarry. From this greenwood retreat I sent my bastard son John to the North.

Hutton. It was for his own safety, but he protested as if banished to far Cathay and looked at me with those injured squirrel's eyes, as his mother had when I left her, which had been often. John pleaded, "My lord father, Your Grace, you went with your brother the King, to fight, when you were fourteen."

I said patiently, "When I was fourteen it was not necessary to go; later I went, but saw no fighting. John, you are not even fourteen until December. No." When I say no, he knows better than to argue. "Afterward," I said, in an attempt to cheer us both, "I'll send you to Calais. My Captain will have to start earning his wages." He smiled at this, looked pleased and proud, but his unease was not entirely dispelled. Sometimes he seems as vulnerable as myself at his age, but less enforced to hide it. I kissed him on both cheeks and hugged him, conscious that I said farewell to the last of my children. He swore to pray daily for a victory over my enemies, especially to St. George and St. Anne, also to apply himself to improving his Latin, French, and law, and to practice hard with bow and weapons so he might serve me well when he is fully fourteen and a grown man. He doesn't know how lucky he is; bastards, if God is willing, more often grow to old age than those born in wedlock. I was sorrier to see him go than he knew; I'd grown used to finding him forever standing in my shadow. Though he is not Anne's child, it is good to have a son.

At Kenilworth, one night near Whitsuntide, I was made to suffer the very thing I had gone there, in preference to Warwick, to avoid. I couldn't sleep and got up from my bed at the hour of deepest dark, to open a window. Sometimes I'm stifled in a closed room. Going barefoot on the tiles, to leave my squire sleeping undisturbed on his truckle bed at the foot of mine, I opened a casement and stood mindlessly looking out. In a sky of fleeing cloud, the moon rode high and full, mirrored on the Mere, where dark clotted shapes of beech and oak lay reflected at its rim. This lake, guarding the castle on north and west, is one of the most attractive features of Kenilworth. One almost expected to see an arm arise from it, clad in white, like that which

brandished aloft the sword Excalibur, thrown by Sir
Bedivere when Arthur lay dying. Not long ago it had
rained: somewhere a gutter dripped loudly and
persistently. The chill of night was sharp enough to raise
hairs on my arms and prickle me with gooseflesh, though
I'm accustomed to bear cold without much discomfort.

I leaned my head against the window frame. The quiet
made me feel slack in body and mind, though pleasantly
so; the days are filled with noise. The room overlooked a
rose garden, where colorless and formless flowers
clustered on dark bushes. Climbers had been trained up
the wall under the window, and their scent on the rain-
washed air was very sweet. I shrank bodily away from it,
stricken by a pain sudden as a weapon jammed in the gut.
I shut the window none too gently and dived back into
bed, shivering between chilled sheets.

Roses were the scent my wife liked best. Sometimes I'd
think Anne bathed herself in rose water; she'd even eat
syrupy preserves made from roses or the candied petals.
The perfume she used, roses warmed by musk and amber,
was luscious enough to make the head spin; it clung to her
warm body, to her hair. That hair would sweep over me
like silk, winding itself about me in the most delightful,
hampering ways.

I pulled the bed covers over my head, trying to escape
the remembered fragrance, but it seemed to have
intruded through the briefly opened window, to linger
and torment me. Through the window of my mind, I saw
only the sheen of hair, the sprawl of limbs, so clear that I
put out my hand to caress the familiar place. She always
responded to that particular caress with a surprised,
indistinct sound, intaken breath dissolving in a small
moan. But my fingers met only a sheet and featherbed,
cold and rough. A poet said:

> Know ye that I would be glad,
> To seek a thing that will not be had ...
> Alone, I lie alone.

I fastened my teeth in my lower lip, to keep the groans in.
She had such tender flesh. At the moment of taking she
would sound even more surprised. A strange banging
noise alarmed me, until I discovered it to be my own

heart, echoing fit to wake the whole castle. Later, she'd make cries like a bird, weird and disembodied. I must have been groaning aloud after all, for the squire waked and came to my side. The sight of his frightened face, sleep bleared and unshaven, acted like a cautery.

I said, "It's nothing...nothing. Go back to sleep." My voice sounded thick, a stranger's. He hesitated, looking guilty, as if troubled to leave me. I sat up and reached for the flagon of wine set on a small beside the bed. He forestalled me, poured wine into a gold cup, put it into my quivering hand. "Fetch another cup," I told him, "and drink yourself." He did so, watching me.

I indicated the white machet loaf on the table. "Eat if you wish. I never do—it's only there out of custom." He carefully cut a slice and ate it. There had been no need to strike a light for a candle—the moonlight came in the room in sheets. Colors in the arras on the far wall were transformed by it; a woodwose clad in silvery leaves capered among ghostly trees.

"Your Grace does not sleep?"

"There's nothing new under the sun—no. I will soon."

"The moon strikes full in our faces," he said doubtfully. "It's ill luck to sleep so."

"Geoffrey, if that were true, I'd have been struck down in infancy, I've slept in a haycock and under a quickset hedge before now and none the worse for the moon having a look at my face. Is that a tale put about by the old wives of Wharfedale?" He grinned at that, for I was teasing him a little. He was a man about my own age, in my service some years, who came from Kettlewell in Wharfedale.

"Aye, that's right," he said. "They heard it from the old wives of Yoredale! Will Your Grace have more wine?" I covered the cup with my hand to signify refusal and had to smile at being paid back so neatly in my own coin. He'd used the old name for Wensleydale too.

I lay down again, shielding my eyes from the bright moon. "Go to bed now." Soon I heard a gentle snore. I often wonder how much gossip leaves the household. The King cannot sleep—he dreams and groans in his dreams. They must think sometimes that I will go out of my mind.

Given another night like this one, I believe I will—
anything, anything, but that—that hopeless, bodily
craving. I hadn't thought it possible to so desire
something of which death had deprived me.

On the first day of June we rode to Coventry for the
festival of Corpus Christi, to watch the guild plays. We
were met without the walls by the Council of twenty-four
and the Mayor, Master Robert Onley, a wool merchant
who is reported rich as Croesus. He was immensely
deferential and entertained us in his town house at the
sign of the Bull, with a lavishness a little inappropriate, as
we were still in mourning and our visit to the town not a
state occasion.

Early next morning, Thursday, an ordinary, gray day
but mercifully dry, we attended the customary breakfast
banquet provided by the Corpus Christi guild. Afterward
a procession was made with the sister Trinity Guild
through the city. Preceded by the senior Company of
Mercers, the Mayor, and the Macebearer, the Host was
borne through the streets under a canopy of cloth of gold.
In the enclosed space between the houses misty-blue
threads of incense from the priests' censers coiled and
drifted, mingling with the voices of the singing boys. The
bells of all the city churches almost split the sky apart
with their pealing. It's said that Coventry is a city close to
Heaven, as the great spire of St. Michael almost touches
the clouds. Though great loads of green rushes, fresh-cut
leaves, and herbs had been laid down, the street was
muddy and ill-paved, and the tang of curshed mint and
sweet woodruff could not disguise that Coventry is also a
city of fullers, dyers, and tanners.

At the open place where the plays would be enacted
before me, the city waits, in their livery of scarlet and
green, struck up on harp and dulcimer, small organ, pipe,
tabor and trumpets, blowing fit to burst veins. I'd heard
the Coventry plays are famous for music and singing;
even the Flood is accompanied by thunderous notes on
bass shawms and large drums. The musicians were well
trained for town players and so enthusiastic they made
me smile for the sheer pleasure of watching them. The

crowd smiled with me, laughing and whooping themselves into holiday mood.

We were to watch the plays from a dais, before which each clumsy-wheeled pageant was dragged by draft horses. The pageant masters of the various guilds were presented to me by the Mayor. The man who'd produced the play of Noah and the Flood smiled nervously and almost dropped his hat at my feet.

To set him at ease, I complimented him on his Ark. "You've employed a skillful carpenter there, Master Colclough. That Ark looks fit for the North Sea in a gale."

He was quite overcome. "Thank you, Your Grace, thank you—how kind. We sent for a Trent barge-builder from Burton to do the job ... Has Your Grace witnessed plays in other towns? The noble city of York, what finer cycle of plays ... I remember some years ago, Your Highness's players passed through Coventry and played the story of Jason—your noble patronage has long been given to plays. Now you have honored us by visiting our city, we hope to show you the equal of any plays."

The Nativity of Our Lord, played by the Shearmen and Tailors, was especially touching. The girl who played Our Lady was very young, little more than a child, with startlingly fair hair and eyes one could see even from a distance were blue as my mother's. Her husband whose misfortune it was to have red hair, played Judas in the Smith's play. You couldn't have found a prettier, more tender mother; the baby, I was told, was her first-born son. She sat low in the straw and suckled him as if she were in her own home, making me believe that Christ might have been born in a humble street in Coventry.

After the offerings of the Kings of Cologne and the Flight into Egypt, a hush fell upon the crowd like the stillness before rain, the next episode being the Slaughter of the Innocents. If it had been London, the crowd would have turned their eyes on me like avenging angels, but here only a few covert glances betrayed that some citizens of Coventry wondered if the English King Herod might be in their midst. Let them wonder. But looking at my hands, I found they trembled and that I was up to the

usual trick of sliding rings up and down over the joints of
my fingers.

Herod strutted like a peacock in his pride, in bright
blue tawdry satin, bedzined with tinsel patterns in gold,
silver and green, and he flourished a fearsome wooden
sword covered with paint and gold and silver paper. Over
his head and shoulders he wore a mask painted with
leering lines, red-rimmed eyes, and grimacing open
mouth and a long black-ringleted wig like the Jew of
Lincoln. When Herod leaped from the stage, the crowd
recoiled with shrieks, leaving a space for him to rage up
and down, proud as Lucifer and horrendous as
Beelzebub, while the property men ducked down behind
the stage and let off charges of gunpowder to lend
thunder to his storm. The reek of it filled the street, as if
serpentines had been fired.

The soldiers marched on in jacks and sallets, armed
with swords, snatched the babies from the arms of the
shrieking women by hanks of yellow hempen hair,
savagely dismembering them, unraveling yards of
swaddling bands. The mothers put up a fight, belaboring
the men with pots and ladles; a fat woman resoundingly
smashed a crock over the steel hat of the burliest soldier.
But Herod's orders were obeyed. At the end an ear-
splitting howl of woe went up from the players and the
crowd, in protest at the ungodly deed. The soldiers stood
and exonerated themselves. "The King," they said, "must
bear the blame." A hard truth, that. The King is a useful
scapegoat, to bear universal guilt until the burden breaks
his back.

After, men came with brooms and cleared up the
remains of the Innocents, and the plays proceeded. Our
Lord's suffering and death, enacted by the Guild of
Smiths, distressed me as it always does. Christ, like the
Blessed Virgin, was young and fair. This is customary,
but perhaps not truthful; Our Lord was thirty-three. I
thought of my friends and of my own battered face, but
one could argue an entirely blameless life must preserve
youth.

Darkness fell upon the Harrowing of Hell, the stage lit
by cressets that threw an evil, flickering glow over the

players, like the flames of the pit, casting their shadows huge as the giant Gogmagog. The Cappers' company possessed a magnificent Hell mouth, built of canvas, glue, and wire, painted in every lurid color conceivable and made still more ghastly by the red coals of Hellfire, on which brimstone burned nauseously. Satan turned cartwheels like an acrobat, firecrackers exploding from his ears and tail, taunting the audience with obscene gestures. His lesser attendants prodded a squirming mass of black damned souls with pitchforks. The Company paid damned souls less than the saved, who wore white and at the end were gathered singing to the hem of God's white robe. With everyone else, crossing myself, I began to pray that at the end of darkness there might be some salvation through Christ's suffering.

The next day we returned to Kenilworth. Robert Percy, who is the only close friend at present in my company, and his sensible, handsome wife, Joyce, rode beside me. Joyce had been endlessly kind to me at the worst time of the scandal, putting herself out to be seen talking to me or to walk with me, when everyone knew that she was a strong-minded and virtous woman who had been the Queen's friend.

Rob had as much a look of impatience as his fair face could show. He had been waging war ever since we came to Kenilworth on a pike that lived in the mere, one of those tyrannical old monsters that lurk in the same territory for years, for the purpose of outwitting fishermen. Rob had tried everything, fishing from the wall at the edge of the tiltyard or having a man row him about on the deepest part of the Mere. Joyce, like Dame Julian Berners, who wrote of fishing, is also skillful with a rod and fly, and fishing parties with friends who share the passion is their chief recreation. I envied them a little this pastime in each other's company.

Rob's mind was not entirely occupied with fish, however, but moved after a while to other slippery game. "One would think," he said, "that the whole royal household would fall about our ears without Lord Stanley to direct it. He enjoys his petty powers as well as his greater. He'd see the world turned upside down to keep them."

Stanley had been under our noses all morning, going about his usual duties as Steward of the Household, seeing that we left Coventry in proper order. He is one of those men who always appear busy, whether they are occupied with weighty matters or trivia. Considering that he had held the Steward's staff for nearly fifteen years, it was a little surprising that Robert had suddenly found his busyness worthy of comment.

Joyce glanced from one to the other of us shrewdly, as if she had known that her husband had been watching Stanley.

"How often," Rob inquired more seriously, "has Lord Stanley turned his coat?" This was difficult to answer quickly.

"If I calculate corectly," I said, "six times in the last twenty-years."

"Then it must be like Joseph's coat of many colors," Joyce remarked drily. "It works miraculously to his advantage every time."

Rob brought his horse around to one side of me, leaving his wife and her sorrel mare on the other. I had a feeling this conversation had been planned between them.

Robert asked another unexepected question. "Has Your Grace ever heard John Howard speak of the battle of Blore Heath, between your uncle of Salisbury and Queen Margaret's men?"

"Yes," I said, "Thomas Stanley was careful to put six miles between himself and the fighting. He was supposed to be loyal to Lancaster, but pledged himself to my uncle just the same. In the end he joined neither."

"And yet he somehow obtained pardons from both parties, though he'd been no more use than a fart in a colander to either."

"My brother pardoned him again, after he'd played safe and deserted our cause during the restitution of poor Henry of Lancaster."

"He makes much of your association in previous years," Joyce observed, "but both Rob and I think that he bears you several old grudges, Richard, of which Your

Grace should be aware." I was surprised that she should put this in such strong terms.

"We've had differences, certainly, and I do not count him a friend, but he dislikes making enemies."

"You frighten him," she said, "and you first frightened him when you were seventeen."

"I hadn't thought he was so nervous. Am I alarming? Are you frightened of me?"

She tilted her head to one side, and a dimple appeared in each cheek. Her smile grew broad enough to show one little gap in otherwise neat teeth, a defect more endearing than disfiguring.

"No." I was absurdly relieved, though I'd been half teasing her. "But I," she said seriously, "am not Lord Stanley."

Rob gave a hoot at this. "By the mercy of Heaven," he laughed, "there's no resemblance!"

"Go on, Joyce," I said.

"Rob should tell the tale. He was with you."

"I see. Did this take place near Manchester, in 1470, around Passiontide?"

"Yes," Rob grinned rather maliciously at the recollection. "Lord Stanley had gathered more than two thousand men, which anyone could have guessed he intended using to aid King Edward's enemies." He did not mention that those enemies were my brother Clarence and my wife's father the Earl of Warwick.

"He had the ill luck to meet us on the road, if you could call it a road—it looked more like a river. He knew us and rode straight to you, furious that he'd been discovered moving his personal army. When you told him to disband his men and get out of your way, he turned redder than a radish and swore he'd be damned if he would. Then you said, flat as you please, that if he did not move aside within the count of ten, you'd see it done by force. He gave way, collapsed in his dignity as if you'd slapped him around the face with a wet mackerel. I'll never forget him, sitting there with rain dripping off the end of his nose and those goggling eyes of his standing out like apples. But he obeyed without a word, though he turned his horse as if to leap a gate from a stand. My knees trembled for an hour afterward, I was so scared you really would set our few hundred against him. A few of them laughed out loud to see him dismissed so summarily, and poor Stanley was quite purple with cold and mortification."

I had to smile a little at this; it recalled Stanley so vividly. "Rob, I was too exhausted to argue with him. We'd gone from south Wales in three days, and if I spoke sharply, it was because I was cold, hungry, and very wet. Also, I was desperate to bring those men safely to join my brother. Maybe I was too young to see the value he sets upon his dignity. You think a few hasty words still rankle?"

"Yes. You all but accused him of treason. He complained to your brother the King, who laughed as if he'd been told a joke, which only increased his chagrin. I remember King Edward's laugh ..." So did I and remembering brought the familiar wrenching pang of loss.

"He had a lovely laugh," I said. Seeing me sad and musing, Rob paused, but he was not long deflected from his urge to provide me with unwelcome information.

"Stanley still thinks himself the hero of the siege of Berwick, because the town surrendered to him, not to you."

"I was grateful for his assistance. He had ample reward."

"But not the acclaim in the streets of London, as you did. If he had endured those two winters we spent preparing war on the Border, he might have allowed more credit where it was due. Winters!—they say the second was the wettest in the memory of man. As for the chilblains, mine lasted until May."

"And mine," I said. My fingers had swollen until no rings would fit them, cracking at the knuckles until they bled. "So you think Thomas Stanley was envious of my command at Berwick? If he'd been in my shoes, he'd have soon wished himself out of them. Besides, I took pains to see that the services of all my captains were brought to my brother's notice and given as much acclaim as my own."

"But not enough to stifle his resentment. Given a situation like that at Blore Heath, with Stanley able to put an army of two or three thousand into the field, do you consider he would engage those men on your behalf?"

"Possibly—more probably not, as I think it unlikely that he will engage in a battle at all, however that busy little wasp of a wife, Lady Margaret, is stinging him. I am convinced he will not join Tudor openly. He knows that if I, with God's help, am victorious, I would have his head, every acre of his northwestern kingdom, and the subjection of every man in his private army. The evil of the situation is that he can maintain such an army outside the King's control. I cannot break his power without first being given cause; it would be unjust, and I would risk a rising in the northwest. Let him stick to his bird in hand. If you want to bet on his circumspection, Rob, you may as well lay a high stake. I am forced to wager my crown on it."

Nevertheless, Robert appeared to have less confidence than myself in Lord Sanley's neutrality. We rode the few miles to Kenilworth in a silence that after a while plunged me deeper than ever into gloom. The towering elms that lined the road made a green tunnel of mols-smelling shade, keeping the way miry as in midwinter. The place had the air of a graveyard. I am not much given to daytime fantasies, but for a short space I lost awareness of White Surrey's solid bulk between my knees and fancied I stood pinned against a tall elm's trunk, unable to move a finger to free myself. I'd been there some time too, waiting for an end—exposed, pinned down, and helpless, like a corpse laid out for a surgeon's anatomy lesson, nails through my hands, neck, feet, and heart. There was nowhere behind for me to go, nowhere in front.

I must have shivered and jerked at the reins, for White Surrey threw up his head and shied in protest. When he was quietened, I thought: I looked too sadly upon the Smith's play, the hammer, nails, and bloody hands. But I knew that my words to Rob had been left unfinished. The crown is not the only stake I must play in this deadly game, this war of which the very thought drags me down to despair; it is my life. Men of God say that to live without hope is a grievous sin. Then among my many transgressions I am guilty of this also, and I admit it daily to the Almighty Father—*Confiteor Deo omnipotenti ... Peccavi, peccavi, mea culpa, mea culpa, mea maxima culpa* ... It makes me greatly afraid.

II

Castle of Care

Told by George Stanley, Lord Strange

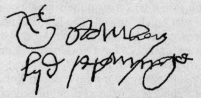

"That dungeon in the dale • that dreadful is of sight,
What may it be to mean • madame I you beseech?"
    "That is the Castle of Care • who-so cometh therein
May curse that he was born • to body or to soul.
Therein dweleth a wight • that Wrong is called,
Father of Falsehood • and founded it himself.
Adam and Eve he egged to ill,
Counselled Cain • to kill his brother,
Judas he fooled • with Jewish silver,
And since, on an elder • hanged him after.
He is destroyer of love • and lies to them all,
That trust in his treasure • betrayeth he soonest."

William Langland, Piers Plowman

In the third week of June, I came to Nottingham to join the King on his arrival from Kenilworth. There I had the briefest of meetings with my father. In his letter he had said that he intended going home for a while, to rest, and that the King had requested my attendance in the royal household in his place.

The great outer courtyard of Nottingham Castle swarmed with servants bearing the Stanley Badge of a gold eagle's claw. Under the close supervision of my

father they were loading chests and coffers onto carts,
trussing canvas bundles with cords, and falling over the
dogs. He bustled to and fro, snapping his fingers at
obsequious menials, with his usual air of the Lord God
ordering the first day of Creation. No one could doubt he
is a great lord—there were enough of his men about to
make me think the King's household was on the move.

He bestowed a paternal kiss on my cheek. "George," he
said, "I'm sorry I am unable to stay longer to enjoy your
company. But affairs—you realize—affairs ..." I wasn't
quite sure of his meaning. "To tell the truth, George," he
went on in a rather irritating undertone, "I can't wait to
get home. I feel a trife unwell. The last few months have
been most wearisome—too much work, distressing
events. It'll be a relief to have nothing more pressing on
my mind than a little hunting in Lathom park. The
sooner I see one of my own huntsmen, in Kendal green,
the happier I shall be. I'm tired of mourning crows." He
gestured vaguely around. Everyone was clad in black. My
father was even more dapper than usual, in black silk, not
a hair of the lavish sable facings on his riding gown out of
place. A grease spot on his doublet will agitate him more
than a bill for a £ 100. He wears well for his age. He's of
medium height, spry and active. For a man of fifty-one,
his figure is trim, a very small potbelly rendered invisible
by a clever tailor. His dark hair is very gray now, but not
too thin, except for the top, which has a bald patch neat
as a tonsured monk's. I've noticed he only removes his
hat when etiquette demands.

"So you leave me to nest with crows," I said, sourly.

He gave me a sharp, reproving look. "My dear son,
things are nothing near as bad as they were. You won't be
overworked. The King has a craze for hawking—spends
more time talking to his falconers than to his lords and
council. You'll be out in Sherwood Forest for days on
end, sitting on the ground to eat your dinner."

"That," I said, "should be pleasant enough." I met my
father's eyes, which are round, brown, and slightly
protuberant. They had a moist, sympathetic look. He was
disposed, as ever, to be conciliatory. Though he
perpetually worries over his health, his only bodily defect

I know of is the long-sightedness of middle age, to aid which he obtained a set of gold-rimmed spectacles from Italy. These, perched upon his nose when reading, elevate him almost to the dignity of a churchman or, as my uncle William put it, "make Tom look like some whoreson bishop, living in hopes of a cardinal's hat!"

As he hadn't mentioned what seemed an important matter, I spoke up myself. "What of Tudor? You expect him to invade?" He looked away.

"Without a doubt, between now and September."

"Father ..." but he was already beckoning to a groom, who led up his horse, a fine, strong animal of the Wirral breed. As a fly alighted, the glossy bay hide twitched; it was groomed so sleek, the blood vessels could be seen pulsing. As he swung himself into the saddle, I tried again. "What will you do?"

He arranged the folds of his gown into comfortable order, while the groom adjusted a stirrup leather. "Hold myself in readiness, of course." He put out a hand and squeezed my shoulder. "Remember, George, you are my son and heir."

As I watched him ride away, raising his hand in farewell, I thought: an odd thing for him to say. The old fox has something on his mind. You might search the breadth of England to find a wilier old fox than my father. Considering the history of his past twenty-five years, one wonders that he has ruled the northwest unchallenged, from his fine houses at Knowsley or Lathom, lord of all the Lancashire plain he surveys and much of its moorland, too.

This departure with a train of baggage carts and servants into his own great territory is dictated by more than reasons of health. The wonder is that King Richard allowed him to go at such a time. He knows my father's reputation, yet has given him leave to hatch whatever plots he may please in the safety of home. No more is demanded than my presence in the household and an understanding that defense of the northwest and Marches of Wales lies in Stanley hands. There is nothing out of the way in this, but I am certain that as the eldest of the Eagle's brood, I am hostage for his good behavior.

This is no surety—he has other sons. Despite a pledge to prevent my stepmother Beaufort from all communication with her son Tudor, letters continue, I am sure, to pass between Lancashire, London, and France. I do not know the full extent of my father's treasonable meddlings or how much is suspected by the King, or, rather, how much he has found out. Sometimes, when confronting Richard, I feel an urge to run a finger under the neckband of my shirt, to still an itching in my neck. I'll admit, I fear him.

My father fears him too, face to face. Though twenty years the younger, Richard is the only man I know who can make my father turn red as a cock's wattles, as if obliged to acknowledge the presence of a despicable or devious thought in his mind. That is painful to him, as it diminishes his self-esteem. At heart he might wish to rid himself of a king he fears: a Tudor stepson, deeply indebted to father Stanley, offers a more reassuring prospect.

As for my uncle William, he swears that he would rather run stark naked in January up Halkyn Mountain in wildest Flintshire than make war on Tudor. Of Richard he muttered, "I'll serve him a breakfast of trouble, such as no subject ever gave a king!" and I've never seen his dark, grim face look grimmer. Apart from wealth he can weigh in gold nobles, for some years he has desired the Earldom of Chester, a prize held tight by the crown for generations. He is as likely to get it from Richard as he is to play football with the moon.

While they sit at home, my father at Lathom, my uncle William at the Deeside fortress of Holt, I am obliged to remain under the eye of the King. Whatever Richard knows, he will not say. He's a strange man; who can tell what currents tug at the deep waters of his mind? Even the direct gaze of those dark, slaty-blue eyes reveals nothing. I felt like a mariner lost between shoals, unable to fathom the depth of his passage. Richard left me puzzled. Like any monarch possessing supreme power, he is in a sense two men. Since I have been thrown more closely into his company, I had discovered a man one would be honored to call a friend; I found myself hoping he thought well of me. But as the King, one fears him, for his strength, his intelligent, thinking mind, and because he is as incorruptible as anyone could be who wields such power. Yet behind these two men lay the black specter of rumor, which he could no more cast off than a sundial can its shadow.

Most disturbing, of course, is the fact that the bastardized King Edward V and Duke of York have not been seen since the late summer of 1483, when they were still in the Garden Tower, under the eye of Robert Brackenbury. Soon after, the King was riding five hundred miles across storm-devastated, quagmire England, dealing with Harry Buckingham's rebellion. No one I spoke to knew if or when the boys had been moved from London. As there was so great a danger of further rebellion focusing on them, it is reasonable to suppose they might have been moved to some secret hiding place. On the other hand, persons who are a political encumbrance might as easily be hidden under ground, sheeted and stiff!

Poor Henry of Lancaster, I remember my father saying, when I was too young to know he spoke with tongue in cheek, had died in the Tower of mere displeasure and melancholy. Yet King Henry's secret execution—or murder, call it what you will—had been followed by a seemly display of his corpse and a decent Christian burial, all done openly in public. Well, I reasoned, if those boys had met a similar fate, why was it not proclaimed, settled, sealed, and buried forever with them? For children, measles or any contagious spotty fevers would have made a good substitute for displeasure and melancholy; they could have been laid out in St. Paul's, like poor Henry. Every time I tried to weigh the pros and cons, my head began to spin with questions to which I'd never get an answer. I could hardly believe that Brackenbury, with his soft Durham voice and amiable manner, could be a party to the murder of children. The King's other intimate friends and councilors I found it impolitic to question, and the King himself is a deep-minded man—no one better at keeping his own secrets.

The mystery nagged at my mind a little, though, and on

my last home-coming had made me shudder. I held up my son, little Tom, to see how he'd grown. He's a beautiful child, with a curly thatch of dark hair, round brown eyes, and rosy skin, as sound and healthy as a russet apple in October. Child murder is a monstrous sin, and I don't believe any penance on earth may absolve it in God's eyes; He will punish it, either in this world or the next.

But it is not good for either one's political or one's personal health to dwell on dangerous secrets. I have to admit, morality in my family is flexible, and I myself have never suffered from the perpetual need to run to the confessional. In all, I am prepared to take the King as I find him, and as he *is* King, I am tolerably content. It remains to be seen if my father will take the same view.

Throughout July, a month of dazzling sunshine, sudden storms, and overcast days of humid, enervating heat, we waited for news of the inevitable invasion by Henry Tudor from France. By the time I had been at Nottingham a full six weeks and July almost ran into August, tempers began to grow a trifle frayed. John of Lincoln, in particular, lost no opportunity to twit me with my father's inconstancy. He and Robert Percy would fall silent on my appearance, suddenly hushed conversations in corners betraying their unease; if they'd been dogs, I'd have seen their hackles rise. Richard himself showed me no hostility; indeed, he went out of his way to make me feel welcome among the small circle of intimates. Often he seemed very withdrawn within himself, his friends perpetually trying to find new diversions to bring him out of brooding silence. He could sometimes be persuaded to shake off these distressful moods by taking part in sport. Before, I'd never thought of him as having either time or inclination for athletic pastimes, but now he seemed intent upon hardening himself, as if visualizing personal combats with giants in the future.

In the court at Nottingham I played many games of tennis with Richard, sometimes singly, sometimes partnering with Lincoln or Percy. This is a game at which I fancy myself adept and one which Richard, as far as I know, has never had much time for. Yet whether we played with the gloved hand or with those newfangled

French "raquets" made of gut stretched on withy frames, I only beat him by a narrow margin, and as he got into practice, increasingly often he beat me. Whatever he lacked in height and reach to command the court, he made up for in speed of movement, and he put the balls over the tasseled rope as hard as anyone I could remember playing against! When I asked him where he had learned to play so well, I received a rather short answer: "In the courts at Westminster, when I was a boy of fourteen, kicking my heels for occupation. I played Dorset, to learn to beat him." Well, Dorset had been acknowledged the best player at King Edward's court. If Richard had beaten him then, out of sheer stubborn antagonism, it was not surprising that even after seventeen years with little practice he played a fast game.

But it was at the more serious sports of a knight-at-arms, that he really astonished me. Lincoln, one evening, half-seriously challenged his uncle to fight with swords, on foot; Richard agreed amiably enough. We all trooped off to the castle tiltyard to watch. After a thundery night the day had been hot and humid, one of the July dog days, when hounds hang out a yard of pink, dripping tongue as they flop about, following patches of shade. St. Swithin's Day I think it was. If we were in for forty days of similar weather, Tudor would probably take advantage of it.

Long evening shadows had crossed the sanded width of the yard, though it remained warm as a summer beach under our shoes. The sky beyond the rim of the jutting castle rock was clear of all cloud, but the distances misty. wheeling in the soft air were multitudes of black, batlike specks—jackdaws coming home to roost. A great twittering and crooning came from the high castle walls, as if all the birds of the air were nesting up there, in cracks and ledges of sun-warmed stone.

We watched the squires arm Lincoln and the King. As they fought with blunted swords, they wore only half-armor—brigandines covered with velvet, breast and backplates, a gauntlet and guard on their right arms, guards on shins and thighs, and neckpieces, the visors of their sallets pulled down over their faces. As Lincoln is a

hand's breadth taller than Richard and, though slim
enough, probably two stones heavier, in addition to the
ten years between their ages, I wondered if he might not
emerge the victor. Bets were laid, about equal on either.
Robert Percy fished out a rose noble, laughed, and
wagered it on his friend the King, saying he'd do the same
if it were himself in Lincoln's place. He should be in a
position to judge, so I followed suit, but venturing only a
couple of groats.

I found myself standing by Captain Salazar, the
Spanish mercenary soldier who has been about the court
for the past year, rather in the manner of a privateer
riding at anchor on a trade route. They call him "Juan *le
petit*," or the lesser, which Englishmen have corrupted
into "little Jack" as a joke, for he is built like a big hairy
ape! He was entering into the spirit of the contest with
glee, tossing up English coins, making it clear that he was
an expert in feats of arms and prepared to offer his advice
freely.

When the slither and clang of sword on sword hit the
walls and sprang back, making the yard echo like an
armorer's workshop, all the birds flew up in an agitated
flock. Salazar voiced his approval in foreign crows of
delight, grinning and displaying a set of horrible teeth
nearly as brown as his skin. Watching Lincoln's efforts,
he said, *No te dispares—poco a poco!*—gently!" The
advice—I suppose not to lay on too hard at first—didn't
work. I began to think it would need a giant to knock
Richard clean off his feet before he gave an inch. If that
lopsided tilt to his shoulders resulted in this, I wouldn't
mind having it myself!

After a while, Richard decided to change his tactics to
attack. He fought with an intent ferocity I'd have thought
more appropriate to a *melee* joined with enemies than to
a practice yard. Lincoln found himself jammed against
the wall, his sword clattering on the ground from a
cracking blow on the wrist. When he pushed up his visor,
he was laughing ruefully between gasps for breath, as if he
had almost expected such an end. Salazar applauded
enthusiastically.

Richard handed his sword to a squire and stood

removing the gauntlet from his right hand, calm as if he had just walked through the door from a stroll in the castle garden. Though the thick, curly hair had been flattened in sticky clusters against his cheek by the sallet's pressure, he breathed more easily than his nephew, who was as I would have been after such an effort—blown. Lincoln turned to me, saying with an underlying, abrasive note of mockery, "Would you care for His Grace my uncle to fight with you now, George? You might have better luck than I, being the second!"

"Thank you! Not tonight." I thought I showed admirable restraint in not answereing rudely, having one eye on the dying light and the other on the King. Richard looked from one to the other of us and gave a little twitch of a smile. "Why don't you two fight, another day? John, I think you might take on more than you bargained for in George." I was secretly pleased at this. Richard has a knack of turning aside sharp words, and his rather soft-toned voice is very persuasive.

Salazar strode up to him and said something I did not catch, obviously a compliment, though Richard, as is his way when flattered, made little response. Then Salazar said, "This 'Enrico the Welsh bastard must take care to say clear of Your Grace in the battle, or else ..." He jerked his thumb explicitly earthward. Richard looked up at him—the Spaniard was a head taller—and gave him one of his fleeting smiles, charming, amused. "Yes," he said, without emphasis, and left it at that.

Eleven days of August were gone when the news came at last. We had begun to worry that it would never come, for a bare month was left before autumn gales began in the Channel and Tudor could not risk an October disaster as he had two years ago. After mid-September he'd have to wait until next spring. Richard said bitterly that such an event would bring himself and the realm to beggary, being not far short of it now, the money swallowed so fast in defense. But Tudor had sailed from the mouth of the Seine with his little fleet to invade England. The winds that favored him perhaps also spun the wheel of Fortune, and who knew what it held for him.

One thing was certain, he would not have the chance to
play the game twice; he staked everything on this August
adventure. I knew, too, that if he had not some certainty
of my family's support, he would not have played the
stake at all.

We had gone to Bestwood, a hunting lodge in
Sherwood Forrest, about five miles north of Nottingham, for a few days hawking. In the forest those days of
high summer seemed as if they could have no end.
Sherwood was greenly peaceful, lapped at last fair
weather warmth, its very quiet lulling one into pushing
the threat of invasion into the farthest corner of the mind.
On the evening of the following day, when the messenger
came from Wales, we were so absorbed in making music,
all thoughts of war banished for a short space, that the
shock hit all the harder. Richard played a lute very
competently, while I have some talent upon the shawm
and hautbois, so together with a few minstrels and boys
of the chapel royal who had come to Bestwood, we
managed very well.

Bestwood is a large house, like a country manor, built
in two stories, with tall, clear-glazed windows that have
been let into the lower floor quite recently. These
windows were now flung wide open, for the night air was
very warm, strong-scented with green bracken. Outside
lay a black gulf where no stars could be seen until you
leaned out and craned upward, for the leaves in the forest
grew so thick. Inside the room, candlelight blazed,
spilling out like a sunburst through the windows, in long,
slanting strips across the grassy lawns around the house.
The King was playing alone an old air by Dufay, the notes
of his lute carrying far out among the trees, I knew the
refrain:

> *Adieu dames, adieu borgois*
> *Adieu celle que tant amoye,*
> *Adieu toute playsante joye...*

A plaintive sound it was, as if the music craved the
company of a human voice, marooned and solitary
within a candlelit island deep in a dark forest. I am rarely
given to melancholy, but this air affected me as a sudden
mist shrouds a traveler; this transient life is full of

farewells.

We failed to hear the soft thud of hoofs on the turf outside until they crunched hastily into the graveled yard. In the corridor, voices gabbled. An usher slipped around the door and whispered to Robert Percy, who nodded, frowning. A man entered, travel-stained and unshaven, flecked with foam from his horse's bit dried white like salt, pale dust thick in the creases of his long boots. As he crossed the room his large-roweled spurs clinked lightly on the tiles.

Richard was sitting in the alcove seat by an open window, bending over a lute, adjusting a new string. His deerhound with the odd name lay flat on her side near him, like a pony indoors. A pair of golden, feather-tailed setters sprawled blissfully asleep, one with its muzzle resting on his foot. A little orange and white spaniel was curled up on the seat beside him. At the messenger's approach, Richard looked up and slowly put down his lute. He must have recognized the man, for he said, in a soft, deliberately emotionless voice, "What news from Wales brings you here, Richard Williams?" I knew him then, Williams, a good Yorkist Welshman, was constable of all the west-coast castles of Pembroke, Marnobier, Cilgerran, Tenby, and Haverfordwest. Richard had appointed him.

He knelt, hat in hand, grimy and furrow-faced with tiredness. The dogs at Richard's feet woke, stretched, yawned, and sat up, pressing against his knees, laying their chins across his thigh, ogling soulfully upward, tails softly sweeping the rushes, hoping for attention. He pulled gently at their silky, hanging ears, waiting for the man to speak.

Williams appeared to take a very deep breath. "Bad, Your Grace. The rebel Tudor landed at Angle in Milford Haven on the seventh day of the month. I could not be holding Pembroke. Four fifths of my garrison laid down their arms and declared for Jasper Tudor, the rebel's uncle, as if he were the prodigal returned and true Earl of Pembroke. Shame it is! They have forgot their allegiance." He paused. The King's face did not move a muscle. He let the man go on.

"The King of France has furnished Owain Tudor's grandson with an army. That is to say, he has opened up his prisons and enlisted every thieving, murdering, frog-fed criminal fit to wield a weapon and some that are not. Nearly three thousand of them, under some mercenary captain called Shanty! Sire, the man must be desperate to take such rabble, even as a gift." The Welshness of his voice came over very strongly as he said, "It is singing they are. All the bards in the valleys are singing and there is the sound of harps in the mountains. He marches under the old standard of Wales, the red dragon of Cadwallader, and at the sight of it, look you, no gate is closed to him. The poets draw men who see a new promised land in Wales, a leader who's a cross between Moses and the hero princes, the sons of Llewellyn. It is Arthur himself come forth from his cave under the green hill that they see. A Bull of Anglesey, they say, the hope of our race!

"Your Grace, this rebel is a pawn of Englishmen who exploit the old cause of Lancaster, seeking to regain their fortunes—red rose favors, they wear. As for angry!—a villainous mob, it is, spreading their poxes through Wales and ready to stab any man in the back. But from a few real soldiers, they'd run, look you, like mice. And their arms! Scythe blades bound on staves with twine, butcher's knives, clubs with rusty nails, sickles to reap legs with—and themselves near naked as makes no odds!"

Sensing that something was wrong, Richard's dogs tried to squirm closer and lick his hands. He put them aside and stood up, beckoning to a page. Williams stood looking down at his own feet, turning his hat in his hands The two men were of a height Williams being one of your little cock-sparrow Welshmen.

Richard said, "I am grateful to you for riding so far with this news. I am glad that he is here at last. I should have guessed that he might return to Wales. He has given Lord Lovell the slip. At least my worst fear was baseless, that he would land at Milford in Southampton Water and march on London before I could stop him." Then to the page, "Fetch Master Kendal, Ralph." He picked up the discarded lute string and wound it around and around his finger in a nervous, jerky way that entirely belied an otherwide calm manner. "Who has joined him?"

"Few, thank God, Your Grace. Rather they allow him to pass unhindered than commit themselves to his cause. Rhys ap Thomas of Dynefor has sworn that the rebel will have to step over his prostrate belly on the ground before he deserts his King. There are a few of Tudor's kin. The rest are wild men from the mountains, poor herdsmen from the valleys, and cattle drovers with beasts to feed the army."

"How fast does he march?"

"Slow Your Grace. When I left, he was heading up the Cleddau valley toward Cardigan. I left Iolo, my brother, to keep watch on him. Stick close to him, boyo, I said. When he has kept his eyes and ears open a while, Iolo Williams will ride to Nottingham."

Richard gave a flicker of a smile at that, though it did not seem able to travel from his mouth to his eyes. "I wish there were more Welshmen as loyal to me as you, Richard Williams," he said.

I was not slow to comprehend the import of the news for myself. That Tudor had chosen Wales, where he had not been expected, meant that between him and the King at Nottingham lay the more northerly Marches— Denbigh and Montgomery—whose defense was the responsibility of my father and Uncle William. Still I do not know what my father intends. The King will summon him to arms with all the rest, but there is no telling how soon cracks in his loyalty will show. I, meanwhile, occupy a very uncomfortable seat.

Late into the night, long after I had retired to be in thoughtful mood and lay tring to get some sleep, shafts of candlelight from the King's room, falling across the grass, brightened my own window. As on some of the bad days last summer, when we had been pounding the length of Yorkshire, Richard and Kendal, his Secretary, worked half the night, so that letters to the Commisioners of Array in the counties were dictated, written, sealed, and ready for the messenger's saddlebags at first daylight.

Our party left for Nottingham that morning. We did

not expect to go back to Bestwood. John of Lincoln rode beside his uncle, now and then trying to prize him out of his long silences, without much success. The dogs ran loose along the broad verges of the road, in grassed-over ruts, sniffing and sneezing as they scattered seeds and scuffed up brick-colored dust or leaving paw prints in mud where puddles still stood. North of the town were several windmills, each on its hillock, stolid as men-at-arms, the white sails turning very slowly in the almost breathless air. On the azure ground of the sky small clouds hung motionless, like painted scutcheons. Below the mills, stretching toward the town wall, lay open fields of barley, whiskery-eared and faintly rustling. A poor crop, patches of it flattened by storms.

Lincoln was saying, "Williams told me he heard that Tudor knelt on the beach where he had landed, with only diving cormorants and the cockle gatherers to watch, and kissed a handful of wet Welsh sand! They recited a psalm, too: *'Judica me Deus et discerne meam causam* ... Judge me, O God, and uphold my cause.' "

The King gave his nephew a somewhat ironic glance. "Against an ungodly nation? And deliver me from the deceitful and unjust man," he said gently, *"amen."* This, from one who had clearly read the psalms of David, emprinted Lincoln's face with a delighted grin.

"Did you kiss the sand at Ravenspur in seventy-one, when you came back with King Edward from Burgundy?" he asked with expectant relish, guessing the tone of his uncle's reply.

His gray horse going delicately over the hard, pebbly road, almost in step with Lincoln's, Richard said, "With a spring tide running on the North Sea in March—one half of me in it and the other being kicked in the ribs by a mad horse dangling from a ship in a sling? And a wind straight from the shores of Greenland? The Lord God wouldn't have heard if I'd shouted psalms the length of Holderness. As for kissing the sand, well, it was down my neck and in my ears already, and far from welcome. I must lack a sense of occasion." Even at this time, Richard is not without his glimpses of humor. As with many a northerner, his wit is unobtrusive—a little while before one appreciates its bite.

Three days later we were still at Nottingham, waiting until further news arrived and, more important, until we had an army to go out and fight with. The King had at first intended to leave for Leiscester and gather his army there, but as no news came, we made no move. Richard seemed curiously reluctant to take any decision, which was most unlike him. On Monday, fifteenth of August, the feast of Our Blessed Lady's Assumption into Heaven, the day in the year most sanctified to Her name, he flatly refused to do anything but properly observe the festival, in the castle chapel.

That morning, at long last, letters came from my father, one directed to the King, one to myself. It appeared that he had left Lathom, but got no further than the manor of Manchester, where he had been striken with the sweating sickness. In bed a week, the man who brought the letters said, sweat pouring off him and weak as a blind kitten. He had been expected up and about again and should be on his way to Derby in a day or two. The Lancashire levies were in the main assembled, but delay unavoidable. The King bit his lip when given this news, but said only, "I am sorry to hear it. I will see him when he has recovered." He didn't look as if he'd hurry to extend a loving welcome, either.

The contents of my own letter afforded me more concern than my father's health. If he really had been taken with the sweat and recovered in ten days, then he must be strong as a Liverpool ferryman. The disease has already taken off young men in a day! His letter was brief: He expected to join the King at Leicester by the appointed time. It was better, he said, that he went there straight from Manchester via Derby, rather than divert to Nottingham. But he asked that I should take leave of the King immediately and meet him at Derby, so that I could be in effective command of his two thousand men, he being still far from well and not yet able to sit a horse. It took no prolonged thought to grasp the meaning of this. He could position himself between Tudor coming from the West and the King, able to join either or remain neutral, without the encumbrance to his conscience of threats to my life! He would not deal honestly even with me, his eldest son and heir. Frankly, I was undecided on what to do. I could ask the King for leave to go to my father, but felt instinctively that it would be refused. Richard can be alarmingly peremptory if he chooses. Also, to make such a request would inevitably make him suspicious of its intent. So for the moment I did nothing.

Later in the day, at dinner, the household sat in formal state, the King at high table. He wore unrelieved black, very rich and elaborate, a long gown of silk damask, figured with pomegranates and lined with black satin, that fell in heavy, gleaming folds, like robes carved from basaltes. Even the collar round his shoulders was of massive lumps of jet set in dull silver, bordered by black pearls and amethysts. I hadn't seen him so deep in mourning since St. Anne's Day, which he had kept in memory of his wife.

Our meal had progressed no more than two courses, when a messenger was brought into the hall, his news too urgent to be kept until after dinner. Dusty, he knelt at the King's feet; one of the men who had been posted to watch the Severn crossings—from Shrewsbury, I heard him say. Into the silence that fell among us all, he spoke words which, in different ways, meant nothing less than disaster both to Richard and myself.

The man's voice forced itself into speech, as if dust still grated in it. His eyes would not face the King's. "Your Grace, the rebels entered Shrewsbury yesterday."

Shrewsbury! But that was the strongest garrison town in the Marches. I watched the King's face turn from pallid to plain sheet white. Slowly he laid down his knife upon the table. The voice went on mercilessly. "The town surrendered—not a stick raised in defense. At first the Bailiff, Thomas Mytton, closed the gates, but within a day or so word came from Sir William Stanley that the town must give the rebel free passage or he'd personally see Mytton hanged.

"They let down the drawbridge on the Welsh side, and this—rebel—marched in over the Severn. Your Grace, I stayed long enough to see him march out over Engish Bridge and take the road for Newport and Stafford. His intention seems either to approach Nottingham or to head down the Watling Street for London."

The squealing noise of wood on tiles as the King's chair skidded back across the floor made us all jump. The dogs shrank under the table. Richard flung himself a few paces away from the messenger. The silk of his gown crackled with the force of the movement.

When he shouted "Shrewsbury!" his voice was loud enough to make us all jump again like plucked harp strings; it ricocheted from the roof. "You tell me he has walked into Shrewsbury unmolested—at the invitation of my Bailiff? He could have been halted in half a dozen places before he ever left Wales. Where was Lord Stanley—laid up with the sweat at Manchester? When I see him at Leicester he'll sweat more, I guarantee! And Sir William Stanley dares use his word to free this bastard Welshman from all hindrance—the word he gave to me. I'll choke his gullet with his treachery!"

We were too stunned by this outburst to do anything but stare at him. Great God Almighty! he had full as much power to frighten men as King Edward when crossed. It was as well, perhaps, that I was given an opportunity to realize it. A subtlety modeled in hard sugar had been set on the table near me, representing the coronation of the Blessed Virgin Mary. I kept my eyes fixed upon the base of this confection, where a scroll picked out in gilt letters read, "Hail Mary Queen of Heaven." All eyes turned on me. Will Catesby gave me a warning look, compressing his mouth. No one dared utter a sound. Even the crouching dogs forbore to whine, but peered anxiously out from behind the tablecloth. Richard's voice lashed us.

"Was there no man in all the Severn towns to lift a finger against him? Men of straw—afraid of burning their tails if they fired the guns. We pay good money to give them guns and they hand them over to my enemies ... Were they afraid of his scrofulous Army! He has no more idea of commanding an army than a troupe of tumblers ..." He laughed, a sound to splinter the air. "I wish the hordes of the Grand Turk were against me, and Prester John, and the Sultan of Syria—for all their armies, I

would show them I am still King! By Christ and His Holy
Mother—I swear that from Lancaster to Shrewsbury,
Holyhead to St. David's I'll tear their castles down, and
parks, forest, and open fields shall take their place. Those
who bear the name of Stanley, knight or squire, will
regret this treachery to their King."

At last, then, he knew his enemy. Sweat broke out on
me as if I'd been suddenly doused, though I sat frozen,
hoping to escape notice. In vain, for the King swung
round on me, his hand, white-knuckled, clenched on the
hilt of the dagger at his belt, as if to withold it from use.
The barely contained violence in his voice made me draw
back in my seat. "Write," he said, and the word had the
sound of a slap in the face, "to your noble father. Tell him
what I have said. That I will see his brother's castle at
Holt fall in ashes in the river Dee before the year is out if
he dares break his oath to me." With that, he walked
swiftly from the room, the door slamming to behind him
with a crash to set the knives jittering on the table. One by
one the dogs went to the door, whimpering and
scratching at the jamb until someone let them out to run
after him.

There was nothing for it but to finish our dinner; I
cannot remember ever having less appetite. Richard had
disappeared somewhere within the castle, none daring to
follow him; no orders had been given for my detention,
though several, I'm sure, were itching to give them. As for
me, the one thought in my mind was to escape from
Nottingham before the situation grew worse. Once my
father knew the tenor of Richard's mind, he might feel
driven to declare outright for Tudor. Richard could well
seal his own fate by threats to our family. Given a chance,
he'd break my father's power, and that of others like him,
forever. I honestly admit I'd see him dead before I gave
him that chance. Kings may turn their anger against
overmighty subjects, but an overmighty King will ruin us
all!

My effort to abscond from Nottingham proved a
dismal failure. To be brief, I took myself off to my own
apartments as fast as was discreet, changed gear with my
father's servant who had brought the letters earlier in the

simply as carving a piecrust. What he had said was an admission as much of my own feelings as his. Yet it seemed strange, to feel Richard, who had become a battle hero when he was very young, shaking and afraid as any green, waged man. With good reason—ordinary men die in battle tossed aside like winnowed wheat, but a king is a coveted prize for which every man jack with a weapon in his hand plays. And Christ help us, our enemies played with loaded dice.

These gripings of battle panic had the inevitable effect on my bowels. It takes almost everyone like that, before hand. We went our separate ways into the dark bushes, weak-kneed, insides somersaulting in alarm. When we emerged, I comforted myself that the waiting would be over soon, and our fears slaked in the turmoil of fighting.

As if to challenge our thoughts, the restive, angry squeal of a horse at odds with its neighbor carried across the camp, clear as a trumpet call over the sea. We both looked up at the sky. Due east a thin line of greenish gray had sneaked into the horizon, revealing the black edge of earth. Our *dies irae* was upon us already.

"It's time to arm," Richard said. "We must be on the move by five." I knelt again then and let my hands rest between his, as I had done in homage when he was crowned. He raised me up and embraced me like a brother, kissing me on both cheeks and drawing a Cross on my brow with his finger. He'd stopped trembling now, was steady-handed. "God keep you, Francis," he said.

I was much moved by this gesture of affection and returned it, kissing my friend's face and signing the Cross on his whole body, brow to breast, shoulder to shoulder, to protect him. "God keep you safe, Richard," I murmured. "God keep Your Grace."

We walked back together, in silence.

I entered the stuffy closeness of the tent with him, woke the squires, who when they had shuffled out of sleep moved about in a dither of nervous apprehension. It was their first battle. Apart from the few Border raids I had ridden and a grisly memory of the aftermath of Barnet, it was my first too.

I began to eat some bread, but my mouth was dry and

swallowing difficult, like trying to chew a dried-out bath sponge. I managed some, but not much, and drank a pint of ale washing down the mouthfulls. His squires tried to persuade the King to take some breakfast, but he refused to eat. This worried me; it was unwise to go without food before long hours in the blazing sun, and for days he'd not eaten enough to keep a fly alive. He drank the cooled ale they offered and after he'd been shaved, let them arm him.

Stripped quite naked, he stood for them within the circle of lamplight. It struck me that though his face had aged too harshly, he still had the body of a very young man, almost boyishly narrow and smooth, the skin milk-pale. The bones showed badly under it, standing out on his chest and back, especially on the shoulder that was slightly malformed from an old injury. He was well-muscled though, and I wouldn't fancy trying my strength against him, having been bettered too often. There weren't many men past thirty who would today wear armor made for them at eighteen; if anything, it would be slack on him now.

Last night the steel had been sanded and burnished glass-shiny, yet still showed scratches like claw marks from the battering it had taken at Tewkesbury field. It was the finest Nuremberg armorer's work, very plain, except for a narrow border of damascening on the larger plates of gold suns and roses; the full weight amounted to about seventy-five pounds.

The body squires did not really need supervising, though they were fumbling a little this morning. I stayed, as I felt it a duty of the King's Chamberlain to see him made ready for war. They laced him into the thickly quilted arming doublet of coarse cloth, the smooth, satin-lined side directly against his skin. It was sewn with link mail patches in all places vulnerable between plates and cut with holes to let air through, which made precious little difference when the sun on steel fairly cooked you, like an egg on a griddle.

I saw the younger squire glance upward as he pulled points tight so that the clothing fitted snugly. If it did not, it could ruckle under armor and become excruciating discomfort. Richard had his eyes shut. The boy looked scared. He went on tying points: the plates now, each one onto the shoes, the blanket-cloth padding to prevent the joints pinching at knees and ankles. Plate by plate they built him up; the golden eyes of the lamps reflected on each fluted surface, their light shivering and running like oil as he moved or breathed. They had got as far as the buckles on breast and backplates, when the King swayed a little as he stood, as a sapling bends before a gust of wind.

The boy knelt and clutched at one of the lax hands and kissed it, in a-fervor of anxiety. I stepped forward. Richard opened his eyes, looking startled; I think he had almost fallen asleep on his feet. He must be close that half-world, where one is so tired that the body screams for sleep and the mind empties itself even of recognition of the hour or where one stands.

"What is it?" he said. "Francis?" He disengaged his hand.

The distressed young face gazed up at him. "If only Your Grace would eat—I beg you—it will be such a long day."

"I cannot. Tom—don't fuss me." His mouth twitched briefly into something resembling a smile. "The day will pass very quickly. At the end of it Lord Lovell and I will see that we eat, drink, and fear war no more."

"But Your Grace looks so ... Sire, you rock on your feet as if ..."

"I'm tired, nothing more. I've not slept. It harms no one. Don't look so worried." Richard looked at me wryly and ran his hands through his hair in an exasperated way, until a mass of dark curls stood out all over his head. He was edgy with tension.

I said, "It's as the King says, Tom. I've not slept much either, but we'll live through another day."

Richard stretched his arms above his head suddenly, irritated, and stifled a yawn. "For God's sake, boy, don't look at me like that. One would think I'd kicked you."

Then he sighed, relenting, and turned the boy's face up, so the light fell upon it, his hand hard under the chin. Fear was written all over it. He was about seventeen, and I

knew he'd come to Middleham when he was seven, a
Metcalfe from Askrigg. For all his training, he had never
seen men mangled and dying. It was useless to allow him
to dwell on his fear, almost a cruelty to reveal it. Richard
snapped his fingers sharply.

"Come," he said, "arm me. We waste time. You may
bear my helm and stay near me today if you wish.
Quickly, now ... Francis, go and get yourself armed,
there's no need for you to stay."

I left rather hastily and soon had my squires moving so
fast that we had no chance to brood on the coming battle.
When I was ready, daylight had almost come outside. I
went back to the King's tent, passing through the press of
his waiting captains, exchanging greetings. Richard was
preparing to leave. The squire tested the free running of
his sword through the steel ring in which it hung, the
blade naked and ready for use.

"They're waiting outside," I said. "There's been some
babble about priests; some of them think you should hear
Mass."

"No." He shut his lips tight. He appeared to have
nothing more to say. He walked over to the little altar in
the corner—a small table with a triple folding painting of
Our Lord's Crucifixion, flanked by two lit candles—and
knelt in front of it. He bent his head a moment, as if
asking absolution for his sins, though as far as I could see,
his lips did not move in prayer. In his steel, he looked a
little frightening, a weapon of war in himself; his spurs
jingled and the sword had clanked against his knee when
he walked. When he got up, I saw that a little ivory image
of St. Christopher was set on the table; we both gave it a
last glance, to keep us safe from a violent death that day.

Then he went out. At their first sight of him, a murmur
of shock traveled around the captains. John Kendal
stepped forward. In his armor he looked desperately
uncomfortable. He stared in dismay at Richard's face.
"Your Grace," he said, "are you sick? You look fit for
nothing, let alone a battle. Man, you're a ghost, all
parceled up in steel plate. You'll melt away in sunlight!"
Poor Kendal, he was far too tense in his own unfamiliar
guise to restrain his words.

It was true, though. Inside, in the lamp glow, I'd not realized fully how dreadful Richard looked. In the dawn light his face was the color of wood ash in a dead hearth. It had been haggard for many months, but now it was ghastly. His eyes had sunk deep into blackened sockets. He looked at us as if from a great distance.

"I'm no ghost, John." Even his voice sounded gray. "I never sleep well." He rubbed his hand over his face and eyes abruptly, as if to wipe away the tiredness, characteristically trying to shrug off their concern. "Last night I had time to think." The words were so low, so beaten, we had to strain to hear. "I must be honest with you, my lords and friends. I can see no future for this realm but an unhappy time of trouble and change. If this unknown Welshman wins the field today, it will be by treachery, and he will rule as a tyrant, by fear, out of his own fear. Mercy will be dead, as it will if the victory is mine. I have reached the end of my patience with treason. I'll stamp it out, by taking the heads of half the noble blood in England, if necessary. Justice I cannot forget, but mercy—no—even I will not be bitten twice.

"If the battle is lost, then I will not retreat. For me, this day will be the end of war, or of life." These terrible words were rendered more bitter by the gentleness of their utterance.

After an appalled silence, a concerted jabber of protest rose up, in which a voice said, "Why are there no priests attending Your Grace? Will you go into battle unhouseled?"

Richard replied calmly, "There are no priests on my instructions. If God regards my cause with favor, then He will absolve me without the aid of Holy Church; if not, to touch His sacred Body and Blood would be a blasphemy." He spoke as if this must be immediately comprehensible to all, oblivious of the dropping jaws and shocked mutterings. I knew he'd left Dr. Roby, his confessor, and his chaplains in Leicester town to stay in the house of Gray Friars. Even so, the bleakness of this reasoning chilled me.

It's my belief he thought that the determination to finish with life in the event of defeat had put him in a state

of mortal sin. Thus he would not claim the comfort of the
Blessed Sacrament. Last night my hand had felt his fear,
the slippery cold sweat on his skin, the mute trembling;
he'd been afraid for his soul, that it might be condemned
to the everlasting death, forsaken by God for all eternity,
and severed from the company of the souls he had loved.
Lord Jesus, I thought, do not let him suffer this. Some of
the others tried to make me plead with him, to alter his
mind. I would not. What could we do, that Our Savior
Jesus Christ would not do out of His infinite mercy and
forgiveness? I let him alone.

A groom who'd been walking White Surrey around in
circles led him up. The horse was lightly armored, his
white ears and nose projecting from the spiked chamfrom
like a metal-disguised unicorn. The blinkered eyes knew
his master, and pink, whiskery lips nuzzled the familiar
hand hopefully. Amazingly, Richard had remembered to
bring him a little apple, which he champed, tossing his
great head and snorting with wet and noisy affection.

The King had mounted and gathered up the gilded
leather reins, when I saw the Metcalfe squire carrying the
helmet with the coronet of gold and gems circling it like a
nimbus. I held White Surrey's bridle for a moment and
said quietly, so the others should not hear, "You'll not
wear that crown in the fighting? Richard, for God's
sake—every whoreson Welsh archer will pick you out as
soon as they're in bowshot. Don't take more risk than you
need."

I thought Richard almost smiled, though it was hard to
be certain, as his mouth was partly hidden by the steel
neckpiece that covered his chin. "Francis," he said, "that
way I'm certain of dying a crowned king. They'll not take
it while I live." The archangel Michael himself, with his
flaming sword, could not have turned him from his
resolve. I acknowledged defeat.

We marched north, back past the village of Stapleton.
The air slid by our faces, very cool, unlike the afternoon
before, and I breathed deep of it while I had the chance.
The sky had a fresh-scoured look, clear and pinkish as the
sun came up from a horizon of mackerel cloud on the
army's right hand. A knee-deep mist wreathed over the

low-lying ground.

The King rode ahead of his heralds and trumpeters, the standards raised over their heads. Priests bore a great jeweled Cross before us and banners of the Holy Trinity, St. George, and St. Cuthbert of Durham—this last to rally the northern men. The horses were fresh and jostled each other, squealing. My Lyard must have been fed too many beans, for he eyed every rising lark and scuttering coney as coyly as a virgin, his ears flipping back and forth and his quarters bunching up angrily, as if I were a gadly on his back.

Norfolk's army had drawn up across the track, waiting. John Howard rode forward on his roan horse, bright with scarlet trappings, to greet the King. He took one look at Richard's face, opened his mouth to remark, as Kendal had, but must have decided against comment. The strained silence of the household knights could have done nothing to dispel his unease. I noticed his son Thomas glance around with his shrewd, dark eyes, calculate the situation, and elect to make the best of it. It was reassuring to see their long, leathery Howard faces, undisturbed as a mud flat by a Suffolk river.

The great host moved on through another cluster of cottages, past a little squat church, and the place was deathly silent. The tramp of feet and hoofs, the jingling creak of harness and clang of arms intruded brutally upon its peace. No dogs barked, even the pigs in the street were gone. There were no roosters to crow in the morning; they had all been stuffed into baskets and taken away by the villagers, who had bolted like rabbits down a burrow. Uncut corn stood in half-harvested fields, until trodden flat as rushes by the advancing army. Eight thousand men made a brave show. By now the sun had climbed out of early cloud to shine slantwise upon the ridge of rising ground along which we marched. You could see clearly across Redmore plain to where, on the flat ground to the west, the enemy gathered. They would approach us around the north side of the marsh that lay between us.

Norfolk was saying, "We have the hill. Oxford will have to kick his hung-over hirelings in their backsides this morning."

Richard nodded, staring into the distance. The light was making him frown again. "Don't understimate Oxford, Jack. If anyone can flog those hirelings into semblance of an army, he will."

On the northwest slope of the rise called Ambion Hill, Norfolk halted his men. They stretched out in a curve—not a deep line, but a long one, designed to act upon the enemy attack like the pincers of a crab, crushing it in upon itself. On either flank stood the guns: serpentines chained together in rows, some brought from Warwick Castle, some from Nottingham, and the great bronze gun I'd heard christened for the occasion by the northerners, out of very vulgar affection, "Owd Dick"! Archers were set in clumps along the front of the line, linked by pikemen and knots of handgunners. They were mostly fair, sturdy men, of the three eastern counties, from Colchester to Lynn. Between the greasy collars of leather jacks and helmets, necks and faces wore a sun-boiled look, angry against the scarlet Howard livery.

A stubble-faced sergeant chivvied his men. "Now, you whoresons," he bawled. "See those standards? Oxford arms. You're going down there, you ugly brutes, to find the lord bearing those arms. You'll lay him on his back—with Jesus' help—and slice him fine as my mother does bacon!" And they all crossed themselves as if facing the Turk and not a mere Essex rebel.

When the King was satisfied with the disposal of his troops, he left Norfolk. By this time Northumberland and his three thousand men should have joined us on the ridge. There was no one in sight. No sound of pipers rent the air. Only in the distance, a mile or so back, were there signs of movement, curls of smoke, and wink of metal.

I strained to see, shifting in my saddle; the arming doublet stuck to me already. "What in God's name is Henry Percy doing?" I said to Dick Ratcliffe. "The sluggard's not doused his campfires yet."

Ratcliffe looked. "If he's doing what I think—nowt," he said slowly. "We're close on three thousand lads short. All the best men from Anwick and Barney Castle to Humberside short. If they find out what he's at ...

Dickon's got two knives drawn behind his back, then."

"Stanley?"

"Aye."

I gave him a sick look and turned to Richard. If anything, he looked worse than before, in the visor's shadow. He was frowning and biting his lip, while the horse leaned against the bit, fretting and circling. He dismounted, and a groom took the reins.

Two heralds went speeding away, bearing a few curt words, summons to our dilatory Northumberland and to Lord Stanley, who stood waiting a mile or so to the south. In the northwest the horsemen of Sir William Stanley were stationed.

Suddenly someone yelled and pointed. "They're coming! Moving up there, on the right of the marsh."

We walked forward to the highest point of the hill, to watch. As they came closer, the devices on their banner became clearer: the two badges of De Vere, Earl of Oxford, a silver star, not seen in England since the fog-bound chaos of Barnet, and the blue boar; the black Welsh-mountain ravens of Rhys ap Thomas; Sir John Savage's silver unicorn; and in front of them all, the great dragon standard of the Welsh princes, scarlet upon white and green. A dragon with claws, forked tongue, and tail; it called to mind the fiery dragon I'd seen so often in the Alpha and Omega east window of St. Peter's at York that made a gift of a scepter to the Hydra-headed beast. Oxford had the vaguard. Tudor himself must be somewhere in the center, nursemaided by his uncle Jasper, so-called Earl of Pembroke, who'd fought half a dozen battles for Lancaster and lost every one! The men sang as they marched, you could hear it in bursts and snatches— no English words, nor French; it was the Welsh who were singing, deep over the rattle of the drums.

Ratcliffe said, between his teeth, "They'll soon shut that caterwauling. Jack Howard's red-faced crew'll stuff it down their leekguzzling throats with ten feet of English pike behind it!" It was stirring, though, the singing; they put their hearts into it.

Whey they were past the marsh, Norfolk gave his signal. The cannon went off with a crack fit for the Day of

Judgement. The ground under our feet shuddered as if it were the graves about to render up their dead. Horses jerked their heads, whinnying in answer to the guns. In the blunt-ended, wedge-shaped mass of the enemy, the rake of shot opened little holes that close again as if they had never been. It must have been like marching over a butcher's slab. Their own guns returned the fire in good measure.

All of a sudden the air quivered with a most magnificent sound. To men brought up on tales of Agincourt, as Dickon and I had been, it was the most exciting sound in all the world. The archers had losed their first flight—an enormous, concerted *plunk!* loud as hitting a huge drum with a hammer, followed by a thrumming whistle. The arrows passed across the sky in a dark cloud as a flock of rooks homing. Arrows came back, flight for flight. Good bowmen had been found to put in the enemy's front rank—Cheshire men most likely, from Stanley country—too many of them for comfort. I knew very well who had put them there—William Stanley. Pray God someone put a clothyard shaft through his treacherous gut!

A blare of trumpets meant that Norfolk had sounded the advance. The vanguard of the King's army began to move forward, in tight-knit order, very disciplined. They went down the slope at a trot, shouting for Norfolk, for Howard, and for King Richard; it drowned even the Welsh singing. As the armies clashed, their din swept back up the slope and half deafened me.

It was not long before Norfolk's line began to sag a little in the middle, buckling back up the slope. Oxford's tactic of throwing every man he had hard against our center was having some success. Norfolk was outnumbered. Richard began to move men quickly in blocks of a few hundred at a time, to bolster the line. Our force on the hill dwindles, and there was still no sign of Northumberland.

I began to taste salt trickling off my upper lip. The sun burned one side of my head through the helmet; its dazzle broke in the open visor. The day was warming up already and we'd not been fighting half an hour. Horses were stamping and tossing, maddened by flies that had invaded the hill to torment men and beasts, worse than all the plagues of Egypt. A brown fog of dust hazed the air. Down there in the battle, the confusion grew. Worse, a worm of fear had begun to slide like poison through our reserve of men on the hill. It was becoming obvious to even the most dim-witted yokel shoving a pike that Northumberland would betray the King. That, and the thought of the four thousand fresh troops waiting only for orders from the Stanley brothers, made my mouth feel as though it were stuffed with sawdust. I pushed through the press of household knights who stood near Richard.

When he saw me, he said, "They don't move a pike's length either way. Our men are less, but better. If I can put some heart into them, we should be able to force Oxford back.

"My lord Lovell will remain here in command—if Northumberland comes, then he knows how to deal with him."

If! Well, I laid no bets on my chance to relieve him of his duties.

Richard was riding around his men, giving last minute orders, when the heralds came back, almost upon one another's heels. The replies from Lord Stanley and Northumberland were alike to the point where grimness verges upon farce. Each supplied ample evidence that the other's actions were treacherous, so both intended to keep a close guard on the other's inactivity! It could have been a dull child repeating his brother's lesson. Seven thousand men stood idle, no more than a mile away and within our sight. Word had only to gain a hold in Norfolk's army for a sickle of panic to slice through it; they'd run fast as rabbits caught in the last swathe of harvest.

Richard swore an oath that was doubly shocking, coming from him. Truly, I'd never seen him so savage. "I'll have George Stanley beheaded—now!—any one of you can do it—over the shafts of a wagon if you like. Stanley may have other sons, but now he'll be one less. Do it, I say!—before the rest of my army turns its coat!"

With that he slammed down his visor, raised his arm in

signal, and dug spurs into White Surrey's sides. The horse threw up his head angrily and leaped down the slope in erratic, stiff-legged bounds. Men under the Lords Scrope, Ferrers, Clifton, and Zouche poured after him, yelling. Norfolk's army took up the cheer and surged to the attack again, bellowing the King's name.

I'd never seen anything like it. The men fought with new heart. As if he were a giant reaching out his arms across their backs to block them from any retreat, Richard held his army together. He was everywhere, the sun glancing on his crown clear as a torch flame to follow. The men could only move forward, for the fear of him harrying their backs was as great as their fear of the enemy in front. Up and down the twisting *melee* of a line he went, like a galley master between ranks of toiling slaves. Wherever the enemy advanced thickest, he hacked a way among them and his men followed—they'd have followed him into Hell mouth itself.

But it was futile, only a prolonging of the agony. Tudor was getting reinforcements from somewhere; it could only be from William Stanley, if not Lord Thomas, too, by now. Watching, I grew frantic to join the fight— anything to tilt the scales in our favor, to stop the killing that looked as if it would become a massacre before we were done. The armies were flagging with heat, straining in a dogged wrestler's clinch, as they writhed over the same bloody yardage of earth. It was hard to see who was dead and who still fighting. Richard must have sensed how bad things were, for he came out of the battle suddenly, riding fast; a group of household knights followed him. Men bundled out an inert body behind them.

Beside me someone was panting, "Norfolk—it's Norfolk—dead—an unlucky shot—the King's been told. He's out of his mind if he thinks he'll hold them without more men. We'll all be butchered where we stand if he won't withdraw. My lord Surrey's in dire straits down there. Where's Northumberland? God damn the whoreson, treacherous, son of a bitch ... We're beaten— the King must know it...."

I had no time to think on this new disaster. White

Surrey's distended, blowing nostrils loomed in my face, and I dodged out of the way of his great gory platters of hoofs. There was blood all over his mouth—he'd savaged men as a dog does. Red-stained froth splattered my armor as he ground furiously at the bit. He was still mad from the battle, and the reins were tight enough to break his jaw. Even so, it could be dangerous to get too near.

Richard was wrenching off his helmet, careless of straying arrows. He gasped for air, shaking out the sodden hair from his neck, so that dripping tails stuck to his face. He flung his right arm up against his forehead for a moment, trying to stop sweat running into his eyes, but it slid down faster than rain water off a window. His arm looked as if it had been dipped in crimson and smeared his face and hair with blood not his own. It had run right up to his shoulder and down his side, was even dribbling over the knee of his armor. The silk tabard he wore, blazoned with the arms of England, hung off him in tatters. He had become a machine for killing, driving himself beyond exhaustion, comprehending nothing but violence.

I'd never felt so afraid in all my life. If we could not get Richard away soon, the battle would become a shambles, and he was certain to kill himself in the middle of it.

Even now, he could scarcely speak, his throat seared by shouting and his lower lip cracked and bitten until it oozed blood. Between the rending effort of drawing breaths, he said to a squire, "Fetch me a drink—water—anything—the sun's so hot."

There were two of us hanging on to White Surrey's bridle, as the horse heaved and trembled, one on either side, myself and the Spanish captain, Salazar. Richard stared down at us as if we were strangers. Christ have mercy! I thought: He's blind, doesn't know me. The blue eyes had turned black, dilating into the frantic, glazed look of a foundered horse.

Salazar pushed up his visor, coughing as the dust rolled up and became gritty mud on our faces. His hard voice rose in a shout. He, the Spanish Hector, who had fought the Swiss, urged retreat.

"Your Grace—more you cannot do! *Madre de Dios,*

this army would have been fled an hour ago ... Never have
I seen one man hold together so many lacking in heart.
They fear treason.

"Sire, you cannot win today. It is not the end—we will
have another battle. Even such a *capitan* as yourself
cannot turn this tide. See—there are fresh horses—fly
now! There is no disgrace, no man can say you lack
cojones!"

The King shook his head, and the sweat drops
showered off him, feel on my hand. I hated seeing him
reduced to such stubborn, anguished desperation. He
knew as well as we that he was beaten.

"God forbid, Salazar," he said, in a strained and
breaking voice. "I will not budge a foot. I'll die King of
England!" He clutched his helmet with the crown as if it
were the Holy Rood to strengthen him. I thought he was
very near fainting.

"*Mierda!*" Salazar burst out. "He will not listen. Will
you take death as a lover?" He slipped into a torrent of
Spanish, by the sound of it complaining to all the saints of
Castile.

Then the squire came back with a flask filled from the
spring on the hillside. He had to push it into the King's
hand. Richard drank as if he could not have enough. He
leaned back to tip the last of it over his head. When he
staightened, water rolled down his face onto the hot
metal shoulder plates, washing freakish stripes through
the dirt. His hair was wet as a water spaniel's. One would
think he'd drunk potent wine, from the way he reeled in
the saddle.

Within my head I gibbered a prayer to God, half
blaspheming: "O Lord God, to whom all things are
possible, take away this cup from him—do not let him
throw away life ... take his courage, weaken this resolve to
die ..." I'd say all the Fifteen Glorious Mysteries every day
for the rest of my life; I'd go on pilgrimage to Walsingham
barefoot in a hair shirt, shave my head, anything ... I
pleaded for intercession. it was intolerably hot, the sun
flayed us. I stood trembling, sick with dread, when one of
the scouts we had sent out came hurtling from his horse to
the King's side.

"Sire, I've found him!" he yelled, "Tudor! He's behind the battle, on the right-hand side, where the ground is flat—under the dragon—on a bay horse. There's not more than a couple of hundred left with him. Men kneel to him ..."

I cursed at that, but Richard did not heed the words. The change in him astounded me. His face was flushed, his smile radiant. "You'll come with me." It was a statement rather than a question and as such needed no answer. I followed wordlessly as he rode back to the remnant of household and northern men on the hill.

His voice was hoarse when he spoke to them, but very clear. "We have a chance to end this bloodshed quickly. Tudor stands behind the battle poorly defended. A hundred men, a sudden attack, could scatter them. You see the terrain; on our right, Sir William Stanley waits with two thousand horsemen. The hazard is great—weighted against us. God give me strength—I will try to kill Tudor myself. Who will come with me?"

They stared at him for a moment, in dead silence, then began to step forward. First Robert Percy, Dick Ratcliffe, John Kendal, who'd never borne arms in his life, Robert Brackenbury, Ralph Assheton, and other men from the north parts: Harrington, Middleton, Pilkington, Markinfield, Metcalfe, Broughton, Harbottle, Mauleverer, Martin of the Sea from Holderness, Ogle, Dacre, Tempest, and Heron—oh, dozens of others, many names from our old reiving days on the border. They amounted to well over a hundred.

The horses were brought up. Men began to mount, adjusting visors and gauntlets. Squires checked the girths. Will Catesby came up to me. The Speaker of the House of Commons looked green as the grass, his habitual air of competence and urbanity vanished, hair lank and face grimy. He was sweating as much as any of us.

"Where is he?" he said.

"Hiding at the back, on the right of the battle."

"You mean we'd have to ride out there under the very nose of William Stanley who is a proclaimed traitor? It's an open invitation for him to cut you all into as many

pieces as there are cards in a pack. Is the King stark raving
mad? He'll be fighting an army alone if they move. How
can this succeed? Francis, you must stop him."

Already on my horse, I wished Catesby would stop
bleating.

"No. I couldn't, even if I wanted to. We have speed,
surprise on our side. Have you ever seen Richard use an
ax?"

"He can't wear it. Not that crown. They'll murder
him."

"If they can get near. You stop him." I was barely
heeding.

Catesby tried.

He turned up at my stirrup again, shaking like a palsied
old crone, his hard, handsome face fluid with fear, ready
to dissolve and run away off his bones. "He looked at me
as if I were crazy, not he. Just shook his head. Francis,
he's weeping; I don't think he could see me properly, for
tears. He can't speak for weeping—and bloody as a
butcher. Jesu! he *is* mad!"

I could have wept too. The unquestioning devotion of
the household moved me beyond anything I had ever
experienced. Each man might have handed Richard a
tally stick with the pledge written on it: a life, offered in
love and duty.

Poor Will; Lyard's rump pushed him aside as I
pricked in my spurs and moved with the others. I did not
see him again. We rode in double rank, Richard a few
yards out in front. I kept as close to him as possible.
White Surrey was pulling against his left arm like an ox
team, sidling and snorting down the slope as if a silly colt
again and daisy-fresh. Richard's right hand grasped a
lance, upright in its rest. That stained, short-handled ax
hung from the saddlebow, a spare one and a mace in the
other side. He wore a sword and a long dagger. He'd kill
most men with the ax; with his strength and skill behind
it, the blade could shear through steel plate and bone
easily as a razor cutting air. Cornered, Tudor would have
no defense ... one blow ... Jesu! we'd have such a victory. I
dared not think. I peered ahead through my visor slit.

Looking at Richard, I was dazzled. The sun struck full

on his armor, so it shone bright rayed as a burning glass.
We followed a faceless, shimmering man of steel, his head
ringed with fire. He was alight, a flame to consume his
enemies utterly. The pennoned points of our lances
swiftly crossed my narrowed vision, high above our
heads. The sky was bright, jewel-enamel blue.

Ave Maria, gratia plena ... I wanted to shout, to call on
the saints for protection. But we rode in silence, with no
trumpets, no war yells, to take them unawares. I dug in
spurs, and we were trotting, then cantering, then broke
into a pounding gallop, going as hard as we could flog the
armored horses. That in itself was lunacy on the iron,
fissured ground, but there was no time to fear falls. It
was all I could do to breathe; dust filled the stifling
confines of my helmet, coating lips and tongue, and a face
on fire behind the metal visor.

Then came the first trememdous crash. Richard had hit
whatever wall of men and weapons had packed itself as a
bodyguard before Tudor. He'd spurred White Surrey to a
bolting frenzy, and the impact of the charge buried him
deep in a mass of soldiery. My own lance crashed and
splintered on them, jerked me backward in the saddle.
Men seethed under our feet, screeching. I rode over them,
felt Lyard Gloucester treading them down with his hoofs,
the ring of metal under his shoes, his lurching slide on
squashy, giving things. I killed a foot soldier by ramming
my sword point in his neck as he turned to take a swipe at
me with a poleax. His blood fountained out astonishing-
ly, like a jet of wine from a broached barrel. Blows landed
and glanced off my plate, but I never·felt the bruises.

The dragon standard loomed in my bleared vision,
with Richard's crown right in front of it. We were so near!
I saw his ax smash down and split a helmeted head so
neatly it flopped apart in halves on either shoulder, red
and pink inside, and juicy as a pomegranate. It must have
been the standard-bearer, for the pole toppled and
splintered over, and a billow of white and green silk fell
rending under White Surrey's hoofs. The dragon was
gone.

We were so near! I could see Tudor, a visored figure on
a big bay that reared up and trampled around as he

dragged on the reins. A huge man on an elephant of a
horse moved to defend him, swinging a two-handed
sword. Dear Christ! only one man in England could be
that big—Sir John Cheney—overtopping King Edward
in his hose! And Richard rode straight at him. The man
was more than twice this weight. A match so uneven, so
terrifying, I all but covered my eyes. It was hard to tell
what happened, it followed so quick. Richard dropped
the reins at the last minute as Cheney's sword lifted and
used both hands on his ax. He hit that vast expanse of
breastplate awkwardly, being so close, but the giant went
down like a plucked weed, his bulk pulling the horse over
him. A broad Dales voice was bawling, right by my ear:
"Ding him Dick! Gaw' lad—ding 'im!"

Tudor dropped back when Cheney fell. It would have
taken a rash dragon to stand firm against the very figure
of St. George. Now he'd glimpsed his enemy, Richard
hacked his way ahead; none of us could get near him. A
man lunged with a bill that hit him and slid off, drew back
for a second jab—too close—his ax flashed in a
downward, slicing arc. The man's forearms were severed
instantly.

Robert Percy, lunatic-sounding, was hauling on my
arm and yelling: "Stanley—Stanley—Stanley!" I knew
what it meant. We both tried to cut through to Richard's
side. I had to reach him, either to help him kill Tudor or
to drag him away before Stanley killed us all. I lost Rob; I
think his horse fell with him.

I was within a few lengths of White Surrey's quarters
when Lyard checked, lurched, and halted, dangling a
forehoof, whinnying in fear. Beside myself, I tore his silver
flanks with spurs, but he could only hobble. On a broken-
legged horse I had no chance. I shouted to Richard to
warn him, shouted until my lungs cracked open, but the
din of battle smothered every syllable. He could not hear.
I threw myself off the horse and tried to struggle toward
him on foot, but he had gone too far ahead.

Then the wave of the charge broke. Nearly two
thousand horsemen, Sir William Stanley had, and they
hit us with the force of a siege ram. We were scattered like
chaff, our horses swept off their feet by a boiling surf of

red-coated men. They closed around Richard. I couldn't
see him anymore. I fought like a madman, until the world
turned dark. The last thing I remember was grabbing
someone—I think I'd fallen on my knees by then—I was
gasping,choking, my lungs threatened to burst one each
fiery breath; sweat blinded me, ran into my mouth. I did
not see my friends die. They were slaughtered like
bullocks. By some miracle, I was not.

But I heard Richard die. In the midst of all those howls
of victory, through the roaring in my ears, I heard it. The
memory will never leave me, until I die too. He cried out
when they took his life. His cries, of treason, held such
anguish ... I grow faint every time that sound comes to
me, it comes so clearly.

I shall never know with certainty how I got away from
Redmore. I think some unknown rescuer threw me up on
a riderless horse. It probably bolted with me; I was useless
as a dummy in the saddle. I cried like a child.

So it ended, the brief moment of glory, victory slipped
through our hands. At the end, Richard knew he was
betrayed, knew only failure, despair, and death. As God
is my judge, I'd have given my life to save him, if it had
been possible. Perhaps it would have been better if I'd
thrown it away and died with him. When all was finished
and I knew he lay dead, my King, my friend, I ran away. I
threw off my coat of arms as I rode and tore off my own
badge, casting it hastily from me. It caught on the thorns
of a bush and fluttered there for all to see, a silver,
running hound.

13

Our Triumph and Victory
Told by a Squire of Sir William Stanley

I wende to deeth, knight stith in stour [stout in battle]
Thurgh fight in feelde I wan the flour;
No fightes me taughte the deethe to quelle—
I wende to deeth, sooth I you telle.

I wende to deeth, a kyng, y-wis;
What helpeth honour and worldes blisse?
Deeth is to man the kynde weye—
I wende to be cladde in clay.

15th century

Two days ago the world turned topsy-turvy, and I landed
feet first in an ill-fitting pair of shoes. I'd never had any
ambition to become a soldier, a murderer, or a jailer, but
now had been all three. I sneaked a look at the man who
sat not a yard from me, my lord's prisoner, whom I had to
guard. Two days ago he'd been one of the greatest lords in
the realm—Thomas Howard, Earl of Surrey—now, I had
to tell myself, his King is no King, and he is a traitor taken
in arms against King Henry the Seventh. The man who
was King Richard is dead.

Who could have foreseen such an event? It was hard

enough to imagine a man of King Richard's repute in war being beaten at all, but to be killed ...! The tale on every tongue is Richard's death, not our new King Henry's victory. To tell the truth, that seems almost an afterthought. Men cannot understand why King Richard died; kings should not get themselves killed in battle. But I knew why. He died because of treachery—my master's treachery—my own.

I can't pretend that I was there in Leicester out of anything but blind family allegiance. My father, who prefers a quiet life, had sent me to march under the hart's-head banner of Sir William Stanley, to ensure his continuing favor to petty gentry like ourselves. I'd have rather stayed at home, near Shotwick in the Wirral of Cheshire. I had been seeking a place at one of the Inns of Court, wishing to study law, when I was forced to become an unwilling soldier. I'm nineteen and not trained for it; Redmore was the first battle we've seen in England for fourteen years. My father will have a seizure when he hears the news.

He'd have another if he could see me now, sitting in a Leicester inn called the White Boar—I'll make a bet that will turn blue within a week!—wondering how on earth to address my noble captive. He'd not said much to me beyond a few grunts and gasps of pain. He had been brought from the field in a litter, badly hurt, and the Earl of Oxford's surgeon had got to work on him. I shared the duty of guarding and serving him as nursemaid, with one of Oxford's squires.

His right arm was a lumpish cocoon of bandages, and he moved his head on his neck gingerly, as if thankful they were still united. He groaned softly sometimes, as if pain grabbed him when he shifted. Probably a few broken ribs kept his arm company. Lord knows what the surgeon had put on his wound; it smelled like horse liniment. He sat in his chair as if he thought he'd never get out of it again, though his spare, stringy frame had a look of great energy. He could have been any age between thirty-five and fifty. The dark hair had little gray in it, though the top was thinning. He had brown, sharp eyes with big bags under them, and his skin was as lined and

tanned as an oak gall. Frankly, he was no beauty; his nose
had a squashed look, as if it had been broken in a fight,
his jaw was pugnacious, and he needed a shave.

"Will you take some wine, my lord?" I ventured, trying
to overcome my embarrassment.

The brown eyes flickered open like a lizard's. "Yes, I
will. Since I am to be entertained with wine, you may as
well drink with me." The voice was hard and abrupt,
though not markedly hostile. It had a queer, rolling
accent that was native to his home in Suffolk or Norfolk,
I supposed. "Thank you," he said, when I set the wine
within reach of his left hand. Then, with a rather nasty
grin, "Don't shuffle your feet, boy. Even if you did stick
your sword in my King, there's nothing I can do now.
This dog has had his eye teeth drawn. To pass the time,
tell me what happened; I've lain here two days and don't
even know who of my friends are dead or prisoners."

"No one knows for sure," I told him, "there was such
confusion. King Richard's men were so outnumbered
and trampled, half the dead were hard to identify. It
seems certain Lord Ferrers was killed. Sir Robert
Brackenbury and Sir Robert Percy were found dead.
Some say Kendal, the King's Secretary, and Sir Richard
Ratcliffe were killed too. No one has counted the
ordinary knights and squires—I think they were mostly
northerners."

Howard grunted. "Did any escape? Who was taken?"

"It's thought Lord Lovell escaped. He must have been
lucky. King Henry spared most of the common soldiers.
Catesby went to the gallows this morning. He knelt to my
master's brother and begged for mercy. He said he'd
saved Lord Stanley's son from death, by ignoring King
Richard's order. Lord Stanley turned his back."

"Which proves Catesby a fool," Howard said acidly,
"for putting his trust in a Stanley. What of our other
hero—great Percy of Northumberland?"

"He is with King Henry. He was supposedly
welcomed, but I hear he is not allowed to go home, and his
inn is guarded."

"If I know anything about it, when he is allowed home,
he'll never dare be without an armed guard."

"Why?" I said, startled.

"Many men in the North will think he deserves to hang from a tree, like Judas Iscariot."

"A man of King Henry's was sent north, to York."

Howard let out an unpleasant hoot of laughter. "they'll skin him alive—if he dares enter the city!"

"Another was sent to Sheriff Hutton, to fetch Lady Elizabeth."

"That," he said, in the same vein, "is indecent, but inevitable."

"Did she really ...?" I wanted to ask: Had she really lain with her uncle and was King Henry going to marry her, but he cut me short.

"She did nothing. Keep your mouth clean, young man, Now tell me how he died—you were there."

"The King?" I was relieved to speak of it; events were all to vivid in my mind. "I was with Sir William Stanley's mounted men, waiting on the north side of the battle, near one of the streams, at a place called the Sandford.

"The path of King Richard's charge led straight past his own right flank. Everyone recognized the white horse and the standards. He smashed through the Welsh soldiers as if they were straw dolls.

"We all sat transfixed. We couldn't believe our eyes— that the King should try to kill his enemy with his own hand. Sir William gaped for a few moments like the rest of us, then bawled: 'Get in between them! Save King Henry! If Gloucester won't bulge, kill him—kill the whole lot. Move, God damn your eyes!' We were confused at this change of kings—he let fly the filthiest blasphemies ever heard!

"We moved. We rode like maniacs, were only just in time. The King's men had fought hard—Sir, I'm not a soldier, I had only time for a couple of blows, Jesu! enough to find out what fighting was like in that heat—we made short work of them. It was nothing but butchery— no quarter given. The standard-bearer was the last left near the King—he had both legs chopped clean of and crawled before letting the leopards and lillies fall."

Howard sat motionless, grimly silent. I must have looked a fool, dazed as a owl in daylight by my own tale.

"King Richard was alone," I said. "Before then I hadn't seen a horse pied white and red. It was a monster, rearing and fighting—took a man full in the face with its teeth, crunching him easily as an apple, hurling him aside like a spat-out core, had the arm off another. The broken reins flew loose. The King was as one demented. He used an ax like a sledge hammer against a solid wall of men and metal. The blows had no direction, only force that threw him half out of the saddle.

"It was hopeless, of course. We drove them back into the marsh near the stream. The horse sank hock-deep in an instant. The ground there was so heavy and holding it only bogged down deeper, struggling to free itself. There was nothing the King could do; he was trapped. The poor beast floundered like a netted fish, hamstrung and belly-gutted. It's not good to see a brave horse burst its heart with effort, but to hear it scream in terror ... When it died, it was stuck fast in the bog to the saddle girths.

"Richard got himself clear of the horse, but he was well nigh finished too, could hardly stand. He sank up to his knees in mud. Christ knows if he had wounds, or how many, he was so covered with blood from other men he'd killed or maimed. He had no weapon left but his bare hands. I don't think he could even see those who plunged into the marsh to be first at the kill.

"Then it was impossible to make out what was happening, only this scrambling mass of men, all yelling. They were throwing themselves off their horses and fighting each other to get near enough to join in. Once they got their hands on him, he was dragged and beaten down into the mud. They knelt on his arms and legs to stop him struggling, while they wrenched some of the armor off, smashed the rest inward. And all the time, as the weapons went into him, he cried out: 'Treason ...! Treason ...! Treason ...!'

"God forgive me, I struck him too. My sword ran right in, I didn't see where—jarred on something—armor plate or bone—I didn't even know if he were alive or dead. I'd never killed a man in my life. I couldn't strike twice, though plenty of others did, again and again, like beasts. It went on for what seemed a long time.

"I left them to it. I claim no virtue in that, but the sight of my sword afterward made me retch and shake for a full five minutes."

Thomas Howard ran his left hand over his face in an attempt to hide his emotion. He could not speak at first. After a while he said, "Murder, and the murderers will claim it as an honor."

That was true. I told him, "They're bragging in the taverns now, of the kill. A dozen Welshmen swear they finished the King, but there's a Staffordshire man, called Ralph Rudyard, who boasts that it was himself. I doubt if anyone could tell, there were so many."

Howard did right to call it murder. It had only been when Sir William Stanley himself had forced a way through that the killing had ceased. The men had drawn aside, muddy and panting, I like a craven idiot in the back row.

Soon Lord Stanley came and stood at his brother's side. He was crossing himself and becoming purple and white by turns; possibly he had not meant things to go so far. But the pair of them had greeted with reverence the man who walked slowly through the dividing ranks.

Sir William had been the first to speak. "Your Grace," he said, very solemn, "My lord King, King Henry, you have proof of your victory." They had only needed to take one look. It silenced them for a moment.

King Henry took off his helmet and drew breath as if just rescued from drowning. He had a face the color of curds, under a layer of dirt and freckles, hair plastered darkly to his head, like fur on a soused sandy cat. He was shaking so uncontrollably his armor rattled, with his relief at being alive. It had so nearly been himself, dead in that wreckage of flesh and metal.

The body had been trampled face down into a churned quagmire that was puddled with crimson for yards around. Sir William heaved himself closer and turned it over with his foot. His contempt was so deliberate—I couldn't look.

King Henry was able to look, though, on the face of his enemy—what he could see of it. He didn't go too near, not joining those still floundering about in mire and rushes, trying to get a last jab. His face went green, and he turned away quickly, out of squeamishness, I suppose. Like me, he was seeing his first battlefield. It comes as a shock that a man has so much blood in him to drain out into the ground.

"Well," Howard said bitterly, "it was done. It would not surprise me to hear they'd crowned his head with paper and mocked him as they did his father. Tudor's triumph stinks, however much he and Tom Stanley try to sweeten it with righteousness."

Merciful Christ! He didn't know how near the mark he was. I swallowed, wondering how much I dared tell him.

"Not, not paper. It was after. King Henry had been crowned upon the field. They found it—the gold circlet— caught up in the foot of a scrubby hawthorn bush. I suppose it had been kicked aside in the confusion or secreted by a thief. Sir Reginald Bray found it. 'Cleave to the crown,' he said, 'though it hang on a bush.' Lord Stanley set it on King Henry's head, after they'd scooped the mud off it, banged the worst dents into shape, and given it a polish.

"A band of King Henry's men—I think they were mostly foreigners—took Richard's body as their plunder, though not until Sir William Stanley had claimed anything of gold or jewels of value. They stripped it and flung it over a sumpter horse, carelessly as an empty sack; bound it fast with cords." I heard my own voice begin to shake.

"He was naked," I said. "They hadn't left even a rag to cover his male member. I'd never seen death by this sort of violence before, and I wouldn't have believed it possible to see so many wounds on one man. Jesus—how they'd torn him ..."

I was one of those guarding the prisoners and found myself an unwilling witness. I'm not usually queasy, but I'll admit I heaved as much as a maid at a pig slaughter.

They broke his body by force, to make it lie backwards across the horse, the arms and legs dangling on either side. The man's own mother wouldn't have known his face, nor the head that hung down so low, the long hair falling from it, plastered with mud. Blood ran down, so it

dripped like a old string floor mop. His feet and hands
dripped too; the ground was marked all around.

I mumbled to Howard, "They took him back the dozen
miles to Leicester, like this. The raggle-taggle of human
kites that always follows an army trailed along behind.
They spat on him, pelted him with stones and filth, lewdly
jeering all the way. The camp women were the worst of
the lot." In the flush of victory they'd got at the wine
barrels; they were animals, drunken animals. Some
things that were done I could not bring myself even to
think on again, let alone speak of. They knew no limit to
obscenity or abuse.

"Queer," I said, "they began calling 'Crookback' as a
taunt, as brats do after cripples. True, with a man
doubled over like a snapped reed, it's hard to tell, but I
couldn't see any deformity."

Those had been slow, dust-choked miles, across the
wide fields, in the heat of afternoon. Slow! I began to
think Leicestershire never-ending; that journey dragged
out for the best part of five hours. Flies swarmed over
everything—you could hear their buzzing in between the
jeers and boos and shrieks of laughter, the brutal thud of
blows. The reapers left their corn stooks to stare, but it
took them a little while to understand who was used
in this way.

Howard was still silent. I did not look at him. "They
even knotted an old rope end around his neck, noose
tight, haltered him like a common felon—or a traitor—as
if he'd been taken on the run and hung for his treason
against King Henry."

Howard heaved hmself upright in his chair then, his
face a sallow gray. "Great God!" he said with difficulty,
his mouth twisted in disgust. "This was done to an
anointed king! To give his body to the scum of the vilest
army of hirelings I've ever set eyes on—to the camp
whores—for a plaything! Whoever allowed that lies very
low in the scale of humanity." He was right. I shivered. A
king was easily branded a felon and traitor, it seemed.

"Have orders been given for proper burial?" Howard
went on curtly. "I am aware that he has been displayed in
public for the last two days; it is customary. We want no

more wars over pretended escapes. Tudor allowed my
father's body to be sent home to Thetford Priory; surely
he cannot have intended this foul game?"

I found it hard to reply. "I don't know ... the Gray
Friars took it ... They bury plague victims and paupers." I
wriggled, though why I should feel guilt on Henry
Tudor's account, I can't say. "King Henry was in
Leicester all the time. He's still here. He leaves for
Coventry tomorrow.

"Some time after he came into Leicester as a
conqueror, we arrived. My lord, I truly wish I hadn't been
there. I was ashamed. We used the same road your army
must have taken to Redmore ..."

"It was a fine army," Howard said, half to himself,
"that part of it which wasn't rotten as a turd with
treachery. Many men from our Suffolk villages won't see
harvest home this year or sail from Orwell haven again.
God knows if I will, either. Go on."

Having told him so much, I found myself unable to
stop. "A guard had been put on the miserable procession,
though there weren't many prisoners. Sir William
Stanley's Cheshire billmen marched on either side. I
wore the same scarlet livery.

"We drummed the crowd out into the street. Some
must have seen King Richard ride by last Sunday
morning. Now all they could see was the once-crowned
head swinging upside down, about as like a human being
as a dead hare hung up by the feet on a shambles stall.
Things were bad enough when we started, but ... The
decent townsfolk turned away, sickened, but the rabble
stayed. They loved it."

It must have been about six o'clock then—Monday
evening. Today was Wednesday. I remembered wondering about King Henry, sitting in his bath and
preparing for a right royal supper, and whether his
victory had seemed sweet to him.

"A few gobbets of rain began to spit down. There was
thunder about, and a smell of too little rain on parched
ground.

"The soldiers hauled out a herald they'd captured,
kicked and beat him almost senseless, then threw him up

on the horse. He doubled over its neck, retching. Blanc Sanglier, he was, the white boar on his coat of arms daubed with blackening blood, like its human namesake. Tears poured through the muck on his face—flying stones cut him. The poor wretch was forced to ride into Leicester exhibiting his King. He had cause to weep.

"The crowd whistled and hooted at this mockery of royal state—made it the target of anything they could lay their hands on. A drunken looter, who didn't know one end of the instrument from the other, had got hold of a trumpet. He blew horrible discords a fool's fanfare, that was drowned in jeers and bombardments of filth.

"Someone began an ugly, slow chant, and the mob took it up, keeping time with the drums and the tramp of soldier's feet: "Traitor! traitor! traitor!' all the way into town. They shoved so hard to get across Bow Bridge, no one could hold them back, and it was too narrow to take them. The noise reached a roar. They were around the horse in a solid jam, pushing it bodily about the road; it struggled and nearly fell to its knees—the herald could do nothing. The horse was too near the side of the bridge ..." I faltered. I didn't want to think of it.

"I saw King Richard's face smashed against the bridge," I said. "It left a wet red smear on the stone. And the crowd laughed. I couldn't take any more—I had to lean over the parapet and spew into the river."

For a few moments there was silence. Darkness had crept upon the room. I could only hang my head. Howard crossed himself, twice. "God have mercy on the dead," he muttered. *"Requescat in pace.* Have pity on his soul, for there was none for his body."

I busied myself with striking a light for a rush taper with which to light the candles. There was no need to tell the rest, how they had tipped the body off the horse and let it lie as it fell, in tumbled squalor. There had been no bier,only the stones and muck in the street. Merciful saints! I dreaded to think what the friars found next morning. I did not go with the others to look.

I knew it would be unwise to speak again as I had this evening. Howard had not so far reproached me for the part I had foisted on me, and I felt relieved. There are few

like him about, who would not betray my bewilderment
to those who might interpret it as treason.

He came out of his silence at last and said slowly,
"What does Tudor wish to prove by taking his triumph in
the desecration of his enemy?"

"That King Richard was no king. Already it is said:
'King in deed, but not in right.' They call him the late
Duke of Gloucester, a traitor, the usurper of King
Henry's right, a homicide and tyrant. For him, no word
or act is too foul. King Henry did not need to order the
details—anyone knows what a mob of brutish hired
soldiers can do. But his orders must have been to mock
and degrade the false King until he was brought lower
than the beasts. Some people think he killed his brother's
children and that his fate was deserved. They wanted to
show how all murderers and traitors meet a Godforsaken
end. You, my lord, are also a traitor. King Henry dates
his reign from the day before the battle."

Howard gave his nasty laugh again. "A traitor! Has the
world gone mad? What security can any king have if he
and his loyal subjects may be branded traitors for doing
their duty? If this becomes a precedent, we may as well
abandon kings in England and set up a rule by apes. The
day before! Harry ap Tudor ap Owen or whichever
bastard you like is King by chance of conquest solely—
conquest by the gracious aid of William Stanley—may I
see him hang himself!

"Listen to me. I fought for King Richard. He was made
King with the consent of both lords and commons to his
right. Most of them will consent to the right of his
murderer. Poor mealymouthed, senile Archbisop
Bourchier will anoint Henry's body and crown his head
just as he did Richard's. They say it is a crime against God
to lay violent hands on His anointed. Let King Henry
remember how easy a crime it is to commit! There will be
too many eager for the privilege. Lincoln is heir to the
throne—will he relinquish his right so easily? And Lovell
will seek to avenge his friend. Tudor may well find
himself deposed and in exile again. Perhaps the way King
Richard chose is better than that fate."

His voice had grown hoarser as he spoke, and he sank

back in his chair, as if the effort had exhausted him. I
hastily poured him some more wine. As he drank, he gave
me a sharp look.

"Both you and I are discreet," he said. "You're an
honest young man; your master does not deserve such
men in his service. Take care what you say, or you may
find yourself keeping me company in the Tower. If you've
any sense, you'll go home to Cheshire and keep your nose
out of Stanley family place-seeking; you might find it
even more dangerous than lucrative."

I took his advice. The next day the victors set out for
London. I was dismissed from the company of Sir
William Stanley, my miliary service over. I rode home on
the same road out of Leicestershire into Staffordshire
that I had come south on four days before and was
continually astonished that it looked exactly the same.
That other journey felt like six months ago. The fields
had broader expanses of stubble in them, and I passed
more loaded wains taking harvest home, but otherwise
the scene was unaltered. The armies of kings might have
clashed as far away as Constantinople as near some
village called Market Bosworth. The men in the fields
might have known there had been a battle, if they had
seen fleeing soldiers, or they might not, having noticed
nothing but their own labor. I could tell enough tales to
keep all Shotwick agog until Christmas. But I doubted if I
should tell them—certainly not as I had to Howard. With
my discarded armor in my baggage, all unknightly in my
shirt sleeves, the sun burning my face, I had time to
wonder on the things I had witnessed, on King Richard,
who was dead and already reviled. What will men say of
him?